The
Drazine
Chronicles

Departure

MARK COOK

Trilogy Christian Publishers
A Wholly Owned Subsidary of Trinity Broadcasting Network
2442 Michelle Drive
Tustin, CA 92780

Library of Congress Cataloging-in-Publication Data is available.

ISBN 979-8-88738-413-9 (Print Book)
ISBN 979-8-88738-414-6 (ebook)

Dedication

To my Lord and Savior, Jesus, who has given my family and me everything. To my mom, Magee, whose years as an executive assistant and science fiction fan helped me throughout the writing, and to my wife and love of my life, Jenna, who supported me in quitting my nine-to-five gig and encouraged me in the writing of this book.

Contents

CHAPTER 1

The Seed Is Planted

Tan'cha lunged forward, using his spear to jab at his opponent; as he did, he could feel his knee buckle under him. The uneven ground caused his ankle to twist and put too much pressure on the knee. His spear missed its mark, and his opponent (a much smaller but quicker fighter) took the opportunity to strike. Dodging the spear point, the opponent pounced to the side to attempt a powerful blow to Tan'cha's upper back, aiming for his neck with a long glistening sword. Tan'cha had fought too many battles in this arena to expose himself; using his war hammer to prevent himself from crumbling, he threw his shield up and over his head and down his back in a smooth-flowing motion. His shield connected with the blade just as it was slicing into his upper left shoulder blade.

Tan'cha feigned a spin to his left. His opponent took the bait and jumped into the attack. During Tan'cha's turn, he was swinging his war hammer with him. The speedy little fighter was ducking the shield and dodging the spear, he even got out of the way of Tan'cha's sword, but when you fight someone with four arms, you learn quickly what happens when one misjudges just one arm or weapon. The hammer connected with the jaw of the nimble fighter. He was lifted off the ground and thrown at least fifteen feet across the fighting pit. He slammed into the ground as his long sword flew out of his hand.

Tan'cha hobbled over to him as the crowd erupted into cheers and applause.

1

The little guy was a crumbled mess; he had multiple cuts which Tan'cha had inflicted upon him during the match, dark purple blood was oozing from several, but the most damage was to the lower left jaw where the truncheon had found its mark. The jaw was crushed, several teeth were cracked, and a few were missing; the horn jutting from the jawbone was shattered, and blood was dripping from the wound.

Tan'cha checked to see that the fighter's hearts were still beating and he was breathing.

"Well done, little guy; Zhuni will fix you up." "Little guy" was a funny expression but true; when you are over nine feet tall most of your opponents are going to be little guys.

He turned, acknowledged the crowd, and, leaning heavily on his makeshift crutch, made his way out of the pit. The pit was the fighting arena where Tan'cha and the others battled in. It was a sandy-floored oval space. Walls carved out of the mountain's sandstone surrounded the pit. The walls were over sixty feet tall and were topped with a force-generated shield to protect the spectators. The arena was several hundred feet long and just a bit narrower across the middle of the oval. The space was large enough for several hundred warriors at a time. Small battles were the most common, but during the main events, hundreds of fighters would battle at a time. This was a lower-level warm-up fight, Tan'cha was one of the locale's favorites, and he often drew a crowd more suited to the upper-level fights.

Tan'cha wobbled through the far gate to exit the pit. The groundskeepers and gate guards directed him down a corridor also carved from the sandstone. It was well-lit and nearly thirty feet high. Down the center were light panels that produced bright but glare-free bluish light. The pale blue light, along with the sandstone color, gave a warm feel and color to the corridor. The lighting also had a calming effect upon most of the creatures.

"Come on, Tan'cha, get over here!"

"Yes, Sir," he said with a smirk.

Zhuni was a young twentyish human dressed in linen scrubs; he was busily taking care of the fighters as they left the fighting ring. He was an arena medic and a favorite of the fighters. He also knew more about the fighters and their biology than anyone else here, as he truly cared about every one of them. Zhuni always worked to heal them to the best of his ability and had been doing so since he was a child. He worked the lower-level fighters where the injuries were usually less serious than the upper-level fights. He was motioning Tan'cha to come to sit on a bench so he could be checked.

Tan'cha towered over the medic; even sitting on the bench, he was tall. He was covered in leather armor, the sides of his head had huge flat disks that were his overly sensitive ears (he could hear a heartbeat), and he had a set of broad horns protruding from the back of his head and angling to the front, just above his ears.

"Get your gear off so I can check you out; I have to go fix your handy work over there," Zhuni said as he walked over to attend to the fighter Tan'cha had just fought.

Tan'cha set his weapons down, first his sweeping sword, which he welded with his upper right hand. He then set down his shield, which had been held by his upper left arm. His lower left arm had held his spear, and his lower right arm dropped his war hammer.

He started to remove his gear, a long leatherette (tanned animal hide covered in carapace and chitin as plated armor) trench coat strapped across his chest, which covered his back like a heavy cloak. Under this, he wore a similarly made vest to protect his chest and abdomen. Before he could remove the vest, he had to remove his strykers, blades on his arms used to deflect and block other fighters' weapons. He also had to take the padding off his shield arm.

An attendant (a smaller version of himself with a lighter blue hue to his fur) came over to assist. The attendant picked up the weapons and turned to place them in the arms of a second attendant. The second turned and walked off with his arms full. The first attendant turned back to assist with the padding wrap. He set the strykers and padding in a neat pile next to Tan'cha. He then knelt to assist with the removal of the armored boots. The second attendant came back with a pair of soft boots and a robe for Tan'cha, which he placed on his feet after the armored boots were removed, then set the robe over his massive frame, which was covered with coarse blue fur patterned with snow leopard-like spots of grey.

"Tell us about the home world," the attendant said.

Tan'cha began, "My father told me stories that his father told him, and I will pass along to you."

"You young ones were born as warriors and slaves of this Gamer's world just as I was and my father before. But his father was taken from our world and told of its wonders. Our world is a wondrous and unique world unlike any other, with some of the most amazing creatures. Many of the creatures here originated from our world."

"What makes ours so wondrous and *amazing*?" the young one says with too much sarcasm.

"To start, our planet has an elliptical orbit, unlike any other known planet with life."

"What do you mean '*eeeliptaacal*'?"

"Oh, so the smart guy doesn't know what 'elliptical' means? It means the planet revolves around our sun in an oval pattern; nearly all other planets with life have a round orbit. This creates a terribly harsh environment."

"Why is that?"

"Our planet doesn't have normal seasons; we have the burn and the freeze."

"You mean summer and winter."

"No. I mean the burn and the freeze, twice a solar cycle there is such heat that the rivers and lakes dry completely, and during the freeze, the planet freezes completely, rivers, lakes, and even seas and most of the ocean."

"How does anything live?"

"That is why our creatures are so amazing; they are able to survive by multiple means; many borrow underground or will even freeze solid and thaw out. Some have thick armor plating, which is nearly indestructible."

"Like the Scrytock, he is indestructible."

"Yes, the Scrytock came from our world, they are not only rock hard and fireproof, but they can freeze solid like a block of ice, then thaw out as if nothing happened. The gamers don't know all the creatures' secrets. Their scientists like to think they know. But you know who knows all their secrets? Zhuni there, he knows about all the secrets of all the creatures, don't you?"

Zhuni was still working on the fighter Tan'cha had sent him, and Zhuni just huffed.

"Zhuni is the best doc the games have seen."

"Did this little guy crack your skull or something? I will definitely have to do a brain scan again; I still haven't found one in your head," Zhuni said.

"Haha, anyway, where was I?"

"You were going to tell us about the Drazine," said the first attendant.

"The what?" asked the second.

"Shhh." Was the response from the first attendant.

"I was?" asked Tan'cha. "Okay. So, the Drazine are protectors of worlds. They are powerful and terrible creatures. They are peaceful until provoked and then can be terribly violent and destructive. Rarely are they seen but do not be fooled; they are there on every planet.

My father said that the Drazine fought the gamers and drug cartels off our world."

"How is that possible if many of the creatures here came from our world?"

"The gamers have always traveled looking for unique creatures to enter into their games. When they first came to our world, they only had small raiding parties; the Drazine did not get involved because they did not see a need to rise up, many tribes fought off the gamers, and a few creatures and tribes were taken. It was not until Starch was discovered. Yes, the same Starch that the drug cartels push and sell. It was a tuber that we grew as our main food source. For us, it was just food that could grow in the short growing seasons and store well. It had a very different effect on other creatures and other races. For some, it heightened their strength and senses making them powerful warriors. Many mercenaries use it, especially the Ryalian. But to most, it became an instantly addictive and euphoric drug. When the true nature of Starch was found, the gamers and drug cartels decided to join forces and invade our world. The drug cartels wanted the Starch, and the gamers wanted slaves and creatures for their games.

"At first, we were able to hide and fight them off as they were ill-prepared for the extremes of our world. But they soon learned to raid during the growing season and started taking entire clans and clearing the plains of all creatures. This awoke the Drazine. They struck the landers and wiped out the foot soldiers. Then some were able to get into orbit to destroy the star ships. The gamers and cartels brought tens of thousands to control the planet but left with a few thousand and are now afraid of our world. They have been able to make synthetic Starch, but it is not as powerful as the real Starch, so some still sneak back to steal Starch; that is why the real Starch is so rare and expensive. There are some who make it to the planet and return, but most do not come back. No one knows if the Drazine are still protecting the planet or not. It is thought that the ones who do not return were killed by the Drazine, and those who do make it back were just lucky. But no one knows for sure."

"So, what kinds of weapons do these warriors use?"

"The Drazine are not warriors like you or me; these are massive beasts that can use their claws to tear apart starships; they can throw bolts of powerful energy and spitfire hot enough to melt or cremate even a Scrytock. The Drazine could breathe noxious gases. Bolts and plasma weapons just bounce off them like raindrops on ceramasteel."

"All right, kids, story time is over. I have to repair this old thing," Zhuni stated as he watched the previous fighter get carted off to the barracks for recovery.

The attendants stood and thanked Tan'cha for the story and headed off to their other obligations.

"It is about time; I am sore," Tan'cha whined.

"Really, that guy was half your size. Getting old, maybe?"

"Yeah, but he was fast, and he had sharpened his sword, see the cuts, and I am not old!"

"I said, getting old, and you always have boo-boos coming out of your fights, especially as you are getting older, excuse me, more experienced, shall we say?"

"Better."

"I definitely do not like the sharpened sword; I will have to talk to Stanton."

"He will do nothing."

"Then I will talk to Klavan."

"As you please."

Zhuni takes out his scanner and, from a short distance, performs a quick head-to-toe scan.

"Several of these cuts are deep and will need attending to."

"I told you."

"I do not like the sharpened sword; this is going to get some of you killed. Who did you upset?"

"I did not like the sword much either, and I did not upset anyone."

"Well, I will just fix you up again." Zhuni reached over to a medical bot and retrieved a gun that he used to secrete a sticky substance to the cuts. As the substance is applied, the bleeding instantly stops, they seal up, and there is a sizzling sound as the cuts become faded scars.

"Ouch, that stings!"

"Do you whine and complain this much in the pit?"

Zhuni has Tan'cha stand, and this time, the bot performs a full body scan, throwing up a teal-blue hologram of Tan'cha. Zhuni looks the hologram over and exclaims.

"Oh there, your lower left hand has not been broken, nor your right forearm! Otherwise, everything else has been patched, stitched, or glued. I am surprised you have any flexibility left at all."

"Thanks, Doc."

"Looks like your knee is torn up pretty well, and your ankle doesn't look much better. He got a couple of good shots in, especially that one to your back. You have a shield, you know, that, right?"

"Yes!"

"Well, it will serve you better if, in the next fight, you use it."

"You think? The ankle is messed up because they did not groom the pit. I stepped in a Scyrtock print and twisted my ankle, which hurt my knee."

"So now they are not fixing the grounds between fights; this just gets better and better."

"Why are you complaining? You are not out there fighting."

"No, but I have to fix the mess they make. I will have to talk to Stanton and Klavan."

"So now I am the mess you have to fix; you make me feel so special."

"Well, after looking at the scan, I have good news and bad."

"Bad news first."

"You are going to live."

"So, what is the good news?"

"Your knee looks so bad that you will be out a few rotations, maybe more."

"That bad?"

"Yup, I will need to slice and dice and stitch and glue, oh and soak."

"Not the soak; I hate the soak; it stinks!"

"Stop fussing and get in the chair."

Zhuni places his palm onto a small orange panel on the wall. A door slides open, and a board twelve feet long slides out; it is covered in a green-tinted gelatin. Tan'cha hops up onto the board and lays back. The gelatin forms to his body and stays in that shape. The board changes shape to form an inverted chair that now has Tan'cha on his back with his knees up.

Zhuni touches a few buttons on the panel and a smaller panel with a keyboard, toggle sticks, and a screen slide out. The bot rolls over to the opposite side of the patient, away from the keyboard. It projects a holographic image of the injured ankle in front of Zhuni. The bot also produces an arm with a sprayer on it. This passes over the ankle and sprays the ankle with a bright green mist.

Tan'cha yells out, "That is so cold!"

"Oh, my, will you stop? It is like working with a screeching Mynog!"

The bot raises another arm with an injector gun on it and places the business end against the ankle just above the injury. There is the sound of a slight metal clang and a discharge of pressurized air.

The hologram projected by the bot now shows a bright orange dot at the point of the injection. Zhuni presses a button on the keyboard, and hologram enlarges to a detail of the orange dot. It is not one dot but several dozen smaller dots, nanobots. He grasps the toggle sticks, twists one, and the dots begin to move. The hologram flickers, then goes completely out of focus, flickers again, and goes out.

"Dagz!"

Zhuni slaps the bot, and the hologram flashes back, flickers, and then restores itself. On the hologram, the tendons show up as bright green, indicating the injured area. He twists and jostles the sticks, so the orange dots weave in and out of the green area; it slowly turns yellow, indicating the tendons are repaired. Yellow highlights an old wound or scar tissue.

The bot moves the injector gun up the ankle towards the knee. The bot now moves the sprayer arm up, spraying as it goes. The orange dots of the nanobots move up the ankle towards the knee. They arrive at the injured area, highlighted in bright green. Now the injector sounds again with the metallic sound and the soft hiss of pressurized air. Now red dots appear and join the orange. A second injection and blue dots arrive.

"I really messed it up, muscles, tendons, and ligaments. Yup, I will be out a day or two."

Now the tears and green areas slowly turn yellow. This surgery is complete; as the hologram slowly changes back to the full body scan, we see most of the hologram is yellow, showing the years of damage this fighter has suffered. Zhuni flicks a switch, and the hologram disappears. He throws another switch, and a large metal collar is brought out of a compartment in the wall by a small control arm. The collar is opened and clamped around the repaired knee. The device begins to hum slightly, and a mist or light smoke begins to drift up from it.

"I hate the soak, it stinks, and the humming gives me a headache; machinery always gives me a headache."

"Funny, you stink and give me a headache, but you don't hear my crying about it. Now put your robe on and hobble back to your quarters. I will check in on you tomorrow."

"See you later. And thanks. Do you, by chance, think you could get me a private room? I have been living with at least ten other fighters every day of my life here; there is always someone around. It is so depressing. I would kill for some privacy."

"Sure, that will happen. It will be easy," Zhuni said in a sarcastic voice.

Zhuni continues to work on the other fighters as the day comes to an end. Being in the lower-level fights is an all-day job; the fights start at dawn and end just before the main event in the late evening. He is glad this marathon of events is only every fourteen rotations. It takes nearly that long just to recover.

He was heading down one of the hallways, having been told by one of the guards that there was a fight with injuries outside of the pit. This gives Zhuni concern as this type of thing is highly unusual.

Zhuni nears the intersection of two passageways and suddenly gets a tremendous feeling that he has been here before. Not just this intersection but this exact situation. It was as if he were experiencing this entire situation a second time. He caught a flash of movement out of the corner of his eye, but when he turned to focus, nothing was there, odd.

In his mind, he could see death around the corner, possibly his death. But he was driven to help; that is all he knew. He was here to help others. That was his calling. He would continue no matter what. If he could save one, he was going to do whatever he could to help.

He rounds the corner to see two Pantaas tearing into some guards and fighters. Three fighters and two handlers are running his way to get away from the Pantaas, and so are two guards. One of the guards looks to have been hurt badly, and Zhuni can hear him calling for help. Zhuni rushes to help. Just as he reaches the guard, one of the Pantaas turns towards him and looks to pounce. Zhuni wasn't sure exactly what happened at that moment; it was all a blur. When he was able to collect himself, he realized the Pantaa had leaped at him; the three fighters had thrown themselves into the fray. One fighter ended up on top of Zhuni, covering Zhuni with his shield and body; another had jumped onto the Pantaa's back as it leaped, and the third had attacked it with his spear. The first fighter was hit with the full force of the Pantaa but was still covering Zhuni. The second was stabbing it with his knife and was barely hanging on; the third was holding his ground, standing between the Pantaa and Zhuni. That was when Zhuni noticed the two handlers were jabbing at the Pantaa with their shock sticks also, and one was actually attempting to keep it from Zhuni by holding its tail. The fighter on top of Zhuni rolled off and stumbled to his knees, holding his shield up to protect Zhuni and himself; he turned to Zhuni.

"Go!" he screamed.

Zhuni was in shock. He did not know what to do; he wanted to help, but he did not know how to fight, and he could not leave these fighters.

"Go! We cannot afford to lose you!" the fighter continued.

What did he mean? Zhuni stood still, not knowing what to do. The fight continued, and the Pantaa seemed to be getting the upper hand; it had thrown the one fighter off its back and was headed towards Zhuni.

"Get out of here!" the fighter exclaimed.

Zhuni stood there, not sure what to do. He saw that the Pantaa turned to look at the guard a few dozen feet away and lunged at him, grasping his upper body in his mouth and shaking him. The sound of bones crushing filled Zhuni's ears, and he saw the lower half of the guard's body fall away. The Pantaa looked back at Zhuni. Chewing the remains of the guard, it took one step towards Zhuni. The only thing standing between Zhuni and death was the fighter who had recently been on the Pantaa's back. The fighter stepped in front of the Pantaa to block his path to Zhuni, but the Pantaa just swatted the fighter across the hall, slamming him against the wall.

Zhuni needed to decide and was about to turn to run when he heard a blast from a plasma rifle behind him. The blast knocked the Pantaa back. A second blast knocked it to the ground, three more blasts followed, and the Pantaa burst into flames. The heavy-strike guards had arrived and rushed past Zhuni, heading towards the other Pantaa.

The fighter who had been on top of Zhuni collapsed. Zhuni rushed over to help him. Zhuni grabbed his scanner and saw the fighter had his chest caved in when the Pantaa hit him. If Zhuni didn't act fast, this fighter would not live very long. He immediately went into emergency medic mode.

Yelling to the handlers and one of the newly arrived guards to grab the fighter and follow. Zhuni ran to the nearest medical station just down the hall. The fighter was set on the platform, which came out of the wall, and Zhuni began working on him.

"Grab the other one and bring him here also," referring to the fighter who the Pantaa had smacked against the wall.

Zhuni had one of the guards go find another medic to help with the surgery. The fighter who had been smacked against the wall had a couple of bad cuts, a concussion, and a broken shoulder, so he could wait until the second medic arrived. The first fighter was in bad sharp. But Zhuni was determined to save him. The fighter was a Ryanlian (a reptilian alien) and, as such, was very tough. The skin alone needed special instruments to slice into.

Zhuni activated the med bot to assist and got a holographic scan projected above the patient showing the extent of his injuries. One of his hearts had ruptured, and Zhuni was not sure how long the fighter would survive on one heart. Zhuni knew the ruptured heart was the secondary heart that pumped the blood to the fighter's muscles allowing amazingly quick reflexes. Zhuni could only hope, as it was the secondary heart, that the fighter's vital organs would remain stable while he repaired it. The fighter's primary heart should keep pumping blood to the vital organs. Zhuni had the med bot inject the nanobots, which Zhuni would use to repair the heart and the other injuries.

Zhuni was well on his way to repairing the heart when the other medic arrived. Zhuni knew this medic was new and may need some prompting but was glad the guard had found him. Zhuni did not want one of the "scientists" working on the fighter.

"Do you need assist, or do you want me to go to work on this guy?" the medic asked.

"Get to work on him; if I need you, I will let you know."

They worked on the two fighters for the next two kolts. Zhuni learned the new medic's name, Tazlon, and was pleased with his work. Both fighters were going to be okay. They needed to be sent to their quarters and monitored over the next couple of rotations, but Zhuni felt they would be fine.

Zhuni told the guards and handlers to move the fighters to their quarters and that he would check in on them the next morning. Zhuni looked around for the third fighter, but he was gone. The fighter must have been okay and not in need of medical attention. Zhuni would have to attempt to track the fighter down later and speak with him.

Zhuni still had a lot of work to do to complete his day. As he headed back to wrap up the normal end to his day, he could not help but wonder why three fighters he barely knew would risk their lives to keep him safe. Why him? There were several medics. *Why?* This question ate at him all evening as he completed his day's work.

One of his tasks this evening was to work on a rather sour Scrytock who had had one of his plates cracked. That is always a major surgery as they require some special attention. The plates are five to six inches thick and have airways under them, which need to be handled with extreme diligence. They tend to be rather angry after a match. This one was no exception. While the guards were controlling him, one of them had an arm broken and another a leg broken, so Zhuni ended up with even more injuries to report than usual.

He is finally able to wrap up his work. He stows his scanner, bandage bag, and info pad into the storage locker next to the medical station. He takes the recorder off his shoulder. (He is wearing the recording goggles he wears all day.) These goggles record all the injuries, vital signs, and procedures of every fighter, creature, and guard he works on, plus everything he sees and hears. He clicks on the scanner screen and does a quick look-see to remember his day and see if he missed any notes. He adds a few thoughts (he is the only medic to do this). There are six medics in the lower fight level. He hopes to move to midlevel to be on the under cards rather than the warmups. The shifts are shorter, and the pay is better. Someday maybe the main event, work one day in fourteen, and get paid at least five times as much plus better quarters and benefits. He thinks he is doing a good job and has been told so by the fighters and by Klavan.

He hits send and knows the entirety of his reports are now in central records, where they will be used to determine the over and under for all the fights. The gamers make their living knowing the injury history and the strengths and weaknesses of each fighter. Without this vital information, they would be at the mercy of just plain luck in making the bets. The house can never rely on luck. The odds must always be in the favor of the gamers.

He places the goggles in the pouch in the recorder's case. He then places the recorder in his locker; he slams the locker shut in a sudden burst of energy as if to say, "My shift is now over; I am ready to enjoy my day off tomorrow." But that was the extent of his energy stores; he touches the blue dot on the wall with his palm, twists his hand, and a metal clang announces that the locker is locked.

He strides off down the corridors heading to his quarters, looking for a solid night of sleep. Tomorrow is his day off, but he must speak with Stanton and Klavan about the conditions of the pit during the fights (it just got worse as the day went on) Tan'cha was not the first nor the last to get injured due to the poor conditions. He must also make them aware of the deteriorating of the medical kit and bot. He wouldn't have this problem on midlevel. He also must check in on the fighters and attempt to find the third and speak to him.

---

*

Zhuni woke up, sat up, and thought about the day before. He was still mulling over the entire incident with the Pantaas. He needed to talk to Stanton and Klavan. He was upset with how the fighting pit and equipment were being taken care of. Some of these fighters were free, but most of them were still slaves. They were still entitled to proper medical care and working conditions. He would have to do something; he did not want to see them killed; it was bad enough that they were getting seriously hurt. After all, many of them were his friends, and the gamers were making a fortune from the fights. The gamers only saw them as slightly better than livestock.

He got dressed, wearing his oldest set of teal scrubs with high brown boots and a brown wrap thrown over everything. His shoulder-length brown hair was pulled back and held in place with a band of brown leather. His appearance was purely for function; there was no one to impress. The fighters were not of his race, and the few of those that were his race worked for the gamers as foot soldiers, guards, supply personnel, or maintenance. They were all humanish anyway. He did not like his race much. He had only seen one or two of his race in his life; they seemed to be few and far between. The humanish were a violent group who treated the fighters and creatures from the fights as if they were insignificant unintelligent animals. The humanish were not truly his race; they were a conglomeration of humans and something else.

Down the corridors, he headed. He was going to take the long way to Stanton; he hated to cut through the luxury box area at any level, and it gave him an uneasy feeling. Almost creepy, it just felt evil and cold. Of course, the cold was felt throughout the corridors on off shifts. They shut down the heat and conditioning when the spectators we not around, anything to save a credit. He also would pass by the fighters from the Pantaa incident and check on them.

Zhuni was an orphan who Klavan had found roaming the space port. Even at his young age, he had an affinity for dealing with exotic creatures. Zhuni knew more about the fauna passing through the space port than some of the gamers scientists. Klavan brought him on board and paid him to be a keeper. But when the creatures were injured or sick, the gamers thought to dispose of them. Zhuni was able to nurse many back to health, so he became a fight medic. He helped train some of the other medics, also. He was given his freedom as part of his pay also. So, he was not a slave to anyone, as most of the fighters were. He was paid well and was able to learn more about the fighters and the exotic creatures. He also had a place of his own. When he was younger, he had lived in the corridors and power ways of the market or the spaceport. The stability and privacy of a space of his own were nice.

He was reminiscing back through his life as he walked and was not really paying attention when he bumped into a Chordentia. Chordentia was Stanton's henchmen; they were roughly four feet tall. Smelled and looked like giant rats. They were never alone, and when

Zhuni looked around, he realized he was in the middle of seven of them. They all looked the same to him except this one. You could tell by of the massive scar across his face, the dead eye, and the torn ear. This was Traxon, Stanton's head hench.

"Look out!" Zhuni growled.

"You watch; you hurry."

"Yes, I am in a hurry."

"Why, where you hurry?"

"Where is Stanton?"

"Boss, you see, hurry we go. Office."

"No, I do not need an escort."

"Idea we take."

"Dagz!"

Zhuni did not have much choice alone; these furry pieces of filth were annoying, but in numbers, they could be downright dangerous. He would just fall in line with them; they were going the same place he was, so they said. This was not how he had wanted to spend his morning.

They entered Stanton's office to find him screaming at several guards.

Zhuni had yet to figure out exactly what type of creature Stanton was. He was a bloated creature who moved smoother and faster than his tremendous girth would imply. He liked to wear elaborate clothing of brilliant colors, but his chest and head were always exposed. His skin was pale white most of the time.

Stanton's office was a grandiose space covered with a reflective and shimmering stone, all the way to the expansive ceiling that soared high above. The center of the room held an enormous table of a dark glistening wood. Behind the table was gargantuan chair, more throne than chair, which Stanton was lounging in. The guards were on this side of the table.

One of Stanton's huge eyes rolled to watch Zhuni and Traxon enter; the other stayed focused on the guards. It was very disconcerting.

"Just do as I tell you to! This is *my* sector!" Stanton bellowed, his skin a deep red, nearly magenta hue; he was furious.

"*Go!*" Stanton hollered.

"Yes, Dwayan," the guards bowed and left as quickly as they could without running.

With that, Stanton motioned for Traxon and Zhuni to come to the table. Stanton's skin quickly faded to a light pink tone.

"Traxon, what have you brought me?"

"Zhuni, in a hurry."

"Yes, I heard you had an exciting evening."

"To say the least."

"Do tell your Dwayan."

"I have no idea how or why those Pantaa got loose, but we almost lost three fighters, two handlers, and I don't know how many guards."

"Only one, no problem," Stanton said with a slight smirk.

"I mean, how many could we have lost?"

"No worries, everyone is replaceable."

"I see. The pit is a wreck, and it is not being cared for properly; I saw several injuries because of this. Tan'cha will be out fourteen to fifteen rotations because of a knee injury from the poor conditions."

"Is that the blue one?"

"Yes."

"That is unfortunate, but the new Game Master has deemed the pit maintenance as a cost we will no longer need to incur. It is not on Her list of priorities; in fact, She is getting rid of the whole section. This will give us more space for other ventures."

"Well, it should be important; we will lose more fighters more often."

"No worries, fighters are cheap. Even good nonslaves do not need much by way of compensation. Some should be at or near the end of their careers and should finish soon. We will find new and more exciting fighters. Tannycha should be near his end anyway."

"It is Tan'cha, and he is one of your most exciting and best fighters, a crowd favorite. He is not ready to retire."

"Oh. Yes. Retire."

"Hmm. You also must upgrade the med station. I was having issues with the hologram again."

"Now that is expensive."

"If you can't or won't do anything, I will speak with Klavan."

"That is fine; he will do nothing. He still must get it past the game master. Just remember, by doing so, you may upset your sector, Dwayan."

"It will not be the first time."

"No, it won't."

Stanton started to look as if he had a sunburn.

Zhuni knew it was time to leave. He turned and saw himself out.

Stanton started to lose his color and glared at Traxon.

"You and the Boyz need to keep an eye on him. I do not like his brashness, and I think he is going to be trouble for us. I also do not like the reports I heard about last night, fighters willing to die protecting him. That may be real trouble."

"Traxon watch."

"You *and* the Boyz need to watch him at all times. We cannot let him ruin this."

"Traxon, Boyz, watch."

"Put a keeper on him; we need to know everything."

"Yes, Dwayan."

---

*

Zhuni found Klavan at the docks. Klavan was easy to spot. He was of a powerful build, intimidating, and stood seven feet tall. Klavan was Septorian, a lizard race; he was a dark teal green with a cream color across his chest and throat. He always dressed elegantly, and his favorite colors were purple and red. He was wearing an elaborate long coat of a blood red hue with detailed stitching in gold; the cuffs were oversized and were marron. He had his jeweled walking staff with him; it was a silver metallic with golden flecks, an exotic wood. It was the only thing Zhuni had ever seen made of that exotic wood. It only grew on Klavan's home world of Septor. Klavan called it Sezonian. He said every Septorian who left the home world had a piece of Sezonian with them. They called it "Lifewood."

Zhuni caught up to Klavan and began, "I am concerned someone is going to be seriously injured for no logical reason if the grounds of the pit are not groomed between fights."

"The Game Master actually liked the uncertainty the rough ground lent to the matches. She has decided we will no longer be needing the large grounds crew. This will save us credits, and She likes it."

"But what about the medical equipment? It was giving me trouble, the hologram kept cutting out, and the bot is no better."

"That will be taken care of; in fact, you will be getting all new equipment."

"What, really?"

"The grounds equipment storage area will not be needed. After reading your reports, the Game Master wants you to take over the space and create a complete medical department."

"I am going to be working as part of a medical team?"

"No, you are going to create a medical department for the Arena. Master was impressed by your record, and She was not impressed by the other medics; She would like you to oversee the arena's medics, all of them. You will train them."

"I am not sure I can do that; I mean, train anyone. I have always been on my own."

"Well, you are going to. The doctors we have are specialists on one or two creatures and are more like scientists who have been doing dissection. They act as if healing was a simple mechanical process. They do not have the deft touch you have nor understand the fighters nor creatures like you do."

"This is not exactly what I was thinking would happen; I just thought I would move to mid-level and then eventually the main event."

"You will be working mid-level and main event."

"When does this all start?"

"Tomorrow, the grounds equipment will be removed. That should take a few rotations. Then we will start building the med lab. This should take two to three rattons once the space is cleared out. So, spend the next couple of rotations figuring out what you need, how you are going to train the others, and anything else you may need, then come see me."

"Yes, sir."

"By the way, do you not think I know about last night? Tell me your thoughts."

"I just did; the pit is dangerous."

"Zhuni, I have known you a long time. I can tell the situation with the Pantaas rattled you. Talk to me; you have been in bad spots before."

"I just do not understand."

"What do you not understand? We work with some strange creatures, some are dangerous, and accidents happen; some will get loose, and some will hurt people. Pantaas are nasty when you have a creature as tall as me at the shoulders, and it has claws as long as your forearms and teeth as big as your lower leg and as powerful and quick. They scare me."

"That is not the issue; I have dealt with Pantaas and worse before."

"What then."

"Klavan, the fighters. They were running away from the Pantaas."

"Wise."

"But when the Pantaa turned towards…"

"Turned towards what?"

"Me."

"Turned towards you? What?"

"When the Pantaa turned towards me, the fighters, a couple of handlers they…"

"They what?"

"They rushed to protect me. Me. Why?"

"Oh. This, this is good. Oh yes, this is very good."

"What do you mean?"

"My plan will be even better."

"What plan?"

"Oh yes."

"You are not making sense."

"Don't you see? These fighters were willing to die to protect you. They have a strong sense of righteousness and honor. They see you as one of them. Oh yes, this is good. Very, very good."

"I do not understand your plan."

"Watch yourself, as word gets around, and it will, there will be those who will see you as gaining influence with the incident and your new position. Some may see you as a threat. Many gamblers and some in the betting syndicates will think you will now have influence on the outcome of the fights, and this may cause some concern for them."

"I never bother anyone; I just want to take care of the fighters."

"I know that. But be careful. And Zhuni. You can't save them all; some fighters will not make it through this."

"What do you mean?"

"You care too much about them. Do not get too attached to the fighters. Changes are coming with the new game Master, and some changes will not be an improvement. The grounds, for example."

"What else?"

"Not now. We will talk later. I do have a plan. I will let you know. This is good."

———————— * ————————

Zhuni left the loading area frustrated and overwhelmed. He wanted to move to mid-level and help the fighters, but to oversee medical training and build a team was a little more than he had hoped for or even dreamed of. Plus, the fighters now see him as one of them. It did not seem right; he did not fight. He was lost in his thoughts and found himself under the luxury box, taking a short cut back to his compartment. He stayed away from this area as much as possible; he felt uncomfortable here; it was eerie.

He did not realize he had come this way until he started to have strong feelings of pain, pity, and forgiveness. There was a strong feeling of confusion also.

He moved along quickly. This section of the complex had highly polished corridors, and everything echoed. Just walking through these corridors made Zhuni uncomfortable. But with those thoughts and feelings inundating him, it made his feeling worse. He broke into a run, and those thoughts and feelings subsided.

He swung by to check on the fighters. The first was in the small medical center. The facility had to take care of any and all injuries. It was drastically lacking for the fighters. There were only four critical care beds. The first fighter, the Ryanlian, was here.

The Ryanlian was still in the induced coma he was set in last night, but all his vital signs looked good, and both his hearts were beating strong. Zhuni was pleased; he had never had to repair a burst heart on a Ryanlian before. Luckily it was his secondary heart, which was a simple pump, only two chambers and two valves. The Ryanlian's main heart was complicated with eight chambers and sixteen separate valves. That would have been a problem. Zhuni knew he could have figured it out, but would he have been able to in time save his life?

The other fighter was passed out but also was showing signs of improvement. He was in the noncritical care unit next door; it had only twelve beds. Zhuni hated the fact that the medical facilities were so lacking. This was the only medical area, other than the equipment in the corridors designed to stabilize the fighters, for the entire complex. It needed to improve drastically.

He made it back to his compartment, sat on his bed, and just started thinking of his next couple of rotations. He was mentally exhausted and could not shake the strong feelings he had earlier, as if someone was being held captive and they felt sorry for and even forgave their captors. Strangely, he fell asleep even with all these thoughts crashing through his head.

———————— * ————————

Pain and suffering, sadness, loss, grief, confusion, and pity fought for control of his head. The pain was excruciating. He felt he was being torn apart. He could see computer screens with images of muscles, bone structures, claws, teeth, and a nervous system. Zhuni was not familiar with the creature he was seeing, but he knew these parts were his. He did not know where he was nor why he was there, only that he knew this was not where he was supposed to be. He did not recognize the strange little creatures who were cutting into him and stitching him back together; they were constantly taking him apart and putting him back together. It was as if he were being cut into and torn apart to be mapped and dissected but left alive for later study. The dream was too real.

Zhuni bolted up out of bed. The pain was gone, but the images were still locked into his head. The feeling of being cut apart was terrifying. It was all too real. He had to get up and move; maybe waking up fully and walking it off would clear his mind.

He put on his linen scrubs from the day before, put on a pair of brown boots, got up, and drifted out of his compartment.

It was early morning, still dark, and few were moving this early. Zhuni just had to clear his mind. The thought of starting a medical department was daunting, but add the strange dream, and he was confused and overwhelmed. Getting out may help. He headed down the corridor to the loading area, making certain to go nowhere near the luxury box.

Even the loading docks were quiet. The guards barely acknowledged him. The night guards were not the regular ones. At night the heavy guards were put out. The Swaklin. They were large, nearly seven feet tall, dressed in their dark uniforms. Enormous and muscular upper bodies topped by broad heads, which seemed to be extensions of their chest and shoulders. The head seemed to be mostly a mouth with multiple rows of large pointed, triangular, and serrated teeth. Zhuni nodded at them and headed out of the dock.

The warm, dry air instantly put him at ease. He walked out past the lights and just before the wall. He stopped, took a breath, and glanced up into the sky. The sky was brilliantly filled with massive numbers of stars. The moons were also visible. The closest of the five moons (Balseck) was just setting; it appeared as a pale pink glowing orb just setting itself on the top of the nearby mountains. Zhuni could see three of the other moons also. One was a dusty yellow, about the size of his fist (Desrod), the largest in the sky was a greyish blue that was Colthon, and finally, there was Mocktuk, a brilliant blue. The fifth moon, Nerom, was a right orange and was the farthest moon, but it was not in sight tonight. He loved to gaze at the moons and stars and imagine traveling to them. Knowing the creatures here at the games being so diverse and amazing, he imagined how marvelous other life could be.

He sat down on the dry and dusty ground. He leaned his head back to look up and, this time, stared at the stars. He would sometimes attempt to count them. That is what he was doing when he laid out on the ground and feel back to sleep.

A huge powerful hand with four fingers was firmly shaking his shoulder to wake him; it was one of the night guards. Zhuni had fallen asleep on the main supply entry to the docks. It was inky black, as all the moons had set, but the guard's natural night vision found Zhuni easily. The guards blinked their eyes and held them shut for a moment, then the thick reddish night lens of their eyes would close and allow them to see perfectly. He was waking Zhuni to let him know deliveries were coming in the gate, and he did not want Zhuni to get run over.

The guard was a Swaklin, the Sargent of the guard. Zhuni knew it was the Sargent mainly because of the massive rifle he had slung over his back. The rifle was said to be the most powerful man-portable weapon known. Zhuni had heard the guards saying that Sarge had been hired as a mercenary in many wars, and in one, he had obtained the rifle. Zhuni had heard that no one had ever seen the Sargent without the rifle on his back, but no one had ever seen him use it. Zhuni just marked that all up as hyperbole. It was probably just a fancy rifle and nothing more; the Sargent probably told that to all his guards to help keep them in line and to build his reputation.

The Swaklin were known for their power and aggression, but Zhuni found they had a strong sense of right and wrong and were actually pleasant, reserved, and shy. Being tenacious warriors, everyone thought they were dumb and prone to violence. Zhuni found once you were able to understand their language and attempted to speak to them in their language, they would carry on a conversation. Zhuni had learned a lot about them other than just being incredible fighters. Most had families, were very loyal to those they trusted, and enjoyed his humor. The gamers had taken over their world and enslaved their race. The Swaklin were not as technologically advanced as the gamers. When the gamers, drug cartels, and slavers combined, the Swaklin lost their world. They were brought into employment with the guilds and cartels due to their tenacity and fighting prowess. They made fantastic bodyguards and security.

The Sargent wanted Zhuni to move on as the morning guards were coming on. Zhuni and the Swaklin shared a disdain for the humanish guards. They were referred to as humanish because there were so few truly pure humans left in the galaxy. Humans were one of the most intelligent but fragile races. They had spent millennia attempting to use their science to create stronger bodies using gene splicing and DNA adjustments. Even so, one-on-one or even ten-to-one, the Swaklin would easily best the humanish. But the Sargent and his guards rarely dealt with the humanish other than to take over their shift and turn over their watch.

Zhuni got up, grunted a thank you and good morning in Swaklineese, and headed back into the loading area, hoping to get through before the humanish came through.

He did not like humanish ones; the only ones he knew were the guards, the gamers, or the drug cartels. All were cruel and mean and looked at anyone other than their race as inferior. Zhuni had made sure to stay away from humanish ones and swore he would only befriend the fighters and creatures of the pit. When your own family abandoned you and left you to die, what possibly could and would other humans do to you?

Zhuni headed to the chow hall. They would just be starting breakfast, and he knew it was going to be a long day. He would need all the energy he could muster. A large first meal would help.

He sat down with his breakfast, Suhmarian eggs, Hamastrion hash (his favorite), a bowl of fruit salad including Ju-johny fruit (purple and sweet), and Slokton coffee. He was thinking you could not have too bad a day with this meal.

Then he heard the voice, "Zhuni."

Tan'cha was entering the hall and stumbled over to sit with him. "Good morning."

"Good morning to you, Tan'cha. I thought you were supposed to rest for a day or two; at least, I thought that those were the instructions from your doctor."

"Well, I woke early and thought a good hardy meal would help me heal quicker."

"You might not have to heal all the way, like back to fighting shape."

"Right, what are you talking about? Did you bump your head or something? I heard about your excitement last night."

"Yeah, that. Why would three fighters I don't even know want to risk their lives to save me?"

"I know you, and I don't get it either."

"Shut up, I am serious, why?"

"All of us respect you and know you care about each of us. Other than each of us as fighters, no one, and I mean no one here, cares whether we live or die. But you do. Many of us will die in the pit, but you give us hope and keep us going; we have seen you cry when you have not been able to save one of us; no one else cares."

"Really?"

"Yes, all the fighters know you, whether you know them all or not. They all talk about how hard you work to not just save us but to make us good as new. You study each of our anatomies as if your life depended on knowing everything you could to heal us properly. The scientists they have here do not know as much about each of our systems as much nor as well as you do. And none of them ever check on us to make sure we are okay. I bet you stopped in to check on the fighters from last night. Am I right?"

"Well, of course I did."

"See, now, what were you talking about not needing to get back into fighting shape?"

"I have to move to mid-level and start medical training and set up a hospital, rehab, center, or something I am not really sure. I thought you could help me."

"Me? What? be a nurse?" Tan'cha could not keep a straight face and started to chuckle.

"No! You are useless when it comes to medicine; I mean, look at you. You broke the collar off your knee already, and it hasn't even been a full day."

"I told you it stinks and gives me a headache."

"I think I will start calling you Mynog, all you do is whine like a baby Mynog."

"Shut up. I do not. Besides, what could I do to help you? I am a fighter, born and breed or breed and born, not a medic."

"Klavan told me to put together a team, and I thought I could use some muscle to move things around, maybe do some help strapping the big ones down, help fill out reports, you know, that sort of stuff."

"So, an errand boy. Okay, it might be nice to not get beaten up every few rotations."

"Something to think about, I mean, you are getting old, and you may need to consider another line of work before you get retired."

"You mean, before I retire."

"Nope, from what Stanton hinted at, it is getting close to game over for some of you, guys, and I would rather you be around a while. Things are changing, and we must at least keep up; it would be better to stay ahead of the game than fall behind. I can put you down as physically unable to perform anymore and then request you be part of my team. Seriously think about it."

"I never thought about what to do when the fighting rotations end. Besides, we fighters are slaves under the gamers, not paid and free like you."

"Well, grab yourself some breakfast, and we can work things out and talk more."

———————— * ————————

Zhuni and Tan'cha walked into the grounds maintenance space to look at their future.

Tan'cha said it first, "Wooh."

The space already had been cleared of the heavy equipment. It was an enormous cavern of a room. The space had been cut directly into the rock of the mountain the arena sat against. Zhuni had not expected it to be this big. Why would he need this huge expanse? Klavan said he was going to be the medical center for the arena, but this seemed a little extreme. Were there huge creatures he had not seen? Were they going to be even more injured and those needing medical attention than he was used to seeing?

This was a little more than he was expecting. He would have to have a better discussion with Klavan to see what was really going on.

Zhuni noticed that there was a large beam running the center of the space out of the hall and directly into the arena. It looked as if it was a rail for a heavy lifter. That may need to stay if they were going to be working on large creatures. A heavy lifter would also help with heavy equipment. Was he to set the area up for large creatures, small fighters, or a mix of all? Was it to be an emergency center and rehab or just operations? So many questions and so many thoughts were going through his head.

They spent another twenty partions in there just bouncing thoughts off each other. Tan'cha had some good concepts about separating different groups, the space would have to be divided and cages set up. Zhuni was used to working on the fighters and creatures one on one at the exit to the fight, but if they were all in this area, it could become interesting.

They started to leave the area as the construction foreman and his crew came in.

"What are you going to do?" Zhuni asked.

"Just getting measurements."

"I mean, what are you doing with the construction?"

"I know we are putting some med equipment in, a few living quarters, and that is all I have been told."

"Do you have the plans?"

"Nope, I have been told there are not any hard plans as to what to do. I was told the guy who was going to set this place up hasn't even been told exactly what they what done to it. Once he figures it out, we will start working. For now, just getting measurements as to what we can get in here, honestly just about anything."

Zhuni turned to Tan'cha, "Living quarters, this just keeps getting more interesting."

"So, if I work with you, will I get my own private living quarters? I would like that, no more living in the open barracks."

"I have to talk to Klavan."

"What about Stanton?"

"I have a feeling that may be why he was a little shorter than usual the other day; I may no longer be his to push around."

"No more Stanton to worry about. Well, then, count me in. I am sure I can do something to help."

"Let's find Klavan."

They turned down the corridor to look for Klavan; he was usually in the loading area checking in supplies or meeting with and entertaining the Game Master.

Tan'cha leaned down to speak quietly to Zhuni as they walked.

"There are a couple of Stanton's Boyz following us. Did you notice?"

"No."

"They have been following us since breakfast. I noticed them sitting in the closed-off section of the chow hall."

"Why would they be following us?"

"I thought you knew."

"What should we do?" Zhuni asked.

"We can lose them when we get to the loading docks."

"This just keeps getting more interesting."

"This does seem to be getting fun."

"I did not say fun."

"That is okay, I did. I am enjoying myself now, seems a lot better than just being an errand boy. If they are following us around, we must be important. I haven't felt important in a long time." Tan'cha chuckled.

"You are going to cause problems being so important."

"Me. I bet it is something you did; I am just a fighter. What could I have done? You're the one who is changing things up."

"I always wanted to move up, but this med lab, med center, whatever wasn't my idea."

"That may be the problem," Tan'cha answered.
"Dagz."

———————— * ————————

It did not take long to lose the Chordentia in amongst the crates, equipment, and bustle of activity. Zhuni noticed a large amount of equipment he had not seen before and wondered what it all was and what was going to happen. There was a lot heavier equipment that looked like it would be used by mercenaries or military rather than gamers or even the drug cartels. It was heavier weaponry than they usually saw. Mostly here, the guards were armed with blasters and rifles, not tripod-mounted equipment or missiles. There was even what looked like some type of body armor.

Things seemed to be changing fast. This new Game Master was serious.

They wandered all over, looking for Klavan but could not find him. They were going to have to go to his office and hope he was there. As they stepped into the corridors heading towards Klavan's office, a night guard, a Swaklin, told them that Klavan had been requesting Zhuni meet with him. The Swaklin also were Klavan's favorite guards and errand runners. They did as they were told and did not deviate from their assignment, and most importantly, unless you were one of them, they did not gossip. The Swaklin motioned for Zhuni to follow. Zhuni grabbed Tan'cha and drug him along.

"You said you wanted to feel important, so you can come with me," Zhuni said.

"I did not say I *wanted* to feel important, I said I felt important, but I am kind of over that right now."

"Too bad you are coming with us."

"Dagz!"

CHAPTER 2

The Plan

Klavan's office was up above and behind the luxury box. They were able to grab a lift as it came down, ready to take a load of equipment up. The Swaklin grabbed it and just looked harshly at the loader, and he knew this was not his lift any longer. No argument there. The Swaklin were very persuasive like that; with their powerful build and shark-like mouths, they rarely had anyone argue.

The office was a large space dug into the mountain, much like the med lab, much smaller, of course, but it was adorned with fine tapestries and art. The desk was an enormous dark wood and cera-masteel bulk work in the dead center of the room. A matching table was strewn with drawings and a hologram hovering above it, glowing a soft green. The hologram was an empty space shaped much like the med lab space. The lighting was soft as to be able to see the hologram.

Klavan nodded a dismissal to the Swaklin, who turned and left, closing the gigantic doors.

"Gentlemen, welcome. I assume Zhuni has informed you of the situation, Tan'cha."

Tan'cha looked surprised that Klavan knew who he was.

"Yes, sir," Tan'cha mustered.

"I must tell you the whole story."

He flicked his hand towards the chairs around the table, insisting they take a seat.

"This is the space we have to work with." Pointing to the hologram.

"Klavan," Zhuni asked, "what exactly are we doing?"

"That is why we are here. I know I threw a lot at you yesterday, and you are still attempting to grasp the complete concept. Here it is in an abbreviated form. We must form a medical facility in which you and several of your team will live. The facility will be designed to heal all fighters and creatures. Long-term care will be transferred. You will be a quick fix and stabilize the wounded. I know you care about these fighters and creatures, and I feel things are going to take a turn for the worse."

"Why do you say that? I know we have a new Game Master, but this doesn't usually change that much," Zhuni stated.

Klavan continued, "I see a lot of death, and I have set this up to attempt to show the Game Master it is too expensive to replace the fighters and to turn all fights into death matches. I came here as a logistics specialist and have kidded myself into thinking that I was doing nothing wrong by being the logistics and entertainment gentleman for the high rollers. If I was not directly involved in the Starch dealing and the fighting, I pretended I wasn't a bad guy. I just worked with the wrong individuals."

"You mean this whole thing is your idea?" Zhuni asked.

"Yes, but I am not exactly sure how to pull this off. This is my attempt to make things right before it all goes too bad."

"You want me to help design and set it up."

"Yes, I value your input and will need to know what surgical equipment you need. I already have the quarters here (pointing to the front left of the hologram). This will be carved out of the stone and will have an entrance off the main corridor."

"We will have our own private quarters?" Tan'cha blurted out.

"Shhhh. You and your privacy," Zhuni scolded him.

"Hey, I am never alone. It is actually unnerving," Tan'cha shot back.

Klavan glanced at Tan'cha with impatience. Then looked back at Zhuni, "I have always told you that you get too close to the fighters, but I believe that is why you are able to heal them and why you know more about them then the scientists. I want you to use that to help them."

"That is what I have always done."

"Yes, but you will be seeing more and more wounded, worse wounds, and new creatures that we have had at the main event that you have not seen yet."

"How do I work on them if I have never seen them?" Zhuni asked.

"The scientists at the main event have written their logs, and I will send you the files."

"Thank you. I will study them."

"This Game Master is evil and demanding. She demands nearly all my time. I do not know how much more I will be able to assist you. I have a terrible foreboding about this one. You should have a security detail. I will provide a pair of my Swaklin to assist with training and to lead your team. I know you do not trust your kind, so find some more fighters that you trust. I will grant your entire team their freedom, and they will be paid contractors working under the medical staffing budget."

"Why would I need security?" Zhuni quipped, emphasizing the "I."

"I know of at least one with influence who sees you as a threat. Plus, as I explained before, gamblers and odds setters will be looking at you as an influencer in the fights, and as such, you are a threat."

"Me? A threat? Come on, I am the smallest guy in the entire complex, less Stanton's minions. Plus, you know I have nothing to do with the betting."

Tan'cha jumped into the conversation again, "Stanton hates you."

Klavan added, "Exactly."

"Why would he see me as a threat? I am just a medic."

"You keep saying that, but you do know you are much more. That is what concerns Stanton." Klavan nodded towards Tan'cha.

"The fighters respect you and care about you, they know you not only care for them, but you care about them. You are the only one other than the interpreters who can speak most languages," Klavan continued.

"So, how is that a threat to anyone?" inquired Zhuni.

"You weld great influence with the fighters," Klavan stated.

Zhuni did not know how to respond to that; it made him uncomfortable.

"Well, let's get started on this project."

They spent the late morning, afternoon, and into evening setting up every detail they could think of. They were able to develop the staff of the medical team. The medics who worked the games already consisted of five others, and two of the scientists plus several Zhuni wanted to be included. The technical crew would operate the cages, lifts, and repair and maintain the surgical equipment. Then Klavan felt the security team had to consist of a full twenty-four-hour team, bodyguards for Zhuni, and three full shifts for the medical space. It was a good thing they had picked such a large space as they now were going to need their own administration.

"Klavan, are you sure this is going to work?" Zhuni questioned as they were wrapping up for the evening. He was feeling that this had grown way out of hand.

"The only expansive part I had not thought completely through is the security. I will have to justify that. The rest of your staff are just moved from other locations or departments. I think freeing some of the fighters from their slavery and giving them paying jobs may be an issue, but I will figure out a way to make it work."

Tan'cha heard Klavan say freedom and pay and glanced at Zhuni,

"Well, looks like I have a retirement plan after all."

"Yup, you sure do," Zhuni conformed.

"So, you are sure this is going to work?" Zhuni questioned, looking back at Klavan.

"No, not at all, but if we got this far, we could just keep it going, and if we make it big enough, no one will want to stop it. That is one thing I have learned in the years I have been here, make it too big to stop. If it is too big for one to see it all, most around here will not get involved," Klavan said with as big a grin as his face would allow.

"So, we will finish up the little details tomorrow, Klavan?" Zhuni said as he stood up.

"Yes, gentlemen, right after breakfast. I will only have a kolt or so. I have several loads coming into the space port tomorrow afternoon that I must attend to."

"About that, Tan'cha and I saw a lot of equipment in the loading area this morning when we were looking for you. What is going on?"

"We will talk more tomorrow."

———————— * ————————

Zhuni and Tan'cha headed out of Klavan's office and started down the corridor back to their quarters. They took the freight elevator down. Zhuni made certain not to go past the lower level under the luxury box again. After his dream and those feelings, he was not going near that area. His mind started to wonder as he was strolling along when Tan'cha gave him a nudge.

"They're back."

Zhuni glanced around and saw that their Chordentia friends were back.

"I wonder if they know what is going on and if they figured out we were with Klavan all day."

"I do not think they will figure it out. Once Stanton finds out where they lost us and where they found us, he will figure it out," Tan'cha chuckled.

"We should have some fun with them."

"What do you mean?"

"They are just following us; if they were out to get us, there would be more of them, and they would not be trying to hide in the shadows; by now, they would have struck. What do you say we do an about-face and lose them outside, then head off to get a good night of sleep?"

"I am up for that."

With that, they spun around, picked up their pace, and headed out of the loading area. They passed the Swaklin, who were on duty, and weaved their way through the transports and armored vehicles until they ended up back at the dock. Stanton's henchmen had a hard time matching their steps and fell behind. With their short stat-

ure, they could not see past the vehicles; they may have had better night vision than either Zhuni or Tan'cha but could not match
Tan'cha's hearing. Zhuni and Tan'cha would stop and listen to them
chatter and wander off in the wrong direction away from the docks.
Tan'cha laughed as he told Zhuni he could hear them fussing and
chattering into the voxes to call in more to help in the search. Tan'cha
told Zhuni there were more than a dozen wandering off toward the
perimeter, looking for them. When it was clear, Zhuni and Tan'cha
reentered the docks. Winked at the Swaklin, at the docks, he just
grinned as they passed by.

*

Another dream. This time, he saw more clearly and recognized
that a few of the creatures tearing him apart looked like gamers' scientists, but they looked much younger. Much younger. It did not
hurt as much almost as if he was getting used to it.

Zhuni washed. Got dressed and headed to the hall to meet
Tan'cha. He exited his quarters and saw the Chordentia were now
stationed at either end of the corridor. He thought, *So this is how it
is going to be. Maybe Tan'cha was on to something. Could Klavan be
right also? Why would Stanton be afraid of a medic? What could a medic
possibly do?*

He walked past the Chordentia, and as he did, he looked at
them and cracked up.

"Come on, we're going to get breakfast."

He saw Tan'cha at the entrance to the hall and glanced back at
his followers, then back at Tan'cha.

"We have company."

"I told you."

"Yes, you were right. Let's just ignore them and get some food.
I am starving."

"You do realize that we had no midday meal or evening food
yesterday."

"We were a little busy."

They ate heartily, not sure if they were going to eat again today. Klavan said he had things to do, but he seemed determined to get this started and quickly completed before anyone could stop it. They started out of the hall and made sure to invite their admirers. They had picked up a couple more, and as they got to the loading area to grab the lift, Tan'cha looked over the supplies and chuckled.

"We have the Boyz behind us, and there are at least four more sets of them by the back gate and scattered around the loading area."

"Do you think they know how obvious they are, or do you think they are trying to be stealthy?"

"I don't think they know. I have had them hide so well it was only their chittering which I heard in the shadows, and I hear fairly well."

"You know what, Tan'cha, I don't care what they are doing; I have nothing to hide."

"That may change; at least, it seemed Klavan was little concerned."

---

*

Klavan was behind his massive desk, dressed in his favorite purple long coat. He always dressed so fine; it was his trademark. He was always impeccable. The coat had fine embroidery trim in an iridescent stitching that was especially heavy around the broad cuffs.

"Good morning. Sit, I will be right with you."

He was in the middle of a conversation with someone, and by his stance, it was important. This took several partions, and Klavan was loosening up and becoming more relaxed. He nodded one final time, tapped his ear, and turned to Zhuni and Tan'cha.

"That was the Master; all our plans have been approved."

Zhuni and Tan'cha both said with uncertainty, "Really?"

Klavan continued, "Yes, gentlemen. We are now running a medical center. I think we will call it the med lab."

---

*

It had been kolts since Stanton had screamed at his night Boyz for losing Zhuni; he was still in a frustrated pink tone. He had spent the last few kolts worrying about his plans and saw Zhuni as a major issue. He had been unable to sleep even the minimal two kolts he usually slept.

Traxon walked in. He had been warned about his Dwayan's mood and was expecting a rough day.

"Nice of you to join me," Stanton said, thick with sarcasm.

"Morning not good; I heard last night, trouble."

"Oh, so you are paying attention. Now explain to me why you could not have your Boyz follow one crumby little human." Stanton started to darken, his skin changing to a rose, then a dark, almost red pink as he spoke. Both his huge eyes were glaring at the tiny figure of Traxon.

"I tell, watch, not lose, stay with. They no good I get others to follow; I follow if have to."

"No, I need you to take care of other things and to stay on these Boyz; one afternoon should not ruin everything. I told your Boyz to station themselves all over the complex; then there should be no way they lose him again. Pick one of your sergeants and give him the job of staying on top of the tracking team. Make sure he knows his life depends on knowing where Zhuni is always. Have him report to you each morning from this day forward." His color started to fade again.

"Yes, I do."

"I need you to get me some information. I know Klavan is working on something. I know he is doing something with the space for the grounds keeping equipment. I cannot have him doing something big and overshadowing me. Find out what he is doing. Talk to the contractors working there, bribe them, whatever you have to do."

"Yes, Traxon, do."

"Just to be sure we are clear, the Sargent you pick will need to stay on Zhuni always. If his team loses Zhuni, even for a nanosecond, I will toss him into the pit during the main event just for fun."

"Dwayan, yes." Traxon rubbed his scared face remembering the time Stanton had thrown him into the pit when Stanton had gotten angry with him. That was during a mid-level event, so Traxon had not been expected to survive. If it had not been for the new medic who had just arrived, Traxon felt he would not have survived. Since that day, Traxon had been hoping there would be a chance to return the favor.

"Now go, get out of here; I have had enough of you, Drogonds, for one day."

"Yes, I leave."

Traxon turned and left the office, wondering why Stanton was so fixated on Zhuni. Zhuni seemed nice; even the night guards and most of the fighters liked him. The night guards didn't like anyone. Swaklin were like that; they never showed their feelings.

———————— * ————————

Klavan, Zhuni, and Tan'cha were finalizing the details of the living quarters when their lunch arrived.

Zhuni had lunch with Klavan before, but nothing like this. The mess crew was bringing in three carts of spectacular-smelling food. Tan'cha had never had this type of food. They both looked dumbfounded.

Klavan noticed their expressions and snickered, "Gentlemen, it is a special occasion; we should celebrate. This is a big deal. I have been working on this concept since shortly after Zhuni came to us. It has taken three Game Masters. I am hoping this will be our legacy."

"This is going to be a good legacy."

Klavan looked at Zhuni, "Good, this is going to be wonderful."

"Yup, this is amazing. Can we eat now?"

"Yes, Tan'cha, dig in." Turning to Zhuni, Klavan said, "You too."

They all enjoyed the meal, for Klavan, it was a little extravagant, but for Zhuni and Tan'cha, it was a feast of delicacies they had never had before. The mood between the three had changed the last couple of rotations as they all worked to design the space and what they were going to do. There was no longer the employer and employee, nor the slave and master. It was a respectful team, almost a kinship or friendship forming.

Klavan jumped up, realizing the time, "Sorry, I must be going; special arrival landing in a moment. You two stay and eat. I will be back in a few kolts. I will send Shazen to see you when we finish with the arrival and have it put away."

Klavan grabbed his walking stick and headed out.

Zhuni and Tan'cha continued eating until they felt they were going to explode.

"Zhuni, I feel like I should take a nap. What do you say we each grab one of the chairs and grab some sleep? The lighting in here is just right for napping."

"You are a lazy Drogond."

"Yup, I am a free Drogond now."

Klavan's office had his enormous desk in the center, the matching conference table off to the left, and then a large sitting area to the right. The seating area had several overstuffed chairs and several other platforms and pads to accommodate all types of creatures. All of these were upholstered in bold colors and intricate patterns, mostly in Klavan's favorite colors of deep purple and dark blue. The stitching was also ornate and of the same iridescent thread that had been on the trim of Klavan's long coat.

"I don't know if I feel comfortable sleeping in here," Zhuni piped.

"It sure looks comfortable to me."

"Fine, let's just sit and relax then."

They both wandered over to grab a comfortable spot.

"You know, Zhuni, things have changed since you got here. No one before worried about the fighters or creatures like you do. It was not until you started fixing us that the last couple of Game Masters even thought of us as anything more than livestock, good for nothing other than entertainment. If we died, so be it. They could always get more."

"I am sorry it has been like that," Zhuni offered.

"Oh, no worries. Growing up as a slave, I just was used to this type of life; I thought it was how it was supposed to be. But you changed that for many of us. Did you know that before you got here, we were trying to kill each other? After you started saving lives and healing everyone, we felt we might have a chance and maybe live long lives. So, we stopped going for the death blow or even the crippling shot and fought hard but not to kill. No one said anything, it just started, and we all kept doing it. The Game Masters never even noticed."

"You all are not trying to kill each other?"

"Nope, we fight hard, but we all made a quiet pact to survive and work to ensure each other survives the fights."

"Do you think we are going to pull this off?"

"Zhuni, I guarantee you that with the support of Klavan and the pit fighters, this is going to work."

"You know what, I am feeling rather tired."

"Look at that, I become a free Toochuk, and suddenly my wisdom knows no bounds; I told you yesterday Stanton hated you, and this morning you were being followed. Then I said it was nap time, and here we are."

"Shut up."

They both chuckled, laid their heads back, and quickly fell asleep.

———————— * ————————

Tan'cha was lightly shaking Zhuni to wake him.

"We have company," he told Zhuni in a whisper.

"What?"

"There."

Zhuni looked towards the conference table to see several small hunched-over figures rifling through the papers. He recognized them as Chordentia.

"Why are they going through that stuff?" he asked Tan'cha.

"I have no idea, but I am pretty sure they were not invited," Tan'cha said as he jumped up quietly.

"Watch this," Tan'cha continued.

The Chordentia were never known for their bravery. This point was proven when they were confronted by Tan'cha leaping up and over the furniture and running towards them. They completely stopped for a split second, then scattered, bouncing off each other, the chairs, and the table as they hastily departed the room.

Tan'cha was chuckling as he turned to Zhuni, "I was hoping to catch one, but that was fun."

"Priceless, but what do you think they were doing?" Zhuni asked.

"I would say they were looking at the plans and trying to figure out what was going on. Seems Stanton not only hates you but is not fond of Klavan either." Tan'cha grinned.

"He doesn't hate me, but yes, it seems he has an issue with Klavan. We need to let him know."

"That Stanton doesn't like him or that he sent some minions to dig through his office?"

"How do you make it through life thinking like that?"

"Hey, simple question, who is dumber, the dumb one or the one who has the dumb one as his chief of security?"

"Tan'cha, chief of security? Is that what you are? How did you come up with that?"

"Well, you heard Klavan. He said we needed security. I am not a nurse, and I surely do not do paperwork, so what else can a fighter do? Be security."

"Great, I have seen you after your fights, so you are my security?"

"Yes, Boss."

---

*

Stanton was furious, his dark purple skin shivering with rage.

"You got caught! I cannot have this happen. Klavan is now going to know who is working against him; that was my advantage."

"I am going to have to get someone in here I can count on. You, Drogonds, were fine when nothing was on the line and mattered, but now it is important."

He started fading in color as several human soldiers came in and rounded up the Chordentia, who were quivering before Stanton's rampage.

"This is what happens when you fail me. You will now be a warmup to the main event." Stanton started giggling. His color changed to a soft yellow.

An android strolled over to Stanton and projected a hologram that looked much like the one in Klavan's office.

Stanton was studying it when Traxon came in. Stanton swiveled one eye to see Traxon and kept the other focused on the hologram.

"Tell me you have not failed me as the others have."

"No, Traxon do good."

"So, tell me, what it is that I am looking at."

"That hologram."

"Yes, I know that. I am not as dumb as you are. What is the hologram showing?" Stanton burst out, losing his soft yellow tone and fading to a light pink.

"It doctor station."

"This is not a medical station; it is much too large. It has offices and cages and equipment." Stanton's coloring shifted to a barely visible blue.

"Boss, yes. Big medical place to fix all."

"Fix all, you mean fighters and creatures?"

"Boss, yes."

"Interesting. That explains the equipment, medical stations, cages for the creatures, and I am guessing those offices are for administration."

"Boss, yes. Boss, no."

"What?"

"Boss, yes, but office, Boss, no. Living."

"Living quarters?"

"Yes."

"Good job, Traxon; I may keep you around a while." Stanton started to change his color back to a soft yellow.

"Thanks, Boss."

"Get me more info; I want to know every detail."

"Yes, Traxon find."

Traxon spun around and left as quickly as he could. He hated Stanton. He was Stanton's number one, but he always felt Stanton hated him and everyone around him. All Stanton wanted to do was become the Game Master and rule over everyone. Only when he was in charge would he be happy. Traxon did not believe, even though it was what Stanton always said, "When I am in charge, things will be better." Traxon knew all it would do was make life worse for everyone else. He had just witnessed it in the office, five of his brothers taken away for making a mistake. The next main event, they would be fed to her, the Demon of Death, but no one survived her.

He knew he had to get out, but what could he do? He was just a survivor. He was not smart, strong, or fast. He could only live. He had no purpose until he came to Stanton. Traxon thought he had made it; he was Stanton's right hand. Then Traxon made one mistake, and he was thrown into the pit to be torn apart; he was lucky he smelled and tasted so bad. When the Bythtta bit into him, it spit him back out. He lay on the ground as the fighters fought over and around him. He was stepped on and left for dead. When the fighting was done for the night, they came to clean the pit, and one he had never seen before helped him. Zhuni fixed him and repaired him. Traxon hated humans, but Zhuni was different. Traxon may have one eye and scars, but he was alive; it felt to be all he was, alive. Just taking up space in this world. No purpose, no hope.

*

The Swaklin Zhuni knew as the Sargent of the night guard and three others arrived. They were hulking creatures with their broad heads set deep into their shoulders. Their huge mouths in permanent grins. Inside the grins were rows of enormous triangular serrated teeth. Their large four-fingered hands held blaster rifles, and on their hips were two different pistols, one a blaster and the other an immobilizer.

Zhuni greeted them with the clicks and growls of their native Swaklineese. This made all the Swaklin smile. Zhuni introduced Tan'cha formally to them.

The Sargent informed Zhuni and Tan'cha that he and the other three were the security team Klavan had assigned to the medical lab and that they were to train the others Zhuni chose to be the remainder of the team. The Sarge would be the head of overall security. He informed them that he had also been a personal bodyguard to Klavan, and he would train Tan'cha on the finer points of that work.

Sarge barked at the others, and they swung their rifles onto their backs and headed deeper into the cavernous space to interview and watch the construction teams as they began to file in.

Sarge turned to Zhuni and Tan'cha, "Gentlemen, I will tell you Klavan is concerned about your safety and the security of this project. He has asked me to take complete control of all security details, including warning systems and alarms. This space will be a completely independent system. From this point forward, only personnel that my team clears will be allowed in here. I will be bringing in several key players to set the systems up. We will be setting up an armory, a security station, and blast doors to keep us in and others out. The only link to any system will be the medical records, and those will go through a filter my security specialist will create."

"How can we help?" asked Zhuni.

"I know you need to get the medical equipment organized and set up, and I know Tan'cha has some fighters he wants to work with. He and I can go talk to them. I will leave my hirelings to watch over you." Sarge gave a three-bleat high-pitched whistle, and in a moment, all three were back. He spoke to them in Swaklineese, and two went back to check on the workers, and one stayed with Zhuni.

"I guess we will be back," said Tan'cha as he and Sarge walked off.

Zhuni watched them walk out of the space, Sarge was stocky and towered over Zhuni, but he was dwarfed by Tan'cha. If he needed security, those two seemed like an intimidating pair.

Sarge was impressed by the fighters Tan'cha had them speak with. He was interested to know Tan'cha's thinking, so he asked him why he chose who he did.

"Do you mean individually or as a whole?"

"I just wanted to understand your thinking; I have my own thoughts," Sarge said.

"Overall, I feel we need a diverse group with different skill sets. I have fought all of them."

"Yes, I gathered that, especially when that little one with the busted tusks looked suspiciously at you as you first proposed your idea."

"He is new; he actually was my most recent fight," Tan'cha said as he patted his knee, he was still favoring it.

"But what makes you think these specific fighters will work?"

"You learn a lot when you fight someone, if they are out to kill you, if they will cheat or do whatever it takes to win, and if they have honor. If they have no honor in a fight, they will have no honor outside the arena."

"I agree, these may not all make it, but I think we have the core of a solid group. The variety of skills will be an asset. I like my hirelings to have varied skill sets; you match each with another who is strong in their weakness."

"They all certainly appreciate the idea of their helotry ending and gaining freedom with better living quarters and a pay scale."

"We need to be careful with that. They still must follow the guidelines we set for them, and they will be on guard every moment. I am a difficult individual who maintains constant diligence even while not on shift, and I will expect that from each of them."

"I do not believe that will be an issue; all the fighters have wanted the freedom to change their circumstances. I understand you will train us hard."

"Especially you. You will be Zhuni's main bodyguard, and you will be my number two. I will expect more of you and will be harder on you."

"I understand. Why are you doing this?"

"It is my job."

"No, I have dealt with you and your hirelings long enough to know this is personal, or at least it is much more to you than your regular guard duty. You do know I have been raised in the arena. I was born into this and have always been around you and the other Swaklin. I know this arena and the staff like family. Whether you know it or not, I observe everyone and everything; that is why I have lived so long in the pit."

"That is why I know you will make a fine bodyguard and number two."

"So why?"

"It is my job."

"There is more, I know it."

Sarge just turned and headed down the corridor back to the med lab.

———————— * ————————

Klavan no longer enjoyed his job. He had started long ago as a logistics expert for the gamers, not realizing what they did and not knowing they were tied to the Starch runners, cartels, and the syndicates. But when he did find out the money was so great, he could not say no. He had made his name refining trade routes and delivery systems; he had also been a great social coordinator, and that helped even more. He felt if he just told himself the Starch and the slaves were just cargo, he would not actually be involved in any wrongdoing. It had worked for a long time, but the truth was coming to the surface, and he was working to correct his past.

He now found himself sitting in the Game Master's meeting room, awaiting another meeting. He had a sense that this one was different; the feeling was odd as the Game Master's attendants directed him in. They were not the usual attendants he had seen before. This new Game Master was not like the ones before; She was mean and nasty and was so greedy. She saw everything as a means of cutting costs or gaining income. He had not seen it but heard She tended towards violence when She did not get Her way. He heard as a cartel leader a smuggler had tricked Her with a technicality on a delivery. Instead of following the basic creed of the smugglers and realizing She had been taught a lesson, She decided to get Her revenge. She waited for the smuggler to leave Her ship, get on his, and started to fly off. That is when She had Her gunners shoot the ship down and then destroy the wreckage to ensure there were no survivors. She killed a crew of thirty-six to say to the others do not mess with me. It was not long after that that She was promoted to Game Master.

This was Klavan's first time in this meeting room. It was opulent beyond anything Klavan had seen. The walls were covered in an exotic wood that he had never seen. It was a warm orange with brown undertones and shown with gold in the grain. The grain sparkled as if it were electrified. The soaring ceiling was a translucent stone with a hint of orange. The gap between the wood and the ceiling had a light tan sandstone embedded with gleaming stones. The massive table in the middle was made of the same wood as the walls, and many of the stones in the sandstone were inlaid to form the Master's personal crest in the center. At the far end of the table was a massive chair or throne with the crest and again embedded with the stones. Behind the chair up on the wall was a massive viewer. On either side of the throne was a less elaborate chair. Down the sides of the table were ten more chairs. Klavan walked over and sat in the chair to the right of the throne.

The doors opened, and several attendants started setting up drinks and foods on the table and along the small tables along the walls. Klavan knew this was the first official meeting with all the Dwayans and administration, so the Master was putting out a spread.

Several of the Dwayans and regents started to file in and took seats along the table. Stanton himself came in and sat about the center of the left side. He eyed all the others as he came in, each eye drifting off in a different direction and pausing only for a moment as he sized everyone up. He did not even glance at nor acknowledge Klavan.

They all sat quietly for several partions. Then the door behind the table head opened, and She entered.

---------------- * ----------------

Zhuni had learned the language of several of the aliens he worked with. The hardest to grasp and vocalize was Swaklineese. The language was a nuanced series of whistles, clicks, and growls. But as he had nothing to do with the humans, he had worked to master these languages. Speaking with the guard he was with, Zhuni found that the Sarge was extremely worried about this project. The guard's name was Slaza; he and the others were handpicked as the Sarge's most trusted and best trained. In fact, the Sarge wanted to add at least two more of his hirelings onto the project. He did not believe the fighters would have the proper discipline for the job.

Zhuni had found out from the construction crew that they had also been handpicked by Klavan, and several had been brought in from off-planet.

This was turning out to be a much more intriguing project than Zhuni had any indication of at the beginning. Why the secrecy? Why the off-worlders? Why the security, and why Klavan's own Sargent. Slaza had no answers. He just knew the facts of the project, not the compelling reasoning behind the decisions. Zhuni had some questions for Klavan.

CHAPTER 3

The Master

She decided to introduce herself simply as "The Master."

Klavan had spoken to Her nearly every day since She arrived. He had even met with Her several times by monitor but had never seen Her before. When they had met, She had simply spoken to him over the vox She had given him.

She was not as large as Klavan had expected; she was, in fact, shorter than he was and looked frail. Her skin was smooth and red with black and orange markings down Her face. She had long blue hair, so dark that, at first, it appeared black. It was pulled back tight to her triangular head and allowed to flow down Her back. She wore armor of the outer edge pirates and Smugglers' Guild, but it was ornately tooled and had more of the glistening stones that matched those inlaid in the table. She had the matching crest from the table on the chest of the armor. The armor was black, which made the stones stand out; it was detailed in crimson. The boots She wore were black lacquer of the type jump troopers of the Stellar Command wore. On Her hip was a blaster pistol of a type Klavan did not know. On the opposite hip was a large sword of a glowing red. On either side and just behind Her stood a personal guard. They were tall, nearly Klavan's height, and wore armor similar to Hers, black with crimson edges. Their armor was not as ornate nor encrusted with stones. They did wear Her crest. Their heads were covered with an odd helmet, so Klavan could not tell what race they were. Each guard had a power staff, a blaster strapped to their hip, and a plasma rifle slung over their back.

She was small, but Her presence filled the room. Her bearing demanded instant recognition.

She informed everyone present that She had accumulated Her power and now was not just the Game Master but "the Master" of the guilds, cartels, and syndicates, including the Starch Traders.

Klavan had an empty feeling in the pit of his stomach and knew his inspiration to create the medical lab was an idea much needed.

The Master informed everyone that they were there to work for Her and any ambitions that would prevent total and undying loyalty would be dealt with severely. To prove Her point, She told the story of Her arrival and how the previous servants had not shown the respect She deserved. She did not go into detail as to what that exactly meant.

Klavan knew She was keeping it vague for a reason.

So, to show what happens to those who do not heed Her desires immediately, She motioned for them all to look up at the viewer. It came on and showed several of the previous group of servants and attendants standing in the arena.

"Go," She spoke.

With that, the gate opened, and several of the Pantaas were released. They pounced on the victims and ripped them apart. As their screams filled the room, She informed all those present that She wanted the servants to die a useful death. There was no event this cycle, so the Pantaas were hungry.

"If anyone here disappoints me as part of my management team, their death shall not be as quick nor as pleasant."

Klavan could see several of the Dwayans and Regents enjoying the show; Stanton especially seemed to be in glee watching the pain and suffering. He was a glorious, glowing yellow. Klavan was not so much watching them but was just glancing about the room, looking at their reactions. He did not enjoy the violence as the others seemed to. He realized She was watching and studying all their reactions.

Klavan saw Her study every Dwayan and Regent. Her expressions and face showed no reaction, nor did Her stance. She glided about the room slowly and without sound. Watching.

Klavan decided now was a fine time to turn away from the carnage and attempt to present himself as uncaring and unconcerned, so he strode over to grab something to drink and a snack from one of the tables along the wall. The screaming and moaning continued as he made his way to the table; he positioned himself, so his back was to the viewer. Inside he was sick and wanted to throw up but knew he could not show that weakness. He caught a glimpse of Her looking at him, and as his eyes caught Hers, he felt a coldness and emptiness that terrified him. He hoped She had not seen that in him because, just as quickly, Her gaze moved on.

The Pantaas had done their work now, and there were just a few moans and the crunching of bones as the Pantaas began to eat.

"I will expect a report from each of you detailing your worth to me. This report will be due tomorrow; I will visit each of you. Klavan, you have proven your worth to me for now, but once we complete this meeting, I would like to speak with you. We have many things to discuss."

She turned to leave, paused to those gathered, "This will be the last time I inform you that upon my entering a space and leaving a space, each and everyone in the room shall stand until I inform you otherwise. Enjoy the meal." They all stood.

Just as She reached the door, "Klavan."

Klavan had been working with Game Masters before and had anticipated the summons; he was already at Her heels.

"Yes, Master, I am here with you."

They entered the chamber. This was a dark room; much of the light came from the sword on Her hip and several simmering torches on the walls.

The room was round, with steps leading up to a grand throne. She ascended the stairs to the throne and as She climbed, the torches on the wall became brighter and brighter until the room was so bright it was hard to see.

Klavan stood at the bottom of the stairs looking up at Her.

Looking down at him, She said, "That went well. I do enjoy an entrance."

"You made a grand entrance, Master, and the exit was just as dramatic."

"Tell me about them. What am I working with? I want details on each, what drives them, what are their ambitions, what are their fears and weaknesses, everything. Start with that bellicose yellow thing."

"As you wish, Master."

—————— * ——————

The construction was nearly complete, the living quarters were finished, and the team had moved in. Zhuni and Tan'cha were impressed by how lavish their quarters were. Both spaces connected for security. They each had a bedroom, sitting room, and a private shower and restroom. Zhuni also had an office at the front of his space that had a viewer and access to the system. This would allow him to run his reports and review records. His sitting room had seating for a dozen. The space had a large viewer for entertainment and a small one in his sleeping quarters.

This had become a city of their own. In the living quarters, a dining hall had been added, and a pair of chefs had been brought in to have their own quarters. The dining hall could accommodate the entire staff, which now counted over sixty. This included the medics, the engineers to maintain the equipment, security, chefs, and admin. For some reason, there were even members of the construction team with living quarters. They even had a motor pool with armored vehicles. They had an exit to the outside and a loading dock.

Security had been set up, and the electronic security specialist was an odd little creature. He was a bit smaller than Zhuni and rocked forward and back on his oversized feet, balanced by his powerful tail. He could leap tremendous distances; in fact, while installing the security system, he would often forgo the lifts and ladders and just jump to the areas he was working. His skin was rough and with tiny scales covering all but his face, throat, chest, and mid-region. His coloring was a grayish blue, with short, coarse hair randomly jutting out at spots but exploding from the top of his head as if it were a spikey geyser. He would bounce around with his tool kit thrown over his back and often had spare parts in a pouch he strapped to his stomach. The little guy was always bouncing around and went by the name Joxby. Zhuni was certain the guy did not sleep.

Joxby had a collection of robots and androids he built to perform specific tasks. He had several drones that hovered around him and would jet off to perform some task, repair a camera, measure a distance, look at areas not covered by cameras or check the perimeter. Zhuni was certain at least one drone could smell because it always shot off to the dining hall whenever the chefs entered and started preparing meals. Joxby liked to eat a lot.

The security team had come together nicely, especially when Sarge had been able to add two more of his hirelings to the mix. That addition had allowed the training to speed up. All the fighters were well trained on hand weapons, so Sarge had them train each other on their special weapons of choice while his hirelings trained others on rifles and pistols. Having the armored vehicles and transports allowed Sarge to train them on driving and heavy weapons. They were all also issued armor and side arms. These they put on racks in their quarters, the rifles and heavy weapons stayed in the armory.

The one thing Zhuni did not understand was the enormous cage opposite the living quarters on the right side as you entered. This had a massive hoist beam connected to the ceiling. This hoist beam ran the length of the med lab, out into the corridor, into the arena, and in the opposite direction to the loading dock. It also turned off to this massive cage. Did they have something he did not know about?

The medical gear was set up, and Zhuni had his first meeting with the technicians who trained him on some of the new gear. He also met with and trained with some of the scientists and other medics. The scientists, there were three, knew about the anatomy of many of the creatures and fighters but had no idea how to heal them. The scientists had studied and done autopsies but had never attempted to heal, repair, or save them. The medics, five Zhuni had brought on, knew how to give basic first aid to a few creatures, but they would all need training on more creature types and on most of the in-depth procedures. Talzon was a team member, and Zhuni hoped Talzon would live up to the promise Zhuni saw in him. Having spent a few rotations with these individuals, Zhuni understood why Klavan had set this all up. There was no coordination; everyone was doing their best but had limited knowledge. Together they could make a difference if they would learn from each other.

The main event was just a few rotations away. There was talk that this would be a special event. This would be the first event completely under the new Master, and She needed to make an impression. Klavan had told Zhuni to expect many casualties. She was a mean one, and Klavan felt She had some tricks they should be prepared for. She had some construction done in the arena, which only the construction crews knew about. The rumor was that She had installed traps to make it more dangerous and exciting for the spectators. Zhuni was working out a way to get some info on the changes, but no one would talk. Either no one knew, or they were terrified to get caught talking about it. He needed to speak with Klavan. But Klavan had been so busy the last several rotations running around with Her that Zhuni wasn't sure they would be able to meet until after the main event. That did not sit well with Zhuni.

*

Traxon was certain Stanton was going to be angry with him, but there was nothing he could do. Zhuni had a security detachment and was now spending all his time in the med lab. Traxon knew he had gotten Stanton a lot of useful information dealing a little Starch to a couple of the off-worlders building the lab. But then they were left out of the final build, and Traxon could get no information. He even attempted to slip some microdrones in on food shipments and kitchen equipment, but the microdrones had gone dark. He had stationed teams at each entrance, the corridor, the living quarters, and the loading dock. None of the Boyz could get in. This was not good. He had dealt some Starch to some of the arena guards and attendants and was going to be able to get them in during the main event, but nothing until then. He had succeeded in what he thought was a coup and got one of Klavan's old microbugs into the Master's office. He was able to adjust the transmission and make it two channels, one imbedded inside the other. If anyone was scanning for frequencies, they would read it as being received by Klavan and should not be able to read the frequency going to Stanton. He resigned himself to meet with Stanton and tell him. This was going to be rough.

"Dwayan, I tell you."

"Yes, Traxon."

"No able to get in lab. We use microdrones for no work. We work on crew build and a little help. Then work on put team at every entrant. No get in. I get informer in at main event until, no get anything."

Stanton started to turn red; he looked at Traxon with one eye; the other was admiring a new set of robes he had purchased for the main event.

"You could not get into the lab, you could not get microdrones to work, you could not get any information from the construction crew, and you can get some information but not until the main event. Does that sum it up correctly?" Stanton was a deep magenta; now, both eyes were staring down at Traxon.

"Yes, but good news I have."

"You had better; otherwise, I see no need to maintain you as my number two."

"Micro recorder placed in Master's office."

"You got a recorder in the new Game Master's office?" With that, his coloring faded to a pale pink.

"On desk we hide. This we listen," he said as he reached up to place the receiver on the desk in front of Stanton. Stanton rolled one eye to look at the receiver; his skin tone slowly changed to a soft yellow, then his second eye locked on the receiver as he reached slowly to pick it up. He cradled it as if it were a precious child.

Stanton listened to the receiver, "There is nothing."

"No one in office."

"You are sure this is working?"

"Yes, I hear before."

"Traxon, this is why you are and always will be my number two." Stanton slowly turned a bright yellow, and Traxon knew he would be around a little longer.

———————— * ————————

It had been a long meeting with the Master. That first evening had been kolts of questions by Her about each member of the staff. She was interested in Klavan's opinion, which surprised him. But he had been working with Masters before, and that may have been Her reasoning. This one was evil and cruel. It made him nervous, and he was intimidated by Her overbearing presence. She was fishing for information; he was not sure exactly what She was after.

Klavan was sure She had made decisions as to who was maintaining their positions and who wasn't based on what he said. This made him uncomfortable. Even when they met with each Regent and Dwayan, Klavan could see Her study them. Some were totally oblivious to this and just rattled on about how important they were.

When the interviews were over, She told Klavan changes needed to be made. "We have too many doing the same thing, and I do not see them all as useful. I may have some fun with a couple to be examples for the rest." Klavan knew what that meant and feared for those She did not want around.

"Klavan."

"Yes, Master."

"Explain to me why you should stay. Why have we spent all this energy and resources to build this project for you."

"Master, You know my value." Sounding more important than he felt. They had spoken at length about his running the entire organization for the previous Masters. He needed to sound confident but not arrogant. She did not want weakness.

"Yes," it trailed off much longer than Klavan liked.

He knew how to play the game and knew how to keep a job just to stroke the Master's ego. This was more than just keeping a job; this was staying alive. He would have to be on his toes, and this would take every bit of his talent to walk the edge. He would have to be strong while not showing too much ambition. He would have to flatter Her ego without coming across as a lackey. This Master was going to be exhausting.

"Your special project is going well. I hope you are correct about the return on our investment."

"I am sure You will be pleased. I have been working on this with the last two Masters, but they were not as wise and as visionary as You."

"They were not willing to take chances; I am. I expect a solid return on my investments."

"Master, we will have a fine long-term return."

"It had better not take too long. Giving all of them their freedom, I am disappointed that I did not know that detail. Klavan, do not keep information of any type from me."

"My Liege, there was no intention, just an oversight. I had worked on that stipulation with the previous master. The illusion of freedom will allow them to work harder, believing they are achieving a personal goal. They have nowhere to go. Even with direct access to the outside. We have trackers on their vehicles and equipment."

"You may actually have a wise idea; I will not be surprised if you have more in the future. My Liege, I do like the sound of that."

"Thank You, Master."

Zhuni, Tan'cha, and Sarge were all sitting in Zhuni's office. It had been filled with fancy overstuffed furniture in deep hues of blue, teal, green, and purple. There was some intricate embellishment in a golden thread. His desk was the old administrator's desk; it was a rich red-hued wood with a serene padded high-back chair upholstered in a dark blue. The furniture was left from the remodeling of the Master's spaces. Klavan had to redo every detail of the Master's spaces to please the new Master. Usually, the furniture was all crushed in the trash shredder or burned at these changeovers. This time Klavan had informed the new Master how much they could save by reusing the furniture. He received all of it for his office and had some reupholstered in his favorite styles and colors.

"Joxby has the systems complete, we have coverage of our entire space, plus he has slipped some cameras into the corridors and out into the loading areas. From the security room, we can see all around us. We can control all entry points," Sarge said.

"So that is good, right?" Zhuni asked.

"Yes, for maximum security, we not only need to know what is going on in our space but what is going on around us. Joxby has also reprogrammed those microdrones we found and will be able to send them anywhere in the complex."

"Why would we need that?"

"We may not. It is good to have two options if we do need. I believe Klavan had a reason for us to be completely independent of the main complex," Sarge insisted.

"Do you think we are in trouble?"

"No. I believe Klavan wanted us to be free from the Master. I have been with Klavan a long time, and I have never seen him so concerned about the changeover. He found out a few rattons before the rest of us of the change and put this all into motion, knowing who was coming in. He knows something he is not letting us in on," Sarge assured them.

"So, Sarge, what should we do?" Tan'cha asked.

"Trust in him. Klavan has never let me down."

"He has always been there for me; he has been my foundation," Zhuni said.

"But he is now the Master's confidant," Tan'cha voice.

"Even more reason to trust him; he will let us know what is going on," Sarge said.

"So, we are ready? The main event is in two rotations," Zhuni asked.

"Security is. I don't know about medical; it is not like that is why we are all here," Sarge said.

"Medical is as ready as we will ever be. I have the three younger medics set to do preliminary evaluations; then, I will confirm, move the injured off to the two older, more experienced medics, and have the scientists assist them. The sterilized tents are ready, and the tech crews have been briefed," Zhuni stated.

"I will be by your side the whole time," Tan'cha said.

"Just don't get in my way. Is he ready?" Zhuni looked at Tan'cha, then turned to Sarge.

"He is. He is also one of the best I have worked with; his instincts are sharp. I will continue to work with him. He can always learn more. The hirelings and I will continue to work with all the security team. Choosing the fighters was wise, and with one or two exceptions, we have a fine team," Sarge said with a proud smile.

"Who do you not like?" Tan'cha asked.

"It is not that I don't like them; it is that a couple need a bit more motivation, umm, encouragement."

"Okay, you worry about that. I need to be by Zhuni."

"Yes, you do your job, and let me do mine. Zhuni, is there anything you foresee as an issue if they are bringing the fighters and creatures in? Anything you need from security?"

"Actually, I would like to have a training session tomorrow for everyone, security, techs, handlers, etc., explaining how to deal with some of the creatures and the different aliens. We need to be sure we do not put any of them in a situation where they will be hurt or someone will get hurt. I need you in security to know which weapons at our disposal to use on which of our combatants."

"Wise, I do not want to upset something. Or kill something. Unless I truly have to," Sarge said.

"Yes, Sarge, I agree we do not want anyone or anything getting hurt or killed."

*

Stanton had enjoyed the meeting with the Master, except that Klavan was there. Stanton liked the Master and knew She was the type of leader he had longed for. He could now work towards his goal and felt She would be helpful. Traxon had the micro recorder in the Master's office, and Stanton had caught a few vague conversations but had not been able to figure out the Master's routine. He would have to figure a way to know when She was in her office. He could not risk sending any of the Boyz in, they had screwed up the information retrieval in Klavan's office, and now Klavan would know

Stanton was watching him. If one of the Boyz was anywhere near the Master's quarters, Klavan would most likely inform the Master. Klavan had stepped up his game and made himself invaluable to Her. This will be a problem.

Traxon skittered in to see Stanton leaning back in his huge chair with his feet up on the table. Traxon knew when Stanton was the orange hue, he was currently, there was a lot of thinking going on. Traxon had learned the color changes in his Dwayan and paid close attention to not react the wrong way to his moods. The only color he had issue with was purple, which threw him off. Was Stanton furious, confused, or sad? Traxon never knew.

"Dwayan."

Stanton did not move but did open one eye and roll it down to look at Traxon.

"How do we know when the Master is in Her office?"

"Boyz, in corridor by door."

"No. The last time we used the Boyz, they were caught; now Klavan will be looking for them. They have earned an invitation to a front-row seat at the main event for their transgression. Next idea."

"Record office, listen later."

"No, I do not want recordings floating around; what if She finds them."

"Microdrones in corridor."

"That may work. We cannot get too close; there are now scanners in the corridors. The only reason you were able to get the micro recorder in is because you put it in during Klavan's remodel, and I am hoping if it is found, we can blame him."

"I talk, Minnda; he fix drones."

"Good; now you are going to get into the med lab during this main event, correct."

"I not, but Boyz or special, yes."

"Special, one of your informants, I presume."

"Yes, guards, human and animal tenders."

"Good."

"Arena change. Master make many changes."

"What? I did not hear of this." His orange color had changed to his light pink tone, but now he started to change to a darker pink.

"Yes, I find talking to guard night late."

"Do you know what She has changed?"

"Guard say construction tell him."

"Yes?"

"Construction say interaction for crowd."

"What do you mean, interaction?" Stanton said, slowly changing to a dull purple.

"Guard said, construction said, crowd help fight."

"Crowd help fight? What does that even mean?" Stanton said, changing to a deeper purple.

"Dwayan, that what guard at construction said."

"Get me more information; I need to know what you are talking about."

"Yes Dwayan. I find," Traxon quickly made his exit.

Stanton thought this idea of the crowd being involved "interactively" was intriguing. This Master may be more interesting than he thought; he may have to adjust his plans. Maybe the arena could use a little excitement and a few upgrades. His mind started racing with ideas, traps in the pit, a moat, spikes in traps, fire; the possibilities were endless. Now, if he could come up with something clever that might get him on the Master's good side.

———————— * ————————

Klavan was dressed as sharp as ever. He was wearing his favorite color, purple. This time it was a long coat with gold thread embroidery in ornate patterns. He had asked to meet with Zhuni, Tan'cha, and Sarge in the med lab. Klavan had told the Master he was going to check on the progress of the construction and to ensure they were ready. The Swaklin guard and his apprentice opened the door to the med lab for Klavan to enter. He had not been here since it was nothing more than an open empty space. It was still a massive space, but it was no longer empty. Medical equipment filled the front third of the space, and there was a wide access path down the center leading to cages and what looked like minihabs stacked three and four high. Klavan was impressed; it looked ready to go. He saw them standing in front of the largest caged-off area to the right and headed over to them.

"Good afternoon, sir. Welcome to the med lab," Zhuni said.

"I like what you have done with the place," Klavan responded.

"Thank you; we had some help."

"You are ready?"

"Yes."

"Good, now we need to speak in private."

"Let's all go to my office."

The four of them walked across the lab to the opposite side and entered the private quarters of the staff. They all sat down in Zhuni's office.

"Looks like you all have everything ready; the minihabs are a great addition." Klavan started.

"We felt it would allow us individual spaces for fighter recovery rather than an open bay type sleeping arrangement. Plus, we put medical monitors in each. This will enable us to handle some serious injuries without too many issues; one of us can actually keep an eye on several fighters at once," Zhuni said.

"I like what is happening here. But I do fear for all of us. This Master is evil, and She has proclaimed Herself Master of the gamers, drug, and Smugglers' Guild also. She wants to control the mining guilds as well. She is powerful and extremely ambitious. She has plans for major changes, and I feel the departure of many. She will quickly consolidate Her power here, so align yourselves carefully and watch out for each other," Klavan stated.

"Yes, sir, what do you mean departure of many?" Zhuni asked.

"I mean, She is going to get rid of those who do not perform nor please Her, and She will not be shipping them out; they will become examples to others."

"Oh."

"Give Her your utmost respect and maintain, no matter what, that you are only the medical team and the medical team's security. Nothing more, nothing less. Only have staff here you trust. You three will have to be the leaders and will have to back each other. If you have any doubts about anyone on the team, get rid of them now."

"We do have questions about the construction crew left here," Sarge said.

"I do believe they will be of use farther down the road as you continue your work, I trust them, and that is why I brought them here. Trust me, you may need their skills. For now, just use them as part of your maintenance team."

"Is there anything we should know that you are not telling us yet?" Zhuni asked.

"I do not believe so."

"Then, can you explain that massive cage on the opposite side of the med lab?" Tan'cha asked.

"That is for your special guest Brynja Ajal."

"What?" Tan'cha said.

"Dark Death," Sarge said with dread.

"That is why that has the force generator and the ceramasteel," Klavan said.

"Force generator, we don't have that built-in," Zhuni said.

"Dagz, we need to get that installed before the main event, in case you get it in here. That is why there is the lift and the force generator. All that is just to keep the Brynja Ajal contained," Klavan said.

"We need to get the construction crew on that now," Zhuni said.

"I can't believe they missed that. We need this to be completed and ready for the main event before She comes down to inspect," Klavan said.

"She is coming here?" Zhuni asked.

"Of course, She wants to see what all this time and expense has gone into. She has put a lot of expense into this and the upgrades in the arena."

"Upgrades in the arena? I thought you said this space was emptied out because She no longer wanted to waste money on the grounds."

"Oh, Dagz, I forgot to tell you about the terrible things being done to the arena. She calls it spectator interaction," Klavan said.

"What do you mean spectator interaction?" asked Zhuni.

The security commlink chirped. It was the guards at the main corridor entrance.

She was here to inspect the med lab.

———— * ————

The Game Master had brought several of the Dwayans and Regents to see the med lab along with Her personal guard. They entered, and everything stopped. All the crews that were finishing up the details could sense She was here. Klavan led Zhuni, Tan'cha, and Sarge down to greet Her. On the way, he reminded them to present their utmost respect and to ensure everyone else did also.

They arrived just in time to see one of two of Her guards grabbing one of the workers and holding him so a third could use the power staff.

Klavan was afraid this would kill the worker, so he stepped in to stop it.

"My Liege, please."

"Klavan?" She asked.

"Each one of these workers has been brought here with a special skill set, and damaging one could cause issues for the smooth running during the main event."

"All these workers and everyone else need to understand my standing."

"If I may, Your Baroness," Zhuni interjected.

"You must be Zhuni."

"Yes, Your Grace."

"Why should I not make an example of him? I should feed him to the Pantaas."

"Oh yes, my Grace, that could be done. But my Grace, they have been working hard, all of them, to please You with the progress here. They do not know the ways of the respect You have earned. If You would allow him, he could complete the work for You, and I could ensure he and everyone here understands without a doubt the respect that You deserve. I just humbly request that this one occasion, You have mercy."

She studied Zhuni up and down, looking for a weakness or too much arrogance in his way. She could sense his slight confidence but no arrogance. She could see he had no idea of his true bearing. He would be one to watch as Stanton had said to Her. She will have to keep an eye on him.

"Very well, Zhuni, you may be correct. I will allow this one transgression, but if it happens again from any of your staff, they will be fed to the Pantaas, and I will have something special for you as well. Besides, I like the way you address me as Baroness and My Grace. I will allow you and your worker a simple apology."

"Yes, Your Grace, I do apologize for his ignorance," Zhuni said, helping the worker up and pushing him into a slight bow. The worker took his lead, turned, and ran off.

"Now tell me of this facility, I have invested a lot, and Klavan tells me it will save us large amounts in the future."

"Why yes, Your Grace. We will be able to repair the aliens and fighters and get them back in the arena without having to replace them. This will save You money on training and replacements. The more fights they fight, the better fighters they will be."

"So, how bad can they get hurt before I have to replace them?"

"We will have to learn with each species as we go along, but I know I have been able to put fighters back in the arena after they lost a limb. With my old equipment, I was able to reattach the limb, and they were back fighting in six to eight rattons, depending on the species. I think that with the team and equipment we have, anything short of death should be survivable."

"What about blaster burns and plasma pellets? Can you repair that damage?"

"I have only dealt with a few of those injuries, mostly training accidents, and a few times, one of the guards shot a creature. They don't use pistols and rifles in the arena."

"No, they do not, but you do know how to treat those wounds."

"Yes, my Grace."

"Good…good. Now show me what my credits have bought me. Show me Klavan has not wasted my money," She said as She looked over to Klavan.

They spent the several rattons showing Her the equipment and layout of the facility. The new medical equipment was set down in the middle of the space allowing access to both the fighters and the creatures that would soon be in the med lab. The left side held the minihabs, stacked four high to allow wounded fighters to monitor recovery. Then the right side back, two-thirds were stacked with cages of dozens of sizes and materials for multiple creatures. There were multiple levels with various ramps, gates, and doors, all enclosed and separated to allow movement of many angry creatures at once. There was also a series of lifts with carts to allow attendants to move incapacitated creatures. The front third of the right wall held one large cage with mammoth bars and vast cross bars. This cage was to also have a force generator added. This cage was massive and went floor to ceiling; the ceiling had dozens of gargantuan six-foot spikes sticking down from it like deadly stalactites.

Klavan made certain the tour stayed away from the security features and systems. He did notice that the number of Swaklin guards increased from Sarge to four by the time the tour was over. Klavan was pleased with his old friend and bodyguard. Sarge knew how to run security well. The Master's personal guards each had a personal guard. Klavan also kept an eye on Stanton as he was part of the group.

Stanton kept prodding Klavan and the Master for the cost of each item and the cost of everything. Klavan knew Stanton was attempting to get a rise out of the Master, and it suggested to the Master She was spending vast sums to maintain this med lab, not knowing if it would return the investment. Stanton kept saying they could just steal more slaves if needed and that the fans would get bored with the same fighters and creatures all the time. Klavan insisted this was not true; the fans would develop favorite fighters and creatures they would want to follow. It would be cheaper to have healthy, well-trained warriors fighting often than cheap disposable ones that constantly needed to be replaced. This argument raged the entire tour. The Master finally stopped the tour long enough to inform those present that She had weighed all the options before the decision had been made. She was going to have no more discussion of the costs or the decision. Klavan was pleased when She said this and saw Stanton turn a nice deep red.

"Looks like you and your team will be ready for the main event," She said to Zhuni.

"Let's leave them," She said and turned to leave.

Two of her personal guard stepped in front of her, and two fell in behind. The guards now wore crimson red capes that clipped onto their armor at the shoulders. In addition, they also now wore armor plating, which hung down to their upper thighs. Seven highly polished black plates became slightly smaller as they progressed down their front. The plates were also attached at the shoulders by the same clips as the cape. These clips had the Master's personal emblem inlaid with stone and held the front plates with crimson red straps. This gave the guards a regal and intimidating appearance.

The entourage fell in behind the guards; as they reached the entrance, She turned and said, "Klavan."

Klavan glanced at Zhuni, shrugged, and joined the entourage. As they exited the hall, guards closed the main entrance.

CHAPTER 4

Trouble Brews

"We are ready. I am pleased with the run-through and how well the gates and ramps operated. This will make moving everyone around fairly easy," Zhuni said.

"Now that the force generator is in, we should be ready to take in the Brynja Ajal," Tan'cha said.

"Can anyone tell me anything about the Brynja Ajal? I have only heard stories," Zhuni said.

"It wins every fight," Tan'cha responded.

"That much I do know," Zhuni said. "I want to know how we are to deal with it. What does it eat? Is it vicious outside the arena also? Can we reason with it? How do we control it?"

"It is vicious and mean; it kills everything sent into the arena with it," Tan'cha added.

"Yes, we have established that," Zhuni said.

"I have never dealt with the creatures and fighters; I have always been in charge of personal and perimeter protection, but I will make some inquiries," Sarge responded.

"Now see, that is helpful," Zhuni said, looking at Tan'cha.

"What?" Tan'cha asked.

"So, during the main event, we will have a lot going on. Tan'cha will be with me. Sarge, you will be in overall charge. I would like the attendants to stay with their creatures as they bring them through if you are okay with it. I think it will help to keep the creatures calm," Zhuni said.

"Not all the attendants are going to have a calming effect. I will step in if I feel a need to. I also do not trust all the attendants and do not have time or the resources to clear them all," Sarge responded.

"We will have to watch who is in and out of here. Can you and your team keep an eye on everyone and everything?" Zhuni asked.

"I have Joxby and his team also keeping an eye on all of us. We will have extra guards set at the main entrance and the loading area, and I have a team set up to control our personal area. We will be fine," Sarge said.

"Good, and the training as to how to deal with each different creature?" Zhuni asked.

"Yes, each team member will be matched with a partner. Those with direct contact with the creatures will have earpieces with a direct line to one of Joxby's boys. He will have your guide just in case and will talk to the teams as to what they are dealing with and how to handle them. Each team will have a force shield, a stunner, a blaster pistol, and a plasma rifle. And everyone will have their pistol," Sarge assured Zhuni.

"Well done, I did not even think about that. They will all be armored up also. Now we will all be tied in together with our voxes, so if anything seems off or there is any trouble, let everyone know," Zhuni said.

"Do we have any concerns?" Sarge asked.

"I have my doubts about a couple of the scientists we were sent. I don't think they really know how to help; just dissect," Zhuni said.

"No offense but that is your problem; I was meaning from an overall did we miss anything point," Sarge responded.

"Roger that. I do not believe so. We have security set, the cage and ramp operators have done a couple of run-throughs, supplies are good, and the medical equipment checks out," Zhuni said.

"One thing we need to get more about, and I have been unable to find out, is the interactive part that Klavan was talking about," Sarge said with a bit of concern.

"I heard that there were going to be pitfalls and traps set around," Tan'cha said.

"I have only been able to get a bit from a few of the construction crew, and they said they saw turrets installed," Sarge said.

"Turrets?" Tan'cha gasped.

"What type of turrets, where?" Zhuni asked.

"All I could get out of them was turrets, six or eight around the edge of the audience area and two by the luxury box. No mention as to what they held. Viewers, snare traps, or weapons?" Sarge added.

"I wonder if Joxby could find something out," Zhuni asked.

"Good idea; if we can't get the info from the construction crews or attendants, maybe he could come up with something. I will also put him on the Brynja Ajal," Sarge said.

"Yes, please. Let's get all the info we can," Zhuni responded.

"Can we keep this going over dinner?" Tan'cha asked.

"Good idea, let's grab something," Zhuni said.

---------------- * ----------------

Stanton was in his usual position, sitting in his huge chair, screaming at the Boyz once again. He was a bright once red again. It seemed lately to be his standard color. Traxon just stood there; he had become so used to it. This was getting boring; always yelling and screaming. For several of the Boyz, this was new. Stanton had all the Boyz here.

"Dagz! Can't you keep me up to date on what is going on around here? There are enough of you that you should be able to watch everything. I just had a tour of the med lab, and you were unable to get me anything on it." Stanton was glaring at Traxon.

"Dwayan, tell you we try, can't get in. Even microdrones not work. We work on main event; several able get in," Traxon said.

"Have we gotten anything from the Master's?" Stanton again looked at Traxon.

"No, guards scramble. They have scramblers built into uniforms, we think."

"Don't think; get things done. I need to get on the Master's good side; She was listening to me during the tour. Klavan is on Her good side now. We must come up with some way to discredit the med lab and that Zhuni. Maybe even get rid of Klavan too. You tried the loading dock, bug a few pieces of medical equipment?"

"Yes, we try. Guard smart he good, check everything with scanner. We attach one to med equipment and left off, hope it come on to listen," Traxon said.

"Okay, so you can do something right. I am going to have to find better than you thought. You and your Boyz are cheap, but not as what I need now. I need professionals," Stanton said.

"We good and get better, we not technical info, we group strong, we keep order," Traxon said.

"Dagz, you and these others are useless; you need to find me some spies. Go to the port and bring me someone with special talents. Information gatherers. I want covert, technical savvy."

"We get good," Traxon reiterated.

"No, you and all of the others are useless. I do not have time for you to continue making your stupid mistakes. Get me real talent, now."

"You pay much?" Traxon asked.

"Don't you worry how much I pay them? Get them in here, and I will negotiate. Now all of you get out of my sight," Stanton yelled as his color slowly faded to a blush.

Traxon headed straight for the port.

If Stanton wanted someone else to do his spying, Traxon was fine with that, everyone knew the Chordentia worked for Stanton anyways. They could never hide their activities. Stanton liked Traxon and his cohorts because they were easy to control. They worked with Stanton because he kept them in numbers and sort of kept them from being picked on by all the others at the arena. But Traxon was getting sick of always fighting for his survival; he could do that anywhere. He would get Stanton his spies and then figure a way to get out. He did not need Stanton; Stanton needed him. Maybe he could get in good with the Klavan or, better yet, the Master. If Stanton could play games, so could Traxon.

Traxon checked in with a few thugs he knew to let them get the word out. Stanton was well-known in this area. He had a reputation.

Traxon knew he could just wait for a few sectons, and several individuals would soon appear.

———————— * ————————

Klavan thought about the events of the last few rotations. As he did, his mind went back to another time. Klavan had a wife, but she and their child died during childbirth; it was rare in his world and tore his heart out. In fact, it was so rare that his people thought him cursed, so he was ostracized and ended up leaving his world. He knew his hospitality and bearing would get him places, and he ended up working for a rich Aashturian. Klavan did not know it when he started working, but the Aashturian was a guild master in the Eastern fringe smuggling guild. Klavan thought the Aashturian was a collector of artifacts. But even when Klavan found out the Aashturian's true work, Klavan did not leave. He was doing well and thought if he wasn't doing the smuggling or any type of immoral thing directly, he was just doing a job. He has lied to himself ever since.

He had always wanted a family and especially a son. Since he saw Zhuni at the spaceport working with the different creatures and alien life forms, Klavan knew Zhuni was special. Klavan had taken Zhuni under his wing and raised him as well as possible without anyone knowing Zhuni held a special place in Klavan's heart. Zhuni should have been a slave. As an orphan, it was unheard of to be given freedom at that young age. Klavan felt the decision had proven the right one many times over. Zhuni never worried about himself; he was always working to care for the fighters and creatures. Klavan told Zhuni he cared too much but knew Zhuni was doing the right thing. Klavan was so proud of Zhuni. Especially today. When Zhuni protected the worker and did it so wisely and respectfully, Klavan was bursting with pride. He had not expected Zhuni to step up so quickly and easily into the leadership role.

Funny how Klavan suddenly had this desire to make amends after all the time working here. He could not explain the desire that recently overcame him, but he was going with it. He had to do something to make things right, and the med lab was a start. He was able to grant freedom to several dozen individuals and was able to protect them. This was not the right place to have morals, but Zhuni had always maintained his. It was as good a time as any for Klavan to reacquire his.

This new Master and Her guards were different than any Master he had worked with before. Most were here to make themselves rich. This one was different; She was here to consolidate power. It was a different type of greed. She wanted to control everyone and everything, the arena, the credits, the Starch trade, the smugglers, the Starlanes, the drug cartels, everything. But there was something not exactly right about Her. Klavan could not figure exactly, but something about Her and Her guards was off. To start, he had never seen Her race before; Klavan held a wide understanding of alien races as he had been at the arena for many, many cycles. He had seen dozens of intelligent races and hundreds of creatures, but nothing like Her. Klavan had never seen them before nor heard of a description matching them.

The main event was two rotations away; time to start worrying again.

The force generator had been installed, so that was one less thing to worry about; at least the med lab would be safe. The Brynja Ajal would be released into the arena again. That had not happened in several rotations. This was going to be trouble; it always has been. This creature was epic and mythical in its destruction and its indestructibility. It was as if it was created just to deal death. It would hold up to blaster bolts, plasma pellets, and nearly anything they threw at it. They had at one time used a flamer on it, and it calmed it down. In fact, it fell asleep with a flamer pouring molten flame on it. Amazing sinister creature. Most creatures had specific behavior to understand or could be trained. Not the Brynja Ajal; it had no logical patterns. It had a mind of its own. It was intelligent beyond any other creatures. It was intelligent as one of the sentient races, but it could not communicate. It did not understand any known language. Klavan thought it was a mistake to have a creature that powerful here, but the last three Masters had loved it. And since they had been able to surgically implant the brainstem controller, the Masters had been able to slightly direct it. A zap and it would send the creature into an orgy of destruction. It would only last a few actas, but it was usually enough to clear the arena of any other living creatures. It was a terrifying sight to behold. It was an unstoppable bringer of death.

———————— * ————————

Traxon sat at a table in the market district of the spaceport. The port was a mix of industry and temporary living spaces scattered amongst landing pads and markets. The main market was centrally located. This was where the majority of business was conducted. Traxon could sit here at his favorite restaurant and watch everything going on. The restaurant had a large patio on a high deck, allowing Traxon to look out over the entire market. This specific restaurant had Traxon's favorite food, and the owner knew almost everyone and everything that was going on in the market. Traxon could see nearly every ship's crew leave and enter the spaceport from this vantage point.

Agón was a planet with basically three zones. The mid-zone, where the arena and spaceport were, was a barren wasteland bordering salty oceans above and below. The top third was a dense jungle, and the lower third was swamp. The planet's temperature was constantly warm as it had a flat rotation, so there was no winter or cold season. The guilds liked this planet; the mid-zone allowed easy ship landings and easy loading and offloading. The other zones offered massive areas to hide if need be and had abundant fresh supplies of swamp and jungle fruits and wildlife. The swamps and jungles could be exceedingly dangerous for those who did not know the areas.

He liked to sit here on his time off; he could enjoy good food and drink and watch all types of creatures, aliens, and such pass by. He waited for the word to get out.

The first to show was an odd creature, smaller than Traxon. It appeared to be a pile of dirty rags. Traxon could not figure out what the creature was, but he did catch a glimpse of red skin at the wrist. It had a mechanical voice as if it were an old model android or it was speaking through an electronic device. The creature said it had worked for many Warlords and had assisted with the Aashturians'

Civil War and made a killing playing both sides. Traxon asked about his security breaching and spying abilities. It said those were his specialties, and that is why he was there. Traxon told him he would speak with his Dwayan and reconnect. Traxon did not like this one—it was too confident; in fact, it was arrogant. Stanton would probably like it.

The second was a Takchee, a creature who towered over Traxon but was only about eight feet tall. It had a green-brown exoskeleton. It walked on its back four legs. Its upper body had two appendages, like arms, one with small hands, which had two fingers and a small thumb, and the other pair with claws. This one spoke with a strange high-pitched hissing chitter. It was amazingly annoying for Traxon to listen to. This Takchee said it was a security master and had special equipment of its own creation. Traxon thought this one might do well but felt there would be better-qualified candidates coming along.

Traxon spent the rest of the day there, speaking with nine different candidates, and decided on the top five. He would get the word out for them to return, and he would take them to meet Stanton. Stanton could decide what he wanted. Traxon knew which he would pick and could save his Dwayan sometime, but Stanton would want to make the decision. Stanton trusted no one to make decisions.

Traxon decided to enjoy his evening and watch the marketplace. This was his quiet place; he could lose himself just quietly watching the world go by. The next three to four rotations would be stressful enough; he might as well relax when he could. Tomorrow would be a day presenting the candidates to Stanton and listening to him fuss about the lack of intelligent cronies he had and how he now had to spend credits to get some competent outside contractor. He ordered a meal of crispy Banteest and a dragen of Splift to drink, sat back, and watched the evening fade away.

---
*

Zhuni woke up to another dream; this time, it was not about being torn apart but stitched back together and then wrapped up and frozen. He felt as if he was dreaming of flight and freedom as if he was having a dream within a dream. He was soaring over a rugged and beautiful landscape. He saw many other worlds that he knew he had never seen and could not even imagine. This dream had not been as bad as the rest. It was as if he had resigned himself to just dreaming as if he were asleep in his dream but dreaming. He had been having strange and terrifying dreams nearly every night since the planning meeting in Klavan's office. They had been nightmares, and this was the first which he awoke without pain and felt almost free. It was too early to contemplate.

It was too late to go back to sleep and too early to get anything working. Might as well get a shower and get dressed. Maybe one of the chefs was cooking something up. At least Zhuni could get some Slokton coffee.

Zhuni's bed was dug into the stone like a rack on a space cruiser. His bed had a firm mat and was covered with bright-colored blankets. He reached up to the head of the bed and touched a pad that brought a light above the bed dimly on. He peeled the blanket back and sat up. He rubbed his head and swung his legs over the side, placing his feet firmly on the floor. He set his head in his hands and his elbows resting on his legs. He leaned like that for a moment rubbing his head. He looked up, scanning his room, stood, and headed to his private restroom. It wasn't a grand space, but it was his, and it was a major improvement over his previous space.

The shower had helped, and now that he was dressed, he left his space to go below one level to the mess hall. He just needed coffee and some quiet before the final day got going.

He got to the mess hall and found Joxby sitting at a table munching on a variety of fruit and having a cup of Slokton coffee; it smelled so rich that it started to wake Zhuni without having to drink it.

Zhuni walked over to say good morning to the crazy little tech guru.

"Morning-Zhuni," Joxby said in his everything is one rushed word way of speaking.

"What are you doing up so early?"

"Lots-to-do."

"Ready for tomorrow?"

"No,-not-yet."

"Really, you have been working so much I would have thought you were ready. Sarge said you were."

"Sarge-yes,-for-me-no."

"What do you mean, Sarge yes?"

"Sarge-asked-me-to-have-security-ready."

"Is it?"

"Of-course,-but-I-want-more-ready."

"All right. You have a good breakfast; I need coffee."

"Yes,-coffee-good."

"Coffee is very good."

Zhuni went over to the kitchen, got some coffee, and looked around for the chef. At least one of them. He heard some banging around over by the cold units. He walked over to see the head chef slicing and peeling various fruit.

"Gooood Moorniing, Zhuuni." It was quite the change from Joxby in speech; every vowel was drawn out. He was a Maxta. Maxta were up to seven feet tall, had four arms, greyish-green smooth skin, and four eyes. Two eyes were very large and positioned where most humanoids had eyes, and the other two eyes were closer to the size of human eyes but set at the temples. He had large, pointed ears, and when he smiled, you could see his dozens of small flat teeth. Maxta were vegetarians, so he enjoyed the abundance of fresh fruit that were available from the jungles. This Maxta went by the name Chef.

"Good morning, Chef."

"Reeaady foooor *biig* daay?

"Yes, I think we all are."

"Breeaakfaast?"

"Yes, just not sure what other than coffee."

"Freesh Fruuiit?"

"Of course, but I need something more."

"Noo thiis fruuiit speeciiaal. Froom deeseert. Riich, gooood."

"Yeah, I have never seen that tan nor the green fruit."

"Taan iis deeseert fruuiit, caall Zomis, sweeet, looots prooteeiin."

"Sounds good."

"Greeeen sweeet."

"Great, set up a plate to go, please; I will head back to my room."

"Goood."

Zhuni left the mess hall and was looking forward to a nice breakfast and maybe some quiet before the day got started. *This may be a good day*, he thought.

"Mister Zhuni."

It was Sarge; he was the only one to call him by that name.

"Good morning, Sarge."

"I notice you are up early."

Zhuni turned to see Sarge with three members of security. Another Swaklin and two non-Swaklin. One was the guy Tan'cha had had his last fight with. A lot smaller than Zhuni, muscular, dark gray-green skin, with two large tusks sticking out from his jawline. Zhuni had been amazed when Tan'cha had picked him.

"Good morning; how is the jaw?" Zhuni asked the tusked one.

"Morning, it is doing well. I don't even notice. Thank you."

"Well, that is my job."

"Yes, sir, and you will be getting plenty more work tomorrow."

"Don't remind me."

"Well then, I was just doing our shift change, sir," Sarge said.

"Everything good then?"

"Yes, sir."

"I am going to my quarters to have some quiet and breakfast. I will see you for our planning meeting then."

"See you then, sir."

Zhuni made it to the entry to his quarters and was leaning in to open the door when he heard Tan'cha yelling.

"Good morning. What are you doing up so early?"

"I couldn't sleep."

"Excited, nervous?"

"Just some weird dreams."

"Do tell." Tan'cha helped Zhuni open his door and then let himself in.

"I was just going to have a quiet breakfast."

"Were you now? Well, that changed; tell me about your weird dreams. You know my people and I love dreams; they tell us about the future, the past, and ourselves. I can tell you about your dream."

"How can you tell me about my dreams? You don't even know what they are about."

"Yes, I know that. What I mean is when you tell me, I can interpret and explain it to you."

"Fine, I will tell you. But we have a busy day, and I can't spend all day telling you about my dreams."

"No problem, I am good at this. It shouldn't take too long."

They sat down, and Zhuni went into detail about the dreams he had been having and when they started. How long they have been going on and the fact that they no longer wake him up in pain and seem to be calming down. They spoke for a bit more than an hour.

"Dagz! Those are some messed up dreams."

"Well, that is helpful. I thought you we going to interpret them."

"I, umm, am not exactly sure. I didn't expect your dreams to be that messed up. You know, I was expecting normal dreams about falling and whatnot. You know, normal. Sounds like you are having someone else's dreams."

"That is what I felt, but who's or what's? Why am I having them?"

"Do you feel you have a special connection with anyone or with any of the creatures you have healed?"

"No. I work to have a connection with all that I work on or work with but nothing like this. So how would you interpret my dreams?"

"This is just too much for me; I thought you were going to have normal dreams, not dreams about being dissected and visiting places you say you have never seen. You are just beyond my understanding. They are too weird."

"Gee, thanks. You are no help at all."

"Yup, too much for my little brain. Besides, you said we have too much to do today, and we must get going. Let's make certain we are ready for the main event."

"Fine, let's get Sarge in here. You know not to tell him, right?"

"Of course, we don't need everyone knowing you are crazy!"

"Thanks."

———————— * ————————

Traxon was standing outside Stanton's office with the interviewees he had gathered from the port. He thought one was a good fit but was not impressed by the others for Stanton's needs. He was sure Stanton would pick the pile of rags. There were other candidates but…

They all were standing in the hallway. The hallway had high ceilings and was a tunnel cut from the mountain stone, just like the rest of the complex. Traxon looked down the hall and could see the day beginning as creatures of all types started to fill the hall as they all went about their daily routine. Traxon enjoyed just watching the world go by. Here at the complex, there was always something new to see. Dozens of creatures of various types wandered by. Traxon chuckled as he watched, large and small all wander by in what looked like a highly choreographed dance, large creatures stepping over smaller ones and medium creatures weaving through it all. It was amazing that some of the tiny guys didn't get stomped by the big guys, but somehow it all worked.

Traxon nearly forgot why he was there. He told them that he would take them in one at a time once Stanton summoned them.

Traxon looked them over. There was the one he called Rags; the Takchee; a Foehlan, tall, thin, almost elegant creature of a dusty grey color covered with feathers, and then the two that intrigued Traxon the most. A Swaklin like Klavan's guards, he was an older mercenary with scars on his face and arms and a tattoo that Traxon thought meant dishonorable discharge from the service. The Swaklin wore all-black dungarees of some long-forgotten conflict; they were once a military uniform but had no insignia nor rank attached. He looked to be the toughest of the group and could probably beat them all at the same time in a fight. He was constantly scanning the area and the other candidates as if he was looking for a fight or sizing up everyone and everything around him.

The other one was the one Traxon thought would be the best for intel gathering; he did not look to be a fighter. He was short, even shorter than Traxon, but wider in shoulder and girth. His mouth was wide and broad and filled with dozens of small teeth; it was stuck in a constant smile. His head was flat and set low into his shoulders; he had nearly no neck. He had large eyes, which were a yellow-brown color. This guy wore bone canvas pants that were baggy and had dozens of pockets containing all types of tools and electrical equipment. He had an ochre vest that also had several pockets. Even the orange hat he wore had storage space and contained a couple of screwdrivers and clippers. This guy did not look like the fighting type, but to Traxon, he seemed to know his way around computers and electronic devices. If Traxon was going to build a team, these two would definitely make the cut.

It would just be a few partions, and Stanton would call for them. Then Traxon would have to introduce each to Stanton and then explain the reason he had brought each to see Stanton. Traxon was getting so sick and tired of the constant threats and abuse of Stanton, but what was a useless little Chordentia like him going to do? He hated the situation he was in, but at least he was alive and at the top of the ladder in Stanton's pecking order, well, for now.

The door opened, and one of Stanton's aids peered out and motioned Traxon to come in.

It was time, and Traxon could feel the apprehension and tension build inside him immediately. *I have got to get a better life*, he thought as he directed the Takchee in first.

Stanton was in his usual place, leaning back with his fat feet up. The huge table in front of him, which served as his desk, had a pile of food summoned for his breakfast. Stanton was gulping his food as if he hadn't eaten in months. Traxon also found Stanton's eating to be disgusting. Stanton barely chewed and spoke while eating, throwing food about. *This is going to be a long day*, Traxon thought.

"Dwayan, I present to you, Sleth."

"What is a Sleth?"

"Dwayan, Sleth name; he is a Takchee." Motioning towards the Takchee.

"So, Sleth, what is your skill set? If Traxon brought you, I am sure you must be useful for something."

Traxon was already scrunching his face in anticipation of that high-pitched hissing and chittering.

"I am versssed in intelligenccce gathering on multiple levelsss, I am…"

"What is the horrible noise?" Stanton screamed, turning a deep magenta.

Traxon thought this would happen.

"Get this thing out of here; it is destroying my ears, such high-pitched grating sounds," Stanton said, covering his ears and motioning with his hands furiously, swishing him to be gone.

Traxon motioned for Sleth to leave, and he beat a quick exit.

Traxon ran to the door after Sleth and grabbed Rags to bring him in to speak with Stanton.

When Rags was in front of Stanton, Traxon received what he was expecting.

"Traxon, you are a useless Pryvlok! What in Dagz made you think that thing was going to be useful? I sure hope you actually have some that are worthy of my time. How many do you have?"

"This Dwayan is the next, and I spoke with eight and brought five before you. I am sorry about the previous one. I did not realize his speech would be so frustrating."

"How could you not? Did you even speak with it? How are you choosing them? Do you just grab something out of the marketplace? Did you even interview them?"

"My Lord," Rags spoke up.

"My Lord. See, Traxon, this is a classy one; he knows his place; he knows how to address his boss. I guess even you can get something right once in a while."

"Yes, Dwayan."

"You can tell the others to wait; I may have found our candidate. Now leave us."

"Yes."

With that, Traxon turned and left. He knew Stanton was going to pick this one. Traxon was glad his plan had worked; introduce the most annoying one first, then the one Traxon knew Stanton would like and choose. Then Traxon could get out of there quickly and not have to deal with Stanton for at least a few kolts. Stanton may think he is so smart, but he just got set, and Traxon was actually feeling good about himself. He felt smug, and it was a feeling he liked.

Traxon would be sure to stay in contact with the two he liked, as their services may come in handy later down the road. He would have to meet with them; he could say it was on Stanton's time, and he could get to know them better and their skills. If he could trick Stanton, maybe, he could get out on his own and get out of this place. Maybe he was going to be okay.

———————— * ————————

Stanton was pleased with the ideas his new spy had. Stanton also learned his name was not Rags but Boshduul. The rags were his look that was effective in disarming most into thinking he was not dangerous. *Turns out Boshduul was an assassin, a wonderful bonus,* Stanton thought. Stanton had already set him up with his first assignment and was waiting for it to come to fruition.

Boshduul was currently doing his recon of the facility for its patterns and getting his intel for the work to be done. He needed to know workers' schedules and the routines of everyday life.

Stanton was looking forward to this new partnership. Traxon was a bit lacking in confidence, and that had been okay with the past Masters, but this one was something special. She was going to need more finesse. Boshduul was a much more confident individual and definitely knew how to treat his boss with respect, not the sniveling and hiding of Traxon. It was his race, even if Traxon was a bit bolder than the other Chordentia.

Stanton thought to himself, *Traxon has been good as an assistant, but it may be time for a change. With the main event coming in just a few rotations, it may be the right time to make it.*

"Where is Traxton?" Stanton snapped at one of his attendants.

"I do…" one of them attempted to get out.

"Never mind, just find him and get him in here. I need to have a talk with him. Useless Mynog, always missing. Have him waiting here when I return from my meeting with the Master."

———————— * ————————

Klavan was in Her conference room once again. This Master never seemed to sleep. It was one more day to the main event. She had all her regents and department heads here again, going over the last few things She felt needed to be announced.

She stood up to address the gathering. All present became even more nervous as the last meeting involved Her making examples of servants thanks to an assist by the Pantaas.

"We are going to have many honored guests arriving for these games. I do not believe I have to remind you of the penalties of causing *any* issues during these events."

Everyone in the room was dead quiet and heeded Her every word.

"We will be entertaining some leading members of the guilds. These will include but not be limited to the guilds of…" She paused, looking around the room to ensure everyone was hanging on Her every word. "…mining, smugglers, slavers, drug cartels, and the assassins. We will also be visited by some viceroys, kings, and several other dignitaries. I do expect each of you to know their customs and proper behavior when in their presence. Klavan has been so kind as to create the information you will need to know about these guests' customs, greetings, and special needs. I suggest each of you study the information directly. I will not stand for any mistakes in courtesy offending anyone."

She started to walk around the room, looking directly at each individual.

"Some of these individuals will be here for the entertainment only, but others will be here for business, and some extremely important contracts may be formulated. I would hate for one of you to prevent this from happening because you insulted one of our guests."

She liked the intimidation She created. In fact, She thrived on it.

"Whatever any of them ask for, provide it."

She had Her guards posted around the entrances to the room in such a way as to suggest no escape; each was stationed not by a door but blocking it. She loved to play mind games with everyone. Klavan was impressed at Her show and was starting to understand Her tactics. It had taken him longer to figure this one out. But he thought, as he watched Her interact with everyone, how She would linger over some for extended time but others not at all. He realized She knew how to intimidate a few enough to control the entire room. Interesting. She would intimidate a few directly, glaring at them, but basically, overlook the others. She would stare down those who were weak or very strong, and some She would nearly ignore. For example, She never looked at Stanton. He was starving for Her attention. He needed Her attention, and with Klavan as Her liaison, Stanton did not know what to do.

Klavan suddenly understood her tactics. This was a game changer; Klavan may be able to make this work to his advantage.

She spun to glare directly at him. Had She heard his thoughts? Klavan felt all the warmth leave his body; he felt as if he had been struck in the chest by an angry Scrytock. He thought he was going to pass out. He was in deep trouble.

———————— * ————————

"We have a slight problem," Sarge said.

"Oh great, the main event tomorrow, and we have an issue," Tan'cha quipped.

"Shish," Zhuni said.

"It is of some concern, but Joxby is on it," Sarge assured them.

"So, what is the problem?" Zhuni asked.

"Joxby said he has been picking up some chatter and impulses that point to someone using some type of surveillance on the med lab. He said he found a borehole also that had been set to accept video to overlook the open area, and he is sending out his search bots to look for more," Sarge said matter-of-factly.

"Should we be worried, Sarge?" Zhuni asked.

"Honestly, I have worked with many spies and surveillance experts in my many roles in life. Joxby is an odd character, but I can only think of one or two who could even match his skill and knowledge. I would want no one else to have our backs in this situation," Sarge stated.

"Okay, so I have a question. Where did the borehole come from?" Zhuni asked.

"Joxby followed it back, and it came out at the back of the loading dock, behind a heavy-duty lifter that has been left to rust. Joxby thinks it was going to have a transmitter attached, so there was no direct connection to the individual who set it up. He has set up a microbot to keep an eye on the spot," Sarge continued.

"Okay, so Joxby is now in position to keep an eye on whoever was attempting to keep an eye on us? Does he think there are other issues?" Zhuni asked.

"As I said, he is sent out multiple search bots and microdrones to crawl over the entire med lab. He has also set up several outside looking in to keep an eye on our perimeter. He has set up a sonic loop to feed back to any surveillance device so the individual will see or hear nothing. Joxby has got us covered; I just felt you should know we do have someone attempting to watch us," Sarge continued.

"Is he closing the borehole?" Zhuni asked.

"No. With the microbot watching and knowing where the borehole starts and ends, Joxby will control the intel that they receive. If he closes the hole, then the individual will know we are onto them. Joxby is sure this is the best way to deal with it. The more Joxby knows about whoever is attempting to spy on us, the better off we are. I agree with him. I am in charge of our security and believe Joxby is correct. Plus, the little Mosnee never sleeps, so I know he is on it all the time. Now onto other issues."

"There's more?" Tan'cha blurted out.

"No," Sarge scolded.

"Then why would you say, 'now onto *other* issues'?" Tan'cha asked.

"He meant let's get on with other business; we are in a meeting to discuss tomorrow's main event!" Zhuni said.

"Oh yeah," Tan'cha squeaked out.

"Sometimes I wonder about you," Zhuni chuckled.

"I am glad I am not the only one who worries about him," Sarge laughed.

"Oh, shut up, you two," Tan'cha snarled.

"Okay, so onto new business and other concerns about tomorrow's main event," Zhuni said, looking at Tan'cha.

"Sarge, you are confident with our security and feel Joxby has surveillance taken care of. Do you have any concerns?" Zhuni asked.

"No, Mr. Zhuni, I have our security ready. I believe we have all aspects covered, and everyone knows their jobs. I checked all our equipment, and each individual will do equipment check again in the morning. First shift is ready and will be starting their day at zero five hundred. I have security at each entrance to the med lab, the pit's main gate, and three roving crews for the hallways, plus two roving crews for the lab. Joxby and his team will be in contact with all security teams. Joxby's team will have your guide to aliens and creatures, so we will be prepared with the best way to handle all creatures. Your med teams know their job, although I am not too sure about those 'scientists' the Master sent to help; I have asked Joxby to keep a close eye on them. For security and proper medical procedures, Joxby may be talking to you if he is in doubt of the medical procedures and, of course, with me otherwise. Do you have any questions?"

That is the most I had heard Sarge say at one time, Zhuni thought.

"I was going to ask you about the scientists, but you have covered that. Same goes with the new technicians, right?"

Sarge nodded an affirmative.

"I know we have some new equipment mixed in with some old pieces; I am worried about something going wrong with the medical equipment. I may need you and your guys for muscle if something goes wrong with the equipment. I know we went through the operation of all the doors and ramps, but things can happen, and we need to make certain we are all on the same page."

"Mr. Zhuni, when it comes to creatures, you will be the lead. I have spoken with all security personnel, and they know to listen to you, but if something goes wrong, I am not going to risk any of our team's lives for a creature, and I will make the call if I feel termination is necessary," Sarge said in a firm voice.

"Agreed. Tan'cha, any issues you foresee?" Zhuni asked.

"Nope, I am just looking forward to not being in the arena this time around." Tan'cha smiled.

"Yes, this will be a new experience for us all," Zhuni finished.

———————— * ————————

Traxon was reentering the facility through the back loading dock. He had met with the two specialists and was looking forward to working with them. But talking to them got him thinking. There were answers he was going to have to find for himself.

Traxon thought he had some time before Stanton would be looking for him, so he decided to do some investigating on his own. He knew Stanton wanted to know what was going on at the med lab, but Traxon felt there was something more interesting to investigate. Something about this new Master seemed off. Stanton wanted to get on Her good side, but Traxon felt there was more to Her and Her guards. They never slowed down; they were always out as if they knew nothing of a normal sleep or eating schedule. The guards never moved their heads, from what Traxon could see with those helmets on, but even so, the helmets never swiveled, but the guards seemed to see everything, and She seemed to know too much about the Dwayans. It made Traxon nervous but very curious, and he had learned long ago to be curious was a bad thing around here. Nonetheless, he wanted, no, he needed to know, what it was that made him feel so strange around them.

He decided to grab a worker's helmet and face shield, lose his clothes, and go undercover. With his scared face covered, he may blend in as just another of Stanton's cronies. He dumped his stuff behind an old rusty shipping container next to a broken-down lifter. He looked down and saw a rag and thought, *I will just pick that up and shove it in my pocket to complete the look.*

Traxon decided today was a busy day as everyone was preparing for the main event, and it may be an excellent time to look into Her quarters and the guard's area; they would be out dealing with the Dwayans and their preparations for the guests.

With his new look, Traxon headed out of the loading dock and to the lift to go to Her quarters. He wandered down the hallway on the uppermost level of the facility. There were only cleaning crews and a few servants wandering about. He came to the last turn before Her quarters, paused, took a deep breath, and made the turn. Standing directly in front of the entrance to her quarters was a guard. Traxon could not tell if the guard saw him or not. The guard did not even acknowledge him. Traxon felt invisible and unimportant. He was sure his new look was the reason; he suddenly felt even more useless than before.

"Need clean," Traxon said to the guard as he pulled a rag out of his overalls.

The guard did not say anything but stepped aside.

Traxon opened the door and stepped in. The guard closed the door behind Traxon. Traxon was alone in Her quarters. It was dark, very dimly lit. In fact, there was only light coming from a small panel across the room. He headed over to it but stopped. Someone else was here. He needed to see; he saw a tall slim figure to his right, he could not make out who or what it was.

"I clean," He said, taking out the rag. No response from the figure.

He stepped back to the door and felt along the wall until he felt the light control panel. He touched the control, and the room started to light up to a level that he could now see all the way across the room. It was another guard. It was just standing there. Did it see him? It had not reacted to the lights; wait, there were more, all lined up behind him. Traxon turned the lights up and could now see clearly that there were seven lined up behind the first one. None of them moved. Traxon waited to the count of ten, and nothing happened. What was going on?

Traxon timidly walked across to them. They were not breathing or moving or showing any signs of life. *Were they dead?* He worked up the nerve to touch one, but nothing. He hit it, and again—nothing. He looked them over, up and down, and all around them. Nothing, they showed no signs of life. Each was standing as if at full attention, and each stood on a platform that clamped their feet down. *Is this how they slept, standing up? Were they asleep, or did they hibernate like some creatures, that maybe it?* That would be why they never seemed to sleep. They stayed awake for long periods and slept for long periods. If She let half hibernate or go into some type of stasis while the others were out, it would look as if they never slept. *But what about Her?* That he did not know. *Did she hibernate also?*

Traxon felt as if he had been in there for kolts already, so he needed to move along if he was going to find anything out. He walked about the room and was surprised there was no sleeping station, food, or a place to relieve oneself. Nothing for bodily functions. Not even a place to sit. He had never seen one of them sitting. They must get very tired and need to hibernate.

He looked at the panel he had seen earlier and noticed it was a control panel that had a platform behind it, just like the ones the guards were standing on. Then on the opposite side of the room from the guards were eight more platforms, but they were empty. The room was barren except for the control panel, the platforms, and two weapons racks on the walls. The one by the guards was full of weapons, and the one by the empty platforms was devoid of weapons.

Traxon lowered the lighting back to the level he thought it was when he entered. He opened the door to the hallway, and the guard stepped to one side. Traxon stepped past the guard and moved away from there as quickly as he could without looking like he was running.

He made it back to the loading dock without anyone noticing him. He dropped down behind the abandoned heavy lifter to retrieve his clothes and get dressed. He went to place his helmet and face shield behind the box, dropped his rag, and then noticed it. A tiny box attached to the wall. It looked like one of Stanton's recorders, just like the one Traxon had set in the Master's office, but a bit larger. If Traxon had not dropped his rag, he never would have seen it. And if he had not planted one, he would not know what it was. *But why was it here? Why was it behind this abandoned heavy lifter? What type of information could they collect from the loading dock?* And it looked like whoever put it in place set it backwards. *How could they ever get information with it facing the wall?* He grabbed the rag and put it in his pocket. It was a rusty brown and reminded him of something, but he could not remember what.

He had a lot to mull over. He had more information than he knew what to do with. He would have to go make mental notes and connect all the information.

Traxon was exiting the loading dock and heading down the hallway to see Stanton when one of the Boyz came running over, saying Stanton was looking for him and he was mad. Well, Traxon was headed that way already and Stanton being mad was nothing new. It was back to his hopeless life. It was kind of fun while it lasted, being a spy for his own curiosity. It was a type of danger, and responsibility Traxon enjoyed. It felt incredible to be on his own for a moment but a bit too scary.

---
*

Zhuni had finished meeting with Sarge and Tan'cha and was now in the med lab conducting his inspection of the equipment along with his staff. He was pleased with the equipment; everything was in perfect working order.

Now for the planning meeting for the staff. Zhuni wanted to assign teams for field work (those who would be in the passageways working on the lightly injured), those who would be escorting the injured back to the lab, those working in the lab and their assignments and the procedures for the various creatures they would be seeing. The big question still to be answered was, what was the Brynja Ajal, and how were they going to deal with it if they got it?

"Zhuni…" Tan'cha said, his voice trailing off.

"Busy."

"Sarge is telling me it is Klavan; there is a problem, and…the Master is calling for you," Tan'cha offered, speaking into his vox.

"What, where?"

"Follow me, Sarge said in the main conference room upper level."

Zhuni grabbed a med-bag and ran out with Tan'cha.

"What do we know?" Zhuni asked.

"Nothing except that during the Dwayans' meeting, Klavan turned a strange color and dropped to the floor. I am speaking with Sarge now as he is getting more information from one of Her guards. Sarge is headed there now. He has a med float from the loading dock."

"Dagz, Sarge is good. I was just thinking of sending for one."

They were making it through the crowded passageways quickly, thanks to Tan'cha's powerful build and ability to push everyone out of the way. Zhuni's head was spinning; here was one of the most important beings in his life with a medical emergency. Zhuni was beginning to doubt if he could help Klavan.

"Sarge is there," Tan'cha said.

"Info?"

"Sarge is saying Klavan has no breath and barely has a heart rate. Klavan is hot to the touch and has mucus exuding from his skin."

"I have no idea; get him loaded and head to the med lab. We should turn around and get one of the minihabs set to take him. We need to stabilize and then figure out what is going on. We will need to run tests. There is no sense in us running all the way up there and back again," Zhuni said, coming to a stop.

"Load him and get him down to the med lab," Tan'cha said, speaking into his vox.

"Let's get back," Zhuni said, turning around.

Tan'cha stopped, turned around, and started running back with Zhuni.

They arrived at the med lab and headed straight to the first minihab. They started it up and began to set up the medical lines and monitors. Zhuni set the vitals for Septorian, at least what he knew of Septorian biology.

Sarge arrived and was directing the med float straight to them. The med float was a platform that was used in medical emergencies to stabilize the injured for transportation. Sarge had been on many battlefields and knew triage work.

"His vitals are nearly nonexistent. He is basically comatose," Sarge said as they moved the med float into the minihab.

"We need to get him hooked up and observe him to find out what is going on. I have never seen anything like this before," Zhuni was starting to worry.

"Sir?" one of the medical technicians said.

"Not now; we have an emergency," Zhuni snapped.

"Yes, but sir, he has been poisoned," the tech said.

"What?" Zhuni spun to look at him; in fact, everyone paused and turned to look at the tech.

The tech was small alien covered with a short brownish-yellow fur, and he was wearing the red and orange jumpsuit of a loading dock handler.

"Why the Dagz would you say that, and how would you know?" Zhuni asked.

"Well, sir, you may not believe it to look at me, but during the Aashturian Civil War, I was a fighter pilot and had a Septorian in our squadron. Once we came back from a mission, and he fell out of the cockpit with some of the same problems Klavan is having. Is he hot?"

"Yes," Zhuni responded, shocked.

"When you see something like that, you never forget. Our pilot's breathing equipment was damaged during the battle, and he was breathing in plasma exhaust fumes from his weapons system. He was hot to the touch, and he was excreting a mucus also. The heating up was his body attempting to burn off the toxins, and the mucus is his body containing the toxin and expelling it from his body."

"Okay, so we need to monitor him and test for a poison," Zhuni said, getting back to work.

"Then we can counteract the poison when we find it. We will need to monitor the air, the mucus, his skin, and bloodstream," Zhuni said.

"Or you could administer the all-purpose antidote that we used. Septorians, especially Septorians of his status, always have a piece of or a family heirloom of what they call 'life wood.' It looks like metal but is actually wood; it comes from a living tree that sucks up all the minerals and biologically forges them into the wood. It is usually a shiny silver color with a hint of gold," the tech said.

"His walking stick!" Tan'cha yelled as he was bolting out of the med lab.

They closed the minihab and headed over to the control room to set up monitoring. The tech was motioned by Zhuni to follow them.

"Tell me about the antidote; how do we make it, and what do we do?" Zhuni asked.

---------------- * ----------------

Klavan was the best assistant She had ever had. He knew about the edicts, traditions, and cultures of nearly every creature She had coming for the main event. He knew everything about everyone here. *How was She going to run things without him?* She had four guards following her as they headed to the med lab. She could tell Her reputation was proceeding Her as everyone cleared a path for Her and Her guards as they traveled down the halls. She was going to have to do something about Zhuni ignoring Her call for him to see Her. That Swaklin had grabbed Klavan and left, said he was rushing Klavan to the med lab.

She did not take kindly to these med people's disregard for Her demands. She knew it was a first and an emergency, but she was going to have to make an example of one of them.

Just as they rounded a corner, that large four-armed bodyguard of Zhuni's dodged Her but ran straight into her guards. He blew through them, knocking three to the ground.

"Sorry, have a life to save!" Tan'cha yelled over his shoulder as he disappeared down the hallway.

Her guards scrambled to their feet. They started down the hall after Tan'cha but then stopped and turned to Her. She had never seen one of them knocked down, much less three of them at once. This was deeply concerning. *She may be in trouble if She does not remedy this.*

She entered the med lab with Her guards in tow.

The place was a hive of activity. Everyone was running about, some seemed set on a task, and others seemed to just be heading to other places. It all came to a halt as She entered. *Good, they had not forgotten*, She thought. She could see several clustered around the minihab control center and was sure that was where She would find Zhuni.

Two guards took up position at the main entrance, and two fell in line at either side of her as She headed to the control center. They were all shadowed by med lab guards.

"I sent for you," She spoke.

"My Grace, I most humbly apologize. I was under the impression You summoned me due to Klavan's condition, and that was Your priority. Was I mistaken? Was there something of more importance than saving the life of one of Your humble servants?" Zhuni said without even looking up or acknowledging Her.

He was getting a bit bold. This one was proving to have more finesse than She had anticipated. He had paid attention to Klavan's tutelage. He was much more versed in the political game than She had thought.

"Of course, when you did not come to me as I had commanded, I assumed I would only find you here tending to Klavan; there could be *no* other explanation."

"Thank You for the understanding, my Baroness. I greatly appreciate it as we all do, and we are certain You are just as concerned as we are," Zhuni added.

"Do we know what his condition is and how to help him? Is there anything you need of me?" She asked.

"My Grace, we believe he has been exposed to a toxin of some form," Zhuni said.

"Someone poisoned *my* assistant?" She snapped.

"We do not know if he was poisoned or if he was unlucky enough to come into contact with a toxin of some type. He works around the loading docks, and all types of material come through there. It could have been a simple mistake. But we are now monitoring, hoping to identify the toxin."

"Report to me your findings. We still have work to do to prepare for tomorrow, and I will need him."

"I will report any news as soon as I have it. We have checked all our equipment and our staff is ready for tomorrow," Zhuni stated.

"Good. Zhuni, when you make your report do it before the end of this day, and you deliver it in person."

"Yes, Your Grace."

She headed out of the med lab. Her guards falling in line as usual. This was going to be an issue; Zhuni was becoming a thorn in Her side. She would have to teach him a lesson. But he had obviously gained great respect for the staff here, and She already knew how the fighters felt. *How am I going to get him back in line? It has to be personal.* She had to do something.

---------- * ----------

Tan'cha entered the conference room, hearing all of the Dwayans chattering amongst themselves. He could make out the individual conversations. Just as he thought, they were all shocked by what had just happened and by the health issues Klavan was having. But they were all worried about who they would turn to for help tomorrow with the guests. Klavan was possibly dying, and they were afraid of how that affected them and their situation.

Tan'cha saw four guards standing there, keeping an eye on the Dwayans, waiting for the Master to return.

Tan'cha did not see the walking stick, so he started to circle the room, looking along the walls and floor towards the outer edges of the room. Once he had made a full circle, his gaze now turned to the conference table and those sitting there. He continued to circle and was not surprised to see who had the stick. Stanton was sitting there admiring it.

"Nice stick you have there," Tan'cha said.

"Nice of you to notice," Stanton shot back.

"I will be taking that now," Tan'cha said.

"Really, you think so?" Stanton asked, one eye focused on Tan'cha and the other flowing around the room, looking for a response from the gathered Dwayans.

"That belongs to Klavan."

"Belonged to Klavan; since he is dying, no sense, it goes to waste."

"No one said he was dying, and even if he was, that does not belong to you."

"No, Klavan left it here, and I found it," Stanton started to change to a rosy reddish color.

"As I said, I will be taking it. I was sent here to retrieve it, and when I passed the Master, She did not seem to be in a good mood."

"Are you saying the Master sent you?"

"Well, when I passed Her in the passageway, I told Her I was saving a life, and She waved me along."

"I think I will just wait for Her then," Stanton said, turning a bit deeper red hue.

"Suit yourself, but I would not want to be you when She returns and finds out you allowed Her assistant to pass away. I bet Her guards would want to ensure Her commands and orders were met. They would not want to deal with an angry Master," Tan'cha said, looking at the closest guard. As if on cue, one guard stepped towards Stanton.

"Fine, here is his stick; I don't really want it anyway. Besides, who cares about this staff? Why would you need it to save a life?" One eye focused on Tan'cha, and the other followed the guard. Stanton was a deep red now.

"Wise decision. Since you do not care, I do not need to waste time explaining it to you." Tan'cha reached out and took the staff from Stanton; as he did so, he saw the guard step back to his original position.

Tan'cha nodded a thank you to the guard and left. He ran down the passageway towards the lift. He was able to grab it prior to its decent and took it to the lower level. He blasted out the door and turned the corner into the main hallway. Once again, he dodged the

Master Herself but ran headlong into three of the guards knocking two to the ground; sparks shot off one when the staff Tan'cha was carrying crashed into him.

"We must stop meeting like this, ma'am," Tan'cha yelled back to Her.

Tan'cha chuckled to himself. These guards weren't that tough. He rather enjoyed slamming into them and watching them crash to the ground. It was as if they were children's puppets, and by slamming into them, he had knocked the strings controlling them off, and they just collapsed. It took a moment for them to gather themselves and stand.

He did not know how long this toxin would take to kill Klavan, so he did not stop to contemplate the issue; he just keept moving as fast as he could and hoped he was fast enough.

His heart was racing as he entered the med lab. Had he been fast enough? Zhuni was leaning out of the minihab control center, hailing Tan'cha.

Tan'cha met Zhuni at the minihab they had set Klavan into, and the tech who had spoken up earlier was also there.

"Give it to him," Zhuni told Tan'cha.

Tan'cha handed it to the tech, and the tech then went into the minihab. He opened the shirt Klavan was wearing, purple, of course, and laid the staff onto his bare chest. The tech then took Klavan's arms and crossed them over, holding the staff. The tech then walked around Klavan until he was standing at the end of the platform at Klavan's head. The tech leaned across Klavan's head and held the staff with both hands and began to hum. The humming was soft and quiet. It was hypnotic, and the staff started to tremble. The humming turned into very slow chanting.

Tan'cha became very agitated and started to head to the minihab door.

"No, wait, it is okay. Kowstee explained to me the process," Zhuni said as he reached and grabbed Tan'cha's left wrist to hold him back.

"Who in Dagz is Kowstee?" Tan'cha asked.

"The tech is named Kowstee, and his friend was a Septorian who had this procedure performed on him. It was something Kowstee said once you see it, you will never forget it. Watch quietly," Zhuni said.

Kowstee continued to chant. The staff started pulsating very slowly, along with Kowstee's chanting. Kowstee's chanting slowly became faster and faster; it started to have a steady rhythm to it. The staff was throbbing to the same rhythm of the chanting, it was a heartbeat, and it was Klavan's. The staff began to lose its shape. It looked to be melting. It melted into Klavan's chest. The mucus covering Klavan started to dissipate into the air as a mist. When the mucus was completely gone, the staff reappeared as a puddle on Klavan's chest, then started to reform in its original shape across Klavan's chest. Kowstee collapsed, and Zhuni let go of Tan'cha.

"Now," Zhuni said as he and Tan'cha made for the minihab door. They got in just as Klavan gasped and grasped the staff, pulling it tightly to his chest.

"Where am I?" Klavan asked.

"The med lab," Tan'cha responded.

"Let's move him to the next one," Zhuni said, lifting Kowstee to a standing position so Tan'cha could pick him up and carry him into the next minihab.

"What happened?" Klavan asked.

"You are fine; I will explain everything once I get Kowstee stabilized," Zhuni said as he put his hand on Klavan's shoulder, gave it a squeeze, and headed out.

"Who is Kowstee?"

———————— * ————————

Zhuni entered Her office. He was dreading this meeting. He knew he had shown a bit of disrespect but had worked to reel it in. He could not believe She was so self-centered or insecure that She was worried about any slight affront in that situation.

The guards were there, as always; She was never without at least two of them. One on either side of Her desk. She stood there looking down at Zhuni.

"Good evening, Your Grace. I bring good news, Klavan will recover and should be by Your side tomorrow evening at the main event," Zhuni told Her.

"I need him in the morning, have him here at zero six hundred. We need to speak about several incidents yesterday."

"Yes, Baroness, we were all a bit on edge and stressed and may have said and done some things that, looking at the situation as if it were a normal day, may have come across as disrespectful, and I apologize for such behavior."

"I must make an example of you but know that would be a poor thing to do at this time. I need you to perform at your peak tomorrow and your team. I am not sure how to deal with the disrespect yesterday. The problem is that many people saw what happened, not only in the passageways and the med lab but also in the conference room."

"I do not understand, my Liege."

"No, you do not. Are you aware of the incidents in the passageway?"

"I truly hate to be ignorant, Your Grace, but I was preoccupied by Klavan's health and was not in the passageway. Please explain."

"You do not know, truly. Well, then, that makes it even more interesting. Tan'cha ran down my guards twice."

"When You say ran down Your guards, do You mean ran into them?"

"Not just ran into them but knocked three to the ground as he headed down the passageway leaving the med lab but then knocked two down on his way back to the med lab returning from the conference room."

"Oh my, Your Grace, they are an extension of You and should not be touched; this is a tremendous breach of etiquette."

"So, you do understand; as your personal bodyguard, he needs to be an example of proper behavior to all others. I will have to do something, but again do not want to cause too much of an issue; usually, I would just dispose of him, but I feel that would be problematic in this situation. I propose you present a solution to this dilemma."

"Your Grace, Tan'cha is a simple creature and does not possess the intellectual capacity we have. After all, until last month, he was but a pit fighter. Lacking the intellect makes him a simple creature, and a simple punishment would strike him hard. I suggest he be assigned to solitary confinement for ten to twelve rotations following the main event. This will isolate him, and seeing he has been surrounded by other fighters all his life would most likely terrify him with the loneliness."

"Isolate and strike fear into him, good. You have a good plan. I think this will please me for now."

"I do need him, as I know he will do everything in his power and training to protect me as long as he thinks it is to his advantage."

"Now leave me, do have Klavan here at zero six hundred. We have a busy day, and I will need him. Thank you for saving him; he is very helpful. Do we know what happened? Was it an allergic reaction? Did he encounter something in the loading area, or was it something else?"

"We are unaware of the cause at this time, but we will be investigating over the next several rotations to find the full story, with Your permission, of course."

"Of course, permission granted, and keep me informed of your progress, daily and personally."

"I would have it no other way, my Grace; good evening."

———————— * ————————

"I am telling you, it was as if they just collapsed. For a moment, they did not even move. It was odd," Tan'cha was explaining his literal run-in with the guards.

"So, you are telling me that when you hit them, they just dropped and went limp?"

"I ran full force into them, knocked three to the ground, stumbled against the passage wall, gained my balance, and started off again. I looked back about three strides down the passage, and they were just starting to get up. One was laid flat. I ran into them again and, this time, knocked two to the ground, and the same thing."

"Neither time did they see you coming?" Sarge asked.

"I don't think so; it all happened so quickly that I did not even realize it was them until I hit them. And they did not have any give."

"What do you mean?"

"It may be nothing; I mean, it was odd," Tan'cha looked around as if he was collecting his thoughts.

"Okay, explain to me what you mean."

"You know when you hit a creature, an opponent, an enemy, there is that split second when you can feel their muscles give, even when they are armored. You can feel the slightest softness of flesh. Even when you strike a shield, you know it gives as the muscles fail and the shield drops. There was nothing like that when I hit them.

"You mean as if they were not real?"

"No, not like they weren't real, but almost as if they were... mechanical."

"You mean a bot?"

"Exactly."

"That is unique; I thought the guilds outlawed bots and droids without specific functions that only bots could do. Like med bots, mining bots, etc. You know AI had so many issues that only very dangerous or specific jobs could be performed by bots," Sarge looked worried.

"Do you think I am crazy?"

"Well, yes, I do, but on this specific subject, no. As a general statement, yes. What bothers me is that I fought bots long ago, and they were nearly indestructible. With AI, they also learned quickly and overcame our tactics. With shared AI, like a central control or a hive mind, they learn instantly. I do not like this. We will need to talk to Zhuni when he returns and have Joxby look into it."

"Something else."

"Yeah?"

"Well, you know my big ears and my extreme hearing; when I am around machinery or computers, the high-pitched sounds most cannot even hear give me a headache," Tan'cha stated.

"You get headaches when you are around the guards?"

"Yes, but until now, with our conversation and me putting the pieces together, I hadn't realized it."

"All right, we have some work to do, add this to our investigation of what happened to Klavan and the main event; it should be a fairly normal next couple of rotations."

———————— * ————————

"Oh, Traxon, you missed all the fun," Stanton yelled; his skin was a bright, happy yellow.

"During our meeting, Klavan passed out. He turned an awful color and dropped to the floor. Dagz, it was a good time. Where have you been today? Our new employee has already got some work done; he had a little to do with Klavan nearly dying. Too bad we didn't get rid of him. But that Zhuni and his crew saved him. They have a way of saving the ones I need to dispose of."

"Tomorrow is the main event, and I need you and the Boyz to be on the lookout for opportunity; we may be able to get Zhuni into some trouble. He definitely got on the Master's bad side today. And that Tannycha thing, the blue one, got on my nerves too much. If you and the Boyz want to do something about him, I am fine with that. This is your time to shine; you must step up and prove you are worth all the trouble I have gone to to keep you around. You worthless Mynog."

"Traxon, I am speaking to you," Stanton bellowed, changing his skin tone to an orange.

"Boss, listen me. I have some…" Traxon tried to get out the information he had found out about the guards.

"You know what, you were gone all day; just keep it that way. Make yourself useful tomorrow somehow, and stay out of my way. I may have your replacement and don't really need you around unless you can come up with something important. Tell the Boyz to keep their ears open and report to Boshduul anything they find out."

"Who Boshduul?" Traxon asked.

"The new hire you brought to me."

"Rags, him new boss?"

"Yes. His name is Boshduul, and yes, he will be my second now; I like his understanding of authority, and he is much more competent than you, so report to him."

Traxon thought, *It is a good thing I made those contacts and gained the information I did, but maybe the information would serve someone else better. So could the contacts.*

—————— * ——————

"Tan'cha, we need to talk," Zhuni said as he entered the med lab.

"Yes, Boss."

"Sarge, I need you also. We will head up to my office."

They all went to Zhuni's quarters and sat down in his private office.

"Gentlemen, I just finished my meeting with Her, and we have some things to discuss," Zhuni said as he turned toward Tan'cha.

"So, you ran into Her guards this afternoon. She is extremely upset about that and wanted to have you 'disposed of' but realized you were an important part of this team. She had me come up with a suitable punishment; after all, this happened twice in full view of all in the passageway."

"She wanted to kill me?" Tan'cha said with a weak voice.

"We know She is vicious, and this just shows how close we are walking on the edge; we must up our 'respect' game. Yes, She wanted you gone," Zhuni replied.

"So may I ask what you told Her was going to be his punishment?" Sarge inserted.

"You are both going to love this. The morning after the main event, you will be arrested and paraded through the passageway to solitary confinement. You will spend twelve rotations there."

"Solitary, as in by myself, no one else? Really? Privacy?" Tan'cha smiled.

"Yup, and remember you are terrified of being alone, so play it up; otherwise, She won't buy it."

"Zhuni, you know I would take a plasma round for you, but now I would even kill for you. You are the best; I love you!" Tan'cha became quite animated and excited.

"All right, now settle down; we don't need it to get weird," Zhuni smiled.

"Too late; Tan'cha has a special way of making things weird," Sarge barbed.

"Shut up!" Tan'cha shot back at Sarge.

"Girls, please, we have other issues to discuss still," Zhuni had to referee the two.

Tan'cha and Sarge spoke to Zhuni of the discussion they had about the guards.

"So, you think the guards are bots?" Zhuni asked.

"We are not sure; we know bots of this type have been outlawed, but…" Tan'cha said.

"All the evidence points to that fact, but it doesn't seem to make a lot of sense for Her to have bots, androids, droids, or whatever rather than real loyal guards," Sarge injected.

"Unless She truly is evil and cannot find any loyal followers because She is always disposing of them. Sarge, you seem to have an honest dislike for bots. Don't you? We will have to revisit that at a later time. If She is so set on Her ideal of respect and it doesn't match up with a sane concept of respect, She may need bots to follow Her. They would have no morals and would therefore be able to simply follow their programming. No greed, no anger, no hate, not even remorse. They would be perfect for Her," Zhuni expressed.

"Dagz! Hadn't thought about it like that," Tan'cha quipped.

"Perfect followers. Great," Sarge interjected.

CHAPTER 5

Chaos and the Main Event

"Good morning, everyone. Today is the main event. We have all worked hard to get here, and we need to remember we are a team. This med lab was set up to save lives. So, let's put that at the front of our minds. You all know your jobs and your responsibilities. Do your best, and we will save some lives. Let's get to work."

Zhuni wanted to start the day on a good note and ensure no one knew how worried he was. He just addressed the entire team for the first time. He had never given a speech before, so he hoped it went well. The team broke up and headed to their assignments.

"Well?" Zhuni asked, looking at Tan'cha.

"What? I was crying; that was so powerful," Tan'cha chuckled.

"Shut up! Why do I even keep you around?"

"Currently, because my job is to protect you."

"I hate you," Zhuni snapped.

"Yup, I hate you too." Tan'cha smiled.

"Sarge, you have my permission to shoot him," Zhuni said, grinning at Sarge.

"Yes, sir, Mister Zhuni, but I have enough to do without having to babysit you also," Sarge shot back, laughing. Tan'cha started chuckling also.

"Oh my, this is going to be a long day," Zhuni sighed.

Zhuni and Tan'cha headed out of the med lab and started down the passageway to the main gate to the arena fighting area. Zhuni wanted to be at the forefront of the event and be in the thick of things until they had serious injuries, and he had to be at the med lab. He also wanted to see a couple of the combined teams of medics and scientists in action so he could tell where to improve with knowledge. He, Tan'cha, and Sarge were fairly sure they had matched personalities, strengths, and the weaknesses of the medical and security teams properly. Sarge headed up to the control room to watch over and listen to the various teams around the complex. Joxby had everyone tied in through earpieces and voxes so they could all communicate with each other. He also had all communication scrambled so no one other than the med lab teams could talk or listen in.

The morning started off like any normal fight day, a few injuries but nothing truly serious. These were the lower-level fights. Zhuni did have to step in and help with one fighter who was in bad shape; he took a spear to the chest, and then the poor slog got trampled by a Scyrtock. He was now in a minihab in stable condition. He had a lot of broken bones; he would be out for a while. As the day wore on, it looked to be just another day at the fights. The fighting stopped in late afternoon for the big banquet prior to the big fights. This gave Zhuni and his team nearly four partions to go over any issues prior to the main fights. Everything had gone smoothly, so Zhuni had all teams head back to the med lab for a large meal their chefs had prepared.

Zhuni checked in with Sarge, who told him there had been no security breaches or attempts. Sarge said Joxby had been feeding the known device a loop most of the day, so that was taken care of. Joxby had told Sarge to have his security boys on point for the evening. With all the extra dignitaries, guilds, and fighters, there would be some chaos and would provide the perfect opportunity for a breach.

Sarge had already told his teams. Zhuni was pleased with the med reports. One of the new procedures with the med lab was that Zhuni reviewed the med reports before they went to central records. This way, he could review procedures and the team's work. He was also given the ability to make recommendations for further treatment or follow-up procedures. When the event was over, Zhuni had already planned to do a thorough review of each medic, their knowledge level, and how each team worked together. He was pleased to be able to do this but knew he now had a lot to deal with. Considering he had been self-taught, and the gamers scientists had never attempted to save lives, Zhuni was feeling good about how everything was going.

Zhuni decided to check in on the patients they had in the mini-habs, including Kowstee.

———————— * ————————

The banquet was going extraordinarily well. Klavan was pleased. He felt fully recovered and was full of energy. He would like to know what or who had attempted to kill him; he had his suspicions. Klavan had done a thorough job with the etiquette reports for all the dignitaries, guilds, and guests. As of now, there had been no mistakes, and even the Master was in what Klavan would call a good mood. Even if he never truly saw emotions, She was not threatening any of the staff at this point. Klavan still felt he knew a secret about Her and felt She knew that he had figured it out. But She hadn't given any indication of that since the conference room. Klavan was certain She was clairvoyant, and that is how She was able to control everyone. But if She was, why maintain him, a Septorian, as Her assistant? Septorians were well known to be immune to mind control in any form. Still, so many questions.

Klavan was surprised by some of the guests. He was sure the guild masters would all be here. But Tazmok, the Mining Guild's master, was nowhere to be found. Moz, the second, was here, but the Mining Guild was one of the larger and more powerful guilds. Tazmok not being here was odd. There was word that he and the Master had a run-in a few years ago, so that may explain the slight. Klavan was sure the Master would not like Tazmok's absence. *Without Tazmok here, how was She going to negotiate a contract?* Klavan knew this was one of Her reasons for this massive main event. But for now, that was something Klavan did not need to worry himself with. He had to ensure everything here and the banquet continued to run smoothly.

Klavan made his way back to the service area to check on the next several courses. They were about half through with the meal.

He noticed Traxon wondering about and did not like that at all. He knew Traxon was Stanton's main stooge.

"Traxon, get out of here!"

"Traxon need talk."

"Stanton is in the banquet hall, and I can't have you wondering around here. You will have to get ahold of him after the fights." Klavan was heading towards him to throw Traxon out himself if that was what it took.

"Not Stanton. You!"

"Get out of here," Klavan said, continuing towards Traxon.

"No, need talk you."

"Traxon, I do not need to talk to you. I do not see any reason to waste my breath; you and your boss are not exactly on speaking terms with me."

"Yes, no like you."

"Well, I didn't say I didn't like you, but if you don't like me, then just get out of here, we have no need to talk."

"Yes, do I no work Stanton more. I have information useful for you. And for Zhuni."

"What do you mean information? Why should I listen to anything you say? You and Stanton have been a pain in my neck for the last four Masters. What do you mean Zhuni?"

"I need talk important, now. Save lifes. Many."

"Look, I have never seen eye to eye with your boss. I do not see any reason to waste my time for him."

"*Not him.* Me. I fix. I know right side. I make mistakes, many. I help. Very Important. Please just two actas."

Klavan did not know why but something told him Traxon was genuine and needed to share what he felt was important information. Klavan had always felt sorry for Traxon and the situation he was in. Especially after Stanton had Traxon thrown into the pit to watch him die. If it hadn't been for Zhuni, Traxon would be dead. Klavan never did understand why Traxon had continued to work for Stanton. Traxon was a sad little creature; maybe he had finally figured out just how power-hungry Stanton was and what he would do to achieve his desires.

"Fine talk. But we need to get out of the kitchen, and you only have two actas. Go," Klavan said, pushing Traxon into the back service hall.

Traxon looked around nervously to be sure no one was around that would understand this important information. He did not want one of the Boyz to find out.

Klavan could tell Traxon was even more jittery and nervous than usual and realized Traxon was putting himself in a dangerous situation by relaying whatever it was he was going to tell him.

---------- * ----------

The evening started well but deteriorated quickly.

"Zhuni, come quickly. We have some blaster burns that are horrible." The cry came from the main arena gate, Zhuni was starting a couple more minihabs, ready for more severe injuries, but he did not expect this. He bolted out of the med lab and headed to the gate. Tan'cha on his heels. Zhuni remembered the Master asking if he and his team could handle these types of injuries, but he did not anticipate horrible injuries. He needed to see what was happening.

He and Tan'cha arrived as the medic was clearing his station.

"Where is the patient?" Zhuni asked. He saw the kill cart but did not believe it was for the injured already.

"He didn't make it," the medic said totally dejected.

Zhuni ran over to stop the cart.

"What happened?" Zhuni asked.

"He was shot by one of the new turrets She had installed. It blew his head clean off," the cart driver said sadly.

"Turrets?" Zhuni seemed to remember Klavan saying something about turrets, but Zhuni had completely forgotten about them.

"Yes, sir. There are turrets around the upper edge of the VIP level. There are six turrets; two are blaster rifles. That is what got Tockma there," a fighter who had just left the arena said.

"When did they start using those?" Zhuni asked.

"The fight before ours. They are allowing the visitors up there to run the turrets; they have only used the two blaster rifles so far, not sure what the other turrets have. Luckily the visitors who have been using them are bad shots, but every once in a while, I guess even a bad marksman will hit something," the fighter said, looking towards the cart.

"We have how many more fights scheduled?" Zhuni turned to ask Tan'cha.

"If it is like normal, we will have four more before they release Brynja Ajal, and then it will all break loose," Tan'cha said grimly.

"Four, did you include the free-for-all She loves so much?"

"No, four fights, then the chaos battle, as we call it, and then She will release Brynja Ajal. So, the two before chaos should be just like the last two. I will bet that She will allow those blaster rifles to be used for the next two fights, and then during the chaos, She will open up and use the other turrets." Tan'cha was remembering how the main events usually went and what he thought She would do.

"Tan'cha, She asked us if we could handle blaster injuries and what else? Do you remember? We need to remember so we can protect these guys," Zhuni frantically asked.

"Blasters and..." Tan'cha was trying to remember.

"And what? Come on, buddy, we need to think! Dagz, lives are at stake!"

"She said it as She was leaving the first time She came to the med lab for Her initial inspection; blaster burns and..." Tan'cha was playing it back through his mind.

"Right, now I can remember Her visit, but I can't..." Zhuni was also trying to remember the details.

"Pallets. No petals. Dagz!" Tan'cha was throwing words out but knew they were not right.

"Pellets! Plasma pellets! Yes. Tan'cha, that is it! You got it."

"I did?"

"Okay, what do we have which can help against plasma pellets?" Zhuni asked.

"I have never had to worry about blaster rifles nor plasma pellets, so I have no idea."

"Sarge, what do we have in the armory that can protect fighters from plasma pellets?" Zhuni asked into his vox.

"Plasma pellets, what the Dagz are you talking about?" Sarge asked.

"The turrets that were installed. They have blaster rifles, and we think the turrets that haven't been used yet are going to be plasma turrets."

"The best thing we have that the fighters could get ahold of is that chitin, which may not take a direct hit, but even a slight angle could cause both blaster bolts and plasma pellets to ricochet."

"Brilliant!" Zhuni exclaimed.

"So, we need to get the old armor," Tan'cha said.

"Okay, you need to get that going; I will head back to get set-up for more injuries."

"Nice idea, but not going to allow that."

"What are you talking about? We need to get this done."

"Yes, we do, but I am not leaving you. I am your shadow; where you go, I go."

"Really? I will be fine just going back to med lab."

"Nope!"

"I am not going to let you do this; you are beginning to annoy me!"

"I would much rather you were annoyed at me then lose you and have to explain myself to Sarge," Tan'cha explained.

"Fine."

"Sarge," Zhuni was once again speaking into his vox.

"Go," was the response.

"I need Tan'cha to get these guys armored up, and I need to get back to the med lab, so we need to be in two places at once."

"No, you don't. I am on my way. Joxby has central control, Tan'cha can bring you back, and I will get the fighters armored; I am on my way," Sarge replied.

"You don't need to do that; I will just head to the lab and leave Tan'cha here," Zhuni countered.

"No! I am on my way, sir. Do not move." With a firmness, Zhuni had never heard from Sarge. Zhuni turned to see a smile on Tan'cha's face.

"See, I told you."

"All right then, I will wait here."
"Wise decision."
"Oh, shut up."
Tan'cha just laughed.

———————— * ————————

The banquet hall was the largest room outside of the med lab in the entire complex. It had high ceilings, nearly twenty feet. It was two hundred feet long and had dozens of massive tables for guests of every size and shape. The walls were glistening as they were highly polished. Every ten feet along the ceiling was a massive chandelier made of metal of a golden tone; it matched the color of the walls nicely. Around the back of the hall were service doors to the massive kitchen. Also along this wall were huge serving tables that the kitchen crew kept restocking, and the waiters continuously removed food and drink to serve the many guests. The hall was behind the luxury boxes overlooking the arena, allowing the guests a short walk to the dinner from the excitement of the arena.

Stanton was having a great time at this banquet. He had not had this much fun in a long time. It seems Zhuni had ruined Stanton's attempt on Klavan's life, but Stanton now had a personal assistant who happened to also be an assassin. Well, he said he was. Maybe he was, and Zhuni was just that good. Anyhow Stanton won't let that ruin his evening, besides, no one even knew about his new assistant. Well, not the important individuals. He could always take Klavan out at a more opportune time. Doing it during this main event was most likely a huge mistake.

Stanton was making some connections he thought would come in handy. He liked the little band of misfits he had under his wing but could always improve his station. Boshduul could prove to be a major addition or a miscalculation. It remained to be seen. But for now, Stanton was just enjoying himself.

He had to get some fresh air. He was only half through the meal and had already stuffed himself to a painful state and just had to get up and move. He excused himself from his table and decided to head back to the service area to be away from the crowd for a moment.

He was not surprised to see Klavan head back that way; he knew Klavan was ensuring everything was just right for the guests and the Master.

Stanton went out into the service hallway; he knew the facility's layout fairly well. He had been here for dozens of full cycles. But as he thought about it, he got angry. He had been here longer than Klavan and should be the Master's number two. Not Klavan. So, what if Klavan knew about etiquette? Stanton knew how to bully, cheat, steal, and all the important things a good crony needed to do.

Standing in the service hall was the Mining Guild second in command, and Stanton felt a need to speak to him. After all, Stanton needed to make all the connections he could; if he could not get past Klavan here, maybe he could move up in another guild. He headed down to see him but was surprised to see a small figure scurry past the guild master. It had come out of the hall behind the kitchen, where Klavan had been.

Wait, was that one of his Boyz up here? No way, they were not that bold. This one was a bit more hunched over than the others and had an odd gait to his movement. That was not just one of his Boyz but his number two, Traxon. Stanton needed to find out what was going on and find out quickly.

Stanton broke into a run and started after Traxon, forgetting all about the Mining Guild second in command right in front of him. Stanton was of great girth and, once moving, was not so easy to stop. But the guild master did not seem to worry about that as he easily took Stanton to the ground and put a blaster pistol in his face.

Stanton suddenly felt that his evening was not going to end as well as he had hoped.

———————— * ————————

Traxon was not being allowed into the med lab; the guards were not letting anyone but their trusted staff in. This could be a problem.

Klavan had told Traxon to get the information to Zhuni. Traxon did not know how to get into the med lab other than through one of the two entrances: the main entry off the arena passageway or the loading dock off the side. Both were guarded. They did not recognize Klavan's ring, which Traxon had. Klavan had given it to Traxon so it could be shown to Zhuni to prove the information was legitimate. But that would only work if Zhuni saw the ring. *What if Zhuni did not come out until tomorrow?* Traxon had to get in and warn Zhuni. Traxon saw his chance. The kill cart was pulling up to the entrance. Traxon slipped under the cover and stayed very still. Just as he got settled, the cover was pulled back. Somehow it was just the front part of the cover; he was at the back. He knew he was next to a pit fighter and knew that with him being on the cart, he was dead, but why take him into the med lab?

The cart moved forward and into the med lab. The massive door closed. Traxon was in. He rolled out from under the cover into the open. He was there for a split acta. There was no one around. He saw some medical supply boxes and rushed over to hide behind them. *Where was everyone?* He thought there were a lot of staff working here. He sat there and peeked his head around to see if anyone had seen him. He was not spotted. He relaxed and scanned the immediate area looking for a way to get over to the other side where he knew the offices and the quarters were. Zhuni had to be there. Traxon got ready to make a break for it when he noticed security guards heading towards him from several different directions. He had not seen anyone. How did they know he was there? And exactly where he was.

The guards surrounded his position and told him if he was armed to give up his weapon, or they would shoot him. Traxon recognized one as a Swaklin, a former night guard at the main loading dock. This guy did not mess around. Traxon let them know he had no weapons and was here to speak with Zhuni; it was very important. The guards escorted him to the far side of the med lab where Traxon had guessed Zhuni was. But instead of having him meet Zhuni, the guards put him in a small room and locked the room's door with him in it. This was not what Traxon had planned on. Now he was in the med lab but no closer to Zhuni.

*

Klavan got back to the banquet. He had some suspicions about the Master and Her guards and knew Stanton didn't like him, but what Traxon told him was a bit much. He knew if Traxon told Zhuni that Zhuni and his team would be better able to find out the information. Klavan could no longer operate around the facility freely. The Master was always needing him and seemed to always know where he was.

Klavan stepped out of the kitchen into the banquet hall and saw the Master looking for him. She nodded for him to come over.

It had been nearly five partions since he left the room.

"You disappeared," She said to Klavan as he leaned over to hear Her. She was standing at the far end of the table from the kitchen.

"I was simply checking on the meal's next course. It is my job to ensure all the details are properly prepared," Klavan blurted out.

"Yes, I was concerned you may be having side effects from your incident yesterday. I need you to be available for these guests and any possible transactions. You have given all the direction you need for the details; I need you available for contracts and agreements. That is what is going to start happening now. I am working a deal with the Mining Guild to come under my control, and I need to ensure you are available, do not leave my site again unless directed to by me."

"Yes, Your Grace."

"By the way, have you seen Moz from the Mining Guild?"

"No, I have not." Klavan waved one of the servants over and asked him if any of the servants had seen Moz.

The servant said Moz was in the back service hallway.

Just then, the door from the main hall burst open, and Stanton came stumbling in. He had obviously had a run-in with something. He was a deep magenta color, a cross between red and purple. He was beaten and swollen more than usual. He also had a flash burn across his forehead that looked bad.

Stepping behind him was Moz, with a huge grin.

"Master, some of your staff are a bit clumsy but quite fun," Moz said, laughing.

Stanton stumbled over to his seat, looking extremely dejected.

"This Mynog ran headlong into me; I don't know if he didn't see me or just didn't care, but I threw him to the ground, had a bit of a tussle, and we are good now. I don't think he will be so bold again." Moz grabbed his drink and took a large swig.

"Stanton is not one of our more cultured Dwayans," Klavan stepped in to settle things down.

"You don't say he certainly isn't as cultured as you, sir," Moz replied, looking at Klavan.

Klavan glanced over at Stanton and saw he was a bright red. He could tell, even without the bright red hue, that Stanton was embarrassed and irate.

"We will have a discussion with him shortly," Klavan said, looking back to Moz.

"No bother, just let him stay. I have some things to discuss with your Master, so we will be heading to Her office for a few partions. We have a contract to work out," Moz said, heading back towards the door.

"Klavan, attend to these guests while I am gone. I will attend to you later," She said as She looked at Stanton.

"Klavan, when we return, I will find you here," She said, looking directly at Klavan.

Moz and the Master left, followed by two of Her guards. Two were left in the banquet hall, and Klavan had the feeling they were there to watch him more so than the guests.

---------------- * ----------------

Zhuni entered the med lab, knowing they were going to be getting some serious injuries in these next couple of fights. He was not sure how bad it was going to be, but he thought if they could get some med floats at the main arena gate, that should allow a few precious actas of stabilization for any grievous injuries.

He motioned to attendants to get the med floats ready and send them to the gate. He heard Joxby asking for him on the vox.

"What's up, Joxby?"

"Uninvited-came-in-very-animated," Joxby shot back.

Interesting, if Joxby was saying someone was animated, Zhuni would hate to see that individual.

"Do we know who?"

"Guards-said-Traxon-needed-to-talk-to-you."

"Traxon, what in Dagz does he want? Who let him in?"

"Uninvited." The way Joxby said that Zhuni understood he snuck in somehow.

"Where is he? I guess if it is important enough to sneak in here."

"Holding-cell-one."

"Thanks, Joxby."

Zhuni rushed over to cell one. If this was important enough for Traxon to attempt to sneak into the facility, it was either a part of a plan of Stanton, or Traxon was taking a big risk. Either way, Zhuni needed to know.

Tan'cha was right with him.

"This is extremely peculiar," Tan'cha voiced.

"The timing is most convenient also."

"It could be one of Stanton's tricks."

"I am thinking that also, or Traxon is taking a big risk."

"How do you suggest we figure out if his information is legitimate?"

"I haven't figured that out yet. But we will listen for a few actas and see where it goes. Now he came to tell me something important, so don't say anything."

"Yes, sir. I wouldn't want to ruin your party."

"Really?"

"Yes, sir, Boss. I will be quiet as I can be. I will not say anything, not at all. Like the dead. That is me dead quiet."

"Shut up."

"Right."

They arrived at holding cell one and saw Traxon jump up to rush to the bars to shove something at Zhuni. Tan'cha jumped in front and grabbed Traxon's tiny little arm pulling him against the bars and removing what he had in the hand he was thrusting at Zhuni.

"What is it?" Zhuni asked.

"A ring," Tan'cha said, handing it to Zhuni.

"It is Klavan's family crest; it is Klavan's ring. How did you get this? Is Klavan okay? What happened? Tell me!" Zhuni yelled at Traxon obviously concerned.

"No hurt, he give me. Prove you my information real. I go him first, he send me see and tell you," Traxon chirped.

"That does sound like something Klavan would do," Tan'cha interjected.

"Yup, it does. Okay, talk. What is so important that you would risk sneaking in here?" Zhuni said impatiently.

"Stanton hate you, want you dead. I find spy assassin to kill you and Klavan, he poison Klavan, but Klavan live. Stanton replace me as number two with rags. Assassin. I call rags. I find him in market. Lot of bad easy find. I not know he try kill Klavan me like Klavan, Klavan good to me. Nice. Zhuni good too," Traxon said, touching his facial scars.

Zhuni save life. Me like Zhuni. I help now. Klavan and Zhuni. No work more for Stanton; maybe he kill me. I knew secret; I go to tell Stanton he tell me no good replace me. So I come Klavan," Traxon was getting excessively animated.

"What is this information you have?" Zhuni asked.

"I find lot of helpful and dangerous information."

"Yes, you have said that. Not getting rude, but we have a lot to deal with right now. Get to the point," Zhuni barked.

"Here it is. I want to find out Master and guards, not right, so I sneak into her quarters. No chair, no bed, no bath, no bio function things. I think not right. I see eight guards, sleeping, hibernating, off. Don't know. They stand on platforms each one, clamps on feet, just stand. No move. Other side room, eight platforms, no guards, no weapons. Weapons on rack by standing guards."

"What are you saying?" Zhuni asked.

"Guards not real, machines. One main platform between both group of guards, for Her maybe, main control panel for all guards and platforms. Maybe guards plug in, charge on platforms. Her to. Cybot. Roborg thing."

"You mean robot or cyborg," Tan'cha jumped in and looked at Zhuni, who just glared at him. Tan'cha just shrugged his shoulders and grinned slightly.

"Yes. And more. I change to work clothes at load dock. I come back to change and see Stanton. I drop cleaning rag. It catch on something; I look it transmitter for spy pictures. Behind broken heavy lifter, I look down and see a rag on floor. I remember color, my rag gray. Gray like all rags for cleaning, rag on ground rusty brown."

"Okay, so what does that mean?" Zhuni asked.

"Rags brown, only Rags brown rusty."

"What do you mean rags brown? You just said gray," Zhuni asked, perplexed.

"No, cleaning rag gray, Rags rags brown."

"You are making no sense. Brown rags, gray rags, who cares."

"I care, you care. Cleaning rags gray. Brown rags come from Rags. What Stanton call him, the assassin, what he call him. Boshde, Boshdoo, something else, I call Rags."

"You mean the assassin is called Rags, and he dropped a brown rag, but the rags here at the facility are gray. So, a rusty brown rag is from the assassin. Right?" Zhuni wasn't even sure what he was saying made sense.

"Yes. Rags spying you for Stanton. Stanton spy on you to kill and try kill Klavan. Stanton want be Master."

"See, I told you Stanton hates you. He hates you so much he wants you dead. I was right," Tan'cha laughed.

"Really. We are in the middle of a million issues we have to deal with, and the one you find most important to talk about is that you are right. What is wrong with you?" Zhuni snapped at him.

"I am just saying. And besides, you are my doctor; you know exactly what is wrong with me," Tan'cha laughed.

"Stanton wants me dead, he tried to kill Klavan, and you are celebrating being correct. And you are the one that is supposed to keep me alive. Great. I feel so safe."

"I promise you I will keep you alive if just to remind you when I am right."

"Well then, now I feel safe."

"What do you mean?"

"If you keep me alive until the next time you are right, I will live a long time."

"Exactly, see. Hey, wait a minute."

"Traxon confused how this help," Traxon piped up.

"It doesn't; thank you for getting us back on track," Zhuni expressed.

"Well, you and Sarge already figured out that the guards were droids or mechanical, but now we have confirmation. We thought someone had tried to kill Klavan, but now we know exactly who. We had already found the borehole to the surveillance equipment Traxon told us about; now we know who set it up. So, to wrap everything up, Stanton and his assassin are responsible for all the trouble outside of the arena. Do I have it all?" Zhuni looked at Tan'cha.

"Seems about right. But what do we do with Traxon here? Do we keep him?"

"Yes, I think we will keep him here at least overnight, for our safety and his. Then tomorrow, we will have him meet with Joxby and locate this assassin of Stanton."

"Joxby, have you seen anything at the lifter in the loading dock?" Zhuni asked, speaking into his vox.

"Nope-I-have-Traxon-there-earlier."

"That verifies Traxon's story," Tan'cha said to Zhuni.

"No one else?" Zhuni asked into the vox.

"No," Joxby responded.

"Nothing?"

"There-was-no-one."

"Was there anything? Like, some rags?" Zhuni asked, shrugging and looking at Tan'cha. Tan'cha shrugged also.

"Well-actually-there-was-a-moment-when-a-cloth-or-something-briefly-covered-the-camera."

"Joxby, isolate the images, do whatever you can to attempt to identify whatever you find in the images during that time. Analyze images around the loading dock entrances and passageways to find similar images. Then see if you can track it," Zhuni instructed.

"Traxon, when did you take Rags to Stanton?" asked Zhuni.

"Yesterday morning, early."

"Joxby, look at images to Stanton's office for yesterday morning, early. Traxon will be among them. Find a figure that looks like rags. Cross-reference that image to every available drone or surveillance device you can and see if you can track him; in fact, if you can, mark him so we can track his every move," Zhuni explained.

"Will-do."

"It is worth a shot; we may be able to find him," Zhuni said, turning to Tan'cha.

"Okay, so how did you know to do all that stuff?" Tan'cha asked.

"I use my brains, plus I have learned a few things listening to you and Sarge, and I spent some time talking to Joxby. He knows his stuff for sure. Confused me at first. But I just think of the facility as a body and the assassin as a disease that I have to find."

"Interesting, your brain is much more powerful than I thought. I did not know that tiny little head could hold so much knowledge."

"I know, right? Like the reverse of your huge head, so much room, so much empty space," Zhuni chuckled.

"Hey."

"We have got to get back to our real work. We have some heavy stuff coming our way shortly."

———————— * ————————

The Master was in Her conference room along with Moz, two of Her guards, and four of his crew. She was standing at the head of the table, flanked by Her guards.

Moz was a stocky built humanoid of the Toztat race. Toztat stood about five feet tall on average and were powerful, making them great workers in the mines throughout the galaxy. Most members of the Mining Guild were Toztat. Moz was a gray color, meaning he was of older age; Toztat changed color as they aged. They started life as a brown color fading to tan, then gray and a pale gray, nearly white, towards the end of their lives. The other members of his crew were also Toztat but were of a brownish color.

"So, Moz, you have followed my direction?"

"Sure have. Just like you told me. Tazmok has been captured and brought to your guards as you requested," Moz responded.

"You have informed all guild members I am now the leader of the Mining Guild?"

"Yes, and I am your number two."

"You have the documents and the guild stone?"

"Documents signed and witnessed by all in this room and, of course, Tazmok himself. Here is the guild stone," Moz said as he handed Her the guild stone. The guild stone was mounted on a necklace, nearly a full chest plate piece of highly polished silvery metal. In the center of it was the Mining Guild crest and a greenish-blue stone; this was the symbol of the leader of the Mining Guild. All other members and guilds knew that whoever was wearing this was the guild master.

She took it and placed it on Herself.

"I am now guild master, and as such, I do not now and never will need a number two. I do acknowledge the work you have done to get here. I do not need someone so easily controlled."

Moz knew he had made a fatal mistake. Moz and his crew stood as one and reached for their weapons, but as they rose, She gave a quick nod, and Her guards were already raising their weapons. Before Moz and his crew could draw their sidearms, they were cut down.

Her guards stepped back to Her sides and stood as if everything that just happened perfectly was normal.

She spoke into her commlink and asked for some servants to quickly come clean things up.

When they arrived, She informed them that the bodies were to be tossed into the arena prior to the next fight so everyone could see them. Before they started cleaning, Her guards stepped in and stripped the bodies of their weapons and anything else of value or use. A third guard appeared and picked up those items and left.

"Make certain there are no stains when I return," She told the servants as Her two guards headed out of the conference room.

She and Her guards were now heading back to the banquet. It should be interesting to see the reactions when She enters as the Mining Guild master.

———————— * ————————

"The fighters are armored up the best we can right now," Sarge said, speaking into his vox.

"Great, get back here to the med lab," Zhuni responded.

"Traxon, we appreciate your information, and for now, we are going to leave you in here so we can keep an eye on you. For your safety and ours," Zhuni told him.

"Now we have to get the equipment ready to not only the normal cuts and breaks but now blaster and plasma. Great. Let's go," Zhuni said, turning to leave the holding cell.

They headed over to the medical supplies and threw together some kits with blaster and plasma injuries specifically in mind. They called over a few attendants and told them to get the kits to the med teams at the arena.

Sarge came in and saw them at the minihabs.

"We found a bunch of the chitin armor and geared up as many of the fighters as we could. They may be okay, but it also may get ugly," Sarge stated.

"We just sent med floats out and some updated med packs. We have done all we can at this point. They will be back at it in less than two partions," Zhuni said.

"We have the fighters protected for the most part from the new issues. But this is your first main event working with the worst issue and an old one," Tan'cha chimed in.

"Brynja Ajal," Zhuni said solemnly.

"Yes, and it may end up in here," Sarge said, looking across the med lab at the massive cage.

"Well, Klavan said the force generator and the cage should hold it. We will just need to deal with it like we have all the other issues that have come up," Zhuni said.

"By luck and a bit of imagination?" Tan'cha asked.

"Exactly."

—————— * ——————

Klavan saw Her coming down the hallway and instantly noticed the Mining Guild's stone around Her neck. He also noticed the lack of Moz. Klavan could only think this was not a good thing.

"My Grace. I see You have achieved a most impressive goal this evening," Klavan said, nodding towards the stone.

"Yes, I am consolidating the reach of a Master."

Just the way She said it sent chills down Klavan's spine.

"And Moz, will he be rejoining us?" Klavan asked.

"In a way."

Klavan was not sure if that meant Moz would be coming back to the banquet or not and did not feel it wise to pursue any more questions.

"May I have the pleasure of escorting the new Mining Guild master back to Her banquet?"

"Proceed."

As they entered the banquet hall, it slowly became quiet as those closest to Her were the first to notice the stone. Then the rest of the hall started to notice. It became nearly silent, only the sounds of the servants hustling about.

"May I?" Klavan leaned close to Her and asked.

"Of course." Standing there with all eyes on Her, She waved Klavan on.

"Good evening, all. I would like to present to you the new Mining Guild Master. Not only is She the Game Master, the Smugglers' Guild Master, the Master of the drug cartels, but now She is truly the most exulted and powerful Master the games have ever had but also the most gracious and wise. She has spared no expense to provide you with the most wondrous meal and pre-meal entertainment but shortly will provide you with the most amazing evening, including the terrifying Brynja Ajal! A creature feared throughout the galaxies! Celebrate and enjoy this evening!"

The crowd of guests took a moment but then started to cheer and applaud Her; She stood looking around the hall at them all. She seemed to take special interest in Her own Dwayans and Regents' reactions. Klavan could tell She was studying each and every reaction. Klavan remembered back to the conference room when he passed out and realized She was an empath and could read emotions. Or She had empathic sensitivity. That is how She knew how to control each and every individual. Through their own emotions. She could read each feeling and thereby control them. Klavan had been working on controlling his own emotions since he returned to work with Her this morning. Either it was working, or She no longer worried about reading Klavan. Being a Septorian may also help.

This was going to be an interesting evening. *What other surprises did She have in store for the guests? Was this the evening that She was going to show all the guilds how powerful She really was? Was She going to consolidate all the power?* She was Game Master, the drug cartel Master, the Master of the Smugglers' Guild, and now the Mining Guild. The only guilds left were the Thieves' Guild, the Renegade Guild, and the Freighters' Guild. Of course, there was also the Assassins' Guild, but Klavan could not see the Assassins' Guild coming under Her control; they were the most enigmatic and secretive guild of all. No one even knew who their guild master was nor where they called home. There also was the Hunters' Guild, but no one had heard from them in ages. And, of course, the Commerce Guild was involved in financing everything and everyone. Klavan thought that covered all the guilds.

If She did control all of the guilds, She would have control of nearly every nongovernment entity in the galaxy. Just seeing Her work here, thinking about Her controlling all of that, put chills into Klavan. He was going to have to watch this whole situation closely. He was a bit apprehensive but had to be sure to push those thoughts and feelings deep inside. Now he could understand why She had become Game Master; it was the one thing all the guilds had in common. A visit to the games for business and recreation. Klavan began to realize this was going to be a ride quite different from any of his previous employers or any previous Master. None had the cunning or the ruthless lust for power and control that She desires.

———————— * ————————

At the beginning, it was bad enough to have the creatures in with the regular fighters; this was already when most of the serious injuries happened. The creatures were wild and did not have the no-kill policy of the majority of fighters. There were several serious injuries, and again, even with the chitin armor, one fighter was killed.

But then She opened the gate under the grand seating at the opposite end of the arena and released new fighters. These were guild masters and guild commanders, which She had apparently been kidnapping and stockpiling as she consolidated Her power. Among them was Tazmok, a former mining guild master. These fighters were fighting to die with as much hatred as they could find. Tazmok was a Toztat and of a light gray color. He was a stocky, barrel-chested, natural leader, so he coordinated his fighters to attack the beasts more than the other fighters. There were about thirty of the new fighters in the arena up against twenty regular pit fighters and three dozen odd creatures and beasts.

The arena was a kill zone. Even with the leadership and coordination of Tazmok, the fighters were getting decimated. They had never been in the arena nor fought any of these other creatures; most were used to using power weapons, blaster and rifles, or brawls in drinking halls. Plus, the turrets along the upper edge of the ring were taking their toll, especially since many of those operating the turrets had a personal or financial interest in this game. Former allies had become enemies. The screams of the wounded were drowned out by the roar of the crowd.

The ring soon consisted of only a dozen or so fighters and a handful of creatures, including two of Her favorites, the Pantaas. Both fighting groups formed opposing circles. Keeping a watchful eye on each other, they prepared for the Pantaa's attack. But something strange happened; the Pantaas retreated to the opposite end of the arena. They started to shiver. The fighters looked up to the VIP box and saw Her raising Her hands, and in a grand gesture, slammed them down, opening the huge gate under the main stand. The crowd went silent, the Pantaas paced back and forth, looking terrified, and then a massive shape appeared in the gate; it strode forward.

This creature was enormous; it had to lower its head to squeeze through the gate. As it came forward and into the light, the creature took shape. Immediately its huge yellow eyes focused intensely on the first set of fighters. These were the guild members who were closest to the creature. The creature continued to move into the arena, and one could see the creature was a deep blue, nearly black in color; as the lights reflected off of its hide, one could see a metallic shine to it. The head was enormous, as tall as Tazmok himself. The head had the massive yellow eyes but also two huge horns atop its head. The mouth was partially open, and one could see teeth as long as a man's arm. The chest of the creature was a tannish yellow and also glistened like a metallic hide. The creature was starting to rise up as the front legs reached center ring. Now the wings on its back unfolded and could stretch across the entire width of the arena, roughly one hundred feet. The front feet were attached to legs as large as a Pantaa and as muscular. The feet had claws as large as any fighter. The hind legs now appeared, and they, too, were massive and muscular with enormous claws. The creature twisted its back end out of the gateway and slung its tail completely out of the gate area. This creature was glorious to behold. It was obviously built for the purpose of destroying whatever it wanted to destroy, and the fighters were its current target.

The Pantaas were now at the far end of the arena howling and screaming and attempting to jump up and out of the arena, but the walls were much too high. They kept looking at this beast and attempting to escape anyway.

The creature glanced at the Pantaas but did not seem worried about them. First, it glanced at the regular fighters, sniffed heavily, then looked at the guild members. Sniffed and looked up to the VIP box as if for instructions. The Master looked down at the situation, raised Her hand, and made a circular motion. With that, doors opened around the arena, one about every twenty feet or so, all about ten feet off the ground. Weapons dropped out of them, heavy weapons. Bolter rifles, blaster rifles, and plasma guns all came crashing around the arena. The regular group of fighters did not move; they maintained their protective circle, weapons in hand. The guild members bolted for the weapons. The massive creature held for a moment, appearing to size up the situation. It then seized up as if hit with a massive electrical shock, but just for an instant.

The creature lurched forward and chomped down on the first fighter to grab a bolter, raised its head up, tossed the individual into the air, then opened its imposing maw and caught him. Chewing briefly and swallowing.

The crowd went crazy, and that broke the silence and the stagnation of the crowd. The turrets once again opened up. Shots rang off the beast and peppered the fighters. The guild fighters did not have the chitin armor of the regular fighters, so they went down to the withering fire. Those that survived the plasma pellets, blaster rounds, and other fighters were tracked down by the massive beast and torn apart. Eventually, there were only three fighters left, one of which was the badly wounded but still fighting Tazmok. She could see why he had been the guild master.

She must have had the turrets disabled as those around the edge started groaning and screaming. She had other plans at this point for the fighters.

The Pantaas were still cowering at the far end. The beast, standing in the center of the arena, had lost interest in the carnage and began to shift its weight from side to side.

Suddenly it dropped to the ground in a seizure, then stopped moving.

The Pantaas calmed down and began to slink towards the three remaining fighters.

She stood up and raised Her hands to quiet the crowd; they were all in shock when the monster collapsed.

"This is the end of the show; Brynja Ajal has been retired for the evening, and the work remaining is for my Pantaas to finish. Tazmok, you were once a great guild master, but you crossed me years ago, and I do not forget nor forgive those who wrong me. This evening you will serve as an example to others." She smiled, the first time Klavan had seen anything resembling joy on her face.

The Pantaas pounced on one fighter and tore him to shreds. The next fighter attempted to fight them off but suffered the same fate.

Tazmok rose from his knees to stand before his demise. He turned to face Her and gave the intergalactic hand signal of defiance and hatred. He then turned back to face the Pantaas. He raised the bolter rifle he had grabbed during the melee and fired several shots, slowing the first Pantaa down to a near stop, but two Pantaas were too much for a single warrior and a single bolter rifle. The second circled around Tazmok as he fired on the first. Tazmok rotated around to fire on the second Pantaa but just succeeded in turning into its attack. Tazmok died standing as a wounded warrior fighting overwhelming odds, not exactly the humiliating death She had hoped for, but at least others would not want to cross Her ever again.

---

*

Standing at the control center for the minihabs, Zhuni was thinking about the day and especially the final event. Tan'cha by his side.

Zhuni and his team had saved over a dozen fighters this evening, but he could not get over the loss of twenty in the final fight. Add in the thirty guild members She had thrown in, and there had been over fifty killed tonight alone. A massive loss beyond anything Zhuni had experienced before. Before this night, the most he knew of being lost in one night were seven in the arena and three guards and handlers in the passageways. But tonight, a total of fifty-three lives were lost, three in the earlier fights. They had seven minihabs with injured recovering. Just an enormously destructive day. Zhuni felt defeated with the tremendous loss of life. What could he and his team do?

"Today was a bad day," Zhuni told Tan'cha.

"There was nothing we could do for those in the final fight. We all know when you are put in the arena with that creature, no one will make it out alive. Well, except for Her pets," Tan'cha responded, referring to the Pantaas, which the Master loved.

"Yeah."

"Zhuni, we saved at least a dozen with the chitin alone. Every one of them would have been killed if not for that. We attached three limbs lost to the plasma pellets and bolter turrets. You were even able to repair that heart when Xatous took a direct blast to the chest. That was amazing. He would not have made it without you."

"I guess we just need to do more, somehow."

"Short of changing the entire structure of this facility or somehow getting out of here, what can we do?"

"Maybe that is what we need to do," Zhuni implied.

"Yeah, right."

"No, I am serious."

"How do you propose we do that?"

"I have no idea."

"Yup, that is the problem; the Master would never let us leave, plus how would we even get off this planet? If we were still on this planet, they would hunt us down. Where would we go? She would pursue us wherever we went."

"Think positive."

"I am positive. Positive, there is no way," Tan'cha insisted.

"Shut up. There is always a way. We just have to figure it out."

"Okay, when you figure it out, let me in on it," Tan'cha snipped.

"Oh, I will. Look where we are now. We never thought we would be running this med lab."

"But the only reason we are here is because of Klavan and the fact that it is good for the Master and entertaining Her guilds."

"Then maybe we need to use that to our advantage. Klavan could help, and maybe we could offer something to the guilds."

"Why would Klavan risk everything for us to escape this place, and what could we offer any of the guilds?"

"I am just starting to think; I do not have all the answers yet."

"Here comes Sarge," Tan'cha pointed out.

They still had to deal with Brynja Ajal coming in. Just what they needed, more of the unknown.

"Mister Zhuni."

"Yes, Sarge?"

"I have security stationed and ready; the handling team is ready, and the force generator is primed."

"I guess we are ready for it then," Zhuni nodded at Sarge.

Sarge raised his hand and motioned for the guards to open the main entrance. The guards stepped back from the doors as they opened.

Once the doors were fully opened, the gigantic central beam, which had been installed on day one of the construction, showed its purpose. Clamped to it was a lift that had a mammoth creature slung below it. The lift rolled into the space and to the largest cage in the space. The hulking gate opened, and the lift deposited its cargo. The creature was placed in the middle of the cage, and the lift retreated from the med lab. The main doors were once again closed, and every creature in the space stopped to look at the monstrosity that was now in their company.

Luckily Sarge was not easily impressed, and while everyone else held their collective breath, he started the force generator.

"Klavan was pretty adamant about this, so I thought now would be a good time to put it to use." He smiled at Zhuni and Tan'cha.

Both responded with a nervous chuckle.

"Now what?" Tan'cha asked.

"I am not too sure," Zhuni let out.

"Is it hurt? Why do we have it?" Tan'cha questioned.

"I don't think it can be hurt. From what I understand. She said that it is under Her control, and after it fights, it collapses and has to rest for a few rotations," Zhuni stated.

"With all that rage, I am pretty sure it is tired," Sarge said.

"Does anyone know anything about it?" Zhuni asked, looking at the staff that had collected around the cage.

"I can tell you what I know; it isn't much," a small Lokrogh stated.

"Then please do share," Zhuni answered.

"I just started working with it a few rattons ago, when the new Master started. She removed all the biologists, xenobiologists, and scientists who had previously worked with it and studied it. I think once She knew all She needed to, She wanted to make sure no one else knew about it," the small Lokrogh said. Zhuni recognized him as one of the scientists She had sent to work in the med lab.

"Are you one of the scientists who worked with it?" Zhuni asked.

"Scientists? No, just a caretaker or handler. The scientists all disappeared. I do not think they will ever come back."

"What can you tell us?" Zhuni asked.

"It is indestructible as far as we can tell. It loves extreme heat. The hotter, the better. It spits out fire that incinerates anything. It has done that once in the arena years ago. It never eats, well, except for its victims in the arena. It sleeps most of the time. It rarely moves and actually has to be awakened by the Master."

"So, what do we do with it?"

"Nothing, really. In a partion or two, it will wake up, look around, and go back to sleep until the Master wakes it again."

"Okay, you watch it and let me know when that happens."

"Yes, sir."

"Everyone else, we still have wounded to help. We all know what to do," Zhuni said, looking around at those standing by.

"You heard him; this thing will be here awhile. You can stare at it later. Get back to your work," Sarge yelled in his most commanding and booming voice.

———————— * ————————

The final battle was over. The Master had made Her point with the demise of Tazmok and his entire crew. She and Her guards retired for the evening, leaving the guests to retire or to continue their party.

Stanton was attempting to make sense of the evening's events. He was worried that his run-in with Moz had caused issues. But the Master did not even mention it. Then when Moz and his crew's bodies appeared in the arena, Stanton was afraid; he was next. But that did not happen. Was She planning something worse for him?

It was not fair, Stanton thought. He had hired a spy who had turned out to be an assassin. So, Stanton had the assassin take out Klavan. But even that did not go as planned. Zhuni and his team had saved Klavan, and he had come back even more in Her good graces because of the incident. Had Stanton hired a poor spy and assassin? Nothing was going right. Was no one on his side? It appeared even his loyal Traxon had turned on him and betrayed him. But was Traxon smart enough to use the knowledge he had to advance his personal position? All Stanton wanted was respect and power, and he was well on his way to at least being second to the Game Master. Then Klavan showed up. Now Stanton could not get rid of his nemesis no matter how hard he tried.

Boshduul would be here soon. They had a lot to discuss. First and foremost, why did he not get rid of Klavan? What had happened? Stanton knew Septorians were tough and rugged creatures, but Boshduul had promised the poison would kill Klavan. Why hadn't it worked? And why was Zhuni such a thorn in Stanton's side now? How had a stupid little human derelict come to have such influence with Klavan and thereby with the Master?

"Get me food," he bellowed to his closest attendant.

"And drink; a strong drink."

This was going to be a long night. He was going to need nourishment.

Boshduul came in as the meal and drink showed. *Nice timing*, Stanton thought.

"So, what the Dagz happened? He is supposed to be dead," Stanton yelled at Boshduul.

"May I have an audience with my master?" Boshduul asked as he motioned toward a seat.

"Yes. So?" Stanton nodded.

"My lord, I administered the poison as we spoke about, and as a Septorian, he should have been dead in a bit over a partion. But I did not account for the Sezonian. I do not believe you knew about the importance of the Sezonian. Septor is a metal planet. It has a massive amount of minerals and ores in its outer crust and on its surface. These minerals and ores are in their food and air. The Septorians absorb them, and in their bodies, it migrates to their incredibly tough hides. The Sezonian people have a tradition of planting a Sezonian tree on the graves of their ancestors. This tree will grow and absorb the minerals, heavy metals, and toxins around the family's home. This helps create fertile soil for them to farm. Being planted over the ancestors' graves, it also absorbs their DNA. When the young ones grow and move away from their home, they are given a branch from the tree. This branch is often fashioned into a family crest, desk, or some other object they have with them the rest of their lives. The wood looks like metal because of the massive amounts of minerals and has amazing healing properties."

"I was not looking for a science lesson. What the Dagz does that have to do with Klavan being alive?"

"Klavan is a Septorian. His staff is made of Sezonian."

"And?" Stanton pondered, his skin tone taking on his tannish gray color of complete boredom.

"And that is why Tan'cha took it from you. If you had held on to it for fifteen or twenty sectons more, Klavan would be dead."

"So, it is my fault!" Stanton screamed, turning a bright red.

"No, my lord. That is not what I am saying; I am explaining to you what has happened and the fact that you did not know the details. Through no fault of your own. We must learn all we can about our enemies; without proper knowledge and preparation, we will be defeated as we were in this case."

"Wise words. So now, what do you propose?" Stanton asked, fading from his bright red to a more neutral beige.

"We will study them more, get to know their routine, patterns, habits, and such. Then we will study their weaknesses. Then we will be ready, and we will not fail."

"How long do you suppose that will take?" Stanton said as he started to darken to a slightly rosy hue.

"We will know when to strike."

"You do not know." Deepening to a red.

"My lord, haste will continue to be rewarded with failure."

"Just kill Klavan and Zhuni; they are thorns in my side I need removed. And do it in a timely manner. Quickly." Patience was not one of Stanton's finer points.

"Yes, Master. I will keep you up to date. I will obtain the needed information as quickly as I deem efficient."

"Make it soon," Stanton said, fading back to a more neutral beige again.

CHAPTER 6

Traxon's Trouble

"Sir, it is stirring," the Lokrogh said.

"Thank you, Ohmdod." Zhuni had learned the Lokrogh's name since he had spoken up earlier.

"This should be interesting," Tan'cha interjected.

They all headed back out of Zhuni's office, where they had been reviewing the events of the day. Zhuni, Tan'cha, Sarge, and Slaza. Slaza was Sarge's second in command for the security teams.

They all headed across the med lab. As they did, they could see that few of the staff had turned in for the night. Most were watching the creature as it stirred as if in a dream. It was truly an awesome creature. The bars of the cage look woefully inadequate for the size of this beast. The humming of the force generator gave a bit of comfort to all who could hear it.

"Now, what do we do?" Tan'cha asked.

"Wait for it to wake," Zhuni said, turning to Ohmdod.

"Can we communicate with it?" Zhuni asked.

"No."

"Well, what do we do? What will it do?" Zhuni asked

"It will wake, look around, get a feel for its surroundings and then go back to sleep until the Master wakes it again," Ohmdod said.

"Why is it out?" Zhuni questioned.

"See there at the back of its head?" Ohmdod asked, pointing.

"That silver pod? That is how the Master controls the monster. One shock, and the beast wakes up and moves to the arena. Another shock, and it goes crazy and kills everything. The next shock knocks it out for two to three partions. It will calmly awaken, look around and go back to sleep."

Brynja Ajal rolled its head to face out towards the center of the med lab. It opened an eye. There was an audible gasp from those who saw it. The eye slowly looked around. The second eye opened, and everyone could see the creature was studying everyone and everything in the space. Everyone could see the gargantuan eyes focusing. With the enormity of the eyes, you could not miss it. Suddenly they opened wide in an expression one could only describe as surprise. It raised its head and started looking around frantically. It quickly studied each individual until its gaze locked on Zhuni.

Zhuni suddenly looked shocked and surprised. He bent over, grabbing his head with both hands, and began moaning. He dropped to his knees, then to the ground on his side. He stopped moaning, and his body went limp.

"Zhuni," Tan'cha dropped to his side.

Sarge and Slaza immediately stepped between Zhuni, Tan'cha, and Brynja Ajal, weapons drawn. Sarge drew the massive rifle off his back. No one had ever seen him draw that rifle. It was said to have been picked up during one of the wars Sarge was involved in and is said to be able to destroy anything it is fired on. It was too powerful for Sarge to ever have a need to use it before today.

"Get him out of here, now!" Sarge yelled at Tan'cha.

An inquisitive expression passed over the beast's face as it reared its head back, looking at Sarge and Slaza. It attempted to move its head off to the side to see Zhuni but Sarge and Slaza maintained a position directly between Zhuni, Tan'cha, and the beast. No matter how hard it tried, it could not get a straight look at Zhuni.

"I have a heartbeat and breathing, but he is unresponsive; I am taking him to the minihab now," Tan'cha said as he picked up Zhuni's limp body.

Sarge and Slaza maintained the position between the beast and Tan'cha and Zhuni as they all raced across the med lab, weapons trained on the beast.

Every medic turned to run with Tan'cha and Zhuni. They were all going to do whatever they could to help.

Tan'cha set Zhuni on the bed in minihab number six. The medics set about attaching wires to Zhuni for monitoring. All his vital signs were showing normal except for brain activity that was off the charts.

Sarge had his back to the minihab and still had his rifle trained on the Brynja Ajal. It was still watching them.

"It is still watching us," he said to Tan'cha.

"What the Dagz was that?" Tan'cha asked, looking at Ohmdod.

"I have no idea; I have never seen something like that."

"What are we to do? We have to kill it," Tan'cha growled.

"You are going to think me crazy, but I think killing it is a bad idea; plus, I am not sure with the stories we have heard that we could. I have seen the damage they can do when I was in the civil war. I would have to turn off the force generator to fire my weapon on the beast, and it would most likely kill most of us in this small space. Then if it didn't kill that beast, it would be loose anyway," Sarge announced.

"So, what do you propose?" Tan'cha inquired.

"Hear me out."

"We are all listening."

"I have an idea," Sarge said, stepping away from the minihab.

"We all saw that the Brynja Ajal had expressions on its face. Correct, we can all agree to that. I mean, I am not the only one who recognized surprise in its eyes and on the expression on its face, right?" sounding slightly unsure that his statement was fact.

"Actually, yes," Tan'cha somewhat timidly responded.

"Yeah," Ohmdod responded.

"Okay, so expressions denote thought; thought would indicate intelligence. Let us suppose the creature is more than just a killer. Let us think it may not be able to communicate in a way we understand."

As Sarge was talking, the beast was tilting its head side to side as it stood watching them.

"So, let's watch the reaction to what I do." As Sarge said this, he dropped his rifle and then slung it onto his back, where he usually kept it. The Brynja Ajal set its back end on the ground like a pet would sit down.

"See," Sarge said.

"Wooh," Tan'cha exclaimed.

"Okay, that could have just been a coincidence," Tan'cha continued.

"All right then," Sarge said as he unslung his rifle.

Brynja Ajal stood back up and lowered its head, partially closing its eyes as a look of concern overcame it.

"See, did you see that?"

Sarge slung his rifle onto his back, and again, Brynja Ajal sat back on its haunches.

"Wow, all right then. But what about Zhuni? It is trying to kill him," Tan'cha asked.

"I do not know; how is he doing?" Sarge asked.

"The same; his vitals are all fine; it is just brain activity is going crazy. I have never seen anything like this," one of the former scientists said.

"And no one else has been affected?" Sarge asked, looking around.

"Seems not," Ohmdod offered.

"Okay, so the beast targeted Zhuni for some reason; it knows he is our leader; there is something different that sets him apart from us, other than him being the only human. Wait. Maybe that has something to do with it; either it is him being our leader or his being human," Sarge voiced.

"It did seem surprised, so it may have been the new environment, new handlers, or it may have sensed something different in Zhuni or us," Ohmdod said.

"All right, we need to figure out how to distract it or figure out some way to break this, whatever it is that it has over Zhuni. We need to speak with Klavan, and we need to get Joxby working on figuring out what is going on. If the monitors can pick up Zhuni's brain activity, I am sure Joxby can figure something out to read the monster's brain activity also. Tan'cha, go get Klavan. Slaza, you stand guard here; I am going to see if I can communicate with it," Sarge instructed.

———————— * ————————

Traxon was worried. He had come to like Zhuni, and from what he could see, things were looking bad for him. Traxon was still in the cell and was still not exactly sure why they would not let him go. He did not like Sarge nor Tan'cha; both made Traxon uncomfortable. Traxon knew he did not have a good track record with those in the med lab but hoped things could be different if he could just help them somehow. He saw how they had a certain freedom none of the others had here at the games and wanted to become a part of that. Maybe this could be the new start and reset he wanted so badly. He just wanted to be accepted and treated well somewhere. His entire life had been about surviving; he wanted more. Zhuni had always treated everyone well and had a following that respected him and wanted to help him. After having been treated so poorly by Stanton, Traxon had finally had enough. This was an opportunity he had to take. Even if it meant spending time in this cell. He knew he would not be thrown into the arena by those in the med lab; he felt safe here. He had never felt that before.

He needed to help them. He could never go back to Stanton, and he did not want to. He may even get out of the spying, stealing, and lying game. It looked to be working for Zhuni and his team. Traxon was amazed by how quickly the Swaklin guards had thrown themselves between Zhuni, Tan'cha, and the monster. Then how everyone had rushed to help get the minihab set up and surrounded it, showing so much worry and concern for Zhuni. Traxon could see everything unfold from his cell. He had to get out so he could help.

Traxon could help them find Rags if he could get out. He had seen the jumpy guy that was their electronic specialist. If Traxon could get out and help find Rags, maybe, then they could see that he was here to help. Maybe he could even do some information gathering for them. The Boyz all hated Stanton, and maybe Traxon could use that to help get some information. He knew they all always gossiped amongst themselves about everything Stanton said.

He would get out of the cell and help.

———————— * ————————

Tan'cha was not sure where Klavan was; he hoped he was at his office. He beat on the office door, but there was no answer; then he thought of the banquet hall. That would surely be where he was. Tan'cha went back down the lift, through the loading dock area, and back into the main hallway to head over to the VIP level via a service lift. Tan'cha caught snippets of conversation as he ran down the hallway. There was great concern among the service personnel about the evening's events, so many killed in the arena, the Master now being the Master of the Mining Guild; this was all so unusual for a Game Master. The Game Master was typically a neutral party. They had tremendous power as a moderator between various parties and guilds, but this Master was attempting to consolidate all power to Her. This was making everyone nervous. They felt something bad was coming soon.

Tan'cha stepped out of the lift into the service hallway. It was bustling with activity as the servants were still serving guests. Tan'cha stopped to ask a servant if he recognized where Klavan was. After the Master had retired for the evening, Klavan had been seen heading back to the kitchen. Tan'cha raced toward the kitchen.

The Master had retired? That was not normal. She usually was the center of attention, and with a banquet going on, Tan'cha thought that was odd.

Tan'cha entered the kitchen through the back. This was an enormous space, and delicious smells hit his nostrils, things he had never smelled before. He had to take a moment to glance around, looking for Klavan but also to see what was happening.

The kitchen had dozens of cooks working, each at a different station. Each station was part of a massive row of ovens, stoves, and open fire pits. There were creatures of all types cooking. Meats, vegetables, and exotic fruits being roasted. To Tan'cha, it seemed like a battle in the pit, creatures going in all directions barking orders, carrying food and spices, delivering items, and taking items. It looked to be utter chaos, but Tan'cha knew it was choreographed and controlled. He was drawn to one particular cook roasting a huge piece of meat under what looked like a space freighter's engine. The cook slowly adjusted the flame output with a large lever he would push and pull with one hand while slowly rotating the meat on a spit with another hand. An assistant was tossing spices on the meat, and another was gently spraying the meat with some type of liquid.

"It is delicious. One of my favorites. It is local and is called Banteest, but the way Doble roasts it makes it amazing. This is his third entire Banteest of the evening. Grab a hunk. In fact, Doble, wrap that up and send it to chef in the med lab; they are going to need it; also, chop off a hunk for my friend here." It was Klavan; he had found Tan'cha.

Tan'cha paused for a moment and thought about it but had more important things to discuss.

"What are you doing here?" Klavan asked.

"I need to talk to you now. Zhuni is in trouble."

"I knew that would happen sooner or later; who did he upset?"

"Brynja Ajal."

"What? What happened? Is he okay?"

"We are not sure; he has good vital signs, but he is in a coma-like state."

"Was he attacked? How did it happen? What happened?"

"We do not know exactly; everything was going well. We were getting everything shut down for the night, and we had Brynja Ajal delivered to us. It was not a problem; it just laid there like it was asleep."

"That is what it does after every fight."

"But then it woke, looked around, locked its eyes on Zhuni, and he grabbed his head and collapsed. He hasn't moved since."

"You said he has good vital signs?"

"Yes, but his brain activity is going off the charts. It is as if the monster has some brain power over him, and we cannot unlock it."

"I have to find Katool and let her know I am leaving," Klavan said as he headed down the counters to find the kitchen manager.

Klavan quickly returned and headed out of the kitchen with Tan'cha. They broke into a slight jog as they bantered back and forth.

"So let me get this straight, Zhuni was knocked out by Brynja Ajal, and he is now in some type of coma?" Klavan asked.

"In short, yes."

"Are we sure it isn't just exhaustion? I mean, he has been pushing hard; maybe he was overwhelmed by the massive creature and just dropped of exhaustion."

"Hadn't thought of that, but it would not explain his massive brain activity; I mean, the scientists said they hadn't seen anything like it," Tan'cha sounded less worried and concerned than a moment ago.

"Had the scientists ever wired up a human before? A true human, not a humanish?" Klavan questioned.

"I do not know."

"Humans have always been one of the most intelligent races in the known galaxy; they can adapt quicker and better than any other race. Humanish have been genetically modified over the centuries as they have attempted to change their physical state. They have lost some of their intelligence and become somewhat angry creatures. Zhuni is the only pure human I have ever met; he is different. Maybe his brain activity is normal."

"Maybe," Tan'cha responded timidly.

The two increased their pace as they closed on the med lab.

---

*

Sarge had been attempting to communicate with the creature but to no avail. It had seemed interested for a few sectons but then turned its back to Sarge, curled up into a massive ball, and went back to sleep.

Sarge walked back over to the minihab to see if anything had changed.

The scientists were still monitoring Zhuni. He was okay by way of his vital signs. He still had not moved. His heart rate was good, and his breathing was normal. Sarge was at a loss. He was a warrior, a fighter, a killer, and a protector but not a doctor. He could only hope Zhuni would be okay. He had to recover.

Sarge had never cared as much about a boss before. He had never truly liked anyone before that he had to work for or protect. He respected most of them but didn't care about them as he did for Zhuni. Sarge had never worked for a human before. He had worked for or with several humanish but never a true human. The humanish tended to be angry and bitter, often spiteful and mean. Zhuni, on the other hand, cared about everyone he had worked with. He would get to know their names, where they were from, their traits and customs, and in nearly all cases, start to learn their native language. Sarge had never known a humanish to even attempt the Swaklineese language.

Sarge thought to save Zhuni, he may have to unsling his rifle and kill Brynja Ajal himself. He would have to clear the med lab, turn off the force generator and kill the beast. The rifle was known as the Army Killer, or Sarge called it Sadbaath. It was a weapon Sarge had taken from an admiral in a long-lost war. Sarge had carried it ever since, knowing its destructive power and hoping he would never need it but knowing no one else should have it. He had seen the general raise it against a city, and the entire city had been destroyed. Sarge killed the general and staff and took the rifle. He left the battlefield, swearing to never get involved in war again.

Now Sarge was here, with the most powerful handheld weapon he had ever seen or heard of, unable to do anything to help Zhuni. What good was this type of power and responsibility if it was useless to help those you cared about?

If he had the opportunity, he would kill the beast, that might break the hold it had on Zhuni. Even if it cost him his own life, Sarge swore that was what he would do.

"It is different this time," Slaza said as he put a hand on Sarge's shoulder.

"It is personal. It is about…family," Sarge said, using a word he had not used since he was young.

"Yes."

"I will kill it."

"And I will stand with you, but we must know more before we react. Is that the correct course of action at this point? He is alive and appears healthy. If Brynja Ajal has a mental lock on him, will killing the monster help or kill Zhuni? We need to know more, patience."

"Wise words and thoughts for such a young one."

"Yes, I tend to listen to the old ones around me and take in what they say."

"You stay on watch; I will make rounds to ensure we are secure and ready for the night. We still have many guests wandering around. We need to remain vigilant. We cannot let this distract us and allow ourselves to become venerable. That would hurt all. I will be back."

Sarge started across the med lab to the main entrance. As he did, he saw two figures enter whose profiles he recognized. Tan'cha and Klavan had arrived.

————— * —————

Boshduul left Staton's office and walked to his temporary quarters. He had a place at the port, but Stanton had provided him a room here in the facility. This made his coming and going much easier.

Boshduul felt he had been robbed. Klavan should be dead. Boshduul had never failed an assassination. This could ruin his future. Stanton paid very well, but his information-gathering network had cost Boshduul a perfect track record. Stanton loved his Chordentia. They could be bullied so easily. The problem was, they were inefficient. Plus, everyone at the facility knew they worked for Stanton. They had no loyalty, no courage, little to no intelligence, and they could keep nothing to themselves. They were always bickering and fighting. Traxon had done a fairly good job of keeping the horde in line. But as intelligence gatherers, their skills were pretty much nonexistent. Boshduul had been able to gather better information and more of it with his few cameras and drones than the Chordentias had. And they lived here and knew the facility intimately.

Boshduul had gotten a video feed into the med lab but felt something was not right. It had been a little easier than he had expected. Knowing that the head of security for the med lab was Swaklin made Boshduul nervous. They tended to be difficult to beat. Boshduul had heard that while the Swaklin known as Sarge had been running facility security, no unauthorized items nor personnel had ever gotten in nor out. He had been told by Traxon that Sarge would not have allowed Stanton to have his interviews within the space of the facility. Swaklin were detail-oriented and missed nothing. How was Boshduul going to get access to the med lab? Maybe that was not actually as important as Stanton thought. Maybe Boshduul could redirect Stanton's plans.

To be successful, Boshduul would have to build Stanton a new team. Boshduul could see Stanton being useful. Yes, he was the client and the boss, but Boshduul could easily use him. Stanton was so hungry to be respected and have power that he would take the power at any cost. He would not even worry nor ask how he could come to a more powerful position. This could easily be used against him. Boshduul could see him bringing Stanton along for a long and expensive ride, which would ultimately make Bosduul rich enough to retire. Boshduul could also set Stanton up for a fall if he needed that safety. Stanton wanted nothing more than to be the Master. Boshduul did not see that happening with this new Master here. Just from what Boshduul could figure out from the brief tidbits of information he could catch from individuals wandering the corridors, this new Master was different. She was beyond ambitious; She was power-hungry and willing to rid the galaxy of anyone in Her way. Boshduul liked Her efficiency, drive, and dedication to Her goals but did not want to cross Her. That is where Stanton would come in. Stanton was just smart enough to get himself into trouble but not smart enough to get out of his own way.

He could start setting everything in motion with Traxon's move. Boshduul had put a tracker on Traxon, which also had a video feed. When Traxon had gone into the Her quarters, Boshduul had lost the feed, but he knew the guard would inform Her that a Chordentia had entered Her quarters. She did not need to know which Chrodentia, and since Traxon had been wise enough to cover his scarred face, She would assume it was just one of Stanton's lackeys. Boshduul could use this to his advantage and set himself up as an informant for Her. Then when Stanton had run out of money or time, Boshduul could set him for the fall.

Boshduul would have to set up more surveillance of his own to gather as much information as possible. He would also have to convince Stanton to spend more money to create a better and more reliable group of informants to get Stanton into the number two spot and relieve Klavan of his position. If Boshduul played his cards right, he could work Stanton into believing they were working to remove the Master and install Stanton as the new Master. The simple thought of this being a possibility should drive Stanton into a state of euphoria, which could give Boshduul the freedom to build a team to take down Stanton and the Master, all at the expense of Stanton. With the correct team, this could work. He could go to the port and find a team. He remembered Traxon had a good group brought together. Boshduul could track them down, plus a few more. He would pay them, then charge Stanton their fees plus a markup of, say, twenty percent for managing and finder's fees. This could get expensive for Stanton.

Boshduul would track down Traxon in the morning and have a bit of a talk. He had not seen Traxon since he had entered the Master's quarters. He had also not been able to pick up the tracker since then. Had Traxon found the tracker and disposed of it? Boshduul did not think so, but maybe, Traxon did not strike him as that intelligent.

Boshduul got to his space and scanned it for bugs and other listening devices. He ensured it was secure. He then set his own security alarms and settled in for the night. He was going to be busy tomorrow.

---

*

Stanton finished his meal and began to think. Had he hired the correct spy? Was he truly an assassin? If he was an assassin, how could he have failed? Had Traxon turned on him? Was that going to be an issue? Could Boshduul deliver on the contract?

Stanton felt the failed assassination was a lack of proper information or preparation. Was that because the Boyz were not providing Stanton with the proper services? Would Boshduul do better? Maybe it was time to up the game and hire more professionals. Stanton had made no progress on the advancement front since Klavan had arrived. But that was also roughly the same time he had started relying on the Chordentia to take care of his plans and enforcement. Was that a coincidence? Maybe he should have a discussion about this with Boshduul. Boshduul should be given a fresh start.

If Boshduul could deliver, maybe Stanton could be more than number two. If Boshduul could dispose of Klavan and Zhuni maybe, he could also assist with the removal of the Master. Staton could not dare think of that this early in the game; he did not even know if he had Boshduul's full commitment. He certainly did not trust Boshduul enough to open up that much to him.

Stanton would need to ponder these issues. He would need to have some food to settle his mind. The banquet had not fulfilled Stanton's insatiable appetite, nor had his snack.

"More food and drink," Stanton screamed.

---

*

Tan'cha and Klavan met with Sarge.

"What do we know? Anything change since Tan'cha got me?" Klavan asked as they all headed to minihab six. Sarge stepped in behind and kept pace with Klavan and Tan'cha.

"It appears that Brynja Ajal has a mental attack it used on Zhuni. But we are not sure at this time," Sarge stated.

"It appears? Why are we assuming this?" Klavan asked.

"As I am sure Tan'cha explained, there was no problem until the creature locked its sight on Zhuni. Then Zhuni grabbed his head and dropped to the ground. Since that time, he has not stirred," Sarge said authoritatively.

"Just for the sake of argument, let us assume this is what happened. Do we have a plan?" Klavan asked.

"Assume we all saw it happen," Sarge snapped.

Klavan came to a stop, looked at both Tan'cha and Sarge directly in the eyes, and with an exasperated look, started to speak.

"Gentlemen, I am not accusing you of a fairytale nor any such thing. I am concerned about getting to the bottom of this and about facts. One, Zhuni has been pushing hard these last several dozen rotations. In fact, he is exhausted and has had a tremendous amount of pressure placed upon him. His entire life has been changed, and suddenly he has the responsibility of the entire med lab dumped on him. In fact, Zhuni has been getting little to no sleep as he has been getting everything in order, training the staff on medical procedures, meeting with each of you about security, etc. In fact, no one here has ever taken the brain wave pattern readings of a pure human before. Is it possible, just for the sake of argument, that he finally just collapsed under the stress of the past several dozen rotations and he has had an emotional or psychological breakdown? We have never had the Brynja Ajal attack anyone or anything with a brain power. I may be wrong, but we all may have pushed Zhuni too much, and he may just need some hard rest."

This sudden logic hit both Tan'cha and Sarge hard.

"You could be correct; we have all been pushing hard and, in our exhaustion, could have misinterpreted what we saw," Sarge said apologetically.

"Yeah," Tan'cha blurted out.

Klavan started back towards minihab number six again.

"Now, let's go check on our patient. You may be correct but before we go all crazy emotional, let's collect as much information as we can and go from there."

They checked in with the scientist who had taken the lead over Zhuni's care and monitoring. She was a Skrenoch. The Skrenoch were extremely intelligent creatures and were known to study any and everything. Many races went to them to gather knowledge. They were collectors and dealers of knowledge. Physically the scientist was roughly the same size as a human, with smooth greyish-purple furless skin. She was dainty in build (the Skrenoch were not strong nor physically menacing) and had much longer arms and hands; plus, their hands only had three fingers and a thumb. Her head was twice the size of a human's and looked much too big for her thin neck. She had large black eyes that blinked sideways, and her eyelids were vertical. She moved with a slow, graceful purpose.

"Hey, Doc, how is he doing?" Tan'cha asked.

"My name is Mazalla, and I am a scientist, not a doctor."

Tan'cha remembered then that Skrenoch has no sense of humor and takes everything literally.

"Mazalla, do we have a prognosis?" Klavan asked.

"I have only read about humans. As a race, they are fairly intelligent and emotional. I have dealt with humanish before, but they are not as emotional. Humanish are tougher and have lost some of their individual intelligence. From his brain activity, I would say he is thinking intently about many important issues or as he is in a state nearest to a sleep, in my experience, he is dreaming. This is an intelligent individual."

"Is he okay?" Klavan asked.

"Okay, as in he is physically unharmed, I would say yes. But I will continue to study and monitor him. I have never seen the brain waves of a human before."

"So, you would suggest we stand by and monitor?" Klavan questioned.

"I would say so. Until we know otherwise, we should just let him rest and see if he comes out of it on his own."

"Okay, for now, we will just keep an eye on Zhuni," Klavan said.

Turning to look at Sarge, Klavan continued.

"Do not kill the beast; the Master would be mighty upset."

"I wouldn't even think of attempting that," Sarge said with a half grin.

"Mazalla, would you please send word if he regains consciousness? I still must deal with the banquet and tie up many loose ends from this evening. I know we are all concerned, but we must give him time to recover," Klavan stated.

"We do not need sleep; I will stay with him at all times. I will care for him. It will give me more of an opportunity to study the human mind," Mazzlla replied.

"If you do need to sleep, we have plenty of others who would be glad to keep an eye on him." Klavan glanced around at all the concerned faces.

"No, I mean my species do not sleep; we spend our time studying."

"But still, there are many here willing to help. Sarge, you are in charge. Is there anything you need from me at this time?" Klavan turned to make his way to the entrance.

"No, sir. Everyone knows their job. We just need to get shut down for the night and keep a watch on him. And I think I will keep an eye on that, just in case." Sarge nodded towards Brynja Ajal.

"Don't kill it," Klavan said quietly but sternly.

"I am not sure I could unless I took the med lab with us," Sarge replied.

"I have known you a long time, my friend; if anyone in this facility could find a way to kill it, you would be the one." Klavan strode towards the entrance.

"Be safe and have a good night," he called out over his shoulder.

Sarge turned to Tan'cha as Klavan left.

"I still feel there is more to this than Zhuni being tired. My instincts tell me otherwise."

"Klavan could be right, we have all been pushing hard, and Zhuni has been leading us. He has not had a break. Relax, Sarge, it will be okay."

"I hope you two are right, but I have been in too many wars to not notice things that add up to a specific conclusion. Two and two rarely add up to five. There is something more here, mark my words."

"You continue thinking that way. Zhuni has taught me that just because everyone around you agrees doesn't mean it is right. You may be the dissenting voice, but you may also be the only one who is correct," Tan'cha announced.

"I would like to be wrong." Sarge turned to again take up station by Brynja Ajal.

"I would like that also, if even just to say you were wrong," Tan'cha snorted.

"There is more to this situation than any of us have figured out yet, and I feel this Drazine has something to do with it. I am telling you."

"If you say so, I think you have a special sense in these things, and until Zhuni recovers, you are in charge."

"Don't remind me."

*

Stanton had gotten no sleep all night. In fact, all he had done was eat and drink. He was unsure why the Master had not berated him nor done anything to him when he had the run-in with Moz. Yes, Moz was killed and dumped in the pit for everyone to see, but Stanton had broken the protocol, which She said was so important. Why was he not in the pit? Was there value in him that She saw? This could be a good thing.

The main door to his office flew open, and one of his Boyz came running in; he seemed more agitated than usual.

"She is coming with many guards," the Chordentia yelled as he stood at the front of Stanton's desk.

"What do you mean, many guards? How many? She usually has two," Stanton bellowed, turning a strange brownish-green color.

"Many, many!" The Chordentia squeaked out, looking nervously at the door.

"Go get Boshduul. Now!" Stanton screamed at the nervous little creature.

"Yes, Boss!" He responded as he ran from the room.

This is it; She is coming for him. There was nothing to do. As nervous as the servant was, She must be close. Hopefully, Stanton could explain his way out of this.

Stanton began thinking of an excuse, a story, something to keep him alive. He could say Moz was drunk and just attacked him. He had to come up with something, and quickly.

Two guards came in first. Shoulder to shoulder, they scanned the room quickly and took up a guarding position on either side of the door. Six more came into the room, again shoulder to shoulder, and proceeded to the opposite wall from Stanton. They lined up shoulder to shoulder along the wall as if in the positions of a firing squad. He was feeling sick and thought he was going to pass out. Bravery was not one of his strengths.

She came into the room with four more guards following her. Two stopped and turned their backs to the entire room facing into the passageway. The other two remained at either side of Her.

"You have the courage to send spies to investigate my personal quarters. Bold, especially for you. I must say I am impressed by the attempt. Stupid though it was. It does show a courage I did not expect from you," She stared straight through him as She spoke.

Oh, Dagz. She found out about the microdrone they had planted, which would explain why it had not been working since it was set up. Traxon was always messing up any plans Stanton had developed. Once again, he had let Stanton down, and this time, it was going to cost Stanton his life.

"During the banquet last night, you sent one of you filthy little creatures into my Personal quarters to gather information. As I said, bold but stupid. Did you think my guards would not inform me of any such intrusion? I am not sure which one it was, it was wearing a face shield and had dock workers uniform, but everyone knows the Chordentia work for you. Point out which one it was, and we will take care of him."

Wait, this was not about the bug in her office. Stanton had not sent any of his Boyz to look into Her personal quarters. That would be idiotic, bold, yes but not something Stanton would dare do. One of his Boyz thought to do this all on his own?

"Well?"

"I have no idea. This was not under any orders of mine," Stanton whimpered.

"I am disappointed; I thought you had shown a new level of audacity. What a shame. So, you would not be able to tell me which one? You exert that much control over your own. Then what we do will not matter." She turned to the six guards along the back wall.

Stanton knew what was coming; they would unsling their blaster rifles and fire on him. This is not the way he had seen his life coming to an end. His body involuntarily released its bodily functions. Stanton turned a pale white, nearly a clear color. He closed his eyes and ducked his head, expecting to hear the cracks of the shots and then the searing pain of the rounds. But it seemed an eternity, and it never happened. He looked up to see the six guards heading out of his office in the same two rows, shoulder to shoulder, which they had entered. She was glaring at him.

"What? Did you think I was going to have them shoot you? No. You are too easy to control. I am going to have them and my others track down and execute each Chordentia in this complex. You nearly surprised me. I was close to being impressed, but you disappointed me."

Looking at the wet spot on the floor under his chair and sniffing, She twisted her face into a look of disgust.

"You are nothing if not totally predictable." She turned to the door and left with all but the original two guards who maintained their positions at the door.

Stanton had gotten off. He did not even have to explain what had happened with Moz. He was not going to die. This was going to be a good day. He may still have a future with Her. How was he going to get back into her good graces? First, he had to get cleaned up. Luckily not all his servants were Chordentia. With Boshduul on his way, Stanton would have to figure something out. Stanton needed minions or underlings to do his dirty work and gather information. Maybe with the Chordentia out of his way, Boshduul could get Stanton to the station he wanted. The Chordentia had never achieved what Stanton wanted. It was a good easy way to adjust his system; this could work to his advantage. It was better them than him; only the strong and wise will survive in this game of political power.

He did wonder who would have the courage to sneak into Her quarters. He could not think of anyone of the Boyz who would do something like that; even Traxon would not. Would he?

Stanton could hear a few far-off blaster rifle cracks, and he could hear a high-pitched scream every couple of shots as the marksman did not make a clean kill. *Well, better them than me,* Stanton thought.

———————— * ————————

Joxby's voice crackled over the vox.

"Gentlemen-She-is-coming," he said frantically. "Four-guards-with-Her." Informing all that things were a bit different than Her last visit.

"What is Her ETA?" Sarge inquired as he headed back towards minihab six.

"She-just-left-Stanton's-office," Joxby stated.

"Roger, everyone on your toes," Sarge yelled.

"More," Joxby added.

"What do you mean more?" Tan'cha got in on the conversation.

"Six-guards-left-Stanton's-office-and-are-killing-every-Chordentia-they-see."

"Traxon," Tan'cha yelled as he sprinted towards the holding cell.

"Yes, get him out of there. Take him to my quarters; She will not think to look there. Tell him not to move until you or I come to get him," Sarge instructed.

"Will do," Tan'cha responded.

"Med team, get prepared for injuries from blaster rifles. I have seen how these guards work, and they will not worry about incidental damage to non-Chordentia. Be prepared for trauma," Sarge commanded.

"I want two heavy response teams at the front and one at the dock. Teams three and four to the front and team seven to the dock, you will be heavy response, so suit up. All other teams' regular response and to your stations," Sarge instructed as he came to minihab six.

"Slaza, you stay here," Sarge told him.

"Yes, sir."

"I do not know what is going on, but in case something happens to me, get Sadbaath and kill that (Sarge nodded towards Brynja

Ajal). I have a sinking feeling I have been exposed to creatures like it before, and nothing good comes from those experiences. Long ago, during the Aashturian Civil War, I saw huge creatures and their destruction. That will be your purpose until I instruct you otherwise. As long as I am here and the med lab is active, protect all here," Sarge said with a serious determination.

"Yes, sir," Slaza returned grimly.

With that, Sarge strode towards the main door.

"Joxby?"

"Less-than-two-secton," Joxby responded.

Just as Sarge came to a stop, he looked towards the Security quarters and saw the heavy response teams running out. Two teams heading his way, and one heading to the loading dock at the back of the lab. All other teams were at their assigned stations. Sarge was pleased; the teams had been quick. He was happy with this groups. He looked around and saw an odd mix of races. They were all former pit fighters and had more loyalty and heart than most soldiers Sarge had ever served with. He felt there was a strong connection with them in their respect of Zhuni and their hatred of the games and the new Master. He would take this group into any battle.

What were they facing today? It was always something different with Her. She took offense at the smallest things and was ready to get rid of anyone who offended Her. Sarge could not understand this thinking. It was so selfish and narrow-minded. It would be Her demise. Sarge had always been taught by his commanders to follow orders but to have a moral compass. If you were given orders you knew were wrong, you spoke up, if you offended them or not. Morals did not change; they were universal, as if they were somehow ingrained in all. Those who were evil did not follow morals. They would attempt to extinguish all who spoke up or those who had morals.

Why was She having Her guards eliminate the Chordentia? Was Stanton eliminated also? Sarge could not see that happening, Stanton would do anything to gain Her favor, and that would be useful to Her. A dedicated idiot is more useful to a tyrant than a wise free individual with an opposing thought.

Sarge was standing by and felt this group was ready for whatever was coming through those doors. He just hoped it was not going to get too chaotic; tensions and stress were high enough with the situation Zhuni was in. Everyone in med lab was worried. He felt a need to calm everyone. He spoke into the vox with it open to all channels.

"I know everyone is worried about Zhuni, we are monitoring him, and all are hoping for a quick and full recovery. We all are tired. But we must all stay on our toes and must not do anything rash. Stay tight."

Why was She coming with extra guards? Sarge did not like this.

————————— * —————————

"I do not know why," Tan'cha explained to Traxon.

"All and me? Kill? Hunt, shoot?" Traxon asked.

"Sadly, yes, we do not know why; we will find out why, but we have to hide you."

"I hide?" Traxon asked.

"Yes, you must stay here in Sarge's quarters until Sarge or I come to get you. No one else. Do you understand?" Tan'cha asked.

"Why, you hide Traxon."

"That is what we do. We help others. You came to us, so we need to protect you. We just need you to trust us so we can keep you safe. Got it?"

"Me got it, me hide, safe. Stay with you, no die."

"Stay."

Tan'cha left Sarge's quarters and went to stand by the team, waiting for Her arrival. Tan'cha did not like when She stopped by for a visit. Especially when she was using Her guards to dispatch specific groups. Why the extra guards? Someone or something was always upsetting Her.

————————— * —————————

The vox squelched; She was here.

"Let them in," Sarge instructed his guards at the main entrance.

The door opened, and two of Her guards stepped in, followed by Her and two more guards. The first two spread out to face the security teams. The second set of guards remained at their usual spots just off Her shoulders and behind Her.

"Well, good morning. Quit the reception this morning. I am just here to pick up our boy Tan'cha as agreed. By the way, where is Zhuni?" She studied the large response to Her presence.

Sarge was surprised, so her network was not that good. How could she not know what was happening with Zhuni? Sarge had not sent anyone to inform Her but had assumed She would find out. Interesting. This was a twist Sarge had not expected. In the world of political games, knowledge was key. And She did not have it as Sarge thought. Good.

"He is unable to join us," Tan'cha said.

"Pardon me. He needs to be here, standing in front of me when I arrive. There is nothing that could prevent him from being here," She raised Her voice and pointed emphatically at the ground directly in front of Her.

"Your Liege, he is in minihab number six," Sarge voiced.

"Well, who in Dagz is the patient who he thinks is more important than I am?" She demanded.

"He is," Sarge blurted out.

"What?"

"He collapsed late last night, and we have been monitoring him since," Sarge continued.

She stepped forward with the intention of continuing to the minihabs. But the security teams did not budge to allow Her nor Her guards to pass. She glared at Sarge.

Inside, Sarge just started to laugh, *Man I love these fellows.*

"Oh, my Grace, I am so sorry. Like well-trained pets, they will do nothing without being told. Gentlemen."

With that, the teams parted to allow Her and Her guards to pass. One heavy response team fell in behind them, along with half of the other teams. One heavy response team stayed at the doors along with the other half of the security teams.

She looked into minihab number six and saw Zhuni lying there.

She looked over to the scientist known as Mazalla.

"Well," She voiced.

"He has a strong heartbeat; his breathing is good, and his brain activity is what I believe is abnormally active."

"So, when will he be ready to get back to work? I want another event, and he is key to how this med lab runs. How long?"

"I do not know; I have never worked with a human before."

"You are a Skrenoch, correct? Aren't your people supposed to be intelligent? You can't even tell me when he is going to wake up?" She screeched.

"I am not sure he is sleeping. I believe he has had a traumatic response to something, and his brain has shut down to consciousness."

"You believe. Great. I need him up and moving. Make it happen; I do not care what you need to do," She demanded.

"I am sure we cannot just wake him. He will have to be monitored and watched for any changes. It is highly possible that if he is shocked, his brain could shut down completely if it has experienced a trauma, and he could die," Mazalla assured.

"Well then, I will put you in charge of his care and will hold you personally responsible if anything happens to him," She directed towards Mazalla.

Turning to Sarge, She said, "Just do what you need to but get him back to work as quickly as possible. Until then, you will oversee the med lab."

"Yes, ma'am," Sarge replied.

"By the way, how is my pet?"

"You are referring to Brynja Ajal, correct?" Sarge asked.

"Of course, you fool," She snapped.

Interesting, She rarely showed emotion, and since She had seen Zhuni's condition, She seemed even more intense than usual. This was turning out to be an interesting visit. Sarge was taking mental notes.

"It is sleeping," Sarge said, gesturing towards the cage.

"That is what it usually does. It was not hurt, was it?" She asked.

"We do not believe so. When it came in, it was asleep, and Zhuni was going to check it. But then, when it woke up, Zhuni collapsed. So, we have not had the opportunity to check it."

"With the blaster rifles and plasma pellets raining down on it, no one thought it may have been hurt?" She snapped at Sarge.

"I am not a medical specialist. That is Zhuni's job, and as you can see, we were a bit busy worrying about him. The creature came in and showed no signs that any of us could see to indicate any injury." Sarge was getting angry but working to keep his temper in check.

"I suggest you check your attitude. I thought you said you were not a medical specialist. How would you know the signs of injury?" She groused.

"My Grace, I have not slept in more than two rotations and in no way meant any disrespect. That must have been unchecked exhaustion. I have served on countless battlefields and have seen hundreds of different creatures killed or injured. I do believe I can tell if a creature has been injured."

"But have you ever seen such a magnificent monster as this?" She said in a much softer tone.

"No."

The entire entourage walked over to the cage to look at Brynja Ajal.

When the Master got close to the cage, the monster stirred and craned its neck and head so it could glare at the Master.

Sarge could read anger in those eyes. He noticed the eyes glanced quickly to the Master's waist. Then back to glare at the Master's face.

"Look at the hate in those eyes. Magnificent beast. Dumb as a stone. But just an amazing killing machine. Our scientists studied them for years, I am told. This one had that implant put in its head, and I can now control it. The scientists were able to install that years ago, and that is when the fights here became a main event and were able to bring in the masses. All because of this creature. I am wondering if it could be controlled outside of the pit. That would be useful, correct? But I digress," She was talking too much and caught Herself.

Sarge had developed the skill of noticing little keys to actions individuals did little quirks. When the Master was talking, She dropped her hand to her waist and reached under her cape to grab something that looked to be attached to Her belt. The eyes of the monster also fell on the Master's waist. *Was that where the control device was?* Something else he heard piqued his interest. *Our scientists studied them for years. Were there or had there been more than one?* Then She said something that made Sarge cringe; She openly wondered if the beast could be controlled outside of the pit. She was consolidating power within all the guilds; if She could also control this creature, the galaxy, as they all knew it, would change.

"Yes," Sarge let out.

Sarge did not see hatred in the eyes of the creature but righteous anger. If he was controlled by another like this monster was, he would be angry also. Plus, when he looked into those enormous eyes, Sarge saw an intelligence and wisdom. This was a creature to be studied. Sarge felt there was much to learn; it was not just a killing machine. He had seen hundreds of creatures designed for killing and had been on battlefields with those who enjoyed killing, and Sarge saw none of that in the eyes of this creature.

"I have work to do. Tan'cha, these two will escort you to solitary for the next ten to twelve rotations, as agreed with Zhuni," She said, indicating a pair of Her guards.

"Master. You have put me in charge, and I knew nothing of this."

"It is all right, Sarge; I will go quietly," Tan-cha said.

"Thank you. But with Zhuni's current condition and Tan'cha as his bodyguard, would you allow me to request that upon Zhuni's recovery, Tan'cha be returned to the med lab prior to the end of his isolation term?" Sarge requested.

"Send for me if Zhuni recovers."

"I will send for you *when* he recovers," Sarge smartly said.

"Yes."

"Master? There is word that the Chordentia are being eliminated."

"Yes, and of what concern is that to you? Don't you tend to stand with Klavan over Stanton?"

"I stand with the med lab as that is my area of responsibility, but just out of curiosity."

"So that you know, one of them apparently did something on their own and overstepped their boundary with me. Stanton does not know which one and does not care. I told him if he would tell me, I would eliminate that one, but he either does not know which one nor does not care if they are eliminated, so to be certain, we will just eliminate them all. If he cannot control his own, I will."

"Wise, someone who does not do your bidding should not be around," Sarge said, hoping it did not sound as snarky as it felt.

"Surly," She answered with a slightly sideward glance.

With that, She and Her guards left, taking Tan'cha with them.

The tension eased quickly. Sarge got back on the vox and opened all channels.

"Good job, everyone; now, back to our regular routines. Zhuni will be proud.

*

Boshduul entered Stanton's office and was hit by the horrific smell. *What was that incredibly atrocious smell?* It made Boshduul think of a sewage pit, just worse and more concentrated. The servants were putting away cleaning equipment and disposing of large trash receptacles. Whatever it had been, these poor things had to deal with it. Luckily one of them was breaking out massive amounts of incense in an attempt to remove or mask the odor.

Stanton was not here. That was strange. Boshduul stood at the front of Stanton's desk and waited. He had a plan to implement, and this was cutting into his time. *Was Stanton even around?*

This had already been a strange morning. The Chordentia who had come to get him had hurried down the hallway ahead of him. Boshduul had heard the shot as the Chordetia had rounded the corner. This caused him to ready his weapon, not knowing what was waiting for him. He saw several creatures run towards him, but there were no more shots fired. As he came around the corner, he could see the body of the Chordentia and two of Her guards stepping over it. They did not even acknowledge him, and he knew they were targeting the Chordentia. Boshduul made his way to Stanton's office and saw two more Chodentia had been dispatched. *Why were the Chodentia being targeted? Was Stanton still alive?* Everyone knew the

Chordentia were his Boyz. *Were they being cleaned up after Stanton's execution?* That would put Boshduul's planning to waste. He would have to go back to the port and find new work. He hated shopping for a new boss.

Here came Stanton. Good, he had not been gotten rid of. With fewer Chordentia working for him, it may be even easier for Boshduul to express the need for change.

"We need to do something," Stanton started.

"Yes, sir, I see this. What exactly is going on?"

"The Master is removing all my Boyz. She had one enter Her quarters and is furious; I am lucky to be alive. I had to do a large amount of explaining just to survive. We need to rebuild our organization. We will need new Boyz."

"She is having Her guards execute them."

"Yes, they came in here first, and She threatened to kill me if I did not abide by Her wishes. The guards were lined up on that opposite wall and were going to kill me too. But I explained to Her that I was too important for Her to eliminate and that it would be prudent for Her to remove the actual problem. Besides, it is better them than me," Stanton stated as his coloring became a neutral beige tone.

"Yes, a very good thing that She came to Her senses."

"So now we must discuss our plans to rebuild our organization."

"I think, with your permission, of course, that we should hire a few new hands. We have a few your former colleague Traxon had spoken with about bringing on board. I would like to revisit them and look to get some local talent here."

"When you say a couple, do not bring that screeching thing back here," Stanton squawked.

"The Takchee? Yes, they are annoying."

"What do you mean local talent? Is the port not local?"

"The Swaklin in charge of security for the night shift has been moved to the med lab. As such, we should hire a few of the humanish crew to keep us in the know as to what is coming and going. I will go to the port for more specialized skill sets. I need to know our budget, my lord."

"I do not care. I have been banking my finances for too many cycles; it is time I spend it on some real help. I will need a few errand runners, six to eight guards for my office and private quarters, and whatever specialists you see fit. We will need to remove Klavan and Zhuni still."

"Not to worry. The team I plan to build may take someone out more important than Klavan. We will just need to be patient."

"More important than Klavan? Really? You would do that for me?" Stanton mussed, turning a bright yellow.

"You are my master; I am to serve you and your needs."

"I knew you were the one when Traxon brought you in."

———————— * ————————

Sarge watched Brynja Ajal. It just slept. He knew it had something to do with Zhuni being in a coma. Sarge's instincts told him something was going on beyond Zhuni being tired.

He had to find Traxon and find out what was going on with Stanton. Brynja Ajal was an issue, but there was nothing Sarge could do right now. He had to get control of what he could.

As he walked across the med lab to his quarters, the wounded started to arrive. Sarge was not surprised by the total disregard of life by the Master's guards. He had seen this action by tyrants before.

Every type of creature and every race seemed to be coming in. Most looked to be glancing wounds and indirect shots. Few looked serious. This was more by chance than by the disciplined actions or control of the guards.

This was going to be a long day. He would be available in case any on the security team needed him, but he was going to have a talk with Traxon now.

"Joxby," Sarge growled into his vox.

"Yes."

"Have we seen any movement from Stanton?"

"No-but-we-have-Rags."

"Do we now? Eyes on him?"

"No-he-is-in-Stanton's-office."

"We need a tracker or something on him."

"Already-working-on-it."

"Really? Good. What have you got?"

"Scanned-images-as-Zhuni-asked."

"Okay, go on."

"Found-rags-image, Tracked-back-to-Stanton's-office."

"Okay."

"Set-microdrone-and-markers-at-Stanton's-door."

"Then when Rags returns, you just set drone and tracker on Rags. Good job. Nice work. Let me know when he is moving and give me updates."

"Will-do."

That was a bit of good news. Maybe the day wasn't going to be a total loss. Something useful out of it, and it was not even lunch.

"Traxon?" Sarge said as he stepped into his quarters.

"Sargey?"

"Sarge, if you are going to call me, do it by the name; I go by *not* Sargey."

"Yes, you."

"I am here; where are you?"

"I scared," Traxon's voice sounded as if it were coming from Sarge's wardrobe across the room.

"It is okay." Sarge opened the wardrobe and saw Traxon curled up on the floor in the back. Poor little guy was shivering. And needed to wash. Sarge was going to need to get all his things laundered. That stink permeated the entire wardrobe. Sarge realized Chordentia smelled.

"It you, glad."

"Yes, it is me, and we are going to get you out of there and have a little talk."

"What we talk?"

"Stanton."

"Me no Stanton. Me work you, Zhuni, Tan'cha, and med lab. Me help."

"I know you say you no longer work for Stanton. How do I know that?"

"Stanton try kill me, and have Master guards kill my kind."

"You are telling me that Stanton is using Her guards to kill all of you? How do I know it is not one of Stanton's twisted schemes? Stanton has tried to kill you before. Why do you want to change now?"

"I scared, I come hide. Before Traxon have no choice, no chance. Traxon see robots in Her place. Stanton try kill Traxon before Traxon tell him story. Traxon know in trouble, come for help, to help."

"You said you saw robots in Her place?"

"Guards and charge stations."

"You mean the guards were on charging stations?"

"Yes."

"Mechanicals. That explains a lot, and you are the one who went in Her quarters."

"Yes, no mean trouble."

"Okay. It looks like you may be the only Chordentia left alive. Joxby said many were killed. We are now getting the collateral damage as the wounded are coming in. Did you know this was going to happen?"

"Traxon know he in trouble, not all. Traxon sad, some friends."

"Yes, I guess some would have been friends. I am sorry."

"Traxon scared. Want help."

"Yes, we have saved you; we have helped you. We just have to hope no one informs Her that you are here."

"You keep Traxon here?"

"That is what Zhuni would want. To protect you, even though you have been trouble for him."

"Traxon no trouble, Stanton trouble. Traxon no more Stanton. Now help you." Traxon gave a twisted smile, the best he could do with the scars he had.

"So, how can you help us?"

"Traxon have many contact and much money. Traxon very rich. Traxon have information."

"How did you become rich? And what information could you give us?"

"Traxon small, weak, not smart like Stanton, but not stupid. Traxon spend many cycles working for Stanton, learn. Traxon put bank much money Stanton not know."

Sarge roared with laughter.

"So, you have been embezzling from Stanton all these years? Classic."

"No, not embezzle; take a little here and some more there. Many years much money. Each time he hire someone, Traxon take a finder fee on his pay. Traxon still have money; deposit last rotation."

"You little monster. I can just see Stanton turning a brilliant red when he finds out."

"Traxon not monster." He suddenly looked terrified.

"I don't mean that in a bad way; I am impressed you are getting over on Stanton. All this time, I was thinking you were his little dumb little stooge. Why do you look so petrified?"

"You tell?"

"Stanton? Dagz, no!"

"Okay, Traxon happy."

"I help. Joxby, expert with electronics, yes? I have information good for him."

"What could that be?"

"I put device in Master's office. I tell Joxby, he read."

"A device in Stanton's office; that could be helpful."

"No. Not Stanton. The Master's."

"The Game Master's?"

"Yes."

"Dagz, you are full of surprises. Why don't we go see Joxby."

"Yes, we go."

They arrived at the security control center and walked in to see Joxby.

The center was a large space at the very top of the med lab and looked down on the entire area. Huge windows allowed viewing. Inside the space were dozens of monitors, and just in front of the windows was a holographic image of the med lab and the entire gaming complex. The space was divided into four separate rows of monitors. There were seats for a dozen different operators, but Joxby usually had two or three with him during normal rotations. The space had been packed during the main event. This was the nerve center for the entire med lab. Joxby could watch the lab from his perch up here and switch between all his microdrones and other devices on any of his chosen monitors. The space had low lighting to make the monitors easier to see. Even Sarge was impressed with the complete coverage and secure communication Joxby had developed.

Joxby was in his spot, which was the back and highest point in the room. From there, he could monitor everyone and see each monitor. He had a dozen of his own, forming a ball of monitors around and over him. But there was a large space between his monitors, which allowed him to look out and see everyone and everything from his elevated position. Joxby was bouncing around in his chair. He never slept and never slowed down. It was amazing to Sarge. All the years he had fought, he had never seen anyone nor anything with the never-ending energy of Joxby. Joxby was always moving and always eating. He would eat anything and lots of it. Sarge enjoyed the energy Joxby had; it was infectious. Everyone working around Joxby became energized.

"Sarge," Joxby said.

"I thought I'd surprise you with a guest," Sarge said.

"Funny-you-know-my-monitors-see-you-no surprise."

"True. But one day, I will. Here is Traxon; he has some information for you."

"Yes, Traxon put device in Master's office. I have info for you to tap in," Traxon said, reaching into a pocket and handing Joxby the baseplate with the frequency information and device ID information.

"Good-this-is-extremely-helpful," Joxby said as he recognized the device.

Joxby reached over to one of the keyboards under one of his monitors, entered the information, and watched as a screen flashed away from monitoring the backloading dock, went blank for a moment, then became a blur of activity.

"Why picture not clear?" Traxon asked, sounding concerned. Having worked with Stanton so long, he knew what would happen if what he said would work did not.

"Wow-this-is-downloading-the-stored-images."

"Stored images?" Traxon asked.

"Yes, this-device-is-designed-to-store-all-sound-and-images-so-as-to-not-transmit-while-recording," Joxby said in his everything-is-one-word way of speaking.

"This good?" Traxon asked.

"Yes-very-much-info."

"Traxon help?"

"Yes-we-will-see-what-we-have-it-may-take-a-few-partions," Joxby responded.

"How long?" Sarge asked.

"Depends-how-long-it-has-been-there," Joxby answered, looking at Traxon.

"Device several rotations there. Stanton have wrong code, no see."

"Interesting. Traxon-full-of-surprises."

"You do not even know, and I have the feeling we will be finding out even more," Sarge said.

"There-he-goes," Joxby yelled, pointing at the hologram map and tapping on a keyboard to bring another monitor up to show an image as if from an individual walking down a corridor in the facility. The hologram map had a bright yellow dot start moving along one of the corridors.

"Rags?" Sarge called out, more of a statement than a question.

"Yes-Rags."

"Nice work."

"Yes-I-am-good."

CHAPTER 7

Assassins' Work

Boshduul headed out of Stanton's office and down the corridor to the main loading area. He knew there were a couple of humanish that would do anything if the price was right. If Boshduul could get one per shift on payroll he would be able to know everything that was coming in and out of the complex. This would be the beginning of his information-gathering network. He would also have to get a few of the handlers and interior guards. But this would be a good start.

He quickly found three of the guards, two humanish and a Krodent, not at their assigned posts but at the side of the loading area playing a game of Achbaon. A card game that was quick and simple but could cause issues as betting took place and was an easy game to cheat in. Boshduul excelled at it and decided this would be a great way to quickly get these individuals indebted to him.

"Achbaon, that is a good game. Care to wager?"

"The pile of rags talks?" one of the humanish laughed.

The other just stared at him, and the Krodent placed the hand he had face down to look down on Boshduul.

"What are you supposed to be? Laundry?" the Krodent roared.

"You should not mess with that you are unfamiliar with." Boshduul had to deal with this type of problem all the time, but the rags hid his identity well. No one ever knew who or what he was.

The quite humanish quickly understood and realized what was about to happen and stepped back.

Boshduul whipped his killing blade out of the case under his left arm; it flashed for an acta and was then placed back into the strap.

The swipe was so fast that Krodent did not even recognize what had happened until the wisecracking humanish fell face first to the ground. His throat sliced wide open and bleeding.

"I was going to play you for the opportunity for you to work for me, but this is faster," Boshduul grumbled.

"Whoa," the Krodent responded.

"He owed me seventy-five credits," the Krodent stated.

"Well then, work for me, and you can get that back plus more," Boshduul stated.

"I am listening."

The surviving humanish stepped back up to the loading crate they had been using as their Achbaon game table.

"You have our attention."

"I just need information. The comings and goings here. What and who arrived, left, and times of arrivals and departures. The amounts and types of items coming through here. Copies of manifests would pay well."

"How much?"

"That, of course, depends on the information, the quality of the information, the usefulness of the information, and of course, the timeliness of the information. If you could give me a heads up about important information prior to arrival or departure, that would pay even better."

"So, how will this work?" the Krodent asked.

"I will contact you for information. I will need at least one individual per shift to speak with your coworkers. Think about it. I have other errands to run and will be back to speak with you later."

He reached into his pocket and tossed the Krodent a two hundred credit bar.

"Clean up the mess and consider that a retainer."

Now he needed to get to the port and find some reliable specialists.

———————— * ————————

"I have dealt with the Assassins' Guild many times. I know how you work. Do not patronize me. I have become the Master of the Mining Guild and am currently working on the freighters," the Master was speaking to Her monitor across from the desk in Her office. The monitor had only a dark image centered in the screen. It was the figure of the Assassins' Guild's Master. The shape and size of the individual were extremely difficult to see. The scene was barely backlighted. This leaned a great deal of mystery to the figure.

"I know how you became the Mining Guild master. I do not feel you are right for our guild, and I will fight you every step of the way. The assassins have a moral standard that is strong and has kept us the most influential and powerful guild of all. You do not have any such code or creed that you follow. You have no loyalty to anyone nor anything other than your power."

"Tazmok and Moz crossed me, and we saw what happened to them."

The voice broke into laughter.

"Yes, a clumsy display of your hunger for power. Tazmok had a price on his head at one point but made his peace with the guild. He was an honorable individual. Unlike you. Do you believe threatening a guild master, particularly of the Assassins' Guild, is a wise move? You are both clumsy and too bold; these traits will cost you everything."

"I was hoping you would say something to that effect. These transmissions are not as secure as you would like to believe." She started to laugh and nodded towards the guard who had been standing in the room with Her. The guard was standing behind a cabinet that had a selection of switches and a knob. The guard flipped a switch, and there was an ear-piercing high-pitched hum. It turned into an ear-splitting scream that resonated throughout the room and into the monitor.

The figure on the monitor dropped to its knees and raised a hand in a stopping motion. But it was too late. The sound reached a horrific pitch, and the figure at the other end began to convulse. The figure then began to violently twitch and fell to the floor, motionless.

"Goodbye, Droughlok. I do enjoy blowing minds. End transmission," She said to the guard. The monitor went blank, and the screeching of the machine ceased.

"I hope the new guild master will be more accommodating," She said as she left the room.

———————— * ————————

"This-creature-rags-is-dangerous," Joxby piped up.

"I am glad we can see what he is up to now. Keep an eye on him. I have a feeling he may not be done," Sarge instructed.

"Rags no good," Traxon said.

"Traxon, you are with me. I am not ready to let you run free just yet. I need to keep an eye on you."

"Yes, sir Sarge, sir, Traxon stay by you."

"Come on, we still have a med lab to run, and we have several wounded coming in. Joxby, let me know anything else this Rags character does, and keep me posted as to his whereabouts."

"Yes-will-do."

Sarge left with Traxon in tow. They headed back down to the main level of the med lab. Sarge was not a medic but had seen these types of injuries before. These were the injuries he had seen on many battlefields.

The medics were all busy. There were over two dozen creatures needing treatment. Most were glancing wounds.

Sarge and Traxon checked in with everyone to see if they needed a hand, but everyone was doing their job well. Sarge was pleased; he had not expected to oversee the entire med lab. Zhuni was indisposed, and Tan'cha was in solitary, leaving everything to fall on Sarge. This was not how Sarge had wanted to spend his time. He had a crazy Ragman killing guards and had to protect the entire med lab from a power-hungry Regent and Game Master. Sarge's main priority still had to be security. Let the medical teams do their job.

"Lots of hurt," Traxon said.

"Yes, I did not expect this. The games were bad enough, but this random violence towards anyone who gets in Her way. This needs to be stopped."

"How we do?"

"I do not know right now. We may not be able to. But we are helping the best we can. That is what we can do for now."

"Bad. Everything bad. Change when She come. She evil. Traxon afraid."

"No worry, you are safe here. I do not believe anyone here in our med lab will harm you or report you. We will protect you and anyone else who needs protection. I have seen enough violence in my life, and that is why I am in security. I use my skills to protect. I am sick of killing and seeing death. I have had enough in my life."

Sarge and Traxon crossed from the medical side to the massive cage holding Brynja Ajal. Sarge just had to check on it again.

Just as he had expected, it was sleeping as if it had no care in the world.

Across to check on the security team at the loading dock, then the main entrance. Everyone was doing their job. The team at the main entrance told Sarge that the Kill cart had been brought out to pick up all the Chordentia and deliver them to the Pantaas. Her favorite pets. She seemed to love them more than anything else except power. They were even more precious than Brynja Ajal.

"Sad, some friends. Traxon no like Her. Want hurt Her."

"Yes, but one thing I know and have seen. Evil does not last forever. Every evil is eventually removed, and good can and will follow."

"Traxon only see evil. No good in life."

"What about this?" Sarge asked, sweeping his hand in a wide arc to indicate the med lab.

"Traxon see, always turn bad. Maybe change. Hope."

"Well. While we speak of hope, let us go see how Zhuni is doing."

"Yes, Traxon think Zhuni good. He only one ever help Traxon," he said as he rubbed his scared face.

—————— * ——————

Klavan knew he was going to be summoned to see Her. She had just left the arena without any word last night, and Klavan still had to ensure the guests who had stayed were fed this morning. He was in the banquet hall's main kitchen when one of Her guards found him. The guards never spoke; they just motioned for Klavan to follow. Klavan let Katool know that he was leaving and followed the guard.

Klavan had hoped to check in on Zhuni, but that would have to wait.

He had heard some talk by the kitchen staff of the killings taking place but caulked that up to hearsay until he saw the scorch marks and the bodies. *Why? Why the Chordentia? Was Stanton also removed? Did this have anything to do with the run-in with Moz? Could it have anything to do with Traxon? Maybe it was both. That would explain the Chordentia being targeted.* Klavan hoped Traxon had somehow survived. He was a tough little guy and was showing to be more resourceful than Klavan thought he could be. Klavan doubted even Traxon could survive this hunt. *But what about Stanton?* That was another issue.

The guard opened the door to Her office and took up position just inside the door.

She was standing behind Her desk with a guard to either side of Her as usual. But there was another guard in the center of the room packing up some type of equipment locker. The guard finished packing up the equipment and left the office.

"Klavan, we have some issues to discuss. I am sure you noticed we are exterminating some vermin. Turns out Stanton had one of his vile little creatures enter my private quarters. He claims he has no idea this happened, so he is either lying, which I did not sense, or he has no control over his own. Either way, I felt we should eliminate the issue."

There it was; She could sense emotions; Klavan knew She had not meant for that to slip. That would explain Her hold and strong understanding of all of Her Regents and Dwayans. As a Septorian, Klavan understood She could not read his thoughts, the heavy minerals of his world formed a strong, nearly impenetrable skin that also made mind control and reading nearly impossible for any creature.

"We also have an issue with the med lab. Zhuni is out. He seems to be in a coma of sorts. I find this highly disruptive. We need to get him back to work. I need the med lab working; we have more events and meetings planned. Check in with the security guard in charge. He is running the show down there; the big blue thing is in solitary confinement for a period of time. Also, the Skrenoch, which is monitoring Zhuni, may have some information for us."

"Your Grace, I was in the med lab last night, and I believe Zhuni collapsed from the tremendous amount of stress that has been building on him and his team. He is still young for a human, and humans are not the toughest creatures. I suggest we give him a few rotations to recover, and everything should be fine. What do you mean the big blue thing is in confinement, Tan'cha? He is an important part of Zhuni's team."

"You knew about the issue with Zhuni and did not inform me? As my liaison, I need you to give me all the important information. I need it in a timely matter, not when you feel like releasing it to me. Immediately. Do you understand?"

"Yes, my Grace. You left last night with no instructions, so I felt You were getting some much-needed rest; You have not stopped working for several rotations, and I was attempting to handle the small issues; my intention was to check on him this morning and give a full report at our morning meeting."

"We are currently in our morning meeting. Do you have any news for me about Zhuni? Did you check in on him this morning?"

"No. Our meetings are typically later in the morning, so my time management was a bit off."

"So, have you become incompetent, or is this just an oversight?"

"Poor timing on my part; I should have informed You of the issue last night with Zhuni and checked on him first thing this morning."

"Yes, poor timing indeed. I knew of you prior to coming here and taking over; I know all about you. That is why you are still here. Do your job as you have in the past. Do not make decisions about the important players here at the games without informing me and getting my instructions. Now, do as I have told and report back by lunch. Go, we will have more to discuss then. I will also assign one of my guards to be with you just by chance if you forget to inform me of anything else."

"Yes, Your Grace."

Klavan left the office with his new friend in tow.

It was because of Traxon, interesting. Stanton was not mentioned as being eliminated, and now he would be without his minions. This was proving interesting. Now, how was he going to communicate with the crew in med lab with this thing by his side?

---
*

Boshduul had the loading dock setup; he now had some informants. With the credits he flashed, there would be more joining the team.

So now it was off to the port to build the talent he would need to pull this off. Traxon was a good judge of talent and character and had brought together some talent, but Stanton was so concerned with his standing and power he had no idea what to do with a team that may have different points of view. This was why he had never achieved more than he had. Boshduul would look for the individuals he had seen the morning he was brought on with Stanton.

Boshduul set up at the same spot he found Traxon that evening. He ordered a glass of Splift and waited. He had put out the word with a few of his contacts, and he knew the unsavory type he needed would soon show.

It did not take long at all; Boshduul had just taken his second sip of the Splift when the Swaklin he had been hoping to hire showed up. He was a tough character, and Boshduul knew, looking at the tattoos, that this guy could be dangerous.

"Evening," Boshduul greeted him.

"Yeah," the Swaklin replied.

"I need talent; I was hoping you would seek me out. You may remember we were interviewed by a client to work at the games."

"Yeah," the Swaklin replied.

"I need an enforcer, among other talents. You look the type. Tell me about yourself, and by all means, have a seat. Would you like a drink?" Boshduul motioned for the Swaklin to sit.

"I was never interviewed by the client. I was vetted by his annoying little sidekick. I heard the gig paid well. I am assuming this is for the same individual?"

"Yes. You would be working directly under me for him. Continue."

"I have seen many wars and been involved in countless battles. My specialty is covert work. I have worked for several, umm, let's say, special interest groups. I have done security for several guilds and some of their masters. I can provide references. I am not one to talk much."

The Swaklin sat down as he spoke. Boshduul noticed he did not take to seat offered but put his back to the wall and kept looking around, studying everyone and everything.

"Tell me more, for example, this," Boshduul said, pointing to the mark of disgrace tattooed on his right forearm.

"Why do you not cover it?" Boshduul continued.

"Sometimes in life, we make decisions that stay with us, whether we are right or wrong. This reminds me of such a decision."

"So, what was the mistake?"

"I said it reminded me of a decision. I did not say mistake. I did not say it was for you to know my decisions and reasons for my decisions."

"Well then, why would I hire a dishonorably discharged soldier to work for me? If you can't follow orders while in battle, what would make me think you would follow my orders?"

"Why assume it was because I did not follow orders?"

"Most who are alive to be discharged dishonorably are cowards or disobey orders, and you do not look like a coward."

"Well then, you have me all figured out, don't you?" the Swaklin retorted, his voice heavy in sarcasm.

"I am not sure. I have obviously hit on a hot subject for you. But it is not important enough for you to discuss, or is it too important to discuss? I know little about you; you said you had references?"

"Life can be full of mystery, and so can those in life. I will provide you with a few references, but until you tell me the job and pay, I will not divulge all my information."

"Good, I would have been disappointed if you just jumped on board without asking anything. Start with a name, I am Boshduul, and you are?"

"I am called Sazon."

"Well then, Sazon, let us talk."

*

"Mazalla, has there been any change?" Klavan asked the Skrenoch.

"No."

"Is he improving, or what?"

"No."

"Can you give me a better answer?"

"I am a Skrenoch; we work in facts. You asked if there was a change; no, there has been no change. You asked if he was getting better; by definition, no change cannot be an improvement. There has been no change in his heart rate, rate of breathing, or brain activity."

"So, what can you tell me?"

"There has been no change, good or bad, no change since last night."

"What are we going to do?"

"I do not know what you are going to do. I am going to continue to study him, and when and if there is a change, I will react to it in the way I believe to be proper."

"Has Kowstee improved?"

"Kowstee is still recovering. But he is improving. He should be awake this evening or tomorrow morning. His vitals are all strong and improving."

"How about our new patients, any serious injuries?"

"We heard one individual besides the Chordentia was killed, but all our patients suffered ricochets or glancing blows. They all are doing well and should recover. None of them want to leave here, though."

"I understand, but they do have jobs to do, and as soon as they are able, they need to get back to work," Klavan said.

"I will pass that information on to them. Is there anything else?"

"No, Mazalla. I will be looking for Sarge. Thank you."

Klavan left the medical control room and started across the med lab towards the main entrance. Sarge was making his rounds, and Klavan knew Sarge would finish up at the entrance.

Sarge came in the main door from the passageway.

"Who is your new friend?" Sarge asked, nodding toward the guard.

"Master's orders. I did not inform Her of my visit here last night to see Zhuni. She should have been informed immediately of his condition."

"Okay then. This will make things interesting. I had to drop off a sidekick of my own. Thanks to my guards giving me a heads up that you had a friend."

"Yes. By the way, what is this I hear about Tan'cha being in isolation?"

"So apparently, he ran over a couple of Her guards while rushing to get your walking stick, and She was irate about it. Zhuni talked Her into not killing Tan'cha and had him thrown into isolation for ten to twelve rotations. The poor thing, he will probably go nuts," Sarge said with a chuckle.

"Poor oaf. I need to get back to the kitchen to see how that is going, and then I have a lunch with the Master. Let me know if there is any way I can help you. I know with Zhuni out, that is tough, and add in Tan'cha being indisposed, and you have a lot to deal with. If you get the chance, have Joxby set something up so we can speak to me about anything at any time. I should be at your beck and call also as Zhuni is down. I know I should be available to you every moment."

"Good idea, thank you, sir. I could use some support, and having you available to me would be a huge load off my mind. I will need to speak with you later."

"No problem. That is what I am here for."

———————— * ————————

Boshduul walked into Stanton's office.

Stanton was an unusual greyish color. Boshduul had so far been able to interpret nearly all the colors this emotional clown showed, but this was a new and odd color.

"What?" Stanton snapped.

"I was just coming by to inform you of the good news, Your Highness." Boshduul could not stand working for someone of such little intelligence, but it paid well, and Boshduul felt it could meet his purpose.

"And?" Stanton was losing the gray and changing back to his usual beige red.

"Yes, I have made the connections; we will need to know the comings and goings around here. I have also found several choice candidates to be our eyes and ears and our enforcers. We will have a solid team of ten hired hands. This will be enough to get the ball rolling to achieve our goals."

"Our goals? I do not care about your goals. Unless they include me being the Master and you being my number two. I have failed to reach my goal at this point and am counting on you building a team to do so. I have put out a large number of credits to hire professionals. I expect results. I have collected vast sums over the cycles to be able to become the Master. If need be, I will spend them for my power grab. If you help me achieve this goal, the number of credits available to you will astound you. But only if I become Master. My accounts have been locked for my protection, so do not think of stealing from me."

"My lord, your goals are my goals. I am not a common thief. I am shocked you would even entertain such a thought. I work for you, and my word is my bond. Working in the field I do, I cannot sign contracts; it becomes a matter of pride. I would never steal from you. Your goals are my goals; I am your slave until our agreement is complete. I will not fail you."

"You had better not. I have many connections in the various guilds; many owe me favors. I will call on them one day; I would hate to have to call in a favor to have you removed."

"I have given you my word; there is no reason to threaten."

"Good; see my accountant for payment, so you can give the team their first pay."

"Yes, your lordship. Thank you."

Boshduul left the office and headed straight to the accountant.

Stanton was such a fool. He had no connections of meaning; he was full of empty threats. Boshduul despised him more than any other individual he had ever worked for. Stanton was honorless, a liar, an unimaginative leader who could not even keep Chordentia in line. Stanton could not hold a position of power to save his life. Boshduul knew that Stanton was alone in this world. Not one of the dozens who worked for him was loyal. Stanton would turn on anyone at any time to get what he wanted. Everyone who worked for him knew that. Boshduul did not even have to use the bribe money he had worked into the budget, but he charged Stanton for it anyway. Stanton was being raked over the coals and was too foolish to realize it. Once Boshduul got his money, he would pay the new staff, take his cut, and at the rate things were going, Boshduul was looking at early retirement. Working for an idiot had its perks.

———————— * ————————

Sarge called Joxby on the vox.

"I need a secure communication device delivered to Klavan. He said he had information he needed to get to us, but because She has put a guard on him, he cannot communicate that to us. I want to be able to talk to him at any time, and I want him to be able to talk to us at any time. Got it?"

"Yes-Sarge. Do-you-want-to-see-also?"

"If possible, he does not need to be able to see."

"Will-get-it-to-him. Also-the-down-load-from-Her-office-is-complete."

"Anything important?"

"I-need-you-look-at-it. Thought-you-would-want-to."

"I will be up in a moment; let me check in on Zhuni."

"Yes-sir."

Sarge hated being around the medical equipment. He had seen too many friends die in medical facilities in the many battles and wars he had been in. He stood at minihab number six, looking in. Zhuni was still as a stone. Sarge could see him breathing and watched his eyelids flickering. Zhuni was a good human. Sarge was glad he had been able to be a part of this team.

The minihab was a room that was a self-contained medical lab all to itself. The space was just a sealed chamber with a bed in the middle. Above the bed were several robotic arms which could be used to perform surgery or any procedure needed on the patient. Above the headboard was a large monitor with the individual's vital signs slowly working their way across the screen. The heart rate, breaths per minute, their body temperature, their oxygen levels breathed in and exhaled, etc. It had a graphic representation of each vital sign plus a count to the left side. Next to that on the left was another monitor, which showed the chemical concentration of the air within the chamber. This allowed the atmosphere to be adjusted to the needs of any creature from any atmosphere. To the right of the main monitor was a screen with a holographic image of the patient showing the injuries. This image would change from the initial injuries and the current state of the injuries. Along the walls were several charts, valves, small doors, and a few drawers. *This was a brilliant design*, Sarge thought. Even not being a medic, Sarge could easily look into each minihab and tell how well each patient was doing and how they were improving. Above the main monitor was one small significant item. It was a clock with the countdown of how long the individual was in the minihab. Zhuni showed over twenty-seven partions, and the actas kept adding up as Sarge watched.

Sarge looked up from the minihab over at the Brynja Ajal; it had something to do with Zhuni's situation. Sarge felt it. He knew it. Klavan may not believe it, and if Sarge had not seen how everything went down, he might be inclined to believe the same thing Klavan did. But Sarge had seen what happened.

Sarge knew he could not stand around watching a massive creature like Brynja Ajal sleep; he had things to do. But he knew something was not quite right. He had to leave and head up to see the information from the Master's office.

"What do we have?" Sarge asked Joxby.

"I-do-not-know. I-told-you-you-look-at-it. I-did-run-it-through-filters-and-found-something-I-have-never-seen-before. Had-to-remove-dangerous."

"What do you mean?"

"I-always-run-through-filters-for-best-quality. Filters-picked-up-high-pitched-waves-which-could-hurt-several-types-of-creatures."

"When was that?"

"Just-before-I-call-you."

"No, I mean, when on the recording?"

"Incident-actually-just-happened-this-morning. Recording-stopped-just-a-few-moments-ago. It-went-back-into-non-transmission-mode."

"It is safe; I am not going to be hurt?"

"You-funny;-I would-not-let-you-get-hurt," Joxby said, laughing.

"I did not think so; I just want to make sure. I don't want my mind melted," Sarge laughed nervously.

"You-watch-and-listen;-you-see. Good-information."

"I thought you said you didn't watch it."

"No,-I-said-you-watch-it;-I-don't-know."

"Right."

---
*

Lunch with the Master. Why? This was new. The Master loved Her games. Now that Klavan had a shadow, he had to be careful. He and his shadow entered the office and found Her sitting at large table She had had set up. The table included three chairs; one was enormous. She had her two guards standing behind Her as always.

"Sit," She said as She shooed away Klavan's guard.

Klavan was dying to know what was going on but did not want to appear too interested.

"Thank you." Klavan could smell something amazing. He could not place it but knew it was familiar.

"I have plans I need to discuss with you. I do not see you as needing or wanting power. I see you as a possible partner, so to speak." She waved the attendants over to the table. They brought over several covered trays, which smelled incredible.

"Partner?" Klavan asked.

"So to speak. I have seen you working hard to satisfy my every need. I have not had an assistant do such a tough job before. I think you deserve a pay increase. I have had time to think about our misunderstanding this morning and realized I did send for you much sooner than I usually do. It is possible you could have made your rounds and gotten the information I needed prior to our standard meeting time. I just wanted to clear the air and ensure we are all on the same page." She motioned for the door from the passageway to open, and in walked Stanton.

So, this was Her game. Stanton was to be involved. Klavan had been wondering what had happened to him since the purge of his Chordentia. Klavan was furious to see Stanton here but had to play it off. He could not let Stanton nor Her see his emotions. Especially Her. Klavan hoped the fact that his Septorian hide could protect him from empaths and mind readers was not a myth. He could feel Her looking at him and studying him, attempting to probe him. *Had She sensed anything?*

"Klavan, so glad to see you doing well. We were worried about you," Stanton bellowed as he walked in. Luckily Klavan could always tell Stanton's emotional state. He was a rosy red, which meant he was just as angry as Klavan was, but hopefully, Klavan was hiding it better.

"Yup, I am just fine. It takes a lot more than a little poison to keep me down."

"Poison, you say. So, you think you were poisoned? Could you have picked something up as you worked the loading docks there?" Stanton mussed.

"I have been working the docks too long for something to affect me like that unless it was a poison or specifically injected, especially considering no odd shipments from exotic locations came through recently."

"Maybe."

"Gentlemen, let us sit and talk. I have a special meal for you," She commanded.

"Oh yes," Staton said as he took his seat.

Klavan loved watching Stanton squirm. He had known Stanton long enough to know that odd gray hue was Stanton's worried coloring. He was so stupid Klavan could tell right away that Stanton thought She had called this meeting to poison them. Klavan had watched how She worked, and a simple poisoning was not Her way. She wanted a show; if they were to die, it would be in some dramatic way. They both were worthy of a show. Klavan just laughed inside.

She made a show of flicking Her hand in the air for everyone to see. This was the signal for the attendants to remove the lids from their trays.

Klavan was greeted with the aroma he had been smelling since he walked in, but now it hit him full force, and he was able to see the dish also. It nearly made him cry. He was greeted with the sight and smell of Trodonian eel. A dish he had not had since he was a child on his home world. This was a delicacy. Klavan had nearly forgotten about them; he just sat and took it all in.

Klavan could see Her smiling, an actual smile. She knew She had done something special.

"I am amazed. How did you know?" Klavan asked.

"As a leader, it is my job to satisfy my most important lieutenants. I have my ways of finding out about your home worlds and your pasts," She implied.

Klavan glanced over at Stanton, who was gorging on something that looked regurgitated.

"What is that?" Klavan asked.

He was asking Stanton, but he was making an absolute mess as he gobbled it down in a disgusting display of gluttony.

"That is Roshdon Hash. A special dish from Stanton's home world of Besev," She said.

Besev? Klavan had never heard of that world. He wondered what exactly Stanton was, and now he could do some research. *Has She made me aware of that for a reason? This is going to be a productive afternoon.*

"Klavan, do you not like it?" She asked.

"Oh no, I am very much looking forward to enjoying it. I am enjoying the aroma at the moment."

"A philosophical type, enjoy all aspects of a special situation. Let each sense experience it. Not an instant satisfaction type," She stated, nodding at Stanton, who was now working on his second serving of Roshdon Hash.

So, this was an experiment. She was studying them again. Was Kalvan reacting properly or putting himself in a difficult position? He realized She was always testing and probing everyone. This afternoon was about who could serve Her better and who could serve Her the best. What did She want? Did She want Klavan, a strong independent who would speak his mind a bit? Klavan knew not to do it too much. Or did She want a yes second who agreed with every decision she made? Klavan felt She was too intelligent to want a lieutenant who blindly followed Her. He would continue to be himself but did not want to give too much away. Stanton was too stupid to even worry about what this afternoon was truly about.

Klavan slowly started to taste his meal, and it was even more wonderful than he could have imagined. The eels had been cooked to the edge of medium rare. Just enough to tenderize the meat but not enough to lose that sweet, spicy flavor. Amazing spice. Balanced perfectly. Klavan was in gastronomic heaven, and he did not care about Her watching him nor the disgusting sounds nor display of the fool Stanton. Klavan had not had a pleasurable moment like this since he had left his home.

"So, I have some ideas I need to discuss with you. Klavan, you have a handful of assistants. Yet you get everything done I ask of you and more. I was unsure of the investment in the med lab, but it seems to be a wise idea. I thank you for that. You also bring a sense of decorum and class that no one else here has. You do not have the underworld nor guild connections I would expect of someone in your position. I see that as a sign that you have achieved all this with your own hard work and your dedication. That is commendable but also slightly concerning."

Klavan was listening and taking in every word She spoke, but he was enjoying his meal too much to respond.

"Stanton, on the other hand, has too much greed and blind ambition to be regarded as my second. You have too many connections in the underworld and the guilds. I have removed all your minions, so you only have your connections and your ambition to see you through. I cannot run this facility without the talents you both possess. You each have a unique set of talents. But neither has the full set I need. So, I will retain both of you as my lieutenants. Klavan, of course, will be my liaison and my cultural attaché and my number one. Stanton has the disposition to run the fights and discipline to keep everyone in check, especially with your new hires."

Stanton started to choke on his hash when She mentioned his new hires. And once again, turning that gray color he has been wearing lately.

"Relax, Fatty, I know everything that goes on around here. I have informants working the port. Your boy Boshduul is thorough but not impossible to keep tabs on. I commend you on rebuilding a solid team so quickly. That is actually why you are here. When I wiped out your boys, it was simply a test to see your reaction. Congratulations, you made the cut. We are clear then; Klavan, you run the facility; Stanton, you run the fights, and I want to see some new things. Both of you report to me."

"I am running the fights; this includes the med lab?" Stanton asked, starting to pale to a light-yellow beige tone.

"No. That is Klavan's personal project, and we know how well you and Zhuni and his team get along. You and your new team members will stay away from the med lab."

"Yes, Your Grace," Stanton replied, changing to a rosy red.

"Being my lieutenants, you may see an increase in resistance to your commands and some increase in the level of threats to you.

So, I will gift each of you with one of my guards every acta of every rotation."

"I don't need one of your guards following me around," Stanton snapped.

"No worries, they won't follow you around; you rarely move nor leave your space. They will just be in the background keeping an eye on you. Protecting you," She instructed.

"Thank You, Baroness; I appreciate the added security," Klavan voiced. *Great, so it is permanent*, Klavan thought.

"Sure, you do," Stanton blurted out.

"We are done here. You can go back to your work. Klavan, I will send the second platter down to Katool to store for you." She stood and waved them out.

"Thank You. For everything," Klavan said as he left with the guard following him.

Stanton just huffed as he left her office, glancing over his shoulder at his new friend.

---------- * ----------

"Sarge, you had asked me to look into the chemicals in the minihab we had Klavan in. I found something interesting," Mazalla told him.

"What was that? Were you able to identify anything?" Sarge inquired.

"Yes, there was a chemical that I have not been able to identify. I am not sure if it was a liquid, a gas, or a solid. There was a minute trace left in the atmosphere of the minihab. I am not sure if the majority of it was absorbed by Klavan's staff or if it was a trace amount to begin with. I am uncertain as to what it actually is. I have transmitted the information to an associate of mine on Skren to see if he can identify it," Mazalla continued.

"Do you have any ideas?" Sarge asked.

"I do not believe it is organic nor that it would have been something Klavan would have come in contact with by mistake."

"Traxon told us that Stanton had poisoned Klavan. Do you think this is the poison?"

"I could not identify any other out-of-the-ordinary substances."

"Once we identify what it is and where it is from, we may be able to identify who this assassin is and where he is from. That could give us an advantage."

"That is my hope."

"I would like to get these minihabs and the rest of the med lab emptied out as soon as possible. What do you see as a reasonable time frame?" Sarge asked.

"The majority of today's injured will be out by the end of the rotation. The fighters in minihabs two and three will be here for five or six more rotations. Kowstee should be up and ready to move out of minihab four by the end of the next rotation. The fighter in minihab five will remain here for several more rotations. That just leaves Zhuni, and I do not know if he will be up and out in a few actas, several partions, or many cycles. I cannot say."

"Good, let us just say with Zhuni, it will be a few rotations," Sarge said firmly.

"That is my hope."

"Keep me posted as we release patients. I have been up for over three rotations and am going to my quarters."

Sarge left Mazalla and started across to his quarters. He thought being in charge of the security to this med lab was going to be easy. He had been watching the perimeter of the complex and did not realize how much intrigue was involved in the interior, nor how many distinct and conflicting personalities there were. He was exhausted. The battlefields of the past were safer and less demanding than this place. He was glad to be associated with the crew here. They were all good, and Zhuni drove everyone with his respect and dedication to each of them. Sarge truly felt this was his family to protect, but it was tiring.

"Sarge," Joxby's voice squawked over the vox.

"Go."

"Rags-has-hired-several-not-so-friendly-types."

"We knew he was going to. Do you have any specific information on them?"

"Not-yet; I-will-look-into-each."

"How many?"

"Ten-total. Six-are-muscle, one-of-them-a-Swaklin."

"Interesting. What about the others?"

"One-is-scientist."

"That leaves three."

"Yes,-one-is-explosive-specialist,   one-electronic-surveillance-specialist, last-one-weapons-machinist."

"Sounds like a well-rounded team. This job just gets better and better."

"I-have-the-interviews-Rags-had-loaded. You-come-look."

"Not now. Later. I will come check out the interviews; maybe you could find out more information about who we are dealing with. Traxon still with you?"

"Yes,-will-find-out-more-information. Traxon-is-sleeping."

"Give me a few partions to get some rest. If it is important, I have the vox, but please just give me a few partions."

"I-forget-some-need-many-partions-of-sleep-a-rotation. I-only-need-half-a-partion.   I-will-bother-you-again-just-before-evening-meal. Unless-emergency. Problem-is-many-emergencies-all-rotation-long," Joxby chuckled.

"Yes, that is a problem. Thank you. Slaza will be available if you need anything."

"One-more-thing."

"Of course, there always is."

"Rags-made-a-stop-before-returning-to-Stanton."

"Okay, where was that?"

"Not-so-much-where-as-who."

"All right, *who* did he meet with?"

"The-Master."

"Wait. What?"

"Yes,-he-met-with-the-Master."

"Oh my. This is interesting. Deals, double-crosses, power struggles...always something."

"Yes,-I-am-happy-to-be-in-the-med-lab. Everyone-help-not-cause-trouble."

"Me too."

He found himself entering his quarters just as he finished the conversation. He unslung Sabaath and set it on its rack on the head-board. That bed looked so inviting. Sarge sank into the padding as he sat down on the edge. If was even more comfortable than he remembered. He would just lay back for a moment, then take his gear and boots off. He fell into a deep hard sleep without removing his gear.

———————— * ————————

Boshduul did not like the idea of the guard being at Stanton's side. This could cause an issue if the guard saw or knew more than Boshduul wanted him to see. When Boshduul had spoken with the Master and planted the idea that Klavan should have a guard, he did not expect it to include a guard for Stanton. Boshduul did get a team together using someone else's funds. This guard would just be a new challenge. The team would start work in the next few rotations. Boshduul did not see a logic to eliminating Klavan or Zhuni at this point in the game. Keep them hanging around to keep Stanton distracted. Boshduul was going to take care of other things. Stanton was a usable front and a sucker to take a fall. The Master already was certain Stanton wanted her position, but Stanton was too dumb to see the big picture the Master was working towards; Stanton thought too small. Boshduul would play Klavan and Zhuni against Stanton, then Stanton against the Master, and report all to the Master to become Her confidant. When the time was right, Boshduul would pull the strings, and while everyone was at each other's throats, Boshduul would slip away, retirement in hand and a well-paid team to work for him. This was better than he could have hoped for. This was going to be fun.

———————— * ————————

"Sarge," the vox was screeching with Joxby's voice.

"Dinner already?"

"No,-sir,-breakfast."

"What?"

"We-let-you-get-some-much-needed-sleep. We-do-not-want-you-to-end-up-like-Zhuni."

"I slept since the last rotation?"

"Yes,-no-problems-overnight."

"No emergencies? That does not seem right. You are sure."

"Much-news-no-emergencies."

"All right, thank you. I will get cleaned up, meet with Slaza and security, grab a morning meal, and come see you. To talk about the news."

"Not-just-me;-Traxon-wants-to-talk-also."

"No problem. Give me a partion."

"Okay,-see-you."

Sarge was sore. He had not removed his gear or his boots and had fallen asleep with his blaster on his hip. Sometime during the evening, he had rolled over onto it. His back was stiff. His whole body was stiff. This was going to be a long, tough day. He had not been this stiff and sore after a long sleep since he was out in the field. He was also not as young as he was when he had been out in the field. He needed to clean up, get some coffee and get moving. That usually loosened him up. He was getting old. Funny, when he was in the field fighting all those battles, he never dreamed of growing old. He smiled as he took in the soreness. Many he had fought beside would never know the feeling of getting old. He felt contentment. He was old.

Sarge slowly rose and got himself into the shower. Since he had moved to the med lab, the showers had improved tremendously, there was always plenty of hot water, and having these private quarters with his own head was a true bonus. When he was part of the team guarding the perimeter, he had his own small quarters but had to share the head with several others.

He got himself dressed, got a coffee, and started towards the main entrance to see how the evening had gone. The guards had nothing to report.

Sarge left the guards and called for Slaza. They met as Sarge headed over to see Joxby.

"You look rough, Sarge."

"Thank you, and good morning to you. I did sleep a bit longer than I had planned."

"Joxby and I felt you had a need for sleep. He wanted to let you sleep until there was an emergency or until you woke on your own. I thought this morning may be too late but figured you needed it."

"Thank you; I did need it. Do we have anything to be worried about today?"

"Around here, there is always something or someone to worry about. The only thing to report that I know of is that all of the injured in the Chordentia elimination have been released, Zhuni is still out, and Kowstee is awake and doing well."

"Well, it is early. There is still plenty of time for any number of emergencies. Good news, I will take it as often as I can get it."

"I will make the rounds as you meet with Joxby."

"Roger that; see you for late breakfast or early lunch."

"Yes, sir."

Sarge walked up to Joxby's security center.

"Sarge-looks-rested."

"Yes, I feel much better. Thank you for keeping an eye on things."

"I-told-you,-no-emergencies."

"Yes, you did."

"I-set-a-monitor-in-the-back-room-there-for-you.   I-have-interviews,-and-the-meeting-I-told-you-about-keyed-up,"   Joxby said, motioning towards what was his office.

"Thank you."

Sarge walked back, closed the door, sat down, and hit play.

He was interested to know why a Swaklin was working for Stanton's number two, who the other hires were, and most of all, what had happened in the meeting with Rags and the Master. As he watched, he realized everyone outside of med lab was out to get everyone else. Every one of them wanted to destroy the other and wanted their power, prestige, or money. They all hated each other and Klavan and Zhuni. Sarge started to wonder if they were all so evil and willing to destroy, and they all hated Klavan and Zhuni, maybe Klavan and Zhuni were very good people. He could not believe he had never taken the time to think about the people he worked for before. He had always stayed away from any type of violence; he was in the protection business. But he had never taken the time before to think about the morals of who he worked for. Strange that he should start to think about it now.

Sarge had seen the Swaklin before; he hung around the port. But Sarge did not know his name nor anything about him. He was going to learn about him.

"Sarge," Joxby was on the vox again.

"Yes?" *What could it be now?*

"I-let-Traxon-get-breakfast, I-kept-an-eye-on-him."

"What did he do?"

"Nothing,-he-just-got-back-and-desperately-needs-to-talk-to-you."

"No problem, send him in." *What could possibly be so important?* Sarge had been surprised by the amount of information Traxon had supplied. Sarge and Joxby already knew most of it or figured it out, but everything Traxon had said had checked out. If Traxon felt the information was important, it could help.

The door to the office opened, and Traxon slowly and timidly walked in. Sarge noticed Traxon was still skittish but had a more confident air than he did in the past. Maybe he was starting to feel comfortable, or maybe his plan or Stanton's was starting to work. Sarge was still unsure what to make of Traxon. Sarge could read most creatures and developed a sense of them fairly quickly, but he was having a bit of a hard time reading Traxon. He had started to like the little guy, but Sarge did not want to jeopardize security. He would continue to have Joxby keep a close eye on him.

"Good morning, sir, Sarge."

"Morning."

"What news do you have?"

"Traxon have account. Large deposit made into during evening. That means two associates hired; they tell Traxon."

"What do you mean?"

"Stanton send Traxon find specialists to hire. Stanton hire Rags. Traxon hire Sazon and Goshnel. Both hired by Rags and tell Traxon."

"You mean to tell me that you hired two individuals in the hopes that they would be hired by Stanton, and when Rags hired them for Stanton, they contacted you to let you know."

"Yes, both work for Traxon. Double work. They associates of Traxon."

"You already have two of these guys on your payroll?" Sarge questioned.

"Yes, Traxon like them and want them for him."

"You surprise me every day."

"Good?"

"Very good; in fact, you kind of scare me," Sarge said with a chuckle.

"Traxon not scary."

"No, you are not scary, just clever."

"Traxon like clever."

"Okay, so tell me about the two on your payroll."

———————— * ————————

Stanton was sure things were going better than he could have planned. The guard She had at his side was annoying. But Boshduul had gotten a team together that Stanton was certain would be a better return on his investment than Traxon and his cohorts. This was slowly coming together; soon, he would be running the facility. Soon he would be the Game Master.

Stanton did not like the fact that She had let Klavan know the name of Stanton's home world. Stanton did not even know that anyone here knew where he was from. This Master was tricky; She seemed to know or be able to find out everything.

Klavan would not be a problem; Stanton was sure Boshduul would have all angles and issues with Klavan taken care of. Stanton's concern was the Master Herself. *How is Boshduul or I going to rid ourselves of Her?* She had become so powerful in the short time She had been here. She had quickly and systematically consolidated Her power and seemed to do it with no outside assistance or ally. Stanton feared and admired Her. *What is Her next move? There was no main event schedule that I knew of for a while, so how would She gain more power?* Stanton knew the Assassins' Guild was not something She could control, nor did he think She could gain control of the Freighters' Guild as the ships' captains were too independent a group, the fact that they had a guild was more for price-setting than anything else.

What to do? How am I going to have secret meetings with Boshduul with this guard here? She is a crafty one, that is for sure. The guard was most likely recording his every breath and move for Her to study later. Boshduul had better come up with a plan.

Stanton was getting hungry. With the Chordentia gone, Stanton was having trouble finding good help. He would need Boshduul to get on this issue as well. Stanton did not like to have to chase down staff to get fed.

"Food!" he bellowed.

This was getting old.

———————— * ————————

So, the lunch had been nothing as Klavan had expected. Stanton was now a part of the inner circle of Klavan and the Master. Interesting. Also, now, knowing where Stanton came from gave Klavan and bit of leverage. *Was that the reason She had let that detail out? Besev, where was it?* Klavan would have to find out; he had never heard of it.

She was certain to have set this whole thing up to play into Her game and Her plan in some way. But why and how? What was She up to? She loved to test and divide. What was the purpose for including Stanton? Surly, She had a reason.

Klavan was headed to the med lab; he wanted to see how Zhuni was doing and to meet Kowstee. Klavan had heard that Kowstee was up and doing well. Being in the med lab may also enable him to get a moment away from the guard so Joxby could get him a commlink. Klavan had hoped Sarge had understood the reference.

The corridors of the facility had become quiet over the last couple of rotations. The main event was over, and things had settled down a great deal. Klavan knew that was not the only reason the passages were empty. With the executions of the Chordentia, few ventured out of their personal areas. Only those working on a specific and needed task were out. The Master had done exactly what She wanted, terrify the general population into submission. Instill fear, and you can control them. It was an ancient tactic.

Klavan arrived at the entrance to the med lab and was greeted by the armed guards. They contacted Sarge and granted Klavan access.

Klavan walked across the main floor, heading towards the minihabs. He glanced over at the monster, who was sleeping. Everyone said that is what it did most of the time. Klavan wondered what type of existence it was to kill and sleep. That seemed to be the only thing that monster did. Vile creature.

This would be a good time to test the guard, Klavan thought as he started to enter the control center of the minihabs.

"Stay here; only specific personnel are allowed in the center."

To Klavan's amazement, the guard took up station at the entrance to the control room and did not attempt to enter.

"Good day, Mazalla."

"Klavan, nice to see you. How are you today?"

"Well, came to check on Zhuni and maybe speak with Kowstee."

"No change currently with Zhuni, but Kowstee is awake and will be released shortly. You can go speak with him now."

"Thank you. I know you have studied biology and medicine. But I have a question for you. I do not need anyone else knowing I asked this question."

"You must be getting ready to ask an interesting question."

"Maybe. What do you know of a planet called Besev?"

"Nothing."

"Would you be able to find out information about it?"

"Of course."

"Good; the information I need is its location, information about its people, its atmosphere, food, just about any and everything you can find out."

"Why?"

"Because it is extremely important, it could seriously affect the way things are going on around here."

"I will inquire."

"Thank you."

"I will send you the information when I receive it."

Klavan nodded a thank you and walked to the minihab, which contained Kowstee.

Klavan opened the door and entered.

"Mr. Klavan, you look good."

"Thanks to you."

"How are you?"

"Ready to get out of here. I just want to get back to normal."

"You look like you are ready. I cannot thank you enough for saving my life. I am amazed someone knew what to do. It was said that you had a friend during the Morian civil war and that you saw the ritual. How did you know to do the entire ritual?"

"The friend was my best friend; I was his wingman during the conflict. When you see a friend dying and then see them saved, you do not forget."

"How is he? Did you stay in touch?"

"The reason the ritual is so vivid to me is that he was killed the next day when our hospital was bombed, and that ritual was the last time I saw him. I left the conflict then and have been running from fighting ever since."

"I am so sorry. How did you end up here?"

"I had been a pilot on a transport. We stopped off here at the spaceport to fuel up, resupply, and get another job. I went into the port to get some food and sightsee. Something went wrong during fueling, and the ship exploded. The explosion killed the fueling team and destroyed the ship. The ship's crew and I had our credits and everything on the ship. So, we were all stuck here. I decided to stay landbound, as this was actually the third ship I had been associated with that had been destroyed. So, I found a job here as a handler; I worked the loading docks and specialized in caring for the more exotic creatures."

"Third ship?"

"Yes, I had two fighters destroyed while in the Aashturian war, but those don't count. My first cruiser was attacked by pirates during a delivery. They shot our engines out, took the cargo, and left us to die. Most of the crew jettisoned with escape pods. I stayed with the ship. A local scrapper found us and salvaged the ship. The second ship had a cracked heat shield during reentry; I was lucky and was in a hardened control center. Only myself, the co-pilot, and the navigator survived."

"Maybe it is a good idea for you to stay planet bound for a while," Klavan said, smiling.

"I miss the feel of a ship. I should be out there in the stars. But life has a way of changing what you thought you were meant to do. Plus, you know here, everyone is a slave in some way."

"I thought you found a job here."

"Oh yeah, but I was hired by Stanton and did not read nor understand the fine print. It was written in a language I did not understand. And I am basically a slave to the facility. I would have been better off being killed in the explosion. My only way to freedom again is to have the Brynja Ajal grant it to me."

"Well, now, that is an interesting contract you signed. I owe you my life, so I will see what I can do for you. In the meantime, rest up and know you are now a part of the med lab."

"Until they send the Brynja Ajal back to its dungeon."

"We will see."

Klavan left Kowstee and the minihabs and started to look for Sarge. He would have already made first rounds; he wasn't in the minihabs, and Klavan did not see Sarge by the monster. That left three possible locations, his quarters, the mess hall, or possibly the security control room. When the main entrance guards spoke to him, he responded so Klavan figured Sarge must be in security. That would not be a good place to take his shadow, so Klavan decided to walk over to look at the beast until Sarge was free.

*

The cloaked figure was surrounded by monitors and a hand full of other cloaked figures.

"This cannot stand! It must be dealt with!"

A voice from one monitor spoke up, "What do you propose?"

"Eliminate her." The cloaked figure said.

"This would be the normal course of action. But we are not in a normal situation. Never before has the Game Master been the head of a guild. We all know we cannot eliminate a guild master; that is in our laws to protect the integrity of our guilds," the raspy voice replied from a different monitor.

"But she killed Droughlok."

"This is true, but our bylaws are what keep the guilds strong. And She was not a guild master when She killed Droughlok. She was the Game Master. If one of the guild masters breaks the law, that is for the chamber of masters to deal with. We need to call a chamber meeting and allow them to decide. We do not need to start a guild war."

"Wonderful sentiment, my brother, but the Game Master holds four votes herself. How do you suggest we overcome this little detail?" from the original monitor.

"We would have the Thieves' Guild with us, the Renegade Guild, and the Freighters' Guild. That would give us a matched vote. The Commerce Guild is always in question; they go with the guilds they feel will be the most profitable."

"We still have one guild."

This simple statement seemed to shock everyone as there was a collective gasp.

Then all the monitors started to speak.

"They have not been involved nor even heard from in far too long; they ignore our requests for communication."

"Of course they do; they were betrayed by all the guilds."

"They are still out there operating as a separate and independent guild, but no one knows where they are nor how to contact them."

"We do not need them nor want their involvement."

"If any guild could bring them back, it would be the Assassins' Guild."

"The Hunters' Guild was the most honorable of the guilds and stood strong during the Wreckoning."

Several voices in unison, "Yes."

There was silence for a moment. Then a cloaked figure from the back stepped forward. He wore a cloak made of a rough material in a dark greyish-brown color. It did not have the pitch-black sheen of the other cloaks.

"I implore you to listen to me. You spoke of us as an honorable guild. We have been silent for a long time, and the guilds have had no need of our involvement. We see this Game Master as a threat to the guilds and realize our time has come to be involved. As a representative of the Hunters Guild, I have been sent to assist with negotiations to reconnect with our brothers. We understand the seriousness of this situation and have been watching the Game Master. We have representatives with the other guild masters and councils seeking collective agreement. We were betrayed by our brothers long ago but never left your sides. The Hunters' Guild will stabilize the guilds once again in the ancient way. And according to the ancient way, we bring friends and allies."

A shocked silence settled over the meeting as those in attendance and those on the monitors realized the gravity of this day.

———————— * ————————

Over three hundred and fifty full cycles ago, the guilds were attacked by the coalition of civilized planets. The Coalition demanded the guilds become part of the coalition's trade agreement or dissolve. The coalition was strong and first attacked with trade agreements and financial gifts. The Hunters' Guild warned the other guilds that they all were under attack and needed to stand together or lose their freedom. The other guilds just laughed and took the money and the deals. Slowly they realized they had been had and attempted to extract themselves from these deals. But the coalition applied blockades and then attacked with their powerful militaries. The Commerce Guild saw great financial greed and jumped on board quickly. The Freighters' Guild fell quickly as they never hid their center of operations. The Miners' Guild was difficult to track down, but after many of their main operations were attacked, they lacked the willpower and recourses to continue the fight. The Smugglers' Guild held on a bit longer but realized the coalition controlled a large amount of space that the guild used to operate in and gave in to become a shipping union for the coalition. The Thieves' Guild just dissolved under the pressure. The Renegade Guild was never an actual guild; they were more of a planet system that had joined with multiple talents and skills; they sort of fit all of the other guilds' abilities, so they just became an independent guild representing a system of several planets. The Assassins' Guild stood strong as the coalition could not locate their home planet or base of operations. The Hunters' Guild found out about an attack planned on the Renegade Guild and prepared to cut off the attack and defend the Renegade planetary system. The Assassins' Guild saw an opportunity to get on the coalition's good side without any harm coming to them and warned the coalition of the defensive plans of the Hunters' and Renegade Guilds. Even with this knowledge, the battle hung by a thread, each side gaining a momentary advantage and then losing it. It started to sway in the Hunter's and Renegade's favor and was going to be a major victory for the guilds, possibly returning them to their former glory. But then the betrayal. The Assassins' Guild appeared on the battle scene, and in an instant, the Hunters knew the battle was won. But instead of completing the destruction of the coalition, the Assassins' fleet turned their weapons on the Hunters, and the battle was lost. The Assassins' Guild had made a deal with the coalition to remain the lone independent guild and betrayed them all. This became known as the "Wreckoning."

Seventy-five short cycles later, the coalition folded under its own massive weight and disappeared. Over the next fifty cycles, the guilds were rebuilt as the Assassins' Guild remained strong and used its influence to rebuild. But none of the Hunters' Guild would acknowledge the new creation. So, it has been for more than two hundred cycles.

———————— * ————————

She knew she put a scare into the Assassins' Guild. They knew She had killed Droughlok, but She was certain they would not want another guild war. They had become passive and content with the current conditions. But with her having four votes on the chamber of Masters, the other guilds did not have the votes to beat her. She was in the driver's seat. She was certain She could, at the very least, hold Her position, but with some more persuasion, She may be able to get the votes she needed to control the guilds. There were eight guilds, well, nine if you counted the Hunters' Guild, but they were no longer involved and had not been since the other guilds betrayed them. Of course, they could always invoke the tyrant clause, but it was so old and buried in the ancient bylaws She doubted anyone even knew it existed. Even if they did, they would have to notify properly.

Even if the Hunters' Guild did come back, She was sure She would be able to persuade the Commerce Guild to see the profits She and Her organization could bring in, which would give Her the votes She needed.

She was pleased with the situation. Things were going better than she had planned and moving along much faster than She had thought they would.

Stanton was easy to control and read, and Klavan was more or less on board; She wasn't quite sure with him. He, at times, seemed to fully understand Her methods and results, and other times seemed lost. He was too competent to make these mistakes. She was certain he was much more involved with the behind-the-scenes than he led on. She felt he had to be watched closely. It was a wise decision to listen to some of the thoughts Boshduul had, especially the idea of having a guard follow both on a daily basis.

She was surprised at how efficient and tricky Boshduul was. *Was it a wise hire by Stanton, or was it a wise decision by Boshduul to be hired by Stanton?* There were so many intriguing situations happening here that it made Her smile. Everyone was somehow pitted against each other, and She knew with enough hatred and anger among the help, She could easily control them all. Keep them divided, and they would be off-balance and easier to control.

The only player She was unsure of was the human Zhuni; he did not care about the power struggles at all. *How could someone not care about power?* He had a loyal group working for him, and that gave Her concern. *With no desire for power, what was his game?* He did not seem concerned by credits either. Neither power nor money was important. *Were all humans this way?* She knew the humanish were all about power and control or greed or lust, but Zhuni was more concerned about the health and well-being of those around him. *What would that gain him? What kind of game was he playing?* He may have no bearing whatsoever on the whole power balance here. He was just a young human with no ambition. That was all he was. But he did his job well, and the med lab was running well, even with him out of the picture for the time being.

*

"Good to see you, sir," Sarge said as he reached out to shake Klavan's hand.

"Nice to see you again," Klavan responded with an outstretched hand and an inquisitive look on his face.

Their hands met, and Klavan understood the handshake immediately. He now held an earpiece and a couple of other tiny electronic devices.

"So, how are things going?" Klavan asked.

"As well as could be expected. We have been able to get the majority of the casualties moved along, and Zhuni is not getting worse. Our guest is full of surprises."

"Really? Such as?"

"He is a plethora of information, and he is an embezzler."

"Wow, really. And from whom has he removed funds?"

"You will love this. For many cycles, he has been skimming off all payments, incoming and outgoing, of your colorful buddy."

"Years? The monster. I must say it could not happen to a better guy," Klavan chuckled.

"He is proving to be a character. I believe he has found a home and truly wants to help. But he needs to improve his hygiene; he stinks."

"Work with him; he has had it tough."

"I know I am amazed at his resourcefulness and his resilience."

"Anything you feel I need to know before we call it a night?"

"No, sir, we got it all covered here."

"I will give you a bit of info you may need to know. The Master has made me Her number two, and as such, I may be busy more often; you and Zhuni may be more on your own as time goes by. I will be in your corner, and She has assured Stanton and me that the med lab is still under my authority and that Stanton and his crew are to stay away for the med lab."

"Good to know."

"Let me know if you need anything; I will be watching out for you guys. And let me know if there are any changes with Zhuni."

"Will do."

"Come on, Skippy," Klavan said to his sidekick, then turned and headed to the main gate.

Sarge began his evening rounds.

———————— * ————————

Boshduul thought about it for a while and felt the key to the entire power struggle and game of control was the one no one expected. Zhuni. He was the key. Klavan loved him and would do anything to protect him, Stanton hated him and would do anything to destroy him, and the Master underestimated him and thought he had no drive to be more than he was. But Boshduul saw it differently. If Boshduul could twist the truth enough in the perception of each player, he could have them all fighting over Zhuni, and that would be his chance to make things happen; after all, everyone wants some power or riches; Boshduul just had to figure out what drove Zhuni. He could use Tan'cha or that Swaklin.

All who worked at the games had respect for Zhuni; most even cared for him. Especially the slaves and indentured staff. Some of the guards and dock workers hated him, he was a pure human, and they were humanish, but even they respected him. Interesting for an individual who held no rank, no finances, or special education to be so respected and hated by so many. But he did not seem to care; he just went about helping those he could. He still showed respect and care for those who despised him. The thought of one caring so much for others unsettled Boshduul. It was something he did not comprehend. But he knew this could be the key to the power struggle. *How can I make it work against Zhuni?*

---------------- * ----------------

Klavan returned to his quarters with his guard in tow.

"I am going to turn in shortly; you may go."

The guard did not respond. He just stood by the door to Klavan's private chambers as a statue.

"I guess you are here for the night; all right then."

Klavan went to his bedroom, grabbed his night clothes, and entered his restroom. He removed the electronics from his pocket, which Sarge had provided him with. He inserted what looked like an earpiece.

"Well,-good-evening,-Mister-Klavan."

"Joxby?"

"Yes,-sir,-I-will-explain-the-equipment-we-have-provided-you-with-and-the-proper-way-to-use-it."

"Thank you."

"Your-earpiece-is-a-two-way-communication-device."

"I figured that out."

"Yes,-but-it-is-self-charging-and-as-a-Septorian-in-side-your-ear-canal,-you-have…have-an-artery-that-rests-against-the-ear-piece-this-pulse-will-keep-the-earpiece-charged."

"Brilliant."

"Thank-you,-sir. You-also-will-see-the-tiny-case-with-a-clear-slightly-concave-circle."

"Yes."

"This-is-a-contact-camera-that-you-will-place-over-your-eyeball,-and-it-must-be-under-your-protective-lense,-or-it-will-not-operate-properly."

"I hate things in my eyes."

"Just-get-it-under-your-tough-protective-lense,-and-it-will-be-fine."

"You do know how difficult that is; our natural reflex is to close that lens with any intrusion."

"I-do."

"How do you suggest I do that?"

"It-may-take-a-few-attempts,-but-I-believe-you-will-figure-it-out."

"Will I have to do this every time I put the camera in?"

"No,-sir;-once-you-put-it-in,-you-will-not-have-to-remove-it-unless-you-want-to;-it-is   designed-to-use-the-fluids-in-your-eye-as-the-electrolyte-to-keep-the-charge."

"Again, brilliant."

"Thank-you,-sir;-another-thing-your-earpiece-is-connected-cryptically-to-our-med   lab-vox. When-you-are-not-connected-to-the-vox,-I-will-be-your-connection-and-recording.-To-connect-to-the-vox,-just-say,-'Vox-on';-to-disconnect,-say,-'Vox-off.'"

"Great, so I will never have any privacy again; between you and my shadow, someone will always be watching."

"Actually,-sir,-Sarge-told-me-to-allow-you-full-control;-so-for-you-to-shut-the-equipment-off,-all-you-need-to-do-is-say,-'System-off-now',-and-you-will-shut-everything-down;-then-simply-say,-'System-on,-restart,'-and-the-system-wil-come-back-on-line."

"Thank you, Joxby."

"You-are-welcome,-sir,-have-a-good-night."

CHAPTER 8

Learning From a Drazine

"Sarge,-Kowstee,-and-Ohmdod…"

"What is it, Joxby?"

"Kowstee-turned-off-the-force-generator-and-is-in-cage."

"What? This is not how I wanted to start my morning!"

"Me-either."

Sarge threw his boots on, wrapped them, grabbed a shirt, threw it on, grabbed Sadbaath, and rushed out the door.

He arrived at the cage to see Kowstee climbing on the creature; Ohmdod was on the other side of the beast. Slazan just arrived also, as did too many others, including two heavy response teams in full load out and nearly the entire security team.

Sarge was pleased with his security teams; he had not had to call them. They reacted to the vox.

"What the Dagz are you doing?" Sarge yelled at Kowstee.

"My job," Kowstee responded.

"Your job entails shutting down the force generator and putting everyone in danger?"

"Relax, Sarge; this is what I do."

"*No*! Get out here!"

"You seem upset; why?"

"Why? *Why*? Are you serious? You shut down the force generator and exposed us all to the very real danger of that thing breaking out."

"I am sorry, sir. You do not understand. I will come out and explain to you."

"Yes, you will, and *now*!"

"Yes, sir."

Kowstee climbed down from the beast and walked over to the bars, stepped through them, and stood before Sarge; Slazan threw the force generator back on.

"What is wrong with you? Did that procedure you did on Klavan cause some brain damage? Why would you risk your life like that? And put everyone else in danger?"

"I am sorry you are so concerned, but I assure you this is what I have been doing since I began working with her."

"Her? This thing is a her? How do you know and why would you turn the force generator off?"

"Well, I honestly do not know if it is a her or not, but it seems to be a her to me; I have to check her for injuries and ensure she is okay. As I said, she is not dangerous. She is actually gentle."

"So, you just walk in there? Nothing to worry about?"

"No, not at all. The only time she is destructive is when the Master controls her. She is docile the rest of the time. I will show you, turn the generator off, and if you are nervous, just turn it on when I am in." Ohmdod just watched the interaction with a puzzled look.

Sarge paused and looked over at Slazan. Slazan shrugged and reached for the force generator switch. Sarge nodded. Slazan threw it off.

Kowstee looked at them and calmly walked back into the cage. Slazan looked at Sarge, who nodded, and Slazan turned it back on.

Kowstee walked around the creature, looking it over carefully, followed by Ohmdod. Kowstee climbed up on its hind quarters and checked it closely. He said he wanted a plasma fusing kit to repair a scale. He then climbed down her side to her long neck and jumped down. He looked over at Sarge.

"Get the plasma fuser, please."

Sarge looked around and saw a maintenance staff member and told him to grab the plasma fuser.

"Thank you," Kowstee responded.

Kowstee then headed over to the creature's mouth and pushed the lower jaw down so he could look into it. He climbed into the massive mouth and disappeared. Everyone gasped and looked at Sarge. He just shrugged his shoulders, not sure what to make of it. Then Kowstee reappeared and asked for a ceramasteel saw and some bars. He then walked to stand in front of the creature's face and signaled for it to roll over. That is when everyone realized the creature was awake. More incredibly, the monster rolled over. Now Kowstee inspected this side of the behemoth for damage.

Kowstee walked over to Sarge and asked for a hand.

"I need someone much stronger than me to get something out of her teeth. During the fight, she had a plasma rifle jammed in between two teeth, and it will take a saw to cut it or bars and strength to remove it."

"And you want me to climb in its mouth to get it?"

"Yes."

"Give me an acta or twelve."

"No problem; while you think about it, Ohmdod and I will repair the scale on her other side." He looked over at Slazan, who shut the generator off. Kowstee walked over, grabbed the plasma fuser, and went back to the monster. He showed it to the monster, signaled for it to roll over, and as it did, he went to the hind quarter he had looked at earlier, climbed up on it, and fired up the fuser. He applied it to a cracked scale. The scale started to glow red, then yellow, and finally white. Ohmdod then applied the tightening tools and closed the crack in the scale. Kowstee turned off the plasma fuser and walked over to Sarge.

"Well?"

"Yea."

Sarge slowly walked into the cage, following Kowstee.

They reached the front of the massive beast; it looked down at Sarge with a look Sarge could only describe as inquisitive. Sarge was surprised as it lowered its head and laid its downside ways, as directed by Kowstee. Kowstee then explained to Sarge what needed to be done and pulled the creature's enormous jowl open to show

Sarge what needed to be removed. Sarge could see the plasma rifle twisted between two huge teeth about halfway into the mouth.

"So, you need me to climb in there, place the pry bar between the two teeth, and pry them apart?"

"Yes, and I will remove the rifle, but do not pry too hard; you could damage her tooth."

"Great."

Sarge and Kowstee both climbed into the mouth.

"Okay, Sarge, now ram that bar in just below the rifle; pry towards the front of the mouth so if you slip, you will not get stuck in her throat and choke her."

"What, you are worried about me hurting her? Are you being serious?"

"Yes."

"Okay, here we go."

"Good, more. The rifle is looser, but I can't get it yet. Apply more pressure and steady. Come on, more, more…almost got it. A bit more."

"I am going to give it a good jam this time, be ready. Three, two, one."

"Got it!"

With that, they crawled out of the creature's mouth to the applause of those who had gathered around.

Sarge turned to Kowstee.

"I do not know if that was the bravest or the dumbest thing I have ever done. I feel great."

The creature raised its head, looked at Sarge, and bowed its head as if to say thank you.

"Did it just thank us?"

"Yes, she did, Sarge."

"Amazing."

"Puts her in a new light, doesn't it? Imagine if she was not controlled and forced to act so violently."

"You do not think a creature like her is naturally violent?"

"I think it is made for violence and can become violent, but I do not think that is its nature."

"It sure did a number on that rifle," Sarge said as he took the twisted rifle from Kowstee.

Sarge grabbed the rifle and the pry bar and headed out of the cage. Kowstee signaled to Ohmdod to remove the clamps and to retrieve the plasma fuser. Kowstee then returned everything but the ceramasteel saw; he walked to the creature's hind feet and began sawing at the claws.

"Now, what are you doing?" Sarge asked.

"Neatening up her claws, usually after an event, there are some cracks and gouges in them."

Sarge stepped out of the cage and looked over to Slazan.

"That was incredible," Slazan stated.

"It was."

———————— * ————————

"We are in agreement then."

As one voice, all monitors responded with a yes.

"The Hunters' Guild is back and, as an original member, will have a full vote and a seat in the Masters' chambers. With the Hunters' Guild back, the guilds now have the original ten guilds. The guilds will have equal votes as before. With this, we once again have a proper balance of power. She can vote however she wants, but we will overcome her power grab. For the guilds to survive, we must come together, forget our past, and move on," the mediator stated.

"No. We should never forget what has happened in our past. If we do, we may repeat those same mistakes. We need to remember and forgive. We need to build on our past. To strengthen our hand, we may need to introduce other forms of security," said the representative from Hunters' Guild.

"We may need to call in or create new guilds; this Master is a serious threat to our ability to survive as properly operating guilds; a war may be brewing even as we attempt to stop it. The time has come for us to decide our true intentions and our allies. Not all forces in this game will have guild members. This could become an intergalactic issue greater than the Aashturian Civil War, and we must prepare," the Hunters' Guild representative continued.

"If it means war, so be it, we must prepare, and we must stand strong," a voice over one of the monitors stated.

"We need to prepare and place ourselves on a war footing, but we also must be prepared for peace; talks and negotiations should continue with Her. We still need to inform Her officially of the rebuilding of the ten guilds. To save the guilds, we must follow the original charters," a faceless voice from another monitor said.

"Make preparations as you see fit for war; it is coming. May our bonds remain true and strong," the Hunters' Guild representative continued.

"Aye," came the voices from the monitors.

The Hunter had his doubts about this new organization, but his Master had warned him. This was their chance. They would come out of this the most powerful guild and would be able to gain the peace they sought.

————— * —————

She could not believe they had the audacity to reform the original ten guilds. She had not anticipated this. Impressed, they had outmaneuvered Her. It was time for Her to get serious. She still had the four votes, and with the Commerce Guild, She felt She could swing the tying vote. But She needed more than a tie. Maybe mediation would not work. Up to now, She had played the political game of finesse. Power was Her tool, and it was time to up Her game. This was not getting the results as quickly as She wanted. Power and control of the guilds were the goal. A guild war would not benefit Her in any way, but coercion to bend the wills of the masters would be needed.

Taking control of the Gamers' Guild, drug cartel, and Smugglers' Guild had been easy. The Miners' Guild had also been easy; greed and power often cloud individuals' minds. Using that as leverage was easy, and Moz was easy to control. The Freighters' Guild was going to be a hard sale, they had always been such a loose coalition, and no one knew who their Master was nor where they were, but if She could just get them on board, She would be in the driver's seat. The Assassins' Guild now hated Her and would take a major investment She did not have time for. The Hunters' Guild came in without Her knowledge, so they were not going to be coming into play. The Renegade Guild may also be an option, they had been betrayed and left for dead, but somehow, they had survived. This impressed Her. They would be worth looking into also.

But She needed to act on Her quickest investment. She would call in other investments She had made and use those as leverage. Leverage in the form of threats, violence, and/or death was Her forte.

As She thought about it, She realized this would be a more enjoyable way to get things done. The more death She dealt, the quicker the results.

Yes, this was the way She operated the best. First, ensure Her control of the Commerce Guild, then get the controlling vote. Her position as the Game Master gave her a moderator's vote, and as such, She only needed five of the ten guilds. Her vote would swing a tie.

———————— * ————————

Stanton could not believe the news; the Hunters' Guild had returned. Now the Master would need two more guilds to control. He had connections with the Commerce Guild and could match their greed. If he could deliver that, he would be in for a great reward.

Stanton could see it all working. Boshduul had built the new team, and being Stanton was Her lieutenant, he could just ride Her coat tails until it was time to strike. If he could help Her get that extra guild master under Her control, Stanton would be highly and rightfully rewarded. Then he and Boshduul could strike and control the guilds simply by removing Her. Power greater than Stanton had ever dreamed. Get Her the power she desired, then destroy Her, and the guilds would be forever in his debt.

It was far too good to be true.

———————— * ————————

Joxby sounded more excited than usual as he screamed over the vox.

"Mazalla-said-He-is-awake!"

"Zhuni is back?" Sarge asked.

"Yes,-yes!"

"I am on my way." Sarge ran from his quarters and bolted across the med lab.

Word traveled instantly in the med lab. Sarge arrived to a crowd of others gathered around minihab six. He had to push his way through.

Mazalla smiled across the crowd when she saw Sarge.

"He is fine and fully awake. Go in," Mazalla said

Sarge opened the minihab and walked in to see Zhuni sitting up and smiling.

"What am I doing here? Why is everyone staring at me?" Zhuni asked.

"Welcome back; you had us all scared there for a while," Sarge told him.

"What do you mean? How long have I been out?"

"Three rotations. What is the last thing you remember?"

"I am not sure; I have been having these amazing dreams. Where is She?"

"Who?"

"Abijah."

"Who is Abijah?"

"She is the Drazine. She has been talking to me for rattons."

"Rattons, Zhuni, you have been out for three rotations. You passed out when the monster glared at you. It looked at you, and you just dropped. What are you talking about?"

Zhuni started to get up and out of the bed.

Sarge pushed him back down.

"You need to relax. You have been in a coma for the last three rotations."

"No, I need to get up and speak to Her."

Zhuni stood and pushed Sarge aside.

"Either join me or get out of the way; I need to do this."

"Okay, I will give you a hand. Put your arm around me; let's go," Sarge said as he assisted Zhuni out of the minihab.

The crowd parted and watched as Sarge and Zhuni made their way to Brynja Ajal.

"Joxby, get ahold of Klavan; let him know Zhuni is back," Sarge said.

"Will-do."

Brynja Ajal was already turned to watch them as they came across the med lab.

"Do you hear Her?" Zhuni asked.

"Are you all right? I do not hear anything," Sarge replied.

"What? You can't hear that?"

"Nope, I don't hear anything."

"Her name is Abijah. She is a Drazine. She is not a monster. She has shown me her world and has spoken to me. She is speaking to me now; I am getting a headache, but I need to see her."

"I am right beside you; we will do this together," Sarge told him, and they stood by the cage, looking up at her. She was focused on Zhuni just as before.

He could hear her. They spoke to each other. No one else could hear them.

"Why can no one else hear you?" Zhuni asked.

"You are one of the few pure humans left in the entire galaxy. You were the first race. The Ancients. We, the Drazine, were created to protect your world; as new races were created, more of us were created to protect the worlds. Humans have always had the ability, as the first race, to speak to us. Ancients of your race spread out into the galaxy; some were good and spread life, others were evil and spread hate. He destroyed your world, as foretold in the ancient book. For a thousand cycles, your world was kept in the death throws until all evil had been removed and those who spread life were protected. Your world had been cleaned. Those of you who survived and spread life continued; those who spread evil began to change their biology through science and interbreeding with other races to attempt to create a better, stronger race. But over time, these other races became known as humanish and never were true races; they became evil and twisted, and yet today continue to attempt to create a 'better race.' But that which was created by him will continue; that which is twisted will eventually rot away or be destroyed."

"I have seen the visions you sent me. Are they real? I am an ancient?"

"We Drazine have a collective memory; everything we have done, everything we have seen, everything we have learned is in each other's mind. The history of the galaxy we hold. The visions you have seen are the truth I have shared. You have seen and will see the history of races long gone and yet unknown. You are an ancient, the first race."

"Why?"

"We know the past, but we do not know the why. Our purpose is to protect life and worlds. We defend the weak. We are built to destroy evil, but our nature is to nurture and protect."

"Why do you kill in the arena?"

"I have been operated on and been surgically altered. I do not have control over myself when in the arena; they have somehow tapped into my violence and have control." As she said this, she lowered her head and twisted her neck to show the implant at the base of her skull.

"I can remove it," Zhuni informed her.

"I know, but we cannot let Her know."

"We can remove the part in your head and leave the exterior case so She will not know. Can you control yourself if we do this?"

"I do believe so. My memory does not show any of us as out of control. We are calm, discerning, controlled protectors."

"Then, as soon as I have my full wits about me, we will put you into a scanner, and I will remove that."

"Yes, I am sorry about your time away from your family. I overloaded you with visions; I have never been in the presence of an ancient and could not figure out how much you would accept at first."

"I am fine; it will take me a few rotations to collect my thoughts, and hopefully, my head will stop spinning."

"I have taken these three rotations to understand your ability to accept our connection. I have already eased back, and that is why you are awake. We will learn each other's abilities, and you will have the ability to communicate and soon have dominion over me as it should be. We were created for you."

"I am supposed to control you?"

"No, you are to command me. We were created to protect you, and as such, we need to be able to communicate and understand."

"I believe I understand. The visions you gave me were of my ancient world, our history, your history, our shared purpose."

"Yes, and our purpose is more important now. We must prepare for action. We will be called home to defend our world soon."

"Our world, I thought you said it was destroyed."

"Your world was destroyed, but our world needs to be defended; the time is coming."

"I need some rest; this is exhausting. I need to connect with my team and tell them what is happening."

"You are using a major part of your brain you have never used before. You will train your brain to continue our conversations. The more we speak, the easier it will be. Your brain is tired and needs some rest. We will continue to speak, but for now, we will stop. Connect with your family, and we will speak when you are rested."

"Family. I have no family."

"No, you have a large loyal family more than willing to die for you. You know in your heart the med lab is your family. You have created an amazing family that loves each other and will do all they can to protect and care for each other. You are spreading life. You have created a family in the ancient way and by the ancient rule."

"What is the ancient way and the ancient rule."

"Simply; to serve and to love."

"I am sorry you are here in this place and having to deal with this."

"Do not be troubled; there is a reason we are here at this time."

---

*

Klavan was worried about the entire power struggle going on right now with the Master. If She could gain two more guilds, she could swing everything in Her favor and Her mediating vote as the Game Master. No Game Master had gained control of a guild before. Now she was two guilds from complete control. The way She was gaining guilds, it would not be long. But with the hunters back, She would have some difficulty. There had been word that the Assassins' Guild master had been assassinated, and the guild was currently in turmoil. The timing of this could not be worse unless it had been planned. Klavan knew he had to do whatever he could to prevent Her from gaining any other guild. How could he achieve this? If he could prevent Her from even gaining one guild, that would make it more difficult for Her to gain the two she needed. The Commerce Guild would see profit in Her and most likely join Her. That would leave one guild, and which was most likely to join Her group. It would have to be the Thieves' Guild or the Freighters' Guild. Klavan had had dealings with the Freighters' Guild, so that would be where he would start. Who was that ship's captain he had spoken with? What was the ship's name? He could not remember. He would have to sleep on it.

Before turning in for an early night, he thought he would check in and see how the med lab was doing. He said good night to his shadow and retired to his sleeping chamber.

"System on, restart."

He was quite surprised to hear Joxby screaming at him.

"Mister-Klavan,-he-is-okay!"

"Mister-Klavan,-please-respond!"

Joxby sounded more anxious than usual.

"Calm down, Joxby; who is okay? What happened?"

"Zhuni-is-awake-and-walking-around-with-Sarge;-they-are-talking-to-the-monster," Joxby happily yelled.

"That is wonderful; I am on my way there. Wait, what did you say?"

"Zhuni-is-awake."

"I got that; what else?"

"He-is-walking-with-Sarge"

"Joxby!"

"They-are-talking-to-the-monster."

"What do you mean they are talking to the monster?"

"Zhuni-and-Sarge-walked-to-the-cage,-and-Sarge-said-Zhuni-is-talking-to-monster."

"Unbelievable."

"I-am-watching,-I-believe."

"I am on my way."

*

Klavan arrived at the med lab with his sidekick in tow.

"Mister Klavan, Zhuni is awake and resting in his quarters."

"Mister Klavan, did you hear the news?"

"Klavan, I will get you through," Slaza said as he weighed his way through the crowd to Klavan.

Slaza pushed through as many clapped Klavan on the back in jubilation. The mood of all was better than Klavan had seen since the Med lab had been created.

"Your bodyguard and I will stay outside to keep the crowds in check," Slaza stated as he opened the door to the quarters and gestured Klavan in. Then closed the door behind him.

"Klavan, glad you could join us," Zhuni said with a huge smile.

"I hope you have a long time; Zhuni has been telling me one amazing story," Sarge said as he rose to give Klavan the seat closest to the bed.

"Really?" Klazan asked.

"Oh yes," Sarge said.

"Do tell," Klavan said, looking at Zhuni.

"Let me start at the beginning. When Abijah came into the med lab."

"Who is Abijah?" Klavan asked.

"Abijah is Brynja Ajal's name."

"You can talk to it?"

"I wouldn't say I talk to her; it is more our minds connect, and we can communicate. It is as if she is in my head, and I am in hers, and we talk to each other that way."

"Telepathy, that is what we call that," Klavan stated.

"Abijah attempted to speak to me when she first came in but was not used to communicating with me, so she overpowered my mind and caused me to pass out."

"See, I told you she caused him to pass out," Sarge affirmed.

"Yes, I remember you saying that," Klavan remembered.

"Anyway, as I was saying!" Zhuni broke in.

"Oh yes, sorry, do continue." Klavan laughed.

Sarge just shook his head.

"Thank you. Where was I? Oh yes. As I was out, she sent me visions of the worlds she saw, and she explained a lot to me."

"Such as," Klavan asked.

"This is where it gets interesting," Sarge said.

"Well, to begin with, she told me that humans were the first race created. We are called the Ancients. The Drazine were meant to protect us. Drazine have been sent to every world to protect the life on that world."

"Protect life from what?" Klavan asked.

"That is the same thing I asked," Sarge said.

"It is a good question," Klavan continued.

"Do you have any idea how hard it is to tell you two a story? I am sure it would be straight-up impossible if Tan'Cha was here," Zhuni said with frustration.

"Oh yes, that reminds me, I need to speak with the Master about Tan'cha. I should be able to get him back here quickly now that you are up and about," Sarge quipped.

"Can I continue?" Zhuni asked.

"Oh, sorry," Sarge said.

Zhuni glared at him and continued.

"So, the Drazine were to protect the Creator's world and those worlds He created. At the time of the creation, the Creator made Drazine be His guards and citizens of the realm. But one of His most trusted became drunk with the idea of power and turned many. It is said a quarter to a third of the Drazine turned to his side and attempted to overthrow the Creator. The battle was titanic and caused the turned Drazine to finally flee. No one knows where they are, but the Creator turned the remaining Drazine into protectors of the new worlds He created. The first world was the human world. This was His first and most loved world, but once again, those created became greedy for power. They turned against the Drazine whenever they encountered them, seeing them as monsters. In fact, they created a new word for them and called them Dragons. The Dragons were hunted down wherever they were found. This saddened and angered the Creator, and with their own inequities and sins over time, He destroyed the human planet and went about creating new life, and, on every world, He sent the Drazine. Many humans left the home world before the thousand cycles of the planet's death throws. Many of these humans attempted to use their scientists to create a mixed race of part human and part other races to create a physically more powerful race. Some even breed with different creatures in the attempt to form a stronger race. These peoples became known as they are today, humanish. Few of us remain, the Ancients, pure-blooded humans."

"There is one Creator of everything? Just one God? We all have a God or gods in our races' culture. Are they all the same God?" Klavan asked.

"No. There is but one God. The Creator. According to Abijah, many cultures have many gods, but there is only one," Zhuni stated.

"So, how do we know which one is real?" Klavan asked.

"The one true God is a God of help, service, and life. He created life; He does not want to destroy it. He has given us all the common and universal morals we have as a foundation for our worlds. Serve each other and care for others. Do not lie, do not cheat, do not kill; these are some of the basic laws He laid down for all," Zhuni responded.

"You mean a god of war or destruction is bad?" Sarge asked.

"Yes. The one true God is a creator, not a destroyer. The destroyer is the Drazine, who started the power struggle in the beginning. He is lurking out there, attempting to cause death and destruction, chaos and hate. These are the things that will cause you to draw away from the Creator, the one true God."

"We Swaklin have always worshipped a god of war as our major god. But we have a minor god of peace and family. She is said to be a weaker god but one we need to speak with," Sarge interjected.

"From my understanding with Abijah, that would be the true God. She would be the one you speak to. Your culture still sees dishonor in killing for no reason other than to protect yourselves, lying and cheating as dishonorable also, correct?" Zhuni asked.

"Yes. Our minor god, Elisha, we call her, is the true God?" Sarge asked.

"Are you getting religious, Sarge?" Klavan asked.

"I am not sure. I do know I have seen changes with everyone here in med lab since we have all been working with Zhuni. He seems to be the epitome of service. He is always putting others in front of his needs; he respects everyone, no matter their place. I believe I have been learning the traits of this God working with an ancient, as he is called," Sarge said seriously.

"Wise words, my friend; I believe you are correct. We are seeing the heart of God in this human," Klavan replied.

"Wait a minute; I am just telling you what Abijah told me. I am not all that. I am just a medic," Zhuni said timidly.

"No, Zhuni, you are much more, and I have known that since I picked you up at the spaceport. You have always been different in the way you carry yourself and the way you treat others. We all are better for spending time with you," Klavan spoke.

"I do not exactly agree with your interpretation, but you believe what you want to believe. To answer your question, Sarge, I would say yes. Elisha would be a god of family, peace, protection, and love?"

Sarge nodded.

"Then yes, she would be the representation of the true God. But the Creator is more a father not a female," Zhuni said.

"But to be sure, we could speak with Abijah," Sarge implied.

"This is fascinating, and I would love to continue this discussion, but I still must deal with the Master. I will go let Her know you are back, and I am sure She will want you to get back to work immediately. She will most likely make a visit. I advise all in the med lab to say nothing of this, no one. We do not want Her to know you can communicate with the monster," Klavan advised.

"Klavan, Abijah is not a monster," Zhuni lashed out.

"Tell that to all those it has killed in the arena," Klavan snapped back.

"She has an implant that the Master controls. Abijah cannot help it. We spoke about that, and I am going to operate to remove it," Zhuni said.

"We need to talk about this before you do anything like that. How do you think that would go over with the Master?" Klavan asked.

"I told Abijah I could remove the implant in Her skull but keep the outside cover, so it looked as if it had not been touched," Zhuni assured Klavan.

"Again, we need to talk about it before you do it. All right?"

"I will not perform the surgery until we talk, but I will look into how to do it."

"I would expect nothing less. Now get some rest; I will be back in the morning. It is good to have you back with us. Sarge was worried about you; he did not want to get stuck with running this med lab," Klavan smiled.

"That is correct; I would not want to run this place any longer. I will go with Klavan so I can report to the Master as I told Her I would when you went down," Sarge told Zhuni.

"Good night; it is nice to have you back," Klavan stated.

———————— * ————————

Dagz! Stanton thought.

It had been nice and quiet while Zhuni was out. Now things were going to get back to the way they were. Stanton was not happy about that. He would have to meet with Bosduul again. Stanton would need to get his credits worth; Boshduul had the past three rotations while Zhuni was out to coordinate his team's skills set. Now was the time to set things into motion. Stanton was not patient.

Klavan would be busy with the Master and now the med lab and his boy Zhuni. This would open him up to some attention he would not see coming. Now would be a great time to get Boshduul busy. Stanton would allow Boshduul to create as much chaos as he could here at the games. Stanton would make his guild contacts and build his value to the Master.

Get me a scripter. I need to get a message out." Stanton yelled to his servants.

———— * ————

Klavan was directed by one of the guards to enter the Master's office, followed by Sarge.

"It is late. To what do I owe your visit?" She asked.

"Your Grace, I wanted to personally inform You that Zhuni has awakened and seems to be just fine."

"Very good, so I assume you are here to request the return of Tan'cha," She said, looking to Sarge.

"Yes, ma'am. You said You may allow the return of Tan'cha once Zhuni became conscious again."

"I am glad you are disciplined enough to realize I did not tell you Tan'cha would return. Because of your request and your tone, I will send for Tan'cha."

"Thank You. This will enable me to concentrate on my obligations and for Zhuni to get back to work and get the med lab back to 100 percent much quicker."

"Your Grace, might I suggest we give Zhuni a couple of rotations to get back to himself, and then we can get the games back to full operations," Klavan requested.

"Yes, I believe that is a good idea; we will schedule another round of games in twelve rotations. This will give Zhuni a rotation of rest and then the standard time to prepare for a major game. I want an even larger display than this last round. I have several more contracts to complete. I need this to be the greatest games ever. I will be down to see Zhuni tomorrow morning; the next day, we will get back to work," She demanded.

"Yes, Your Grace. We will make preparations," Klavan told them.

"Take this to solitary and release Tan'cha," the Master said as She handed Sarge a release chip.

"Thank you; we will receive you in the med lab early," Sarge said as he turned to leave.

"Klavan, we will meet early to discuss our plans for the next round of games. Good evening," She said, dismissing him.

"Yes, Your Grace," Klavan said, departing with his shadow.

--------------- * ---------------

This will improve things greatly. Zhuni is back, and that means the games can continue. There was no way Sarge was going to run things properly. She needed to get back in the political running. She still needed to do something amazing, which had never been done at the games. What could she do? She had dispatched several of Her problems and provided excitement, but this had to be something special. Something which would amaze and impress the Commerce Guild, and then She would have them. They would vote with Her and support everything She planned. But how would She make such an impression? She had control of the Brynja Ajal. What else could she present? She only had twelve rotations to come up with something.

She would invite all the guilds, all of them. Then She would demand a meeting of the Masters. This would force their hands. With them all on Her home ground, She would have the advantage. If need be, She could create some issues or overcome some issues with them all in Her territory. With the resources She had at Her hands, she could force the issue and become the greatest Master and control all. Yes, now to figure out how to create the greatest event in gaming history.

--------------- * ---------------

Boshduul would need to get the team to build Stanton's confidence. Now that Zhuni was back. Stanton would be depressed with the current situation. Building Stanton's confidence was key to the project. The Master needed the guilds, and if Stanton could deliver a guild, he would become more important to Her. Boshduul would put the team on guild relationships to see which one they could persuade. This would create the situation needed for Boshduul's plans.

For finesse, Boshduul would use the Swaklin. The Swaklin knew the importance of stealth. He would be able to scout out the guilds. He would be Boshduul's best option, as they only had a few rotations. Boshduul knew the Master was itching for a new event, and now that Zhuni was back, it would be happening soon. The Swaklin would do. The little one would read all communications and give feedback of any chatter he heard from the guilds. Boshduul did not know their names nor care what their names were. Just as long as they got the work, he needed it to be done. He would be done with them shortly anyway; he did not need a team in retirement. This was going to be more fruitful than he had thought, so he would skim as many credits off them as possible and be gone.

Once he had the information he needed from the Swaklin, Boshduul would contact the guilds himself. He could then control the contacts and information. He could control the contract with the information he could gain. This was just getting better and better. Boshduul was going to come out of this so well off he could not contain himself, he usually did not allow himself to get excited about a situation, but this was too good.

Get Stanton on the Master's good side and make him invaluable to Her. Create unbearable friction between Stanton and Klavan by leveraging the hate Stanton has against the care Klavan has for Zhuni. Get the Master to become occupied by their bickering, causing a split between Klavan and Zhuni, even if just a little. And watch them all go at each other. Create all this to come to a head during the main event; then She will become irate, lash out at both of them, maybe even at Zhuni, then Boshduul can clear his accounts and part ways as they pick up the pieces. Brilliant. This is a foolproof payday.

Boshduul would contact the Swaklin and the little guy and give them their assignments. That would keep them busy for now. Boshduul would head to the docks and dig for information. He still needed to know what was happening locally. He always needed to keep a touch of the locale pulse. Plus, he just needed to get away for a break.

———————— * ————————

"Good morning!" Tan'cha screamed as he bounced Zhuni's bed to wake him.

"Good to see you. Now go away," Zhuni snapped in a groggy response.

"I have coffee."

"Fine, I will get up."

"Come on, you have been sleeping for three rotations. Let's go. I hear you have a lot to tell me!" Tan'cha said excitedly.

Zhuni sat up and was handed a mug of coffee. He cupped both hands around the mug and took in the strong aroma. He smiled and looked over at Tan'cha.

"It is good to see you, buddy. How was your vacation?"

"It was wonderful; no one bothered me."

"I wish I knew that feeling," Zhuni laughed.

"Oh, shut up! Tell me the story. Sarge told me a bunch as we walked back last night. Tell me the rest; I want to hear about it."

"It is amazing the things Abijah told me and showed me."

"Yes, so tell me everything."

"To start, she is a Drazine."

"Wow! She is from my planet! And the Drazine are real! This is amazing. I always knew my world was an amazing planet for variety of life," Tan'cha squawked.

"Not just an amazing planet for life but the source world of the Drazine."

"The source world? How does that work?" Tan'cha asked.

"The Drazine are the protectors of all worlds. A galaxy Drazine, as they are known, is born with the eggs of every type of Drazine. They are born on your planet. They then use their enormous wings to fly up to the solar winds that they ride to the planet they are called to. There they fold their wings to protect themselves from the crash and burn to the planet. Their wings are torn off, and they spend the rest of their life laying the eggs around the planet. Placing the eggs in the proper location for each type of Drazine. They will then stay eggs for thousands of cycles until they are needed. They will then hatch as danger to the planet comes to light. Sometimes the planet is safe, and the Drazine will stay eggs, but when the danger comes, they come out," Zhuni stated.

"So, the stories are true. The Drazine are protecting my planet. This is amazing."

"The Drazine protect life on all planets."

"I only worry about my world. I don't know other planets except this one, but I don't care about this world," Tan'cha said.

"Of course, why would you worry about a planet you live on? This planet has its own issues, but it is not in danger; otherwise, we would see the Drazine. They are here, have no doubt."

"How do you know?"

"Abijah told me that every planet with life has them. They are just waiting to be called," Zhuni said.

"This is wonderful. My planet is the origin planet. See, I told you my planet was special. I amaze myself," Tan'cha laughed.

"Yes, Tan'cha, you are amazing," Zhuni said, rolling his eyes.

"Leave me alone. I think I liked you better when you were asleep."

"I agree; you were much more agreeable when I was out," Zhuni snapped back.

"Continue your story, please. I am interested in every detail."

"I am sure you are, and if you would be quiet, I may be able to get the whole story out."

"I am so sorry, sir; I have had no one to speak to the last three rotations, so I am just letting a bit of steam off. I would think you missed our banter."

"Yes, you are right. I missed being interrupted each time I attempt to tell a story or share a thought."

"I don't understand. I do not get interrupted."

"Nor do you share a thought."

"Well, now, no need to get snippy; just continue."

"As I was saying, the Drazine."

"Wait, I do have a question," Tan'cha interrupted again.

"Yes?"

"There are different types of Drazine? And what did Sarge mean, one God, a Creator."

"This is going to take a while," Zhuni said.

"Good, we have the full rotation."

"I will need more coffee."

———————— * ————————

"Sarge,-he-is-heading-to-the-loading-dock," Joxby stated over the vox.

"Roger that, Joxby. I am heading to the far end to catch him. Let me know if he gets past me," Sarge responded.

"I-will-do."

Sarge had been waiting for the right opportunity to meet Boshduul's muscle and now seemed as good a time as any.

Sarge rounded the last armored transport to find the Swaklin he had been looking to meet waiting for him.

"It is a pleasure to meet you, Shem."

"You do your homework; that is a name I have not been called in many, many cycles. I do prefer Sarge."

"Well then, Sarge. My name is Sazon, but I go by Rue. Traxon said you wanted to meet."

"Yes, I want to know who I am dealing with," Sarge stated.

"What do you need to know?" Rue asked.

"Why?" Sarge asked simply.

"Why am I working for Traxon? Why am I a mercenary? Why am I not in a steady, secure position as most Swaklin are? Does that about cover it? Or are you asking about the tattoo?" Rue said in a matter-of-fact way.

"Yes."

"Where to start? I think I will start at a point you will know. The Aashturian Civil War. More specifically, the battle for Mudagor Nine. I was there, part of our Army, Listus One, Third Brigade, Seventh Company, Command Squad. The One Thirty-Seventh."

"That cannot be. They were wiped out."

"That is the official story, but the truth is different. We were marked for deletion due to our ability to adapt and win over any situation. The upper command, the Aashturians, saw us as a threat. They felt if we did not follow their exact plans in their exact orders, we were a problem. The Aashturians do not adapt nor change their battle plans. As we continued to win despite their commands, they became more nervous about our need to have them as commanders and even for us to remain in the war. During siege or Dryduun, we were ordered to attack the fortifications. We were sent to advanced positions to scout the attack."

"I know the story well; your Listus advanced and came under unending artillery fire and orbital bombardment and were wiped out."

"Yes, but the bombardment began at our rear, and pushed us forward into the open, then the orbital bombardment began. I realized what was happening and took my company directly through the advancing artillery. We took seventy percent casualties, but we made it past the artillery just to see the rest of our Listus wiped out."

"You mean the Aashturians wiped out the entire first Listus?"

"Yes, and when they saw my company, what was left of us, break through and get back to their lines, their troops looked at us as heroes. The command could not let what happened to get out, and they could not wipe us out as we rejoined their lines. As the ranking officer left from the Listus, I was given the choice to stay quiet and take a dishonorable discharge or have my entire command destroyed in a transport 'accident' as they were sent home for much-needed recovery."

"Just for argument's sake, let us suppose you are correct."

"Oh, but I am; Listus One was the spearhead of nearly every successful action the Aashturians mounted. But when the first died, so did the civil war, but notice how the 'losers' of Mudagor Nine are now the ones running the show there?"

"I have never been much of a political follower, but that part did bother me. The way the battle went never sat well with me."

"Of course not; you were the 'Great Shem, the Admiral Killer, the Holder of the Great Sadbaath.'"

"It sounds to me as if you are saying that with respect," Sarge said, slightly shocked.

"Of course. You are a legend because of your courage. You obviously do know that. You were part of the cause of the death of the Listus First. When you rose up and killed the admiral, that is when the Aashturians saw us as a threat. If one Swaklin had the courage and fortitude to stand up to the wrongs of a single admiral, what could a full Listus do?"

"I cannot bear that responsibility; it was not my fault the Listus was wiped out. I did what any Swaklin of honor should do. The Aashturians had predetermined that the city of Bethleem would be wiped out. The people were peaceful and surrendered honorably. But the admiral raised Sadbaath and was going to fire on the city and wipe it out."

"So, you stopped him and, with the rules of engagement, took his weapon and position as your own. You did the right thing. Don't you see, that is when the Aashturians knew we were people to deal with. They then and there had to end the war and wipe out our ability to wage war against another race. That is the day *you* signed our freedom clause. We still are a powerful people, a brave and honorable people. We are too spread about to be a force. But if we could reunite, oh, what a force we would be."

"True, it would be grand to restore the old realm."

"Someday, we will be reunited and be a sovereign society once again."

"Until then, we have much to discuss."

CHAPTER 9

New Plans

"Get that off now. I need that delivered immediately. Make certain it is delivered with pomp," Stanton roared.

"Yes, Master," the scripter replied. He would send it with a courier immediately. Stanton seemed overly concerned about this message.

"My lord. I have the Swaklin investigating the moods and reachability of the guilds. We will have you set shortly. I am certain we will have the Commerce Guild on board with you. You have sent your message off, and between our connections and the Swaklin, we should be able to work from the top and the middle," Boshduul stated.

"I do not need you helping me. I need you to get the job done. If this does not work, you will be out. I can run these boys without you if I need to. Remember that."

"Of course, my lord. I am here simply to serve you," Boshduul said, irate. This fool can't run across the room, much less run an organization. Boshduul suddenly smiled, realizing it would be a few dozen rotations, and Stanton would get his.

"Now get me results. I need you to get me information as to what is going on in the med lab. With Zhuni back and the Master talking about the games coming back, She wants something special. We need to figure out what that could be and deliver it."

"Do you want to create something different for the games?"

"Of course I do! We must constantly be indispensable to Her."

"Do you have specific ideas?"

"I do, and I need you to produce ideas also."

"She loves her Pantaas, and the Brynja Ajal is her greatest beast. I would think a battle between the two types of creatures would be exciting."

"You Drogond, She would never allow that. It would possibly injure the Pantaas. She would never let that happen. She had the turrets installed, and that added excitement. Maybe we could upgrade the turrets, or we could have some traps installed and have the crowd activate them."

"What do you think would be the upgrade? What type of traps would you want installed? Maybe we could find some type of new creatures or maybe even new warriors," Boshduul insisted.

"Plasma guns in the turrets would work; that would wipe out instantly any creature in the line of fire, not those little plasma pellets. That would be exciting. New creatures or warriors? Such as?" Stanton asked.

"I am not completely sure, but let me do some investigating, and I will get back to you, my lord."

"Get info from med lab and get me your ideas tomorrow. Now leave me."

"Yes, my lord."

---------- * ----------

"Yes, your world is the source world for all Drazine. The Creator made the Drazine to protect life on all worlds. There is a Galaxy Drazine, a female, massive. She has huge wings and mates with each type of Drazine. Then she swoops to the interstellar winds and rides whichever one will take her to the new world. When she reaches the new world wraps her wings tightly around her and plummets to the planet like a meteor. Her wings burn off as she burns through the atmosphere. Once she recovers, she will travel the planet, laying the eggs until they are all placed. They will stay hidden and unhatched until the planet needs protection. She will stay and keep an eye on the eggs until then," Zhuni continued the story Abijah told him.

"Amazing. So, every world has Drazine?" Tan'cha asked.

"Yes, and there are evil Drazine attempting to end life on each world."

"What do you mean, evil? I thought you said the Drazine were good and protected life."

"Yes, most are. But remember the story of the battle for your planet and some of the Drazine wanting the power of the Creator? Those are the ones life must be protected from."

"Yup, that is right. I forgot. See, I have been telling the young ones here how important my world was; I just did not realize all of life's balance hinged on my world."

"Yes, Tan'cha, *your* world is the most important in all of known space," Zhuni responded sarcastically, shaking his head.

"What? I can't help it if my world is so important."

"Somehow, it always is about you, isn't it?"

"Of course, what do I care about other races?" Tan'cha chuckled.

"The most amazing story in the history of history, and you're stuck on you."

"Yup. Now let me ask, if a planet comes under attack, how do the Drazine protect it from other Drazine, and how do they let other planets know about the attack?"

"The Drazine have a hive mind."

"A what?" Tan'cha asked.

"It means all their minds are connected, and their memories also. If a world is attacked, all the Drazine will have that information in their minds as if they were there watching. They also know everything each Drazine has experienced since the beginning."

"Like you and She spoke through your minds?"

"Yes, but imagine if I could communicate constantly and install memories also, but it happens instantly and all the time."

"That would give me a headache, and I would get so confused."

"You are always confused."

"Not always."

"Our brains are not wired for that type of communication; that is part of the reason I passed out when Abijah attempted to communicate with me. But being ancient, we were actually designed to communicate with the Drazine. We were just not designed to receive all the information the Drazine carried, just be able to communicate with them. With the correct training, I may be able to talk to Abijah more naturally."

"Keeping pushing that 'ancient' thing, but it is my world that holds the key to life in the known universe."

"I don't think it matters which planet is most important; we all have an important part to play."

"You only say that cause your world was destroyed."

"You know, sometimes you can be an absolute drogond!"

"That is not the first time you have said that."

They both laughed.

"So, what is your plan for Her?" Tan'Cha asked.

"What do you mean?"

"What do I mean? I know you; you are going to get that controller off of Her and then want to help her escape. Right?"

"I never said that."

"Nope, but that is what you are thinking."

"Now, how the Dagz would we be able to get her off this world?"

"Off this world? Are you thinking we could just magically fly to the stars on her back or something? There is no way we could get her off this world. We would need a freighter and a crew completely out of their minds. To go against the Master, she would kill us for taking Her prize."

"A freighter, that is a good idea. How could we get freighter to get down here and then load her and get out of here?" Zhuni smiled.

"No! That is insane. We would all be killed. She would hunt us down, so would the entire Gamers' Guild, the Mining Guild that She controls, the Drug cartels, and Starch traders, and by the time we got off the planet, the Commerce Guild would probably be under Her control. Oh no! No way!"

Zhuni just looked at Tan'cha and smiled.

"No! No, no, *no!*"

"What if we took her home?"

"What? To my world?"

"It is the most important world in all of known space."

"No?" Tan'cha whimpered.

———————— * ————————

The craft was a small armed transport. It was built to track down bail jumpers and assassins. Also to evade planetary blockades and travel across the known galaxy with no support. It was armed well and could, if need be, fight its way out of a tight situation. This was the ship of the Hunters' Guild's messenger who had made the surprise visit to the guild masters' meeting. He was in the pilot's seat speaking with an individual over the interstellar communicator. He could see a figure over the monitor but could not truly make out the shape or size of the individual. The voice was muted and muddled, metallic as if spoken through a machine.

"Guild Master, the game has been set in motion," the hunter said.

"Your guild knows their part and is ready for reconciliation?" responded the voice over the monitor.

"Yes."

"Has your guild accepted a leader and Master yet?"

"We are currently having discussions."

"Discussions? You do realize this will all come to a head in ten to fifteen rotations of the gamer's planet. The fleets need to be in the proper positions and be able to jump instantly to work."

"Yes, Guild Master. We are painfully aware of the importance of stealth and timing if this is to work. The Assassins' Guild still has the largest fleet. Our fleet is settling into its positions and will strike at the proper time. We all are in and will perform our task. We have yet to decide on our master. Each clan has its leader. You know we have three hundred clans. One of the clan leaders will be the master."

"I had assumed that would be the case. In fact, I had figured that your clans would ultimately choose a Master and a Vice Master, plus two dozen submasters. With three hundred clans, I know you also have three dozen worlds. It would be logical to have several leaders representing the various worlds. But I thought by now, you would have that all sorted out."

"Guild Master, our people are an independent group. We rely on each other and no one else. We will be ready."

"How?"

"We have our leaders chosen. The only question is who the master will be. The clans have their representation, and we are down to tbunehree leaders; one will be the master. One will be the Vice Master, and the third will be our Prime Minister to deal with the other guilds."

"Who are the three?"

"The clans chose well. The front runner is Hotha the Wise. His second will be Kamon the Warrior, and the prime minister will be Chaytan the Patient."

"The clans choose wisdom over warrior. But with the warrior as their number two, ensure power and force is an option, and patience as an arbitrator for the other guilds. Yes, the clans chose well. When is the final vote?"

"The next two to three rotations, prior to the fleet's deployment. Once the vote is complete, there will be no further need to communicate until launch. They will be ready for battle."

"They, you say? What about you, Lemuel? Where will you be?"

"I will be standing by; I have a personal issue to take care of."

"Will you join the fleet?"

"I will not. I cannot risk my ship at this time. I have an important task to perform. My ship will be needed later. My ship is not built for a fleet-size battle. I will accomplish more if I use my ship for another mission."

"Lemuel, I can provide you with another ship. I have access and dominion over many."

"I know, Guild Master, my ship is perfect for my assignment."

"Lemuel, you will be remembered, and the clans will know your name. You have been instrumental in reforming the guilds and will be remembered as Lemuel the Loyal for your loyalty to your clans and the Hunters' Guild. Know this, the Freighters' Guild master is your friend and will be on call if you need. Your diplomacy will be the reason so many wrongs will be righted."

"I hope this will bring the balance and peace we are all looking for. Until I complete this, you will not hear from me; my work is done."

"Do contact me when your personal issue is complete so I know you are well."

"Yes, Guild Master, I will."

"Until then, Lemuel, be safe and without fear."

Lemuel shut off his monitor, sat back, and thought about the last several rotations. This was going to be a historical time; to be a part of it was an honor. He had fought in the Aashturian Civil War and had seen such death and destruction on Mudagor Seven that he never wanted to be in a land battle again. He thought he might see more death and destruction on his next mission; he just hoped it was not his. He knew he had to do this; it would be the honorable thing to do. He had done his best to do the honorable thing since Mudagor Seven. He had learned a lot then about honor. One of the most important things was to have the back of those who needed you. Clans were important, but family and battle brothers meant more than anything, and you had to have each other's backs, or else there was no hope.

———————— * ————————

"Joxby."

"Yes,-Sarge?"

"I need you to find out everything you can about Rue. You should be able to run back the audio and find all the information you need to do a background on him."

"Yes,-Sarge,-I-will. Are-we-looking-for-anything-specific?"

"I do not think we will find anything we should not know about him; I just want more information on anyone we are dealing with."

"Yes,-Sarge, I-like-him;-I-think-he-is-a-good-guy."

"I feel he is also, but it never hurts to get all the information you can."

"Yes. Also,-Boshduul-has-met-with-Stanton."

"Did you get the meeting details?"

"Yes, they-are-just-worried-about-the-guilds-and-attempting-to-come-up-with-an-idea-to-make-the-main-event-more-exciting-for-the-Master."

"Great. When you have more details, let me know. How is Zhuni doing?"

"He-and-Tan'cha-were-still-talking-Zhuni-has-been-in-medical-records-about-the-monster-and-and-has-been-looking-at-medical-equipment."

"No doubt he is looking into how to release Brynja Ajal from her brain control thing."

"Yes."

"Oh yes, also get information on the little guy Rue spoke of. He would be the electronics expert Boshduul hired. He is also working for Stanton but also, Traxon, let us see his situation. I do not know his name or any details. I hope you can figure out which one I am speaking of."

"Yes, I-have-him,-and-I-will-check-into-his-background. I-will-give-you-the-full-report-on-both-shortly."

"Thank you. I am on my way back."

———————— * ————————

She would have to look into the archives, wasn't there something about the beast and the research about her? She seemed to remember there was something important that may help the games. What was it? She would have to deal with the scientists.

"We need to check in with med lab. Come," She said to Her guards.

They fell into formation, as usual, one on each shoulder just behind Her as She headed out of Her office.

She could see him coming towards Her as they turned the corner.

"Good morning, Grace," Klavan called as he saw Her round the corner. Everyone in the corridor parted as She came through.

"Are you headed to see me?"

"Yes, Your Grace."

"Talk as we walk."

"Yes, ma'am. Where are we headed?"

"Med lab, I wanted to see how Zhuni is doing, and I need to reacquire one of my people."

"Perfect timing; I was going to check in on Zhuni myself after meeting with you. I need to ensure he and his team have all the supplies they need for the upcoming game."

Klavan stepped in next to Her on Her right side and just behind Her, just ahead of Her guard. Klavan's guard stepped in behind all of them.

"This is why you are my number two. I was going to ask about supplies and equipment this morning. You seem to anticipate my ever need."

"That is my job."

"Keep it up; you are doing well."

"In a hurry this morning, I see," She said, nodding at the large mug Klavan was carrying.

"No, Grace, I did not sleep much, just needed a bit of liquid energy."

"Excited to have Zhuni back, I would suggest," She noted this was the first time She had noticed him drinking coffee. Interesting. She knew Klavan had a soft spot for Zhuni, but if he was having a hard time sleeping, there could be more.

"Maybe, it is good to have the med lab back to normal efficiency."

"Indeed."

They proceeded down the corridors discussing the upcoming event. The logistics of the guilds, the actual event, and issues of quarters came up.

"If all the guild masters are here, it will be an immense proposition. How do we placate everyone? You know the assassins see themselves as the most important guild."

"Of course they do; they were the ones who decided the fate of all the guilds hundreds of cycles ago. Placating everyone is your job."

With that statement, they arrived at the med lab. The main doors opened.

"Good morning, Your Grace, Klavan," Sarge greeted them.

"Sargent," She replied.

"How are you this morning?" Klavan responded.

"Very well, it has been a good day," Sarge turned to escort them into the Med lab.

"This way, Zhuni is just finishing his rounds and getting inventory complete," Sarge stated.

"Completing inventory and doing rounds. That was one of the first things he did with his cycle off?" She asked.

"He said it was relaxing and gave him peace of mind knowing everyone and everything was in order," Sarge replied.

"With you and Zhuni running things, I do not know why I have to worry about the med lab," She said, glancing at Klavan.

"What can I say? I trained him well."

The entire entourage walked across the med lab to the back of the loading dock area. Zhuni and Tan'cha were discussing the inventory when the entourage arrived.

"It is good to see you up and about and hard at work. I did give you the rotation to relax," She said as they arrived.

"Yes, Your Baroness, You did. But I have been down for some time already and must get caught up on my obligations to the med lab and my staff. And, of course, to You."

"Very well, do not allow us to disrupt you. I was just checking to see how you were doing and to take one of my staff back."

"Thank You for checking on me. Who would You need to speak with?"

"My scientist," She spoke.

"He has been helpful, and I would like to keep him on my staff, especially with the main event coming up again," Zhuni implied.

"That should be no problem. I just need to go over some things with him. He should return by the end of the cycle."

"Sarge, would you please take Her to the scientist, I believe he is with Mazalla at the minihabs," Zhuni ordered.

"Right this way, Your Grace," Sarge motioned.

"Klavan, join me later," She said over Her shoulder.

"Yes, Your Highness," Klavan replied.

She and Her guards followed Sarge to the minihabs.

"I have loaded all our needs onto this info card; I have added some notes for you also," Zhuni said to Klavan.

"I will place the order as you need, and I will follow your notes."

"Please respond quickly to the notes. They are important and have relevance to our honored guest," Zhuni implored.

"Oh, yes. I will check out your notes as soon as I return to my office and send a response."

"It is of utmost importance."

"Is everything else okay? Do you have all you need to be prepared for the next main event?" Klavan asked.

"My list is on the info card, and my notes will cover anything not noted in our standard inventory format."

"I will head to my office and begin ordering."

"Thank you, sir; I look forward to your confirming our needs and informing me of our supplies' arrival date and time."

"I will get you the data prior to my meeting with the Master," Klavan turned to leave.

"Thank you; I look forward to hearing from you."

*

"Thank you, Sargent," She said as She, the scientist, and Her guards headed out of the med lab.

"That is my favorite view of Her," Sarge said to the guards at the main entrance.

"The back of Her?" asked Sarge.

"Just Her leaving is what I like to see," Sarge said as he turned back to head to the minihabs again.

"Mazalla, you said you had some information for me," Sarge stated.

"Yes. You had asked about some information."

"I asked about several items; which are you speaking of specifically?"

"I have much information on all subjects," Mazalla stated.

"Great, let's get started."

"To start, the trace element in Klavan's minihab is from a world named Gehenna. It is a desolate world deep into the Aashturian region. The planet is a large rocky planet known to have only one race. That race is known to mainly stay on their planet. They are a secretive and violent society; little is known of them. The few times any of their race have left the planet, they have become assassins or bounty hunters. They tend to be smaller than humans and have deep red humanoid bodies. They breath hydrogen, so often have a rebreather or wear an entire pressure suit. The planet's atmosphere is 65 percent hydrogen. The element is fairly common on Gehenna. There is one other place it is found, and that is a planet called Besev. I have been unable to find much out about Beserv other than its thought of location."

"Thought of location?"

"Yes, it is a planet that has not been truly confirmed."

"Not confirmed?"

"There are planets that are said to exist, but there has been little evidence of their existence. Sometimes planets turn out to not exist. On a rare occasion, a planet turns out to be actually part of an existing planet."

"I am simple; I do not understand. Part of another planet?"

"A hidden race on a planet creates a story of another planet to protect their location, or in one case, an entire planet was trapped in a rift in regular space, and the warp the planet would materialize every twelve to fifteen cycles. There is even a story of a planet with a cloaking ability."

"We need to get more information about Besev. I have a feeling I know who would be from Gehenna."

"That would be interesting; I have never seen a creature from Gehenna. Let me know when you find them; I would like to add to our knowledge of Gehenna."

"I will, thank you. I will follow up with you later."

"I look forward to the meeting."

Sarge turned to head towards Zhuni's office.

---
*

"You are sure these are the visions you received?" Abijah asked.

"Yes, they were very disturbing," Zhuni replied.

"I do not understand. I never communicated with you until I came to the med lab. How would you have similar visions unless you communicated with another Drazine?"

"I know, there must be another Drazine here, or there was one. You were passing through the lab and research area; suppose there was a Drazine that died, and you ran into its memories," Tan'cha interjected.

"What do you mean, memories?"

"We believe we have visions from our ancestors. We believe these are their memories left behind when they pass on. A sharing of their knowledge with us. This happens when they are released from their physical forms. Just memories remain," Tan'cha continued.

"Their memories float around?" Zhuni asked.

"Not really, they pass on and release their conciseness, and they are connected to their next of kin, like a gift to the next generation," Tan'cha explained.

"I do not believe that is how it works with Drazine," Abijah stated.

"You don't think?" Zhuni asked.

"What did she say?" Tan'cha asked.

"That is not how the Drazine work," Zhuni said.

"Fine, what is her explanation?" Tan'cha asked.

"He gets snippy; I like him," Abijah quipped.

"Yes, he is a good friend," Zhuni replied.

"I know when you are talking to each other. You move your lips and look off into space. So don't be rude; include me in your conversation," Tan'cha stammered.

"He is right; you do move your lips," Abijah stated.

"Really? Fine, what are we going to do about these visions? Do we have any ideas?" Zhuni said out loud so they all could hear.

"I told you my thoughts," Tan'cha reminded them.

"Yes, but we do not think that is the case in this situation. Maybe there is another," Zhuni said.

"We need to be certain. With this device in my head, it would make sense if they had done research on another Drazine. I just do not understand why I would not have received the visions if there was another," Abijah questioned.

"Yes, they would have had to understand your physiology and your nervous system. The only way to do that is to work on you, and as you have no memory of that, it would have had to be another. That would explain the details of the visions," Zhuni explained.

"I agree; there must have been another," Abijah agreed.

"Come on, I can see your lips moving again," Tan'cha whined.

"Oh yes, sorry. She was just saying there must have been another Drazine that they did their research on. That would explain their ability to insert that device. Which I have a plan to remove," Zhuni stated.

"So how do we find out if there was or maybe still is another?" Tan'cha asked.

"We will have to do some investigating, and we will have to get into the archives or the labs," Zhuni implied.

"You know what? I just thought of this. We need to act quickly," Tan'cha said excitedly.

"Okay, why?" Zhuni asked.

"Dagz! I cannot believe I am the only one thinking this. I am so smart. I am the only one thinking this?" Tan'cha continued.

"He is too funny," Abijah interjected.

"Yup," Zhuni chuckled.

"Come on, seriously. I can see your lips moving again!" Tan'cha snapped.

"You were saying," Zhuni said, attempting to back on track.

"As I was saying, why do you think the Master just came down here and took the scientist?" Tan'cha said with attitude.

"Good point. I cannot even believe we did not think of that," Zhuni said.

"No, you guys did not think about it, but I did," Tan'cha snapped.

"He is just too funny. He is correct. We need to speak with the scientist," Abijah said.

"Yes, he is funny, and he is correct. My only concern is if we can even get to the scientist before it is too late, and then how do we get into the labs?" Zhuni questioned.

"I can still see your lips moving," Tan'cha said with frustration.

---- * ----

"Continue," She said.

"We were brought the two eggs and told to do research on the creatures' biology. We decided to hatch one do the exams and dissections, but we wanted to keep it alive. We would work on it in short sessions and then put it back together. One large problem was how quickly they grow. They grow to full size quickly, in less than a cycle. They are ravenous during this time. Feeding it and learning about it at such accelerated rates made the research difficult. But we did learn about it, and then we put it into cryo-freeze when we were finished. The creature should still be frozen in the lab. The Master determined that this one would be too damaged to be a fighter in the arena, so we hatched the second monster, and that is Brynja Ajal. We kept strict and exact records of all the procedures. This is how we were able to develop the control device," the scientist stated.

"All these records are in the archives?" She asked.

"No, the Master at the time did not want anyone to know the information. So, all the records were sealed into the research lab."

"I found no such records when I went through the lab," She stated.

"You went through the known lab; there is another lab that is under the grandstand and on the back side of the corridor. It has been sealed and is only accessible if you know where to look."

"You know how to access it?"

"I do not. I was not part of the team sealing it. I was moved with Brynja Ajal to work with the monster."

"You are the only remaining scientist who worked in that lab; how are we supposed to access it?"

"There is one who was part of the team that sealed the lab, and there is one other that knows about the research monster."

"I am listening."

———————— * ————————

"Sarge."

"Go ahead, Joxby."

"I-have-much-information-for-you."

"Roger that; I am going to meet with Zhuni and Tan'cha, then be up to see you."

"Okay,-see-you-soon.-By the-way,-you-are-heading-in-the-wrong-direction.-They-are-at-the-cage."

"Thank you." Sarge turned to head towards the cage.

"Sarge, how are you doing?" Zhuni asked.

"Well, I have been busy checking on some things."

"What have you found out?"

"For starters, the Swaklin working for Stanton and Traxon served at Mudagor Nine the same time I was there, and he knew about me. Joxby is looking into his background, but we both have the feeling he is a good one. Second, I spoke with Mazalla, and she informed me that there were traces of an element that, as far as she knows, is only found on two planets. This is what she believes was used in the attempt on Klavan's life."

"What two planets?" Tan'cha asked.

"I was going to ask that," Zhuni said.

"Sure, you were." Tan'cha laughed.

"Anyway, the two planets are two I had never heard of, Besev and Gehenna," Sarge said.

"Anything special about them?" Zhuni asked.

"Mazalla is attempting to confirm that Besev actually exists. It is a mysterious planet that Mazalla had never heard of," Sarge responded.

"That is interesting," Tan'cha blurted out.

"What about Gehenna?" Zhuni queried.

"It is a harsh world deep into Aashturian space; it has a hydrogen atmosphere and is mostly rock," Sarge informed them.

"We will have to do some digging for further information about those worlds, then?" Zhuni asked.

"Yes. I will continue to get as much information as I can. I have other resources," Sarge assured them.

"We have more for you to look into also," Zhuni told Sarge.

"Such as?" Sarge asked.

"We have been discussing the fact that we believe there was or may still be a second Drazine," Zhuni informed Sarge.

"Of course, there is; you said they were on every planet just waiting to be awakened," Sarge stated.

"No, that is not what we mean. We think there is another one here at the games, hidden in a hidden lab under the grandstand at the back of the complex," Zhuni asserted.

"Oh. Now that is something. We need to find this secret lab and find the hidden Drazine? Then what exactly will we do with it?" Sarge questioned.

"The same thing we are going to do with Abijah, rescue it and get it off the planet," Zhuni uttered.

"We are going to do what? You do know I have been through several wars, including the Aashturian Civil War, but you all are dangerous. You are going to get me killed," Sarge blurted out.

"We are not," Tan'cha cackled.

"Let me just say, when I do die, I think I will be around all of you," Sarge laughed.

"So, you are ready to get this rescue and escape figured out?" Zhuni inquired.

"Why not? None of us will live forever. I have survived too many battles already; I always hoped I would die doing something important," Sarge shrugged.

"I feel the same; if I am going to die, I figure it will be with and because of you all. Might as well plan it. Let's do something exciting," Tan'cha exclaimed.

"What is the plan?" Sarge asked, looking to Zhuni.

CHAPTER 10

Preparation for the Next Event

"There is word all the guild masters will be here for the next main event," the humanish told Boshduul.

"This I know; I need good information," Boshduul responded.

"There has been a lot more military hardware and weapons coming in. Also, I have heard something big is coming."

"Again, I know. You are useless. I need information I do not know."

"Okay, I have heard She is preparing something new and unique for the main event. Word is, She has a monstrous creature that will battle the Brynja Ajal. She is gearing up to arm Her guards with heavier gear to protect Her and the facility from this thing. I have also heard that there is a secret chamber they are going to open. She is going to have the arena reinforced, and that is why more ceramasteel and a more powerful field generator are being installed."

"Interesting; get me more details, and then I will pay you." Boshduul scolded.

"Details? Come on. I am not the engineer or anything. I don't know the details; I am just telling you what I hear," the humanish said.

"Well then, that is information I could have gotten from anyone, if you just heard it. I need information that is not known by everyone. I need detailed information worth paying for," Boshduul told him.

"Come on. What more do you need?"

"If I have to teach you the things, I need to know you are a waste of my time. I need details, names, places, times, specific locations, and information, not just hearsay. Got it?"

"Fine, I will dig for more information. What is it going to pay?"

"Worry about the information, and I will worry about the payment," Boshduul snarled.

———————— * ————————

Klavan did not understand the need for the massive amounts of Banteest She wanted. He understood there was going to be a massive gathering of all the guilds. But the amount of Banteest was ridiculous. Why was She having more work put into the arena? Why was there a crew strengthening the force generator? The surprises during the last main event were enough. Now it was more and more. At what point was this insanity going to end? What other surprises was She planning?

Klavan needed to get down to the docks and see what else was going on. He had been in meetings and by Her side so much that he had not even been to the docks in several rotations. He needed to get down there and see what was actually going on. He was keeping Her happy, but he had to get back in touch with what was going on at the docks; this was how he knew what was always happening at the facility.

"System on, restart."

"Mister-Klavan,-welcome."

"Thank you, Joxby. How are you?"

"I-am-well,-thank-you.-May-I-help-you?"

"Yes. I am going to the docks, and I need you to record what I see and to keep track of everything we see."

"I-can-do-that;-is-there-anything-we-are-looking-for?"

"I am not sure. I have not been to the docks in several rotations and feel out of touch. I feel something is going on, but I am not sure what."

"Would-you-like-a-microdrone-to-escort-you-and-perform-a-more-through-search?"

"Actually, if you could have one or two join me and reach spaces I do get to, that would be helpful. I need everything looked into."

"Three-microdrones-inbound."

"Thank you. Have them all record, visual, audio, and all spectrums."

"I-will-record-all-spectrums,-visual,-audio,-and-thermal."

"Perfect; if you see anything unusual, let me know."

"Will-do-so."

Klavan knew the microdrones were with him only because Joxby had told him. Klavan could not see them nor hear them; they truly were microdrones. Klavan knew they could be sitting on his shoulder, and he would not know.

Klavan noticed the activity going on. Several freighters had recently unloaded, and still more were sitting, waiting to unload. Klavan had seen the manifests of the cargo but knew they did not always match the actual cargo. Being at the docks would allow him to see what was truly going on.

Several humanish loaders were making an effort to exit the loading dock quickly, so Klavan headed that way to see what was going on. He headed them off and requested the unloading forms.

One of them turned away from the crew to look for the forms; Klavan had been in the business long enough to know the intent was to turn Klavan away from the loader skid and the cargo. Klavan turned back to the loader to look into the container.

"What do we have here?" Klavan asked.

"I am not sure, sir," the one humanish said.

"What is the hurry?" Klavan questioned.

"We have many ships to unload and little time to do it. The Master is pushing to get all unloaded before the main event," the humanish answered.

"Good job; now let's open this and perform a standard offload inspection," Klavan demanded.

"Yes, sir, no problem, sir. But please inform the Master you are the one slowing down the unloading. I would not want to be responsible for upsetting Her," the humanish who attempted to distract him said.

"No problem; I know Her fairly well and know She would be more upset with improper procedure than a delay in unloading," Klavan said, glaring at the humanish.

"Yes, sir."

Klavan reached down and ripped the top access panel off the shipping container; looking inside, he saw several military weapons power cells. These would power up dozens of heavy bolters or medium laser cannons. Klavan looked around and saw several more of the same. This container alone would power more weapons than the entire facility had, including all the armored vehicles. With at least five of these containers within eyesight, Klavan knew this was enough to power a small army. He would have to find out more about what was going on. This was a massive amount of firepower.

"How many of these have you moved off the loading docks?" Klavan asked.

"This is our third, sir."

"Let me see the manifest," Klavan demanded.

Stuttering for a response, the humanish stared at Klavan.

"We have no manifest."

"That makes things interesting. Just because I have not been down here the last several rotations do not mean we will not be doing our jobs properly. Get me the freighter's information. We still need to have documentation."

"Yes, sir."

Klavan was shocked by the amount of firepower this container would provide. *Was the Master doing this, or was this Stanton's doing?* With the power cells, there had to be weapons systems also. Klavan knew Joxby was busy recording all this and would be chasing the microdrones off to gather more information.

"Klavan,-sir."

Klavan turned away from the loading team.

"Yes?"

"I-found-something-very-interesting, you-need-to-go-to-the-cargo-lift-at-the-east-end. Go-to-level-seven."

"One moment."

"Now,-sir."

"Continue offloading and bring me the information, including the freighter's registration, past port, and their manifest, also the captain's name."

"Yes, sir."

Klavan turned to head toward the lift. Joxby was even more thorough than Klavan thought. He already had the microdrones on level seven. Sarge knew talent for sure. Level seven was the Master's quarters level.

Klavan got to the lift and exited it at level seven. There were four massive shipping containers that had to take up every bit of space on the lift. These containers were unlike anything Klavan had seen before. They were smooth and shiny with no visible seams and ebony black; there seemed to be no access panel nor handles to open anything. Then he noticed the seal. It was Her seal. As soon as Klavan saw the seal, he realized these containers matched the armor the Master and Her guards wore.

"What are these?" Klavan asked.

"They-match-the-armor-and-signature-of-Her-and-Her-guards-armor," Joxby responded.

"I got that much. Can you tell me anything else?"

"Not-much-more,-I-am-getting-a-low-energy-reading,-but-that-is-all."

"Low energy?"

"Yes,-just-a-small-level.-Not-enough-to-support-life-but-more-than-a-standard-container."

"What do other spectrums show?"

"No-other-spectrums-work-on-this-container.-No-thermal-scan-just-showing-space-temperature-infrared-has-nothing,-and-audio-is-giving-us-a-low-level-hum."

"It has no signature at all?"

"Just-that-it-is-there-has-the-temperature-of-the-air-around-it,-and-there-is-a-low-hum-of-equipment,-I-say-whatever-is-giving-the-power-reading. All-are-the-same."

"I guess the only thing we can do is watch them and analyze the sound to see if we can figure something out."

"I-have-set-our-microdrones-and-turned-them-off. I-have-all-the-data-downloaded,-and-microdrones-will-come-back-on-line-on-a-time-delay-after-the-containers-are-moved."

"Great, thank you. I think we have enough to know something out of the ordinary is going on. Analyze the drones' information and see if we can find anything else out."

"Yes,-Mister-Klavan."

"I will head back down to the loading dock for a few and then meet with Her. I am out. System off now."

*

The three of them were once again in Zhuni's office discussing the plans leading up to the main event.

"I received the go from Klavan," Zhuni told Tan'cha and Sarge.

"By go, do you mean the rescue mission and planned escape?" Sarge sarcastically asked.

"No, I have not gotten that far, but he said we could research how to remove the device on Abijah's head," Zhuni responded.

"So how exactly are we going to do that?" Sarge asked.

"I am not exactly sure. I need to run a scan, but our equipment is not sensitive enough. We could fit her head into the scanner we use for the Scrytocks, but it would not give us the details we need because of the thickness of her skull."

"You mean her skull is thicker than a Scrytocks plating?" Tan'cha asked.

"Much thicker, plus I need to see what material the probe is made of so I can install the correct nanobots," Zhuni implied.

"Have you spoken with Joxby about building an amplifier for the scanner? I am sure he could work something up. We could remove one of the large scanners from the corridor and have it under repair if anyone asks," Sarge suggested.

"Good thinking. I will get with Joxby and tell him what I need. Sarge, could you get a couple of the engineers to get the scanner in here for the repairs?"

"Will do. I will get the crew on it after our meeting."

"I will speak with Joxby about what I need done."

"What can I do?" Tan'cha asked.

"There are a lot of things I will have you working on. We still have to work on our main focus. Get the controller removed from Abijah, figure out how to get out of here, find transport off the planet without raising an alarm, and figure out how to get to your world while the Master and all the guilds are looking for us; it should be fairly easy," Zhuni quipped.

"Great, what can I do?" Tan'cha repeated.

"Actually, I have the perfect job for you, and it is important," Zhuni replied.

"What?"

"Sarge, you get the scanner relocated, then get information from the contacts you have around the spaceport as to who could handle this large a transport. We will need room for Abijah and possibly a second Drazine, a route to Kashtuu, fuel, and most likely an armed transport with jump capability and blockade runner abilities. We may even need a couple of transports if one large one is too easy to move undetected. And they will have to be a non-guild member or someone who dislikes the guilds and wants to do something amazing."

"That should be easy enough. Oh, and I need to arouse no suspicion, correct? Easy," Sarge said with more of his sarcasm.

"Great, what can I do?" Tan'cha pleaded.

"We need you to speak to the team members about who would be willing to escape with us and if they would be willing to fight if need be. We need to know who is with us and how many, but you cannot let everyone know exactly what we are doing. Understand?" Zhuni asked.

"Yup, let everyone know what we are going to do without them knowing what we are going to do. Got it," Tan'cha inquired.

"You do know we are all going to die attempting this. And just wondering, how are we going to finance all this? It is going to cost us hundreds of thousands of credits," Sarge inserted.

"If it is meant to be, it will happen," Zhuni stated.

"Yea, Sarge, besides, it will be an adventure," Tan'cha quipped.

"You two are going to have an adventure getting us all killed, great," Sarge mumbled as he stood up to leave.

"He seems a bit grumpier than usual," Tan'cah said.

"He will be fine; now let's get to work."

---------- * ----------

The engineers and construction team completed their work in Her quarters. They turned to leave but were met by several of Her guards, standing between the construction team and the entrance to Her quarters. The team just stood there for a moment, expecting the guards to step aside as they had the last few cycles when the team completed their work for the cycle. Their quarters had been set up temporarily in a storage compartment. The team felt it had been to allow them complete isolation from the rest of the facility.

The guards raised their weapons just as She walked in.

"I want to thank you for the work you have done here, but I will no longer be in need of your services nor of any of you."

The rifles started blasting until every member of the construction team had been cut down. Their lifeless bodies were thrown into the construction debris bin they had just filled.

Two guards re-slung their rifles across their shoulders and began to push the bin towards the loading dock. When they passed the black shipping containers left on level seven, more guards swung those containers around and pushed them towards Her quarters. The shipping containers were placed at the entrance to Her quarters. She removed the jeweled chest piece from Her armor and inserted it into a matching slot on a small panel on the end of the container. With an audible hiss and release of air pressure, the container end opened upward and then slid over the top. She retrieved the crest and now set it into a machined space on a small panel just inside the opening. The interior space now lit up, and standing within the container were twelve guards. She pressed a few buttons on the panel, and the guards started to step out of the container.

"Take up station inside," She commanded.

The guards all stepped out of the container and went into Her quarters. Once inside Her quarters, the guards each stepped up to and onto one of the newly installed stations the construction crew had just completed.

She completed this with the next three containers until She had a new army. Forty-eight new guards.

She looked at the room full of guards.

"I am sure with these, I will easily control the guilds, and no one will be expecting this type of power."

"Dispose of these," She said to the guards who had just brought the containers. Two guards turned to move the now empty containers back down to the loading dock. Two more guards took station at the entrance to Her quarters, and two took up their standard station on either shoulder.

"No one will enter," She said to the guards standing at the entrance.

"With me," She said to the other two.

She turned and headed down the hallway towards the loading docks.

—————— * ——————

"Mister-Zhuni,-Traxon-needs-to-talk-to-you;-he-said-it-is-important," Joxby stated over the vox.

"I can be up there in two to three actas. On my way," Zhuni replied.

"We are done?" Tan'cha asked.

"For now, you know what you need to do, Sarge has his project, and I need to talk to Joxby about the scanner and what I need him to do. Might as well see what Traxon wants while I am up there. See you at evening meal."

Tan'cha left Zhuni's quarters and headed across med lab; Zhuni walked off towards Joxby's area. Thinking about what he needed Joxby to adjust with the scanner and attempting to come up with something to change their situation permanently.

"Hello,-Mister-Zhuni,-Traxon-is-in-the-back," Joxby stated as Zhuni stepped into the monitoring area.

"Thank you, Joxby. I will need to speak with you once I finish with Traxon."

"Yes,-sir,-Mister-Zhuni.-I-am-here-when-you-want-to-talk."

Zhuni opened the door to the back office to see Traxon scrolling through a computer screen. Traxon looked up and smiled his happy, twisted little grin.

"I thinking hard. Looking at finances and think I have idea," Traxon smiled. He took one more glance at the screen and then back to Zhuni.

"What have you been thinking about?" Zhuni inquired.

"I hate here. I want leave. I want help many. I have plan, part plan."

"Actually, we are attempting to protect you, but you are able to leave anytime you would like. You are not a prisoner."

"I know that, thank you. I want to leave Agón; I want never come back. I need help."

"I would be glad to help; what do you need?"

"I need no; I help you."

"How could you help me?"

"I have many, many credits; I help with escape."

"What do you mean?"

"I have associate who has connections with the Freighters' Guild master. I can buy transport for you, Sarge, Tan'cha, Joxby, everyone. I have come here and take everyone away. We go where masters cannot find."

"Supposed I am interested. What if we go with you? Where would we go? How much in credits do you have?" Zhuni was becoming intrigued.

"Right now, I have seven hundred million, eight hundred and ninety-six thousand, three hundred forty-seven credits." He glanced at the computer screen, turned back to Zhuni, and smiled.

"Excuse me?" Zhuni stammered.

"Joxby help secure my credits and in a Commerce Guild high return money market account, and tomorrow I have eighty-two thousand more."

"Wait a minute; you have that much in credits. How much did Stanton pay you?" Zhuni asked in complete shock.

"Stanton bad, I take a little from him every day. I take some from all his contracts; I take some from everything he buy. I make deal with accountant; we fix Stanton. More credits coming."

"You and Stanton's accountant embezzled millions from him over the time you were there?" Zhuni asked.

"Really, the accountant was doing it when I got here, and I found out. I was not sure what to do. Accountant tell me he set up retire plan for me. I say good. When I talk to accountant about idea to take cut from every deal, he sound happy, and we start making many credits."

"Okay, so tell me what you are going to do with all those credits."

"I tell you; I help. I give to you so we can leave."

"You want to finance an escape?"

"Yes. I want help everyone, and I want to make Stanton very mad. This be good, yes. I buy ship?"

"You want to buy a ship?"

"Good, yes?"

"Yes, I do not know anything about ships, but I know someone who was a pilot."

"I buy ship, and he fly, take us where we want go."

"Let's hold off buying a ship until we know what we need. I have never flown, so it may be a bit more involved than just buying a ship and leaving."

"Yes, you right; we need map."

"I think we need more than a map. We need to find out who is going with us, where we are going, how long it will take to get there, what problems we will have to get through, and all that."

"Okay, I wait. You tell me when we go. I give credits."

"Actually, I think we should include you in our next planning meeting."

———————— * ————————

"Great, just what we need now," Sarge said with disgust.

"Zhuni is on his way," Tan'cha said.

"Let Her and Her guards in," Sarge ordered the gate guards.

"You should just open as we arrive; this having us delayed is not proper treatment for the Master," She stated as She entered.

"Your Grace, there is no disrespect intended at all. You understand the pressure we have from the bettors to attempt to get in here and learn more than the house, so they will have an advantage. We take our security seriously, especially if a lapse would cause any hardship on Your Majesty," Sarge assured Her.

"Indeed. Where is Zhuni?" She inquired.

"He was up checking in with Joxby. He is on his way," Sarge said.

"I am here for Ohmdod. I will be taking him with me; I have a special job I need him to do," She ordered.

"I will take you to him, but before you leave, I would like to ensure you speak with Zhuni before taking anyone from the med lab," Sarge informed Her.

"Of course, Zhuni will catch up shortly," She spoke.

"He will. Ohmdod is at the beast." Sarge turned to lead the Master and Her guards.

"He is watching my pet. Such a good keeper," She implied.

"Hello, Your Grace," Zhuni caught up with them.

"Nice of you to join us," She snapped.

They arrived at the cage and called for Ohmdod.

"Yes? I am coming," Ohmdod replied. He put down his rags and tools and walked around the beast into their view.

"I need you to come with me," She informed him.

"Yes," he replied, looking at Zhuni.

Zhuni nodded.

"You do not need his approval; you are coming with me," She demanded.

"Kowstee, open," Zhuni told Kowstee as Kowstee turned off the force generator.

Ohmdod stepped out and was immediately grabbed by the arm by one of the guards, and they all turned to leave. Ohmdod looked worried, as did everyone else.

"He will be back soon, and he can go right back to his work, do not worry," She informed them.

She, her guards, and Ohmdod left the med lab, and the main gate closed.

"I do not like Her in the least," Tan'cha said.

"That is one thing I know we all agree on," Zhuni said.

"I wonder what that is all about," Sarge said.

"I do also," Zhuni agreed.

"Joxby."

"Already-on-it,-Sarge,-as-long-as-they-do-not-go-to-Her-quarters.-She-has-set-up-an-electronic-void-I-have-been-unable-to-penetrate-at-this-point," Joxby replied.

"Just get eyes and ears on them and record."

"Thank you," Sarge responded.

"So, funny thing we are all together again so soon. I have found a financer for our excursion," Zhuni said.

"What is a *fine-ancer*?" Tan'cha asked.

"That was quick. Who is stupid enough or crazy enough to finance this expedition?" Sarge stated.

"I will give you a clue; he is short, smelly, and used to work for Stanton," Zhuni puzzled.

"Traxon? You do know we need some incredible amount of funding," Sarge questioned.

"Wait! Do you two ignore me on purpose to annoy me, or am I just not important enough to speak to?" Tan'cha whined.

"Yes, we do," Zhuni said.

"You do what? Ignore me? I just asked a simple question," Tan'cha said.

"What?" Sarge snapped.

"What do you mean what? I asked a question," Tan'cha asked.

"Yes?" Sarge asked.

"Yes, is that answering my question?" Tan'cha asked.

"No, it was a question, as in what was your question," Sarge said.

"Oh," Tan'cha stated.

"So, what was your question?" Sarge asked.

"Oh, yea. What is a *fine-ancer*?" Tan'cha asked.

"A financer is someone who will give us credits to pay for our plan," Zhuni informed Tan'cha.

"Oh, so you are saying Traxon is going to have enough to do this?" Tan'cha asked.

"You do know we will need hundreds of thousands to just get this started. We will need to find a freighter and a crew crazy or stupid enough to tackle this job, plus supplies, including fuel, most likely bribing guards and loading crews, and much more. How is stinky going to cover all that with a couple thousand credits?" Sarge informed them.

"We continue to underestimate him. He showed me his account, and I verified it with Joxby," Zhuni said.

"All right, I'll bite. How much is he worth?" Sarge asked.

"Let me just say, Stanton never realized who he had working for him. Stanton was never truly an intellect," Zhuni said.

"Yes, we know Stanton is not a good judge of character or talent," Sarge agreed.

"Great, but how much is Traxon worth?" Tan'cha voiced.

"Millions!" Zhuni replied.

"Millions?" Both Tan'cha and Sarge expressed.

"Hundreds of millions, to be more exact," Zhuni continued.

"What?" Tan'cha blurted.

"Yup, we have a truly talented cohort," Zhuni said.

"I just want to say I am glad he is on our side now," Sarge said.

"He has become a much-needed member of our team. I am also glad he is now on our side and that Stanton is so arrogant that he so overlooks the talent he had around him," Zhuni said.

"Agreed," Sarge and Tan'cha said in one voice.

"Kowstee?" Zhuni turned to look at Kowstee.

"Yes?" Kowstee asked.

"You are a pilot. How much would it cost to buy a transport?" Zhuni asked.

"For what?" Kowstee asked.

"To move something," Zhuni stated.

"Move what? How much? Where is it going? Is it on the planet, or is it going to another planet close by, or do you need it to go across the galaxy?" Kowstee inquired.

"It doesn't matter; we just need you to be able to fly a transport," Zhuni said.

"Okay, let's get something straight. People who do not fly think a pilot can jump in any ship, throw some switches, and shoot across space. It doesn't work like that. There are ships that fly in the atmosphere and never leave the planet, ships that can go from planet to planet, and then there are ships that just soar through space and never touch down on a planet. All these ships can be called transports or freighters. But they all have different engines and control surfaces. Plus, they are built by different races. Which can be too large for someone of my size to operate or too small for someone to operate. Imagine a ship built by my race and Tan'cha attempting to even fit in the pilot's seat. You cannot just purchase or rent a ship and hope it will work," Kowstee informed them.

"So, if we purchased a ship, you could not fly it?" Tan'cha asked.

"I have flown dozens of ships, including fighters. During the Aashturian Civil War, I flew several types of fighters, the *Cyphoon Mark 6*, my favorite ship ever, the *Czartyn 367*, and the *Matadurn 3, 4,* and *7*. I also flew a *Titidium Larz* gunship. Transports that I flew were the *Septorian 923*, the *Toztat Meg*, the *Klazin 3327*, and several Ryanlian transports. All were interplanetary craft. You will have a hard time finding someone more capable of handling a ship, but you would most likely be better off hiring a freighter and crew," Kowstee implored.

"Hire a ship and crew? What do you mean?" Zhuni asked.

"Why did we not think of that?" Sarge groaned.

"You will need a navigator, especially if you are making light leaps. Even more so if you are planning to travel across Aashturian space or any other disputed space. Many smugglers and freighters will take a contract to move special cargo. You would be wise to do research on the ship and crew you would use," Kowstee continued.

"What is so bad about Aashturian space? Would you be able to help us with this type of research?" Zhuni asked.

"Of course, but I need to know exactly what you are looking for, why you are doing it, and where you are going. Aashturian space is mined," Kowstee replied.

"What do you mean, mined?" Zhuni asked.

"During light leaps, you have navigators and navigation computers that have to take into consideration the movement of every known object in space along the intended flight path. Imagine going so fast that a rock the size of your head could destroy a starship. Your ship is traveling so fast that a piece of debris or a small asteroid could tear the ship to pieces before you even know it," Kowstee informed them.

"Humor me. I do not understand travel in space. Explain," Zhuni spoke.

"How could a rock destroy a starship?" Tan'cha asked.

"It is a matter of physics and velocity. Imagine a starship traveling at a speed of a thousand light years. A rock would hit the ship with billions of pounds of force; it would blast directly through the debris shield and rip through the ship. The Aashturians used this knowledge to mine their space with hundreds of millions of Udminuim spheres. These spheres have a homing signal that the Aashturians use to avoid. If you were to blast through their space without knowing the signal, you would be torn to shreds without ever knowing it," Kowstee stated.

Zhuni, Tan'cha, and Sarge all looked back and forth with each other.

"I supposed we need to add Kowtsee to our committee," Zhuni said.

"He has proven to be helpful already; he was the only one who knew what to do with Klavan. He seems to be the only one who understands the concept of space travel. Plus, I am beginning to think we may need to rethink our resources. We seem to keep finding useful talent in the most unlikely places," Sarge divulged.

"Tan'cha?" Zhuni questioned.

"Our chances of success increase the more talent and skills we involve," Tan'cha told them.

"But so do our chances of failure as more and more become involved and the risk of the word getting out increases," Sarge exclaimed.

"Always the pessimist, aren't you, Sarge?" Zhuni sighed.

"Nope, the realist until proven otherwise," Sarge grunted.

"Okay, so we now have our financer and our travel expert, and our planning committee has increased to the five of us," Zhuni announced.

"I-would-say,-the-six-of-us," Joxby blurted out over the vox.

"Oh yes, the six of us. Sorry, Joxby. I sometimes forget you are in on all our conversations," Zhuni apologized.

"Out-of-your-sight—out-of-your-mind,-I-understand," Joxby interjected.

"So, we will have to set a planning meeting to have us all go over our ideas. Lunch, next rotation?" Zhuni informed them.

"Joxby, remind us of our meeting," Sarge reminded them.

"Will-do,-sir," Joxby replied.

———————— * ————————

Stanton was bright red and was foaming at the mouth. He was screaming at the messenger.

"Where is the scripter? He must have written it wrong; he will pay. Find him!"

"My lord, the scripter wrote exactly what you asked him to. You even checked it prior to sending it. Killing him will gain you nothing; you may need his services later," Boshduul assured Stanton.

"Then kill this creature," Stanton bellowed.

The guild messenger was used to hearing this when he delivered bad news. But he was also aware of his standing and understood that even with this ignorant Pryvlock, he was most likely safe. Plus, this rag of a creature was speaking sense.

"Again, not a good idea. If the guild will not come to you at this point, killing their messenger would surely ruin any chance of making amends," Boshduul declared.

"Fine, what do you suggest?" Stanton stopped foaming, and his tone was not quite the brilliant red.

"I suggest we return the guild's messenger with a gift and send him safely on his way," Boshduul demanded.

"So be it." With that, Stanton waved his hand to bring one of his attendants forward, leaned over, and whispered something in his ear. The attendant ran into the next room and returned with a large box made of a gilded shiny silver material. It was detailed with a teal-blue cluster of stones. The attendant handed it to the messenger, who took the box, bowed, and left the chamber.

"May I inquire as to the contents of the box?" Boshduul asked timidly.

"It is pure natural Starch. That always makes the guild masters happy. The box itself is Platinium." Stanton was slowly losing his bright red coloring.

"Correct me if I am wrong, but Platinium is the lightest and strongest metal in the known universe," Boshduul questioned.

"Yes, and that box and the Starch are worth a fortune. But they do nothing for me in my quest for power. I have so much of each I could purchase several medium-sized planets. That room and the next are full," Stanton let slip out. He was under more stress than normal and would never let that slip out in any other situation.

Boshduul was dumbfounded when he heard that and had to hold it together. He would move quickly past the breach in knowledge, hoping Stanton was so stressed he did not realize what he just said.

"Well, lord, I and several of our esteemed colleagues are still working several other angles. Not to worry, sir," Boshdull reassured.

"Not to worry, you say. We are only eleven cycles from the main event, and we have nothing. Not to worry, if this does not work, remember it is you and your team who failed *me*," Stanton screamed, turning blood red once again.

"Lord, as long as we have mere partions, we still have hope and a chance," Boshduul disclosed.

"You should know by now I do not work in hopes and chances, I want results, and I want assurances prior to any issues. We only have eleven rotations."

"I assure you; we have several avenues under review and several options still available. Do not think we have failed. I gave you my word, and my reputation is still on the line; I will not let you down," Boshdull announced.

"Fine. Get it done and deliver the Master position to me. Or else I will not be pleased, and I do not believe you would like the results when I am not pleased." Stanton was still a dark red.

---------- * ----------

Klavan had looked over several manifests and realized several were not reporting what was being loaded and offloaded. He was also concerned that several of his informants had been unable to get him any useful information. It was as if they were not even attempting to get him the information he wanted.

The amount of weaponry flowing through the docks was something to worry about. Klavan knew he had to inform someone of the situation; he felt the guilds needed to know what was happening. It felt as if the Master was turning the facility into a battle zone.

Assassinations. That is what she is planning. Klavan knew what was going on; She was planning to have all the guild masters here to force their hands and make them bow to Her, or she was going to assassinate each of them. This was supposed to be neutral territory. The masters had always been safe here; that was the reason the games were set up. The Master was supposed to be a neutral member. This was meant to be a place of entertainment and safety. There had never been the death and destruction wrought by any Master before Her. If She succeeded in Her plan, the galaxy could be set on fire as the guilds would turn on each other, and everything would disintegrate. It was the last guild wars that forced encroachment on Aashturian space and ultimately brought the galaxy into their civil war.

Klavan had eleven rotations to inform the guilds. But which ones? The Assassins would most likely see an act of war and want to get the jump and start a war themselves. The Commerce Guild only cared if there was a profit; the Gamers and Drug Guilds were under Her control and would not care anyway. The Miners' Guild was under Her control but may consider a change as Her killing of their guild master was not the standard changing of the Master. But Klavan would have to figure out to who and how to contact them. The Thieves' Guild could not be trusted anyway. That left the Freighters' Guild, which could be useful, the Renegade Guild (Klavan did not know how to contact nor even who, he did not even know their strength. Had they become stronger with their time away, or had they collapsed), and the Hunters' Guild was back. Klavan knew enough about their history to know they were actually the most honorable. He would have to contact the freighters, renegades, and hunters.

Klavan would also have to inform med lab of what was happening.

"System on, restart."

"Good-evening,-Mister-Klavan.   How-are-you?"   Joxby responded.

"Good, Joxby, I am doing well. I need to speak with Sarge and Zhuni.".

"Klavan-needs-to-speak-with-you."

"Hey, Klavan," Zhuni replied

"Sarge and Joxby?" Klavan asked.

"Here," they said together.

"I am also here," Tan'cha chimed in.

"Good. Joxby, did you tell them about the crates you found?" Klavan asked.

"No,-I-have-been-attempting-to-identify-them," Joxby replied.

"Well, they are gone," Klavan stated.

"What crates?" Sarge and Tan'cha asked.

"Gone? Not-good," Joxby interjected.

"No, not good at all. Joxby and I were looking around the loading dock since I had been so busy, and I realized I had not been to the docks in more than a few cycles. So, I went down and asked Joxby to search with his microdrones. We found many interesting things; the most reviling was a set of three massive shipping crates made of the same material as the Master's armor and had her crest on them. They were located on the seventh level."

"That is the level of Her quarters," Sarge informed them.

"Correct, but when I went back this morning, the crates were gone. But of more interest right now is my belief that She is planning an assassination of the guild masters. We are seeing a massive amount of weaponry and power cells. I believe She will either force them to submit to Her authority or execute them. I am not sure how the missing crates play into all of this, but the humanish dock workers and the exterior guards are having their weaponry upgraded, as is their armor."

"If that happened, the survivors, the number twos and threes, would start a guild war. That could engulf the entire galaxy. It would be complete chaos," Sarge stated.

"That is my fear. We do not need a war. This facility was built to provide a safe haven for all the guilds to be able to meet on neutral ground," Klavan continued.

"She destroyed that concept when She killed Tazmok, Moz, and their crews," Sarge exclaimed.

"Yes, She has perverted the purpose of this facility," Klavan responded.

"What do you suggest?" Zhuni asked.

"I believe we need to be prepared for the worst. If She creates a guild war, we will be in trouble. The med lab may need to be fortified more. I will siphon off some weapons and power cells and another force generator. We may need to consider a plan to attempt to leave the facility," Klavan said.

"We have a planning committee working on that plan," Zhuni spoke up.

"What?" Klavan exclaimed.

"Yes, I know it is a bit of a shock, but we have been thinking of getting off the planet. We are looking at our options and setting a plan in motion," Zhuni informed Klavan.

"So, I guess you are not worried about removing the controller from the monster, then?" Klavan inquired.

"No, we have actually figured that into our plans," Zhuni said.

"You are not even close to normal, any of you. I cannot and will not stop you, and I definitely do not want to know anything about your plans. But of course, if you need anything, let me know. You are going to get each other killed. Good luck," Klavan sputtered.

"That is what I have been telling them, that they are going to get us killed. But of course, they do not listen," Sarge announced.

"I thought at least you had some sense, Sarge; keep an eye on them," Klavan implored.

"That is my job," Sarge responded.

"I will be sending you some packages; keep me up to date on your needs," Klavan told them.

"See you soon, Klavan," Zhuni said.

"Goodbye," Tan'cha said.

"Klavan," Sarge replied.

"Good luck," Klavan said.

"System off now," Klavan stated.

---------- * ----------

"Sazon, what have you heard from the guilds?" Boshduul asked.

"The guilds are all extremely nervous about this upcoming main event. They are also wary about Her. The addition of the ancient guilds has also put them on edge. None of them are willing to put themselves in a situation that would cause them any stress. None of them will be willing to help," Sazon informed Boshduul.

"You just give up that easily? I thought you were a warrior and had courage. This disappoints me," Boshduul snarled.

"There are times that you know the answer will not change. In this case, the attempt to force the issue could cause more issues," Sazon stated.

"You could be correct. What do you propose we do now?"

"I do not know, nor do I care. I am a warrior, not a diplomat. That would be your and your boss's job. I was told to gather information, which I did," Sazon scorned.

"True, I may need you for something else. Wait to hear from me."

"I will head to my quarters. Let me know when you need me," Sazon stated.

"Make sure you are available," Boshduul demanded.

"I told you I would be in my quarters," Sazon snapped back.

Boshduul watched Sazon walk off. He did not feel this Swaklin was totally committed to the cause. He knew something was not right with this one. Boshduul would look to find a route to get the boss his power; he knew he had to do it himself but did not know what to do now.

CHAPTER 11

A Needed Procedure

Ohmdod was standing with the Game Master and four of Her guards at the back wall of the research facility. The room had a greenish-gray glow of the backup lighting. The lighting was slowly getting brighter. Various vague shapes could be seen spread throughout the lab. As the lights brightened, the shapes became microscopes, lasers, analyzers, and other equipment used in the lab for experiments and research. This room had not been entered in many cycles. Not since the last Game Master.

"I was informed you helped seal this chamber," She informed Ohmdod.

"Yes, I did," Ohmdod responded.

"I need it unsealed," She told him.

"That is not a good idea. It was sealed for a reason."

"I know it was sealed for a reason, and I will have it unsealed. I have need of much of the sealed information."

"There is more than information. There is evil; the last Game Master was afraid of what had been created."

"The last Game Master was a fool who did not understand the power he possessed. Now open it," She demanded.

"I will need some time and equipment," Ohmdod replied.

"You tell my guards what you need, and they will get it. Time you do not have; it needs to be opened now!" She stated.

"I can rush, but it will take a full rotation to get it opened, and we will need to go to two other locations."

"Where else do we need to go?" She demanded.

"We will need to go to Your office and to Your grandstand. There are secret controls we must access," Ohmdod informed Her.

"Interesting. Well then, we must get started. Proceed."

Ohmdod told the guards what he needed, and two of them left the research lab to gather the equipment. The other two remained at Her side watching Ohmdod. He did not think this was going to end well. He started to think he would not see the outside of the lab again.

*

"Zhuni, I cannot have you and your friends risk your lives for me. It would not be right," Abijah thought to Zhuni.

"We want to see you safe, and we need to leave here. She, the Game Master, is evil and will continue to attempt to control us and others more and more. We are all in danger if we stay here."

"This may be true, but I can feel that you and your friends could escape easier without me. Your plan to remove the controller is dangerous."

"Joxby has recalibrated the scanner, and we should be able to remove it without harming you."

"You do not know that."

"No, I do not. Not right now, but I believe if I am able to get a clear scan, I will know what I am dealing with, and with Jozby's help and Mazalla, we should be able to safely remove the device."

"You two are talking again; I can see your lips moving. What is she saying?" Tan'cha jumped in.

"She is worried about the procedure and all of us," Zhuni told him.

"Did you tell her not to worry? With the correct equipment, you can fix anyone and anything. I would let you operate on my brain," Tan'cha chuckled.

"Well, thank you, but I would have to perform a scan to see if you even have a brain!" Zhuni laughed.

"Fine, be like that," Tan'cha huffed.

"Stop whining; you know I am just messing with you," Zhuni cracked.

"Yeah, sure. Why is she worried about us?" Tan'cha asked.

"She feels we are putting ourselves at risk attempting to help her. She doesn't want us to put ourselves in danger for her," Zhuni stated.

"Tell her it is too late for her objections; we have all decided to do this, and there is no stopping us once we set our minds to an objective," Tan'cha announced.

"He is a good one, very loyal, as are most of your friends," Abijah declared.

"Yes, he is. And he is right we have all decided this is the best course of action. We are determined to see you free. During the process of freeing you, we will free ourselves also. We just now need to figure out how we are going to do this," Zhuni replied.

"I am happy you and your friends are here and willing to help. The Creator has placed us together for a reason. We all must have a greater calling than just being here. How can I help set us free?" Abijah asked.

"I am not exactly sure. We have to figure out a plan, put all the pieces together, and then start the plan in motion. I may need to remove the controller's inner workings but keep the exterior parts attached to you. I may need you to continue to pretend you are still under Her control, at least until the main event."

"I believe I can do that. I have realized the controller is losing its control on me. Each time She touches it, there is less anger," Abijah said.

"What do you mean, anger?"

"The scientists attached the controller to the anger and hate part of my brain. When She touches the controller, it creates an incredible feeling of hate, anger, and violence that I cannot control. But the pain of the controller is dissipating more and more each time. It is as if my need to control my anger and hate is causing my brain to reprogram," Abijah exclaimed.

"Fascinating. I have seen fighters with brain damage rewire their brains to bypass the damaged parts and use the undamaged parts of their brains," Zhuni informed her.

"The Creator has done an amazing job in the biology of each and every living organism. Truly amazing the Creator is," Abijah said.

"Yes, I see His handy work every time I help heal a fighter. The more I learn about the biology of all the creatures, the more I am sure there has to be a creator or designer of all the lifeforms I work on. I see it all the time. Everything in creatures' bodies works too well to just be an accident. Then take into account how the various planets' atmospheres allow different life forms to survive. Truly amazing," Zhuni agreed.

"Yes. Life itself is the most powerful force there is in the universe. Think about how precious life is but also how resilient it is. A planet can have thriving life, then be utterly destroyed due to war. Totally devoid of life, but then life will start to appear again. No matter what attempts to destroy life, it will always come back. Always. The most determined force known is life, the will to survive, and the need to reproduce. So powerful and determined."

"Yes, I do not fully understand the full concept of the Creator, but with what I have seen, there is no doubt someone or something created all we see."

"And the Creator put that determination into life so it will continue. He created the order of the cosmos and everything to give life a chance. He created order; you can see that in the way planets, stars, and everything work together," Abijah continued.

"I wish I could talk to you forever, but I have to get ready for our planning meeting and also prepare for the main event. I also have to check in with Joxby to ensure we are ready for the procedure on the controller."

"I can still hear you when you are not near me. I will listen to your meeting; you may hear my thoughts during the meeting. I cannot hear you when you are with Joxby as there is too much interference with all his equipment," Abijah informed Zhuni.

"Feel free to give your input; we will need all the help we can get."

---- * ----

Boshduul realized he did not need to get Stanton his guild. If Boshduul could hire a freighter and load it with the Starch, Stanton had Bosduul's retirement complete. He could load the Starch while Stanton was at the banquet; once the Game Master revealed Her plan, the guild masters would rise up to fight Her, and their number twos would be scrambling to evacuate the planet. In the massive confusion, one small freighter would not even be noticed. He could escape with the credits he had and all the Starch. He would have no need for the crew he had, and they would be left here to fend for themselves. As long as Boshduul stayed open to adjustments as they presented themselves, he could come out of this better off than he had planned.

This would involve hiring some of the loading area guards to help load the Starch and find and hire a ship and crew. Once the Starch was loaded, he could eliminate the guards. That would send a clear message to the crew of the ship; they would not mess with Boshduul after that.

He was spending much more time at the spaceport than he had originally planned. But as long as he could hire a ship and crew, he would be fine. He needed a fast blockade runner with a small crew. It would need to be built for a long haul.

He would not need to even pay the crew just show them the Starch, and they would receive a cut of the Starch. That would give them the incentive they would need. Once they arrived at their destination, he would just eliminate the crew and would not have to worry about payment. He could then sell the ship and add to his retirement. Boshduul loved the new plan; there was less that could go wrong. It was much more profitable.

He would get the word out at the spaceport that he needed a small blockade runner able to carry a small, rich cargo. The Swaklin may be useful in this situation; he had many contacts at the port. Boshduul would tell the Swaklin that the Master needed the ship to transport an offering to one of the guild masters. That should work.

---------- * ----------

"Ohmdod, once the chamber is open, I will return you to the med lab. I just need this opened," She informed him.

Ohmdod knew She was lying. He also knew that if he did not get the chamber open, he would die. But he was sure it would be a slow, painful death as She would attempt to remove the knowledge he had of the correct way to open the chamber. His only chance was to open the chamber and hope, somehow, that he would make it back to the med lab.

They were at the back of the lab, and all the tools and equipment he had asked for had been delivered. The lights were now at full power, and it was bright in the space now. One could see from one end of the lab to the other. The room was full of equipment and tables on which many pieces of equipment sat. The guards were there; they were always by Her side. At least two at all times. They never spoke nor acknowledged Her demands; they just did as She commanded. No hesitation. It made Ohmdod nervous.

He knew he had to get this open. But he was wondering if it would be better for him to die than release what was in the chamber.

"Yes, ma'am. I will work as quickly and effectively as I can," Ohmdod responded.

"You said it would take a full rotation, correct?" She demanded.

"Yes, it will."

"I have other things to attend to then. I will leave you two of my guards. They will attend to your needs. I will return when you are ready for the final step in opening the chamber. The guards will keep an eye on you until my return." With that, She turned and left, a guard on either side as usual. The other two stayed with Ohmdod.

Ohmdod thought to himself, *This is going to be a long rotation.*

———————— * ————————

Stanton did not have much trust left for Boshduul.

"As long as we have a few partions left, there is hope," Boshduul had told him. What idiotic talk was that? Boshduul was not going to be the answer. Stanton needed someone else, but who? What about the Swaklin? Yes, that could work. Get the Swaklin to do Stanton's bidding and cut out the middleman.

"Get me the Swaklin!" Stanton bellowed to his attendants.

As soon as he arrives, Stanton will tell him that he is secretly working for Stanton and report any and all behavior to him. This will work; the lower-level mercenary reporting directly to the boss. Mercenaries hated the people they worked for. This was brilliant. Stanton could not believe he did not think of this before.

"Yes, sir?" Rue responded.

"I need you to work for me directly," Stanton stated.

"How much do you pay?" Rue asked.

"What? What do you mean, you work for me," Stanton started turning a rose color.

"No sir, I was hired by Boshduul. I work for him; he pays me; he is my boss."

"I pay him. He works for me!" Stanton screamed, turning a brilliant red.

"I was hired by Boshduul, not by you. I work for Boshduul. You may pay him, but he hired me."

"Using my credits." Still bright red.

"I do not work directly for you, sir, but I could."

"Fine, if this is what it takes. How much will your fee be?"

"I would assume you want me to go behind his back and inform you of his dealings. I would have to do your bidding directly while attempting to ensure I am fulfilling his bidding. That will be at least twice the work, so I would assume it should be twice the pay."

"What? Are you insane?" Stanton roared.

"No, sir, it is a simple matter of math. Twice the work, twice the pay. I assume you know how much you are paying for our services. Oh, and I have to have my assistant's pay doubled also as he works with me."

"Your assistant?"

"Of course, Elu and I are a package deal."

"Who is Elu?"

"My assistant."

"We have established that but exactly who is he?"

"The Salvon."

"The short little one is with you?"

"Yes, he is," Rue commented.

"Fine. Get with the accountant and get her your information. I will deposit the credits," Stanton snapped.

"Yes, sir. As soon as the deposit is secure, I will be at your beck and call," Rue stated.

"I will need you to keep an eye on everything he does." Stanton's color started to return to normal.

"As you wish, Boss. He would you like me to report?"

"With this," Stanton said, handing Rue a small communicator.

"I will inform you when the deposit is secure and then will be available to your needs."

"Now leave me," Stanton said.

"As you wish, sir."

Stanton started to chuckle. He was impressed that he just had to pay an employee he was already paying twice as much to continue working for him. What audacity. This Swaklin was clever. He would be perfect. Maybe Stanton should have the Swaklin remove Boshduul. A plan for a later time, maybe during this upcoming main event.

---------------- * ----------------

The scan had gone well. Joxby was amazing at his ability to work with such varied equipment. Now Zhuni had to have Mazalla assist with creating nanobots that could remove the spikes in the controller probe.

The controller on Abijah had a receiver bolted to the base of the back of her skull. This was the visible part. The part that gave Zhuni concern was the probe that extended from the receiver and into Abijah's brain. The probe was roughly as large as Zhuni's arm. The probe was smooth and made of Zirbronium. Zirbronium was used often in medical and surgical equipment, robotics, and prosthetics due to its strength and nonreactive qualities. The problem was the spikes built into it would rip her brain apart if the probe was removed. Zhuni had to create nanobots to remove the spikes. This was not an easy task as the spikes were made of a metal Zhuni nor Joxby were familiar with. Zhuni had to take the information to Mazalla. She would know what it was, or she would find out about it.

Zhuni would do the surgery as quickly as he could create the nanobots. He needed to remove the spikes, and the probe should slide out safely. He would head over to Mazalla now.

"This is the scan," Zhuni told Mazalla, handing her the info disk.

"I am unfamiliar with the material the spikes are made of. I need those removed. We need to create nanobots to target the spikes."

"I am pulling it up now," Mazalla responded.

"I see. Interesting. The spikes are made of Boratine. A brittle material. They are sharp, and I am surprised there is no trauma to the surrounding tissue. Most often, Boratine causes infection and tissue damage. It was outlawed during the Aashturian Civil War. It was used as an additive to the missiles, bombs, and such the collective used. It caused massive infections and was considered a weapon that was too cruel. The Boratine was so brittle it often broke apart during surgery and would migrate to other body parts spreading infection. It was a cruel, evil weapon. If the Aashturians outlaw it, you know it must be bad. When you perform the surgery, get a sample of her brain tissue. I would like to study it. If she is able to have Boratine in direct contact with her brain and suffer no infection or tissue damage, she must have an incredible physiology. It would need further study. Imagine the healing properties."

"You help me create the nanobots, and I will ask Abijah if I can study her."

"That is fine. Let us begin."

————————— * —————————

"Lemuel."

"Go ahead, Rue."

"I am going to need some help from you."

"I told you I was on my way. I just needed to complete some other work."

"I know that, and I know you will be here as we spoke, but I need more. It is an incredible opportunity, and it is for a very special client."

"What is the mission? And who is the client."

"I need a medium to large transport to get some others off this rock and transport them across Aashturian space."

"What? Why would I risk my ship or anyone else's through Aashturian space? That is for Starch dealers, and you know I do not have anything to do with Starch."

"The client would be Shem."

"The Shem? From Mudagor Seven? The Savior of Bethleem?"

"Is there another?"

"Tell me what we need."

"I thought you would say that. Timing is going to be of the utmost importance; we will have several parties to coordinate. Yes, we will eventually need to follow some Starch routes. We will need to get transition across Aashturian space."

"My ship can handle our original plan, but I may need to get another or several other ships. I can do that. I have a strong connection who will help. I will need to get your exact needs."

"Thank you; I knew I could count on you. I will get all the details and contact you within a rotation or two."

"I will need three to four rotations just to get the ship or ships coordinated. Is there anything else I need to know?"

"We will have a massive creature to transport, we may have sixty or more civilians to deal with, and we may need to shoot our way out. Oh yes, we may have several guilds after us."

"Great, sounds like old times. At least there will be no trouble! Please explain a large creature. Get me the details as quickly as you can; I have some great connections that may come in handy for this."

"You are familiar with the mystic creature, a Drazine?" Rue asked.

"Of course, every culture has the story of a Drazine, or Drachma, Angels, Guardians, Watchmen, Overseers, or whatever."

"Well, we have one, and it is very real," Rue stated.

"Dagz, really? How big is it? Is it as hateful as the stories say?"

"No, it is not a hateful creature, more a violent protector. And it is huge, about the size of four to five Banteests."

"You certainly are making this an interesting mission. Get me further details, and I will make arrangements. I will be standing by and waiting to hear from you. Sounds like you are in deep again. Be safe and watch your back."

"I will. I am in with some bad people, but I am also involved with some great ones. I will watch my back, and I will talk to you soon."

"Until then, my friend, I am with you."

---

*

Traxon realized he had found a home. These were good people, and he would do all he could to make up for the trouble and evil he caused while he worked for Stanton.

The credits he had siphoned off Stanton never were going to be used by Traxon; he had no idea how to spend that much. But he had a good purpose for them now. He would use all of it if he needed to. In fact, more kept coming in. Rue had contacted him and informed him of Stanton's hiring him directly and the rules of Traxon and Rue's agreement that brought Traxon a percentage of that contract. It was as if Traxon was now cursed with so many credits. But he would put them to good use.

Traxon had spoken to Rue about getting some ships, and Rue said he would look into it. Rue was proving to be honorable and straightforward about his intentions. Elu was also helpful and friendly; Traxon had not expected that from mercenaries. Traxon felt he had a good crew under him, and with the med lab team watching out for him, he may be able to make a difference. He could not bring back his friends and some of the other Chordentia, but maybe he could prevent this from happening to others or even save those helping him.

Traxon had spoken with Rue and Elu about the breakout and escape, and they had some good ideas that Traxon was looking forward to sharing at the planning meeting.

There were still a few of the contractors in the med lab who had done the original work on the building of the space. They could work on part of the plan. Traxon had a good plan, and with the input of the rest of the team, he felt they had a good chance.

*

"We are here to plan our escape from this world and the troubles here. The Game Master is going to attempt to pull all of the guilds under Her control, and if She cannot do that, She is willing to start a guild war. Either way, it will be more dangerous for us," Zhuni started the meeting.

"So, we are all agreed, either escape with all members of the med lab or die attempting the escape," Sarge stated.

"I am ready to see my home world," Tan'cha interjected.

"This is more than you're seeing your home world," Sarge replied.

"I know, but that is the best part," Tan'cha smiled.

"Really, escaping this oppression and danger is not the main focus?" Sarge snarled.

"Stop, you two drive me up the walls sometimes. Let us come up with a plan. Stop fussing at each other," Zhuni blurted out.

"Sorry," Tan'cha apologized.

"Yes, sir. You are right," Sarge said.

"Any ideas?" Zhuni asked.

"We need a large transport that has light leaping technology. Then we need a few medium or several small transports to get us up to it," Kowstee announced.

"Rue working on transportation ships," Traxon implied.

"Really. Good job. I believe Rue is solidly on our side. I have spent time speaking with him and feel I am a good judge of character. He is attempting to redeem his fall from grace," Sarge stated.

"I-have-investigated-his-history-and-found-no-issues-in-his-past.   He-has-worked-for-many-good-and-bad-organizations,-but-there-are-no-wants,-warrants,-or-bounties-other-than-Aashturian-rites-against-him," Joxby put in.

"Let us say we get the transports. Any ideas as to how we get everyone out of med lab, onto the transports, up into orbit with the interstellar starship, and then across the galaxy through Aashturian space?" Zhuni asked.

"I know a bit about Aashturian space, and if we can find the correct ship and crew, they should have run the drug cartel or smugglers' routes through Aashturian space. They should have a homer to assist with navigation and their mined space," Kowstee said.

"My concern is getting out of med lab and into orbit," Zhuni said.

"Distraction," Abijah told Zhuni.

"What do you mean?" he asked her.

"Create a distraction. Draw the guards away from the location of the escape," she said.

"Abijah said we should create a distraction," Zhuni said.

"I have idea," Traxon quipped.

"Okay, tell us," Sarge said.

"Make tunnel to cliffs have ships on cliffs. Fly up from there," Traxon declared.

"We have the contractors still here that built med lab. They have done nothing since they finished, but they know who to tunnel," Tan'cha added.

"They could start at the back of the loading dock area, which is closer to the cliffs. Are there cliffs large enough for a medium transport?" Sarge asked.

"We look, find," Traxon chirped up.

"All right, we will look into that idea. We can put the contractors on that. But how do we get everyone out, and when do we do this?" Zhuni questioned.

"I believe we will have the opportunity at the upcoming main event. Klavan said the guards are being up armed, and he believes She is going to attempt to strong-arm the guilds. We could be ready to act as this conflict builds. There may be dozens of ships fleeing the planet's surface at the time we are attempting to leave. They could help cover our move. Imagine two to three midsize transports leaving at the same time as all the others; we would be lost in the crowd," Sarge said.

"So, timing will be everything. Klavan is getting us heavy weapons and another force generator. If Joxby can redirect the force generator for the cage to the entrance, that would keep the guards out for a short time and give us a much-needed delay," Zhuni divulged.

"When you remove this controller, I could create a scene in the arena when you need it. That could create a good distraction. I may even be able to fight the controller myself if needed. The last time She used the controller, I had a massive headache and was able to feel a bit of control," Abijah spoke to Zhuni.

"Abijah would like to help by creating a disruption in the arena," Zhuni told them.

"That could give us the diversion to get everyone to the med lab," Sarge said.

"Okay, but how would we get her back into the med lab then?" Tan'cha asked.

"Let us think about the disruption in the arena. If we could knock out the force generator there and have her go crazy, we could then reactivate the force generator and have it knock her out. We would then have to use the heavy lift to get her back to the med lab. After all, that is why we are here," Sarge cackled.

"That could work," Tan'cha said.

"I could shut down the force generator, I could even make it look like a power surge, and I could set it up on a remote control," Kowstee declared.

"I-could-help-him," Joxby said.

"Great, how do we move everyone at the correct time?" Zhuni asked.

"We will have to set a signal for everyone to understand," Tan'cha said.

"We will need to have everything go perfectly, and everyone will have to work together. Do we have a head count?" Zhuni asked.

"The med lab has run smoothly and perfectly well in the middle of chaos; I believe we will be fine. The team will work like they always do. As for our headcount?" Sarge said, turning to Tan'cha.

"Everyone, their families, some of the fighters, and a few handlers," Tan'cha stated.

"How many?" Zhuni asked.

"Total?" Tan'cah asked.

"Yes, how many want to leave," Sarge demanded.

"I am not exactly sure, but about one hundred and twenty-seven," Tan'cha mumbled.

"Well, this is going to be easy. We just need to sneak one hundred twenty-seven people out of the med lab and a Drazine during the main event and the possible beginning of a guild war while the Game Master is assassinating the guild masters and get into various transports, on cliffs, fly into orbit and offload all of them onto an interstellar transport. You people are going to get me killed," Sarge growled.

"Maybe, but I bet it will be a grand adventure, especially if we survive," Tan'cha laughed.

———————— * ————————

"Well done. I must thank you for the work you have done. I am impressed," She told Ohmdod.

"You are welcome, ma'am." He had a shiver shoot up his spine as he felt he had just sealed his death warrant. The chamber was now open, and the evil was about to be released.

"Now, what is it we have in here?" She asked Ohmdod.

"I am not exactly sure; I do not remember it all."

"Really? When we started you working on this, you said it was evil, so you must remember something."

"I mostly remember the evil feelings I had and the research they were doing and the raising of Brynja Ajals."

"Evil feelings and the Brynja Ajals, you say. As in more than one?"

Dagz, Ohmdod thought, *I am going to die now.*

"So, there were others?" She asked.

"I am not truly sure; I know they were doing so many experiments that it seemed there were many creatures being researched," Ohmdod hoped She would buy that.

"Yes," She said, looking down at him.

Ohmdod was certain today would be his last.

"You have done your part, and I will honor my word. Let us take you back to the med lab," She stated as She motioned two guards to stay put, and the other two took their stations just behind Her.

She motioned Ohmdod to head out of the research facility ahead of them.

They headed out of the research lab and back to the med lab.

———————— * ————————

Klavan knew something was not right about the shipping containers, but he was not sure what they could be. They had been on level seven and were now gone. Joxby had been unable to find anything out about them. Klavan knew they had to have something to do with the main event and the assassinations, but what?

Klavan headed back to the loading dock to see what else he could find out.

The loading docks were busier than usual. The Game Master had sent notice to all the guild masters, and they were sending their preliminary crews to set things up. Some of the guild masters were sending their number twos, and they were now arriving.

Many of the higher-ranking members of the local cartels and gangs were also arriving in anticipation of this massive event. So were mid-level guild members. This was going to be massive. The spaceport and the arena's landing pads were filling up, and the masters had not even started arriving. Klavan was going to have to shut down the supply deliveries to the close docks and reserve those for the masters. Klavan knew he needed to start using the supply trucks to move some of the supplies from the plains rather than load up the docks.

Klavan called the spaceport captain to explain his plan. The captain agreed to send Klavan a dozen extra transport vehicles to assist. The captain also said he would send the supply transports directly to the plains to expedite the unloading.

One problem out of the way. Klavan figured there was going to be a need for four to five times the amount of food and drinks as the last event. This would be the first event since the Wreckoning to have all the guild masters.

As Klavan entered the loading dock, he noticed a group of guards playing a game of Achbaon. He headed towards them. They were so busy playing they did not notice Klavan until he was on them.

"We have a massive main event coming up in a few rotations, and I need a crew to hunt down and bring back six to seven Banteests, and it looks as if you have volunteered; thank you. See the Sargent of the guard to get ground transport," Klavan ordered.

The humanhish guards grumbled, gathered up their card game, and headed toward the Sargent of the guard.

There was some fussing, and the Sargent came towards Klavan.

"I have a job to do, and I need these guards. They are my guards, not yours to boss around," the Sargent informed Klavan.

"No problem, let me go tell the Game Master that She will not have the feast She demands because the Sargent of the guard would rather his men play Achbaon than hunt Banteest for Her. I would like to see your corporal and explain his new position as Sargent of the guard because once I explain to the Game Master that you are in no mood to follow my directions, She will be very happy to have you removed; in fact, you may become part of the entertainment at the upcoming main event," Klavan bellowed for all to hear.

The bustle of activity came to a halt as all eyes were now focused on Klavan and the Sargent. The guard that the Game Master had assigned to Klavan stepped forward to make its presence known, and that was the effect Klavan was hoping for. The bustle of activity in the loading dock increased, and the crew Klavan had told to hunt headed towards a transport and started to head out. The Sargent gulped, took a deep breath, and stood before Klavan.

"Yes, sir. You are correct. I apologize and will fulfill every need, sir," the Sargent grumbled.

"I thought you would see things my way, and do not worry, as long as you perform my needs from this point forward, neither you nor any of your guards will be reported to Her. Now do your job, and I will do mine," Klavan growled.

"As you need, sir."

Klavan hated these humanish guards. Since the Swaklin had been reassigned to med lab, the humanish had taken over the duties, and they had no discipline. Klavan was constantly fighting to keep them in line. Klavan decided he was going to make the Sargent's shift impossible today. They were going to go over all the manifests and loading dock equipment. If Klavan could overwhelm this fool, then it would be fairly easy to siphon off the equipment the med lab needed.

"I have been at the beck and call of the Master over the last several cycles and have been remiss in my responsibilities here at the docks. So, with your helpful attitude, I believe now would be a fine time to review all the manifests that have come through since my last visit. I would also like to see what is incoming and how you and your team are handling the security of the deliveries. Let us go to your office and then see the loadmaster," Klavan demanded.

"I would be honored, sir," the Sargent huffed.

"Please go ahead," Klavan motioned for the Sargent to lead the way.

"Joxby, watch the schedules, the rotations, and the security. Also, take note of all details that could assist in your planning meetings," Klavan stated in a low, hushed tone.

"Yes,-sir,-I-am-recording," Joxby stated.

"Note the gear you may need so I may have it reallocated," Klavan murmured.

"Will-do-so,-sir."

———— * ————

Zhuni, Sarge, and Tan'cah entered Zhuni's office and sat down.

"We need to get Rue the details of the numbers," Zhuni stated, looking at Sarge.

"Yes, I have gotten him the info we have so far. I gave him the race mix so the ships could be prepared for the atmospheric needs. That is something I had not thought of until I spoke with Rue. There is so much we need to continue to work on. We have so little time to plan this properly," Sarge said.

"If we can get the ships here and set them up, would we be able to make some of the builds and such they would need?" Zhuni asked.

"Rue told me the people he is working with often have multiple sections of their ships set up to have several different compartments have different atmosphere," Sarge said.

"How does that work?" Tan'cha asked.

"It was rather interesting to me. Rue said they have a central live support system with many different gases and chemicals available to pump into the different sections. Sometimes they are able to pump the exhaust from one section into another as different races have different gas and chemical needs. The whole science of it all was fascinating to me," Sarge disclosed.

"So, the mix of races is not going to be a problem? And what about Abijah? How is she going to be?" Zhuni asked.

"No one has ever transported a full-size Drazine as far as we know. The ships should have no problem with size; it is just the thought of a vicious creature that large in a ship that gives some captains concern," Sarge continued.

"You did explain the truth about her," Zhuni scolded.

"Of course, but some are still not too sure. Remember, many of the captains have heard stories of the destruction the Drazine have wrought on smugglers' ships. Especially those who have attempted the Starch trade," Sarge exclaimed.

"Klavan is getting us a few more workers and some equipment to assist with the tunneling. He is also getting us a second force generator and some stronger weapons," Zhuni said.

"I do not feel we will need the weapons systems, but the power cells will help," Sarge stated.

"The details of the personal movement and the timing of the operation are going to be paramount. We will have to coordinate with the rush of the assassination attempts or the power grab. I believe She will show Her hand, and that will be our opportunity," Zhuni declared.

"I think the best way is for all of us to spread ourselves out and about the staff, and when we see the chance, jump on it," Tan'cah exclaimed.

"Yes, I agree. With our voxes, we should all be able to stay in touch and keep each other updated," Sarge commented.

"Joxby has been and will continue to be our eyes over the facility. He will let us know the best time," Zhuni implored.

"Yes,-I-have-new-monitors-set-up-in-the-grandstand,-the-banquet-hall,-and-other-areas," Joxby interjected.

"Good, we may find that prepositioning some of the staff may allow things to go faster. Including loading and transport," Sarge told them.

"What do you mean?" Tan'cha asked.

"Have the nonessential staff, families, etc., come into med lab prior to the main event and start heading to and loading on the ship or ships before everything starts," Sarge continued.

"Yes, good idea. We would be able to get them in and through med lab even before any of the event's activities."

"Sorry-to-bring-bad-news,-but-She-is-on-Her-way.-She-will-be-at-the-main-entrance-shortly."

"We will continue this discussion after we see what She needs," Zhuni informed them.

They all left the office and went to the main entrance just as She and her guards arrived with Ohmdod in tow.

"I have come to return your assistant to you as promised. I believe he was working with the beast, so he can now continue. I would like to see that he is making it ready for the main event," the Game Master stated.

"Yes, of course, we are preparing for the main event. This should be the grandest event ever," Zhuni said.

"Indeed. Go on, check my creature," She commanded Ohmdod.

Zhuni glanced at Sarge and nodded.

Sarge stepped over to the force generator and turned it off. Then opened the gate to allow Ohmdod in.

Ohmdod stepped in and began his scan and walk-through to check Abijah.

Sarge closed the gate and turned the force generator back on. Abijah was in her usual sleep position but was awake.

Abijah spoke to Zhuni.

"I do not like this. I feel something is not right."

"What do you mean?" Zhuni asked.

"I just feel evil more than usual when She is here."

"Is there someone else? More evil as if there is another evil creature?"

"No, evil as there is intention."

Abijah jerked and shot awake; she stood up, her eyes became slits, and she glared at the Master, then spun to tower over Ohmdod.

Zhuni grabbed his head and dropped to his knees, then fell to his side as before.

Abijah snapped her mouth down onto Ohmdod, whipped her head back, and he was gone.

The Master chuckled, turned, walked away towards the main entrance, and left. On Her way out, She clicked the controller, and Abijah dropped back into her sleeping position.

Sarge and Tan'cha rushed to Zhuni's side; Sarge and Tan'cha lifted him up and headed straight to the minihabs and Mazalla.

Mazalla opened the first minihab and set it up for Zhuni. Sarge and Tan'cha placed Zhuni onto the bed, turned, and left the minihab.

"That evil, vile creature. I must rid the universe of her!" Sarge spun away from the minihab and started to run to the main entrance.

"No!" Tan'cha exclaimed as he grabbed Sarge.

"Now is not the time. We need to ensure Zhuni is okay, and our responsibility is to get the others off this planet and away from here," Tan'cha informed Sarge.

Sarge stopped. Slowly turned to Tan'cha.

"You are correct, thank you," Sarge apologized.

"I am? I never thought I would hear you say that," Tan'cha chuckled.

"That is okay; I never thought I would say it." Sarge smiled.

They stood and looked into the minihab at Zhuni.

The vital signs looked good; he looked as if he was sleeping. They both hoped Zhuni would be okay again.

Mazalla informed them that Zhuni looked good, but his brain activity indicated extreme pain. That was not the case the last time he was in the minihab. This concerned her.

CHAPTER 12

The Hole in the Plan

"Klavan has given us explicate orders to build a tunnel large enough to get a full transport and several armored trucks through it. The homing device is set, and that is our target. We need to come out at the exact level. This needs to be completed a full cycle prior to the mani event. With that goal in mind, we will work through the entire cycle with three shifts," the construction foreman informed the crew.

The crew was stationed at the back of the med lab's loading dock. The loading dock was a large area that opened up to the main loading dock of the facility. The main loading dock was not connected; in fact, it was several hundred yards apart. But they shared the large, guarded courtyard that constantly had ground transport vehicles moving in and out.

The med lab loading dock was offset from the med lab's back entrance, an L-shaped area. To unload supplies and equipment, the transport would have to pull through the massive main loading area, back up to the med lab's dock, unload, and immediately turn right to enter the back of med lab. The loading dock had four spaces for the transports to unload, which lay along the upright part of the "L." Then the receiving and open storage area, then the back controlled entrance to the med lab, the base of the "L." There was a large amount of open space that would often be filled with shipping containers and power sleds to move the containers.

The construction crew had created a solid wall of shipping containers from the med lab doors to the back wall. This was a screen to prevent prying eyes from seeing what was going on. The crew had set their equipment behind this wall. The wall was created at an angle. The angle started at the back of med lab, where it was barely wide enough to allow for their equipment to pass through to the back wall, where it was wide enough for several ground transports to pass by. This created a wide enough workspace and, at the same time, with the angle, gave an optical illusion of space. When the crew had repositioned the lights, the illusion was complete.

The crew foreman split the crew into the three teams, and the first group began their work. This was going to need to be hurried. The sandstone was easy enough to dig through, but the cliffs at the opposite end were a more difficult rock to cut through. The crew was concerned about the depth that stone began.

---------- * ----------

That would put some fire under them. She thought as She left the med lab. They all seemed to take the loss of anyone heavy. Ohmdod was just an unimportant player in an important game. His part was over, and the information he knew could not leak out to anyone else, so using Her monster to eliminate him was a brilliant move. No one could have seen that coming.

She had to have Her guards ready for the main event. They had to be in the right positions, but She could not afford for anyone to know she had reinforcements. The few original guards were placing the explosives as She headed back to Her space. She still needed to be ready for any response from the guilds. They could fall in line as She wanted, or they could force the issue and need to be eliminated. She had to be ready for each response. Klavan was taking care of the landing spaces for the Masters; unbeknownst to him, he was helping Her set up the plan to perfection. He was responsible and reliable to a fault.

She now had time to get the research lab ready for the main event. This would blow everyone's mind. They would not expect what was coming.

In just a few rotations, She would control all the guilds and have the power She craved.

She just hoped the scientists She had brought in had not been noticed; if Klavan found out about them, he would look into them and wonder why they were here. She had sent Her guards to get them and had not brought them through the loading docks, so they should go unnoticed as they entered through the main public entrance.

It was time to meet the scientists at the research lab.

*

Boshduul noticed the guards at the public entrance. This seemed unusual; he would watch to see what was going on.

It did not take long for Boshduul to see two Skrenochs appear. They headed straight to one guard who motioned them to follow. They did, and the three of them entered the facility and withdrew from Boshduul's sight. This was no concern as there were three more guards standing waiting. Boshduul knew Skrencochs were scientists, so he assumed they would be heading to the research lab under the grandstand. That made sense, but what exactly were they doing? What could be down there that would cause the Game Master to bring scientists in this close to a main event? He would wait to see who or what else the guards met with.

The second guard left with a Foehlan, the third guard escorted a Toztat, and the last guard also met with a Skrenoch. This was a large group of Skrenoch; Boshduul had never met this many in one place. It was normal to have one, rarely two, but three was unheard of. The Game Master must be into something impressive.

Boshduul dropped down to the first level and dropped in behind the last guard at a good safe distance. He was far enough behind that the guard would not notice him, but he was close enough to not lose them.

They headed down toward the grandstand as Boshduul had predicted. They turned the corner to the research lab, and Boshduul saw the Game Master standing there welcoming the scientists as they entered the research lab. Boshduul had to stop before he was seen.

So, the Game Master had something big going on. Interesting.

Boshduul would head to speak with Stanton. This was worth letting Stanton know. Bosduul could distract Stanton with this while he attempted to figure out how to gain good standing with a guild.

*

Zhuni sat up. His head was throbbing. All he could remember was the Game Master telling Ohmdod to check on Abijah, and as soon as Ohmdod entered the cage, Zhuni had excruciating pain and collapsed.

What had happened?

"Welcome back. Are you okay?" Sarge asked.

"You have to stop doing this," Tan'cha said.

"What happened?" Zhuni asked.

"As far as we can tell, the Game Master hit the controller as soon as Ohmdod entered the cage, and the force generator was reactivated. Abijah went nuts and ate Ohmdod. Then the Master walked out, chuckling. When She got to the entrance, She hit the controller again, and Abijah collapsed," Sarge informed Zhuni.

"How long have I been out?" Zhuni asked.

"Just a short time; you only missed the evening meal," Tan'cha laughed.

"How is Abijah?" I cannot feel her nor talk to her."

"She is still out; I think she is okay," Sarge volunteered.

"I need to see her," Zhuni said, getting up.

"Mazalla?" Sarge asked.

The door to the minihab hissed and slowly opened.

"I advise against it; he is still showing extreme pain," Mazalla responded.

"Thank you, but we are going to get him. You know how stubborn he can be," Tan'cha said as he and Sarge entered the minihab to help Zhuni up and out of the unit.

They wrapped their arms around Zhuni's shoulders and assisted him across the med lab to the cage where Abijah was still sleeping.

Zhuni was reaching out as well as he could to attempt to communicate with her. He felt she was in a fog and was working to clear her head and thoughts. Zhuni's head was still throbbing.

Abijah hacked and lifted her head a bit. She hacked again, coughed, and gagged as a figure stumbled out of her massive mouth. It was Ohmdod, and he was alive. He was not even harmed.

He fell down to his knees and stumbled away from Abijah.

"Get me out!" Ohmdod cried.

Sarge looked at Tan'cha, shifted Zhuni so Tan'cha had him, and ran to the force generator. Sarge threw the switch to shut it off and opened the gate to allow Ohmdod out. He stumbled and fell out, but he was out. He was wet and smelled horrid, but he was alive.

Sarge reached down to assist Ohmdod to his feet and away from the cage.

Zhuni and Tan'cha joined them as they all sat down on the floor to check that it really was Ohmdod and that he was okay.

"I do not ever want to do that again," Ohmdod exclaimed.

"What happened?" Zhuni asked.

"She tried to eat me. Can't you see?" Ohmdod said.

"No. If She was going to eat you, you would not be here," Sarge informed him.

"The Master did not want you all to know what she was doing and wanted to kill me, but She must have hit the controller too soon and shut her down before Abijah was able to swallow me," Ohmdod insisted.

"I am attempting to talk to her, but she is still dazed," Zhuni put forth.

"How are you doing? Do you think because you have been communicating to her, that connection caused you to pass out?" Tan'cha asked.

"If that is how she feels every time the master hits the controller, I can understand her rage. The pain is nearly unbearable," Zhuni informed them.

"I am sorry. I did not have time to explain; I hope I did not hurt him," Abijah spoke to Zhuni.

"He is okay. How are you? What happened?" Zhuni asked her.

"I told you that I was feeling the controller was losing its control over me and that I was able to stop it. When She hit the controller, I was able to fight it a bit, but the only thing I could control was my mouth and throat. She wanted me to eat him. But I stopped it. I told you I felt an evil intention," Abijah told Zhuni.

"Is this excruciating pain what you feel every time?" Zhuni asked.

"Yes, I am sorry; I did not have enough time to prevent you from feeling my feelings and fight the temptations the controller forced on me."

"Thank you for saving him."

"You are welcome; it is not my nature to harm good people nor cause undue harm. I am slowly able to fight this thing. You need rest, sleep will allow your head to clear, and you will be fine shortly," Abijah informed Zhuni.

"I need to get that thing out of you. I will remove it as soon as my head is clear," Zhuni promised.

"Tell him I am sorry."

"I will; you rest also."

"What did she say?" Tan'cha asked.

"How can you tell I am talking to her?" Zhuni inquired.

"I keep telling you, your lips move. Often, I can tell what you are saying, just not what she is saying," Tan'cha replied.

Zhuni looked at Sarge.

"Your lips do move," Sarge responded.

"I could see them move also," Ohmdod interjected.

"Shut up," Zhuni snapped at them.

They all laughed.

"What do you know that the Master doesn't want us to know? In fact, what is so important that she would want you dead?" Zhuni asked.

"When the previous Game Master was here, he had some of the smugglers gather several Drazine eggs from Kashtuu. He had the scientists hatch them. Two Drazine died immediately after hatching. One started to grow. The scientists dissected this one, they experimented on this Drazine and mapped out the nervous system, the muscular system, the skeletal system, and kept it alive as they cut it apart and repaired it," Ohmdod explained.

"The dreams I had. Whenever I passed through that lower level under the grandstand, I would get these intense feelings of pain and suffering. I had visions and the pain of being cut apart and put back together. It was horrifying," Zhuni blurted out.

"See, I told you they sounded like someone else's dreams. I was right. I told you I could interpret dreams," Tan'cha voiced excitedly

"Really, that is what you get from all this; you can interpret dreams?" Sarge snarled.

"Thank you," Zhuni affirmed.

"What?" Tan'cha asked.

"When they felt they had learned all they could from that Drazine, they sewed him up and set him into a cryogenic freeze chamber. They collected all their notes and used that information to create the controller. Then they hatched her and introduced her to the arena. But they were so afraid of her that even being able to control her, the idea of a second or third terrified them that they sealed the cryogenic freezer chamber and all their notes and research into the back room," Ohmdod continued.

"How do you know all this? Were you one of their scientists?" Zhuni inquired.

"No, I was a member of the cleaning team and was then tasked with sealing the chamber up. But the last Game Master was not as paranoid as this one and did not watch over everyone and everything like this one, so I was able to look at some of the information before the chamber was completely closed," Ohmdod said.

"The design and build prints for the controller are there?" Zhuni asked.

"Yes, everything is there. The prints, the entire biology of the Drazine, everything," Ohmdod confirmed.

"Now we have to deal with this in addition to our main plan," Zhuni declared.

"Why do we have to do anything about this? Why even worry about it?" Tan'cha asked.

"Think, if they have all the research about the Drazine and they use that to control them, they could easily create weapons to harm the Drazine," Sarge said.

"But it wouldn't matter if we were not here," Tan'cha said.

"No, but if they want the Starch, and they can create weapons to eliminate Drazine, don't you think they would create the weapons, travel to Kashtuu, and kill the Drazine?" Sarge asked.

"Oh," Tan'cha quipped.

"How do we deal with this issue?" Sarge asked.

"If they bring another back, and you have been communicating with him, you should be able to speak with him. You have made the connection," Abijah voiced.

"Yes, I was having dreams before we met. I did not know what they were then," Zhuni affirmed.

"If he was reaching out while being frozen, that would mean he was still alive, and it could help us determine what type he is," Abijah reported.

"How?" Zhuni questioned.

"Freezing and having a conscious thought would indicate a frost, plasma, or a freeze Drazine. A Drazine of one of these types is basically the opposite of me. I am a Fire Drazine. I was created to protect planets during the heat season, to use my flame and heat resistance. A frost or plasma Drazine was created to protect during the cold. We are both powerful during our seasons," Abijah declared.

"On Kashtuu, you would be most powerful during the burn, and he would be most powerful during the freeze. Interesting," Zhuni disclosed.

"Yes, and if he is a plasma Drazine, he is a most powerful Drazine. Even with the experiments they did to him, he would still be powerful. Drazine heal quickly, and that is why he was able to survive," Abijah told Zhuni.

"What is she telling you?" Sarge asked.

"Let me finish up with her, and I will tell you," Zhuni stated.

"If he is a plasma Drazine that would give us an amazingly powerful ally to escape with," Abijah informed Zhuni.

"I will assume they will put a controller on him. If they do, we will have to hope they use the same design as the one on you. We can use the same procedure to remove it from him. But we will not be able to operate on him. So how will we do that? If he is under her control, that could be a major issue," Zhuni divulged.

"Yes, if we cannot get him free, it would be a major problem. He is young and would be inexperienced, so I could hold him off, but he would start to learn his ways from the collective, and in short time he could overpower me. You will have to communicate with him and tell him."

"We will still have to remove the controller; otherwise, we can do nothing."

"We also have to train you to ignore the pain and anger of the controller. We saw what happened when She used it on me, and you were unprepared. I was attempting to block that out of our connection. He will not be able to do that. You will have to."

"What if we both speak to him and teach him?" Zhuni asked.

"That may work, it has taken me a long time to get to this point, but if we guide him, he may be able to achieve success much quicker. We must remove the controller as soon as possible; we may have only a moment to do this."

"I will remove the controller from you and use that knowledge to figure out how to remove it from him," Zhuni implored.

"We have a lot to achieve for this to work. There will be a need for timing and coordination," Abijah stated.

"We have been working on the plan; this just adds a new layer."

"Sarge, lock down med lab; I am going to perform the operation on Abijah," Zhuni ordered.

"Yes, sir. You heard him, let's lockdown," Sarge commanded.

————————— * —————————

The research lab's newly opened chamber was full of equipment that was not in the front section of the lab. The scientists were pouring over the information in the recently opened logbooks and computer files. The Skrenoch were digging into the files.

313

The Toztat was working on the research equipment. He was the electronic specialist and was figuring out the purpose and operation of each piece of equipment. This would be important for the other researchers.

The Foehlan was investigating the freeze chamber. She was more interested in accessing the creature than anything else.

The Game Master was watching over the entire operation. She had six of Her guards standing over the scientists. The scientists were too enthralled with the information they were looking over to be bothered by the guards.

The Game Master had told them they would have access to all the information She had about the Drazine if they could help Her bring the frozen one back to full growth by the main event. She had one condition; they would not be allowed access to transmissions until the main event was over. The scientists were all happy to comply. None had had the opportunity to study Drazine before. To them, the Drazine were mystical creatures, they knew the stories of Kashtuu, but there was no evidence of the stories being real.

With this group of researchers, She knew they could get the Drazine up and ready for the main event. With two Drazine, the event would be unbelievable. Then with two Drazine under Her control, she could rule the entire galaxy; She would not need the guilds. But they would be the pièce de résistance.

In just a few short rotations, Her control would be complete. There would be no resistance; no one could stand up to her guards and two Drazine. She would soon have enough guards to say She had troops. With the two Drazine and troops, nothing could stop Her.

She would no longer need to be on this desolate planet; She could leave Klavan in charge with Stanton and move on to bigger and better planets. Her planning and work were coming together better than She had anticipated. To think all this began because of Her involvement with the Aashturians. The civil war had been better than She could have ever imagined. Timing was so important in a power struggle knowing when to listen, when to learn, what to learn, when to speak up, and when to strike. All that She learned at others' expense. Now fate had come full circle, and She was soon to get all She had worked for and all She deserved.

———————— * ————————

"Yes, sir," Boshduul replied.

"She has these scientists working in the research lab?" Stanton questioned.

"My sources say not just the research lab but a section She had to have unsealed to access."

"The last time the lab was used, they produced the Brynja Ajal. I wonder what she could be working on now."

"I will find the answer for you," Boshduul assured.

"You Dagz better! I am paying you and your team too much not to know everything that is going on around this facility," Stanton bellowed, changing to a dark rose tone.

"The problem I have been having is that all my electronic devices are experiencing interference when around Her and Her guards as if they all have scramblers."

"I do not care about that. That is your problem to overcome, not my issue."

"Yes, I will work with our Toztat to remedy that. I will work to get you more details. This could be a major development. If we can figure out what they are working on, it could be better than the guilds," Boshduul boasted.

"Yes, that reminds me. What is our situation with the guilds? We only have a few rotations to coerce one of them to stand with us. You have been stalling," Stanton yelled, turning a deep red.

"No, sir. Not stalling, attempting to force a response. The guilds are all a bit insecure about this massive meeting She is setting up. They are also extremely busy preparing," Boshduul informed Stanton.

"I do not care for your excuses. I care for results. You are beginning to disappoint me. I would hate to have to start over again. But I would not hesitate if need be. Get results! Now leave me." Stanton was nearly purple.

Boshduul left quickly.

Just a few rotations, Boshduul thought. In the chaos of the main event and the massive number of ships in and out of the spaceport, Boshduul was sure he would be able to make his escape quickly. Just a few rotations.

Now how would they overcome the interference? He had to see what was going on in the lab. He could not get close to it with the guards in the corridor and attached to the scientists. There also seemed to be more guards; was that just his frustration, or were there more? Maybe She just let them all out at once to guard the research lab. Boshduul would have to figure something out; he only had a few rotations to go.

He would head to the Toztat and get him to do something. Rue had made Boshduul hire both of them, but only Rue had made anything worth payment. If this Toztat was worth it, now was the time to show his worth. An electronic specialist should be able to overcome an interference problem.

―――――――― * ――――――――

Klavan had spent the rotation hovering over the Sargent of the watch and the dock's loadmaster. Both had been newly assigned by the Game Master, so Klavan had to impose his position on each of them. Klavan had found many manifests which did not match the actual cargo. They appeared to be arming for a small war. They were a large amount of body armor, hand weapons, squad weapons, heavy weapons, and massive amounts of power cells. Klavan liberated several loads of armor, weapons, and power cells to the med lab. If there were assassination attempts by Her against the guilds, the guilds would see all facility personnel as a threat, and they would have to defend themselves. Klavan had also relocated some mining gear to help them with their tunneling project. He had also been able to get some gear to Joxby for a special project he had been working on. Klavan had little knowledge of electronics, but Joxby was insistent on the items he needed when he saw them in storage.

If She asked about the equipment, Klavan would have to inform Her of improvements to the med lab.

The Freighters' Guild was a loose confederation of ship captains who worked with the other guilds in many ways. They would hire themselves out to the Smugglers' Guild, move cargo, and assist the Assassins' Guild with transporting their equipment or assassins for assignments. They would often hire themselves out to the drug cartels and the Starch traders to move cargo. This was the reason Klavan had made so many contacts with the Freighters' Guild; they had their hands in everything. Not all guild members had their own ships or enough of their own ships to accomplish their needs.

Klavan found it interesting that whenever he made inquiries into ships and captains, he trusted that they had spoken to Rue about the need to be hired and make the dangerous run through Aashturian space. Rue knew many of the same contacts Klavan knew. This gave Klavan comfort as he trusted these captains and knew if they trusted Rue, there was something good about him.

Klavan had been led to contact a few ships of the Freighters' Guild and a few of the Hunters' Guild, which Klavan found surprising. He had not expected such trust in a newly joined guild. He was awaiting their response. With all that was going on with the guilds leading up to this main event, it was becoming hard to contact these ships, many were in the process of light leaping, and some had contracts to move guilds and guild members here. With so many ships scheduled and scheduling to arrive here, Klavan was confident he would find a proper transport soon.

---

*

"You understand I have to find a way to insert these nanobots into you," Zhuni informed Abijah.

"Yes, and the best way would be through my eyes, under my protective lens, or through my nostrils. My body is designed to be nearly impenetrable. Even if they are introduced, my body's immunity may fight them off and destroy them," Abijah responded.

"I have taken that into account. Many of the creatures I work with have strong immune systems. These are designed to be neutral to most immune systems," Zhuni assured her.

Zhuni climbed up onto the bridge of her nose and faced her. Her eyes were as large as he was. He looked tiny, sitting on her snout like that. He held a syringe and leaned forward toward her eyes.

"How does your protective lens work? Should I attempt to inject it under the lens, or will you open the lens?" Zhuni asked her.

"The lens is involuntary, and I cannot control it like my eyelids. It perceives a threat and closes. Just inject the solution into my eye, and it should be fine," she told Zhuni.

"I am just going to drip it into your eye; I am not going to insert the syringe."

"That would be fine."

Zhuni placed the syringe close to her eye and applied pressure to the plunger. The solution squirted out and into her eye until the syringe was empty. He then climbed down and took position at a control panel.

Ohmdod handed Zhuni the hand scanner, and Zhuni raised it to her eye.

"Great, they are in, and we should be ready to begin."

"I need to rotate my head over to the larger scanner, correct?" she asked.

"Yes, just a bit more to your left, there. Now I am going to send the nanobots into along the optical nerve. Your optical nerve runs to the back third of your brain close to the stem of the controller."

Zhuni was watching a monitor screen similar to the one he had used so many times before to perform procedures on the fighters and creatures of the arena. This monitor was attached to a huge scanner, and the screen was large enough that a crowd had gathered around to watch the procedure. Mazalla was by Zhuni's side taking notes. Znuni would not allow recording of the procedure as he wanted no record of a Drazine's brain structure, just in case it fell into the wrong hands. Zhuni was worried about the future of the Drazine.

Zhuni had a control panel that had been removed from one of the surgery stations to be used for this procedure. Joxby had done an excellent job upsizing the scanner while matching the tools Zhuni usually used to perform surgeries. Zhuni was sending the nanobots deep into Abijah's brain. They arrived at the stem of the controller and immediately started to attack the spikes. The gathered group started to cheer as they could see the tiny blue dots swarm over the spikes and devour them. In short order, the monitor showed the spikes were all gone, and the nanobots started to disappear from the monitor.

"How do you feel?" Zhuni asked Abijah.

"No different. Should I feel something?"

"No pressure? No headache? No different at all?" Zhuni asked.

"No, nothing different at all."

"Wonderful," Zhuni exalted.

"Now what?"

"Now we will remove the controller, remove the stem, and reattach the controller body. That way, you will no longer be controlled by the Game Master, but She will see the controller's body and believe She still controls you," Zhuni informed her.

"What do you need from me?" she asked.

"Ohmdod, Kowstee, and I will step up to the back of your neck and to the base of your skull and remove the entire assembly. We will then remove the stem and reattach the housing. Will you be able to remain perfectly still, or do we need to strap you down?" Zhuni inquired.

"You do what you need to. I will trance," Abijah informed them.

"Trance? I have not heard that before. What do you mean?"

"It is a state we put ourselves into when we shut our minds to the world around us and open communication to the Creator. I believe the 'Ancients' called it prayer, or meditation."

"Let me know when you are finished; I may not be very responsive. I trance deeply," Abijah said.

She set her head down and closed her eyes. Everyone became aware of a soft humming or purring sound she created. It was soothing to all.

Zhuni, Ohmdod, and Kowstee climbed up onto her neck and walked to the base of her skull. Kowstee attached a large gun to the bolts holding the housing to her skull. He pulled a trigger, and the gun whirled, backing out a bolt. There were six bolts; Ohmdod and Zhuni held the housing as still as Kowstee removed the bolts. Tan'cha was standing next to them and assisting with holding the housing with two hands and holding the removed bolts with another. His fourth hand he held on to his hip, not sure how to help.

"This is the last bolt," Kowstee announced.

"Tan'cha, I will need you to take the weight of the housing as we slide it out. Be very careful and extremely smooth; we do not want to bruise her brain tissue. We need to just slide it out smooth and easy, got it?" Zhuni asked, looking down at Tan'cha.

"Yes, sir," Tan'cha assured.

"Slowly," Zhuni ordered. Slowly they slide the housing, connected to the stem, out and away from Abijah's skull.

The bolts had been attached to the skull, but as they began to remove the stem, some fluid began to drip out. Zhuni was ready with medical packing but was amazed at how little fluid was escaping; Abijah's body was repairing itself as fast as he could apply the packing. The stem was now fully removed.

"All right, now take it to Joxby; he is standing by and will remove the stem so we can reattach the housing," Zhuni told Tan'cha.

Tan'cha lifted the housing and stem over Zhuni, Ohmdod, and Kowstee and carried took it to Joxby in security. Joxby had used their preliminary scans to develop the plan of removing the stem.

Zhuni was amazed by the incredible healing process of Abijah. The stem was as long as Zhuni's arm and as large around as his waist. Yet the hole the stem had been removed from was already the size of his fist. That was as small as the hole had become. There was a mucus filling the hole. The skin had already scabbed over the majority of the hole.

"Look at this," Zhuni said to Kowstee and Ohmdod.

"Dagz! That is amazing," Kowstee said.

"Get a sample and see if we can recreate it. Could you imagine the healing properties we would have and the issues we could solve?" Ohmdod stated.

"Good idea, I will get samples of the mucus and the scab, but we will have to inform her and get her permission to study it," Zhuni declared.

"Of course," Ohmdod replied.

The three of them climbed down off of her neck and began cleaning the area and putting things away. It would be a bit of time before they continued their work and were able to attach the housing.

———————— * ————————

"I am working on the interference issue. It is taking time. I believe they are using frequency variant jammers. This is way some information slips through for a bit. It is extremely difficult to match the varying frequencies. I am working on an algorithm to correct this. It will take a few rotations to get this right," Elu told Boshduul.

"We do not have a few rotations that will take us to the main event. I need this to work prior to the main event," Boshduul screamed.

"Increasing your octaves and your stress level will not enable me to work faster. I have been at this for several rotations and may be completed shortly," Elu calmly replied.

"Dagz! Just get it done quickly; I need to know what is going on in the research lab."

"Yes, Boss," Elu told him.

"Dagz, I thought I had competent people, and I have just hired a bunch of Drogonds!" Boshduul griped as he left Elu's quarters.

Well, that type of attitude is certainly going to hurry my work up. I am only here for a few rotations anyway, Elu thought. He was looking forward to leaving this place. He did not care for their employers. Sazon had always taken care of him, and Elu trusted Sazon but was getting a bit nervous about these people.

Sazon had contacted Traxon, and Traxon had put Elu in touch with Joxby. The two of them had figured out the interference issue. The Game Master and Her guards were using an old Scatter Frequency Scrambler. The theory was, the device would jam all frequencies but would increase the power of varied frequencies from time to time, so standard anti-jamming readers would be overwhelmed at certain frequencies. This random variation caused issues with standard modern equipment. This was used before the Aashturian Civil War and was difficult to counter, but once you had the correct algorithm, the signal came in clearly.

When Joxby had sent Elu the scans of the shipping containers, Elu had presented the idea that they could use container ten to fifteen more guards. As they both looked over the scans, they realized the guards were not living creatures but were, in fact, artificial intelligence, robots, cyborgs, or androids of some type. With this information, Elu contacted an old friend who specialized in ancient warfare. Elu showed him images of the guards, the Game Master, and Master's crest. Elu's contact did some research and found the guards were from a planet destroyed by the Aashturians during their great expanse. This was long before the civil war. The guards were the palace and personal bodyguards of the planet's ruling class. They were created to protect the royal court from the non-noble subjects. They had put a major dent into the Aashturian invading force and had nearly driven the Aashturians from the planet. But then, one of the builders of the guard became greedy and was paid handsomely to create a way to disable them. It was a specific electromagnetic pulse that short-circuited their controls. Elu's contact was working on the details and some other information they would need in the near future.

Elu had never worked with a Monsee before. He felt they were two of a kind. They worked well together. Joxby was excitable, brilliant, and innovative. He often looked at problems from a completely different view. This often overcame problems Elu had not even thought of. Elu hoped this was the beginning of a long working relationship. They could be of use to each other in the future.

———————— * ————————

The three of them, Zhuni, Ohmdod, and Kowstee, climbed back up onto her neck and had Tan'cha raise the housing up to the back of her head. Just as before, Tan'cha held the housing up and handed Kowstee the bolts. Zhuni and Ohmdod assisted in lining up the housing, and Kowstee reattached the bolts. Once the housing was reinstalled, they all climbed down.

Zhuni went around to the front of Abijah and looked up at her face while everyone else cleaned up and put the tools away.

"Abijah. Hello? We are finished," Zhuni spoke to her.

There was no response for a moment. Then her eyelids flickered, and she opened her eyes. She focused on Zhuni.

"Finished?" she asked.

"Yes, the stem has been removed, and the housing has been reattached. Joxby attached a sensor to the housing, so you will feel a slight tingle when the stem is supposed to be activated. This should enable you to continue the ruse until we can remove the housing," Zhuni informed her.

"Thank you. I have never had anyone treat me and care for me as you have. You and your team are extremely special. It is as if the stories of the 'Ancients' are true," Abijah implied.

"What do you mean?"

"The 'Ancients' were to be a loving, caring society, then the evil got a hold of them and turned many. Many remained loving and caring. They followed the teachings. They put the needs of others before their own, just as you and your team do. But your teaching and example cross many races, which is amazing."

"I am just caring for others. I am not teaching anyone anything. Why is it amazing? We are all the same. We just want to care for each other. Different races mean nothing," Zhuni replied.

"That is how the Creator wanted it to be. But many do not act that way. Evil has a way of twisting things. Many see the different races as inferior or superior to each other. You see all as different but equal. That is rare," she stated.

"I believe all life is special. We are all different, built differently, look different, and think differently, but we can all contribute to help each other. That is why we are leaving and taking everyone we can with us. To hopefully create a better environment for all of us. Including you and hopefully the other Drazine," Zhuni announced.

"Yes, the Creator likes variety. Life is the most powerful force there is in the galaxy. But love and care for each other is what makes life worthwhile," Abijah informed Zhuni.

CHAPTER 13

Ancient Issues

They were all standing around the monitor, looking at the familiar figure.

Elu had sent Joxby several images, which Elu's contact had sent to him; Joxby had to show them all the images.

"Isolate-and-enhance," Joxby said to the screen

There was an audible gasp from everyone present.

"Dagz! That is her!" Sarge exclaimed.

"How old is she?" Traxon asked.

"These-images-are-from-the-Aashturian-expansion," Joxby stated.

"That was hundreds of cycles ago, right?" Tan'cha blurted out.

"More like thousands," Sarge informed them.

"You said there were more images?" Kowstee asked.

"Yes,-these-are-from-the-Aashturian-Civil-War," Joxby motioned toward the monitor.

Several images flashed onto the screen of the Game Master standing beside or behind several of the known Warlords of the Aashturian Civil War, then other images of Her standing with other rulers of different wars throughout the ages. None of them had ever seen anyone who looked like Her, and She was of an unknown race. Some of the images were not photos but carvings on temple walls or in ancient manuscripts. But the images all were without doubt Her. The same triangular-shaped head, the same jet black-blue hair. Her red skin with the black and orange markings; it could be no one else. But some of these were thousands of rotations old. How could it be?

"How can this be?" Sarge asked.

"Is it same one?" Traxon questioned.

"Using-face-pattern-and-physiacal-struture-and-race-based-information,-they-are-all-the-same-individual," Joxby assured them.

"One thing for sure, each time She shows up, there is war and destruction. Look at who She is with. Gron, 'the Butcher of the Southern Rim Worlds,' Toopon of Sednod, Stadnor, 'the Killer of Galaxies,' Frod Maaloth, and Mord of the Aashturian Civil War. Plus, others, a who's who of evil," Zhuni told them.

"My question is, does She show up during the events, or does She shape the events?" Sarge revealed.

"Seeing what is happening now and how She is preparing for war, I would say She creates the events," Zhuni said.

"Evil, not like. She means," Traxon interjected.

"Yes, exactly," Kowstee exclaimed.

"What do you mean?" Tan'cha asked.

"Suppose for a moment that She is evil," Kowstee uttered.

"We know She is evil; that is why we are all here and planning a way to get off this rock," Tan'cha blurted out.

"Yes, to a point. But consider She is evil. I mean pure evil as if evil were a person or a living thing, not an action or an emotion. Every society and race has a Dark One, a Demon, Hellions, Djinns, Devils, etc. What if they are real, and they are all Her?" Kowstee proposed.

"That is a good point and a terrifying one. How could we possibly beat pure evil?" Sarge offered.

"As a family. We have beaten Her to this point, and we will continue with our plan. It keeps needing adjusting, but we keep making it happen. If we continue to work together, we can overcome anything. Abijah said love and putting others' needs before us is what makes life worth living. So, we will continue with our plan and put everyone else's needs before our own. Maybe Abijah will have some insight to help us. After all, she said the Creator made her and the other Drazine to protect life from evil," Zhuni demanded.

———————— * ————————

Klavan was in the loading dock area of the med lab. He was informing the construction foreman of the project and the importance of the work and time frame.

"This needs to be completed by the morning of the main event. It also has to be large enough for one of the transport loaders to drive through. The explosives must also be in place," Klavan informed the foreman.

"Yes, I understand. We are currently ahead of schedule. My team has surveyed the tunnel route, and we have found that with the exception of a small portion near the cliffs, the ground is all this sandstone that the equipment cuts through easily."

"Good. Do we need anything to stay ahead of schedule? More equipment, better equipment, a larger crew?" Klavan asked.

"No, sir. The equipment is perfect for this type of work. The crew we have is the correct size, more, and they would be running into each other, less, and we would be short-handed."

"The location is correct, and there is enough room for the landing?" Klavan asked.

"The landing area we are tunneling to should be able to handle a large space freighter."

"You have not seen the area? Why are you not at the site ensuring it will work?"

"Sir, you asked me to run this, and as a former siege breaker, I can tell you the last thing we need to do is give any indication to anyone of the work being done. That is why we have the loading area and the work area separated by these shipping containers, and our crew is staying hidden. If I send a crew to the cliffs now, they will arouse suspicion. We will wait until the evening for a rotation before the main event. Then there will be so many ships and so much activity no one will notice. I will have the area ready for the ship the morning of the main event," the foreman assured Klavan.

"Very well. I trust your judgment. I just want to ensure everything is going to go properly."

"I understand, sir. I will let you know if we need anything."

"Thank you." Klavan walked back to the med lab.

Klavan could see Tan'cha standing near the monster and then saw Sarge, Zhuni, and everyone else over there. He walked over to them.

"I thought you were going to remove that thing," Klavan said, pointing at the housing for the controller.

"We removed the controller part and reattached the housing. If She pushes the button, Abijah will feel a tingle and know what to do. We will remove the housing once we get out of here," Zhuni informed Klavan.

"Well done. How is everyone doing? Ready?" Klavan asked, scanning everyone's expressions.

"We are all doing our part to make this work. How is the tunnel going?" Zhuni asked.

"The foreman says he will be ahead of schedule," Klavan responded.

"We will be able to preposition personnel and equipment," Sarge interjected.

"Yes," Klavan replied.

"What about our ship?" Tan'cha asked.

"Thanks to Rue, or his given name Sazon, and a few connections I have, we will have a few ships at our disposal. And thanks to this guy, we will have plenty of credits to finance all of them," Klavan said, looking at Traxon.

"Traxon happy help," Traxon stated.

"Yes," Klavan said.

"How are the guilds handling this?" Zhuni asked.

"Good question. Several are looking forward to all of this happening. They believe it is high time something shook things up. I have been unable to get a read on the Hunters' Guild, but I have a feeling they have a plan of some sort going on also. The assassins, I am sure, are not happy, nor is the Commerce Guild," Klavan spoke.

"Those two have always hated everyone else. I have been speaking to Rue and my contacts, and I have a feeling the guild war we all are afraid of will take place no matter what. Several guilds have been fighting a break of their own, and with the pressure of Her power play, it may push them to collapse. Some of the guilds no longer want to be a guild and have been talking of breaking away. The only guild that seems to want the guild system maintained is the Assassins' Guild. They are willing to fight to keep the guild system," Sarge declared.

"Interesting, that could play right into our hands. If they are all at each other's throats, our small group of ships could disappear into space and not be noticed in the turmoil," Klavan stated.

"Our group? Are you contemplating joining us?" Sarge asked.

"We would welcome you; you know that," Zhuni said.

"Yes. Come with us," Tan'cha chimed in.

"I am weighing my options," Klavan affirmed.

———————— * ————————

"Elu, this is going to get ugly. I may need you to join the med lab crew at the main event. I will have some things to take care of," Rue told Elu.

"I will help."

"No, the things I must do will not require your skills, and you will just get hurt getting in my way."

"Thanks for the vote of confidence."

"I do not need you getting hurt. I have to do this; I can make a difference this time. I know it. I have a plan."

"Are you going to let me in on it?" Elu questioned.

"Of course, I need your help executing it. But I do not want you involved on the last day. Do you understand?"

"Yes, you are still working to clear your name."

"No. I am no longer worried about that, I need to do something right to help others, and I know this will make a difference. Will you help?"

"Why do you ask? You know I am with you always, no matter the job or odds."

"Thank you. Have you and Joxby figured out the interference issue?"

"Yes. Joxby and I have also worked on disrupters. We are all certain that Her guards are artificial intelligence, maybe even full-on androids, and as such, a charge of the proper wavelength should either destroy their controls or at least disable them for a short period of time. That should be even the odds for you. We should have several ready by the main event."

"That will be extremely helpful."

"Has Lemuel completed his part of the mission?" Elu asked.

"You know him; he is always on schedule or ahead. He has contacted several freighter captains, and we will have a large transport: two medium transports and four small transports at our disposal. All are armed runners. He has ensured that their nav computers will interlink, and the captain of the large transport has Aashturian passcodes and mine maps."

"Lemuel has always been the most efficient and reliable friend we have."

"As long as med lab performs properly, all the pieces are in place, and all should go as planned," Rue assured Elu.

"You know that is never how it works. Something will cause issues. It always does."

"Yes, but this time we have more help and assistance than usual."

"Hopefully, that will help."

---
*

The small transport had recently had some weapons upgrades added to it. It also had an engine upgrade. This was no longer the small transport that it had been just a few rotations ago. It was faster and harder hitting. This ship packed a solid punch.

Lemuel was seated in the pilot's seat, speaking over the interstellar communicator to the same mysterious individual he had spoken to about the plans for the guild overthrow. He was speaking to the Freighters' Guild master, a known friend of the Hunters' Guild.

"Yes, Guild Master. The cliffs to the southwest of the facility. The contact informed me of the homing beacon's frequency that I sent to you. It will be turned on a cycle plus one prior to the main event. The departure will be hurried and may be tracked and under threat."

"I know the topography of that area; I have been to the planet of Agón several times. We will have many options for departure routes. It will be no issue." The guild master was sitting in the captain's chair on the bridge of the *Palti*. Since the master had been communicating with Lemuel from the bridge, there was no longer visual communication. It was only audible.

"You said you know the topography. Does that mean you will be flying the mission?" Lemuel inquired.

"No. I have a ship ready and willing to go, the *Palti*," the guild master lied to him.

"The *Palti*? I know that ship. She is the greatest smuggler the guild ever had. She could get in and out of any blockade. Most often without being detected. If she was detected, she would just shoot her way out and speed by everyone. This is historic."

"No, the *Palti* is a good ship with a good crew, but no better than any other freighter."

"If that is so, why are you sending her?"

"Because she is available. And is willing to take on the mission."

"The cargo is unique," Lemuel stated.

"To say the least. I have had the crew prepare the *Palti* as instructed. I expect payment prior to their arrival. Just to be clear, if that creature acts up in any way, they will jettison it rather than lose the ship and crew."

"That has been communicated to the client, and your terms have been excepted. I must say I am intrigued by the concept of the *Palti* and her crew being the ship to take this mission. I could not imagine a ship more suited for the mission."

"You most likely said that to every captain until you found me, and I was crazy enough to assign a ship to take this on." The guild master laughed.

"No, that is not wholly true. I know the capabilities of the *Palti*. She is a legend in the smugglers' and freighters' world," Lemuel assured.

"We left the smugglers a long time ago; we are no longer smugglers. We have gone legitimate and no longer run illicit cargo," the guild master insisted.

"Really, and yet you are taking on a task no other sane captain would touch because they would be going against the guilds," Lemuel declared.

"That is exactly why we will make this run. Because it goes against the guilds and will bring freedom to many. The guilds have become soft and evil, which is why their rotations are numbered. The *Palti* has a meaningful mission; it is not just about payment."

"Really? So why the need for payment before arrival?"

"I have incurred many expenses upgrading the ship. The supplies alone are more expensive than most assignments. I need to cover my costs and feed the crew."

"You seem to have taken a strong interest in this mission."

"I have taken an interest in it and will continue to monitor the situation. As the guild master, I feel responsible for all my ships. Especially when I assign them tough tasks."

"That is why you made guild master; your wisdom and care for those working for you is impressive."

"No need for further flattery; we will be taking the mission. Keep me posted as to the details, and I will pass them on to the crew of the *Palti*. When they make orbit, I will have you contact them directly."

"Thank you. Until then, I am with you."

"Until then, be safe and without fear."

---------- * ----------

The project was going well. They were ahead of schedule. They would be complete and ready for a full rotation ahead. The angle was perfect, and the passage would come out at the exact level of the cliff. The foreman had run out to the cliff to do a back read of the passage and was pleased. The cliff space was larger than the dimensions he had been given for the space transport. A good pilot should be able to set the ship properly and have room to spare. The area was high along the sea cliffs, and a ship arriving and leaving should go nearly undetected. With the expected traffic on the main event, this will be perfect.

The foreman was pleased with the job. He and his family were going to be on the transport. Klavan had explained the situation and the ensuing plan, and the foreman realized this would be a good new start for the family. He also realized there would be a need for a construction team once they made planet fall. Several others on the construction team would also be going. The foreman was the only one who knew about the transport landing and departing from here. Many of the others knew where the passage was going, but only he knew the transport would be there; this should keep those who stayed behind safe due to their ignorance.

When Klavan had approached him about the plan, the foreman thought it was crazy but seeing the details, and how well it was planned, the foreman was not only willing to do the job, but he was putting together a list of equipment and talent they would need at the final destination. Klavan had not told him the name of the planet but had told him about the climate and type of geology and topography they would be dealing with. The foreman felt they could create a livable colony in short order.

———————— * ————————

"Joxby, we are going to need to administer these nanobots from a distance," Zhuni informed him.

"Yes,-I-know;-I-think-you-administered-them-to-Abijah-through-her-eyes;-we-need-to-do-the-same."

"How?"

"I-am-working-with-Mazalla-to-create-nanobots-that-can-survive-a-blast-from-a-plasma-rifle."

"Wouldn't the plasma destroy the bots?"

"Yes,-but-instead-of-plasma,-the-rifle-will-fire-a-capsule-containing-the-bots."

"Good idea, but the capsule will not be able to penetrate the Drazine skin."

"The-capsule-won't;-it-needs-to-explode-at-the-eyes," Joxby explained.

"Yes, then the bots can be deposited on the eyes from the distance the rifle can fire, and we should be safe, and so should the Drazine," Zhuni exclaimed.

"I-work-on-delivery-system;-Mazalla-works-on-bots."

"Thank you; I will go speak with Mazalla."

Zhuni left Joxby's lair and walked down to the med lab floor. It made Zhuni a bit nervous to see Joxby because his space was so high above the med lab, and for a few strides, one had to walk across an open metal grate stairway. Joxby had the open grate installed with explosive bolts in case the med lab was breached, and he had to keep things operating. He could close the blast door to his space and drop the grate. This would form a twenty-foot gap to make it difficult to access security. Zhuni hated this part. You could see sixty-five feet straight down. It was nerve-wracking for him. To add to the security, the stairway up was open to the med lab and had several narrow sections and tight turns to prevent anyone from being able to bring up ladders or heavy equipment, like blasters, to get through the blaster doors. Tan'cha had a tough time negotiating the passage up.

Zhuni looked up once he got down to the med lab floor. He realized that Joxby had built a nearly impenetrable fortress high above everything. He even had weapons systems dug into the walls to protect the stairway and to sweep the med lab if it was ever over run. This could be useful on the day of departure. Zhuni thought to add this to the plan.

Zhuni walked over to the med lab's research area just across from the minihabs and found Mazalla hard at work.

"Good morning, Mazalla," Zhuni greeted her.

"Morning, it is good; I am not so sure. It is not bad."

"Joxby told me you were working on the nanobots."

"Yes, interesting challenge. Several things to take into account. Pressure from the rifle, the need to be delivered in a gaseous form after being fired, the need for the capsule to explode on impact but not from the gun pressure, and we have not spoken about the need for the nanobots to do the work without guidance. Much to be done and figured out. I have done much to complete this assignment," Mazalla groaned in a fashion Zhuni had not heard before.

"Mazalla, are you okay?" Zhuni asked.

"Yes."

"No, you seem stressed or upset."

She stopped her work, lifted her head to look directly at Zhuni, took a deep breath, and began speaking.

"I do not understand. I am a young researcher. I am used to observing. I have been forced to operate outside of my abilities and my knowledge. I have lives depending upon me. I am not used to that. I am feeling great weight and responsibility. I do not like this, it is a mix of emotions I did not know I had, and I do not like it," Mazalla disclosed.

"I nor anyone else is forcing you to do anything. Everyone is free to leave the med lab any time they want; we believe in freedom of choice," Zhuni stated.

"No, that is not the problem; I do not feel forced by you or anyone. I feel forced because I must perform for everyone because you are all relying on me. I understand my responsibilities."

"We are all under pressure and are doing our best to work as a team to overcome the situation we are in. I completely understand. Just a few dozen rotations ago, I was just a lower-level medic. Now I have hundreds of lives under my control. All I want to do is do what is best for all of us. We are all going to die, whether it is here as slaves under an evil regime or across the galaxy looking for freedom. We all have a similar goal, freedom. I can only lead; I cannot do it all. I need each of you to do your best. You have the abilities no one else has. I believe what you are feeling is the responsibility and love we all have for each other. We are all under tremendous pressure, but in the long run, we will all be better for putting everyone else first. When we put others' needs before ours, we feel pressured to begin with, and then we start to feel it is the correct way to be."

"I am feeling properly?"

"I only know you from our interactions; I am not familiar with you and your race emotionally. I believe you have been around us long enough to have feelings for all of us, and you are beginning to feel a part of the team rather than an outsider, like when you first began here. You are doing wonderful work, and we are all counting on you as we are all counting on each other. There is no more pressure on you than there is on anyone else. If you can make it work, that would be fantastic. If not, we will develop another idea. We must be flexible in our goals."

"Thank you. I feel better. I am not usually an emotional species."

"Again, the only way you can let us down is by quitting. Continue your work, and we can all help you to the best of our abilities," Zhuni assured her.

"I would like to inform you of the progress I have made now that I am more understanding of my purpose."

"Great, tell me," Zhuni exclaimed.

"I believe I have overcome the pressure issue by placing the nanobots in a liquid; this should protect the nanobots from the pressure and provide a delivery substance at the same time. Now the nanobots we developed to remove the spikes will need guidance. The Boratine needs to be removed completely. I have developed hunter nanobots that will locate the Boratine. Then I need to develop the ability for them to guide the Boratine removing nanobots to the Boratine. They will all need to be in the liquid delivery system. Joxby is developing a two-stage capsule. The outer casing will break away once fired from the rifle allowing the capsule to explode on target," Mazalla informed Zhuni.

"There you have it. The reason we have you working on the project, brilliant. You and Joxby have it all under control."

"What if the delivery system doesn't work properly, our what if the shooter misses? We only have time to create one or two capsules," Mazalla worried.

"This is where you have to stop worrying. I have learned that you can only do so much. The capsule is not your problem; Joxby will take care of that; the shooter missing is not your problem; that is the marksman's job. You can only control what you do; you must trust and rely on others to do their jobs. We all count on each other," Zhuni assured her.

"Well then, I will continue my work and hope everyone else does their jobs properly."

"I assure you, they will. No one has let any of us down so far. I do not see that changing in the next few rotations."

———————— * ————————

The *Palti* slid into a low orbit around the middle moon of Agón. The moon Colthon. The *Palti* had ejected a repeating as she approached the moon. The *Palti* would remain on the far side, away from Agón, and the repeater would continue to a spot that would allow transmissions to be bounced off of it to the surface of Agón without exposing the *Palti*. The facility would not be able to see the repeater as small as it was.

The captain ordered communications to be opened and requested Lemuel be contacted and informed that the *Palti* was on station. The captain was a humanoid figure who wore a crisp, clean jumpsuit of dark blue. The jumpsuit had several patches on it; the most prominent was the seal of the *Palti* on the left upper chest. The Freighters' Guild emblem was on the right upper shoulder. Over the jumpsuit was a brownish-orange vest. The figure also wore a greyish-blue helmet with a wide slit across the area which appeared to be where the figure's eyes would be. The slit was filled with a red material which gave a slight glow. The figure was small compared to the others on the bridge, but just by the gate and reaction of those around it, you knew this individual deserved attention and respect. The figure walked over to the captain's seat and sat down, glancing over the bridge.

The bridge was always a bustle of activity, especially after coming out of a leap. The various bridge crew were checking their stations, equipment, and fellow crew members in their departments.

The *Palti* was a massive ship for a transport. It was unique in the fact that it had a hanger bay and a cargo bay. It had once been a battle cruiser. This ship had two landing craft, six starfighters, and four atmospheric fighters. It could launch and recover its smaller ships while in flight. From the bridge, the crew could coordinate the smaller ships and track them from the flight control station at the back of the bridge; the station had seats for two controllers who sat with their backs to the rest of the bridge crew. Directly in front of flight control was weapons control. This station had four operators who were currently checking their systems. Their backs were to the flight control station and faced the front of the bridge. Both stations were set higher than the rest of the bridge. Directly in front of the weapons station was a raised platform with two chairs for the captain and executive officer. Directly in front of the captain's and executive officer's chairs were large clear viewers that had the information from each station projected on them to allow the captain and executive officer to see the status of each station they needed to see. Just past those monitors were damage control and countermeasures; a station below and in front of them had plotting and secondary navigation. On a lower level and toward the front of the oval bridge were stations for navigation and leap control, life support, and cargo along the outside edge of the oval, as were security and communications. Pilot and copilot were at the front of the oval, and to the sides, each was on opposite sides of the bridge with navigation and leap control set between them.

This was a large bridge compared to most transports. It was a battle cruiser, after all. Most transports did not have fighters, leap abilities, and such massive weapons systems and countermeasures as this ship had. She could force her way through any blockade and insert her cargo wherever it was needed.

"Captain, we have Lemuel," communications informed the captain.

"Thank you, Comm; the *Palti* has set their orbit and is on station," the captain stated.

"Welcome; glad you made it safely. As you can see, the full deposit has been made. Your surface contact is a Monsee named Joxby. You will also be able to contact an individual named Rue. Joxby is their main contact. Rue works for the client and is your secondary or emergency contact."

"Are we certain that the area has the homing beacon and is properly prepared?"

"That is something you and your crew can contact the surface and ask. To my knowledge, they are ready."

"Well then, we will contact them. Until next time."

"Until next time," Lemuel responded.

"Come out," the captain commanded.

The guild master claimed they were not going to run this mission, but even without visual, Lemuel was certain the voice was that of the guild master. The voice was disguised, but the rhythm, Lemuel was certain it was her. This mission could not have a better ship or captain.

———————— * ————————

Boshduul could see the idea of presenting a guild to Stanton was not going to materialize. He also had not been able to get close to the research lab yet. He had nothing to present prior to the main event. It was just a few rotations away. He may have to just cut and run. He still had a good nest egg to head home and retire, or he could continue his work and retire very rich shortly. It was just not going to be as foolproof as he had planned. It may be time to put Stanton's fall into motion. Boshduul loved the action and the death he wrought as an assassin, but it was getting too dangerous here. He would get his escape started.

The med lab still had not seen him nor knew of his existence, so that was a good thing. He could use that to his advantage. He would sneak in by way of the loading dock and plant some of Stanton's listening devices. Then while meeting with the Game Master, he would "find" a few of Stanton's listening devices. This would put the pressure on Stanton, and he would have no idea why. He would get irritated and would not be able to handle it. This would allow Boshduul the time to load the Starch. He just needed a few hired hands.

Boshduul only had a few rotations left. The Swaklin and his assistant would not be a part of Boshduul's future, they would not be a part of the Starch pilferage, Boshduul did not trust them, and they would be difficult to eliminate on a small ship. It was time to cut all ties and be gone.

He would go to the loading dock and gather some equipment that would be good for his future. He would also grab some help to load a ship in preparation for departure. Now he just needed a ship and one pilot he could trust. He would go to the marketplace and begin making inquiries. He may even be able to contact some old friends who could help him.

Boshduul went to the loading dock and spoke with a few of his informants. Now he had the crew remove the Starch and load the ship. These fools were so narrow-minded and greedy that they would never see their own elimination coming.

Now to find a ship. It had to be fast, armed, and large enough to take on enough Starch to make Boshduul rich and small enough to not threaten any blockade or other guild ships.

Boshduul sat down at the cafe he liked; it was in the central part of the marketplace, it had two levels, and Boshduul liked to sit at the lower level under the upper deck. He would sit with his back to the wall but be close enough to the crowd as they went by that he could often pick up bits of conversation. With his rags hiding him for the most part, others pacing by would often stop right by him and talk. They did not realize he was a living creature under the rags. He was able to hear details he would not hear otherwise.

Boshduul did not realize as he walked over to the café a small furry figure seated on the upper deck had spotted him. That small figure called in support, and immediately a microdrone was on sight, watching Boshduul and recording everything.

————— * —————

Klavan had gotten the Banteest hunted and had them delivered just as the Drazine was coming out of its thaw. It would be hungry and had a lot of growing to do in the next few rotations.

She had the guards bring the Banteest in and deposit them into the chamber the Drazine was in. It would need to feed.

The scientists informed Her that they had a controller built, and it would be ready to install as soon as the creature was fully grown. They had been going over all the documentation that had been written, and they were certain they would be able to control the creature and install the controller by just adjusting the atmosphere in the chamber. Then the controller could be attached.

She was pleased with the progress. This was going to work well. The scientists had informed Her that this Drazine was a winter or cold Drazine and was the opposite of Her current pet. This should prove interesting. The scientists had also told Her that this Drazine could generate plasma and electric blasts rather than the fire and slag like Her current pet.

Having two pets under Her control should impress the guild masters; if that did not do it, then the explosives and extra guards would. The galaxy would be Hers in just a few rotations; nothing could stop Her.

Klavan had made the preparations for the guild masters, their landing spots, their quarters, their seats at the banquet, and their seats at the main event. All the minor and major details were ready. She had informed Klavan to tell med lab to expect more casualties than even the last main event. She did not need them to know most of the casualties would be from Her guards and the explosives She had them set up.

Once she had full control over the guilds, She would no longer need to be stuck here at the games. She would turn that over to Klavan and Stanton. Klavan would be in charge, and Stanton would assist. She could then travel at Her leisure and handle only what she found important.

———————— * ————————

Klavan had spent his last few years attempting to make up for his earlier failings. The med lab had already saved many lives, but the staff, the best part of the med lab, was going to take their chances and attempt an escape during the chaos of the main event. Klavan could most likely claim ignorance about the escape plan; after all, if he knew about it, why didn't he go also? But the idea of staying and reorganizing the facility was intriguing. This Game Master was not going to stay here. Klavan was certain he knew Her kind. She would be leaving and leave someone in charge while She traveled about consolidating Her power. The logical choice for Her was Klavan himself. He knew how everything ran, knew all the players, and understood the fights and the fighters. Besides, there was no way She would leave Stanton in charge. Klavan was beginning to rethink his thought of leaving. This could be the big break he was looking for. He might be able to revisit his home if he was the Game Master. That would be a huge honor.

Maybe he was playing this all wrong. If he could stay focused and maintain his morals, he could run the facility in a proper way without the humanish guards, without the crooked deeds. He could turn it into a legitimate facility that may attract more than the guilds. He would need to do that anyway. The guilds were going to fight amongst themselves and eliminate each other, or they would fall under Her control. Either way, Klavan's best play may be to stand strong where he was.

This was not what he had been thinking just a few rotations ago.

———————— * ————————

Joxby was working on the interference issue. He had lost communication and tracking on the rags thing when he got too close to the guards down at the research lab. But now Joxby had that issue figured out and was hoping "Rags" would show up again soon. If he did, Joxby should be able to set a microdrone and tracker on him again with the upgraded signal scrambler. That would protect the drone from the interference.

Elu had just sent the final frequency that was needed to create the electromagnetic pulses. Joxby would begin working on this project.

Then the vox squawked. It was Traxon.

"Joxby, find Rags."

"No,-I-have-not-found-rags."

"Yes, I find."

"You-found-rags?" Joxby asked as he reached over to one of his many screens, pushed a few buttons, and suddenly had a visual as a few microdrones dropped out of the bottom of the security center.

"Yes, he under me. At market. The Smuggler's Nova. I on top deck, he under me."

"Yes,-I-have-your-location-on-the-vox;-I also-know-where-the-tavern-is."

"He order drink and food; he here for bit of time."

"Great,-microdrone-and-tracker-in-bound."

"I watch him; when you find, tell me."

"Drones-coming-out-our-back-loading-dock."

Joxby could see the construction crew as the drones flew out their small doorway, flew up over the shipping containers, and headed out across the loading yard. Joxby could see the humanish guards and dock workers loading and unloading equipment. The drones flew out past the main entrance to the facility and towards the market area. Joxby broke one drone off and circled back to the main entrance; something did not look right. He had the single drone hold position as he guided the others into the target. There he was, up against the wall under the large upper deck. Joxby flew the tracker and two drones up until they nearly touched the underside of the upper deck. He then dropped the tracker down, and he saw it set properly. Now the drones moved forward; one hovered above "Rags," and the other moved across the alleyway to get a wide view. He put both drones on auto. Joxby had programmed them to follow the target and use the architectural and engineering drawings loaded into the med lab's computer to navigate their flight.

Now Joxby returned his attention to the lone drone he had placed into a holding pattern at the main entrance. Why were there two of Her guards mounting a crest of Hers on the wall? It looked to be awkward and heavy. It looked too heavy to be just decorative. The guards were spending too much time looking around at the crowds wandering through the area as if they were placing the crest to cover as much of the area as possible; they kept looking at the crest as if to target something. Targeting. That is exactly what they were doing; these were being set up as bombs. Bombs to create as much death and chaos as possible.

Joxby jumped over to a different screen and monitor, touched the screen a few times, and another microdrone dropped from under the security center. Joxby guided this one to the crest but positioned it above and a few yards from it to continue to watch the guards, the crest, and how they were setting up their targeting. The previous microdrone was sent on its way to join the others at the Smugglers' Nova.

Joxby turned back to the screen and touched it a few more times, and again a drone dropped. This one was sent on a search to see if there were more crests set around the facility. Joxby quickly found several, all at what would be considered choke points around the entrances. There were also several at the landing areas, especially the sites set aside for guild masters. He hoped the guards would finish quickly so he could get samples and find what type of explosive these were. He should contact Zhuni, Sarge, Rue, and Elu and inform them.

———————— * ————————

"I have to go report to the Game Master. She wants all departments to report their readiness for the main event. Sarge, you are in charge while we are gone," Zhuni informed Sarge as he and Tan'cha walked across med lab towards the main entrance.

"Joy, thank you. Have fun," Sarge shot back.

"Oh yes, we are looking forward to the excitement," Zhuni called back.

"Always a good time," Tan'cha added.

They entered the conference room. This had recently been redone. The walls were covered with what looked to be the sides of the shipping containers that they had last seen in the hallway on level seven. The room felt oppressive. It was overbearing. This conference room was massive. The ceilings were eighteen feet high. The table everyone was gathered around looked to hold over fifty. The floor the table sat on was highly polished stone that had been heat-treated to be a nearly ebony color to match the wall coverings. The heat treatment had darkened the stone but also brought out the silver specks in the stone, so looking down, it seemed you were looking into the night sky.

Everyone gathered was dead quiet. There were all of the Dwayans, the department heads, the loadmaster from the loading docks, the head of the humanish guards, the head of security, the fighters' managers, the arena maintenance department head (they were newly formed to clear the arena between fights, the Master still liked Her uneven arena floor), even the kitchen staff was represented with Katool being here. As was maintenance and climate control for the facility. This was a massive gathering, and every one possible that had any part to do with this facility in any way was represented. Against the wall at each entrance was a guard of Hers. There was a total of six, plus the two outside brought the total to eight. The largest group at one place. By anyone's reckoning, that would be the full count of Her guards. But why were they all here?

The room was silent; no one wanted to break the silence until She arrived. They all sat there, just looking at each other.

After a long uncomfortable period of time, the guards all snapped the rifles from their shoulders and held them straight up in front of them in a royal salute; they there stood there motionless. The initial movement startled everyone. Then the main doors opened, and She walked in, followed by more guards. There was a notable gasp as the guards flowed in. But the shock of more guards did not prevent anyone from jumping to their feet at Her arrival.

"Well, hello, everyone. Thank you for joining us," She announced in a tone no one had ever heard from Her before. It took everyone aback.

"Notice everyone is here, plus a few more of my friends."

A dozen more guards filed in. There was now a total of twenty guards.

She strode to the front of the room, Klavan by Her side as usual. She stopped at the tall chair at the head of the massive table. She motioned for Klavan to sit. He pulled his chair out and sat down, glancing around the room; when he saw Zhuni and Tan'cha, he gave a slight smile.

"We are going to go around the room and give a status report. I want each and every one of you to tell me exactly how prepared you are for the main event and your plans to improve your readiness. You will also present to me your departments' plans for closing down as the main event comes to an end. Klavan, take note of any glaring disappointment you hear in my voice as we receive their reports. Also, remind me as to who the executives or assistants to each that disappoints me. Give me their status and ability to take command if needed."

"Yes, of course, Your Grace."

With that, the meeting began. By the end of the meeting, nine department heads and Dwayans had been replaced, and four of those were told they would be a part of the main event entertainment. Those four were immediately marched out by guards. Their replacements were brought in to now stand in their former bosses' positions. She was rather pleased with any detail not covered nor taken care of. She had berated everyone and implied, with what could be stated as nothing other than joy, that none of them were fully ready. She was in an especially evil mood and made everyone pay for their most minute discretion.

Zhuni could see Klavan was more distressed than usual. He kept wiggling around in his chair. Each time She looked to him, he obviously was uncomfortable giving Her the information She requested. Especially when the information would cause the removal of a department head or Dwayan.

Zhuni was wondering how She thought She was making the situation better by removing several of the department heads and Dwayans. Then thought, *She doesn't care. She knows everyone will kill themselves to achieve Her goals.* They were all terrified of Her.

When it came time for Zhuni to report the med lab's readiness, She was disinterested and just nodded. Zhuni was not sure if they had proven their abilities during the last main event or if She was no longer interested in the med lab. Zhuni was both relieved and concerned by Her indifference. She was always playing games, but this tactic was new.

The meeting ended late the next morning. All were physically, mentally, and emotionally exhausted, and now only two rotations away from the main event. Was that also part of Her plan to ensure everyone was completely exhausted going into the main event? Of course, that would ensure complete compliance. That is what She craved.

Zhuni met up with Klavan on the way out.

"What was that all about?" Zhuni asked Klavan.

Klavan glanced towards his guard.

"Not much to tell. She is ensuring everyone is on the same page and that it is the page She has written. Not much else to say right now," Klavan voiced.

"I can see that. She is making sure everyone is following even Her tiniest request. This main event is the most important one for Her. This is the one that will make all the difference. Everything will be different when this main event ends. Do you see your position changing?"

"I do, but not in the way I thought a rotation ago. I believe I am destined to achieve a higher position when this is over," Klavan stated.

"Well then, I wish you the greatest luck and safety. I hope for a brighter future for you. I think I will just continue with my work."

"We all must do what we think is best for us, even if that means leaving those we care about behind," Klavan insisted as he looked at both Zhuni and Tan'cha with deep concern.

"Yes, sir. See you soon. Hopefully, again before the main event," Zhuni replied.

"Yes, I hope so. Continue your work and take care of everyone you can. I will always be here for you," Klavan stated.

"Klavan, we have much to do, and we only have two rotations," She said as She passed them heading out of the conference room.

Klavan immediately stepped in beside Her, and they were followed out by the guards. Klavan glanced back and nodded.

"They are fine; we have other things to deal with," She said as they exited the room.

"Zhuni, what was all that?" Tan'cha asked.

"He is not coming with us," Zhuni grumbled.

—————— * ——————

"I hear you are looking for a ship. With the guilds here, you will be offered many. But the *Transgression* is the ship for you," the stranger stated.

The stranger was a tall Krodent, a lighter brownish green than most Krodents, indicating little to no time in the light of a natural source. He wore an olive drab flight suit. The suit had no insignia. The stranger had a blaster pistol in a holster on his lower left hip and a huge knife in a scarab on his right hip that nearly reached his knee. He was also wearing a flight cap, which was a light brown. This led Boshduul to believe the stranger had left the ship in a hurry.

"And why is that?" Boshduul asked.

"You have not heard of Her?"

"Apparently not; what makes it special?"

"During the Aashturian Civil War, she was the first to navigate across Aashturian-occupied space. She delivered weapons and supplies on many occasions to the city-states of Kapernium and Kazoriam prior to their fall."

"Sounds like your ship didn't accomplish much," Boshduul jabbed.

"Not much! Eleven other ships were lost attempting to deliver supplies and weapons. We were the only one to break the blockade, and we did it on nine separate occasions," the stranger growled.

"Very well then. I may consider you and your ship. I have others to consider. My journey would pass through Aashturian space. The cargo is of none of your concern. I may or may not have associates join me."

"I would need your cargo's weight and area. I would also need to know how many associates you would have. I figure you would have no desire for the authorities to know of our arrivals or departures; there would, of course, be no manifest."

"Is the *Transgression* armed and ready to fight?" Boshduul questioned.

"Did you not listen? We ran Aashturian blockades; of course, we are armed."

"I will contact you. Where would I find this ship?"

"Landing bay two twenty-seven."

"I will contact you."

"What is your destination?" the stranger asked.

"I will let you know that it is passed Aashturian space by four leap frames."

"Aashturian space is wide. I need more detail; what is the final destination?"

"If I choose you, I will inform you of the details; until then, I will keep it to myself. The departure would be in a rotation or two, so be ready."

"We are ready to go now."

"All you pilots say the same."

"Grod, first mate. Let me know," he grumbled as he turned and left.

Just a moment later, another stranger walked up. This one was a Toztat. He was a young one with a light tan skin tone and dressed in what looked to be miners' overalls in a worn and faded bright orange with several oil and/or hydraulic fluid stains. It was once a brilliant orange to provide high visibility in the mines. He had a belt with a power spanner hanging from it on the left side, and a small plasma pistol clipped to the right side. He was wearing the helmet of an engine mechanic or flight engineer. The helmet was small and barely covered his full head. It had a large light on the forehead and would project a hologram of the engine or ship into space in front of the helmet. The projectors were small dots along the sides of the helmet and just under the light. This would allow better diagnostics. The helmet was a pale yellow. His hands were gloved in a brown leather, which matched his high boots.

"Heard you are looking for a ship to hire. I am Jasp, the flight engineer and copilot of the *Hatred*, at your service."

"Why would I want to make a cargo run with you? I have never heard of your ship."

"Of course not. We stay below the radar. It keeps the authorities off us. I can provide you a list of those we have worked for," Jasp informed him.

"Provide me the list."

"What is your cargo? We will run nearly anything; I need weight and destination."

"The weight will be under ten, and the destination is beyond Aashturian space."

"When do you anticipate departing?"

"Within the next two to three rotations."

"Busy time; there will be a lot of traffic."

"If it is a problem, there are other ships available."

"No problem; we are loading our final supplies and will be ready in the next two rotations. Contact me at bay one-K fourteen-nine," Jasp stated and walked away.

*

"Zhuni."

"Go ahead, Joxby," Zhuni replied.

"Rags-has-been-found-again,-and-he-is-at-the-Smugglers'-Nova-hiring-a-ship."

"Interesting; where is he headed?"

"Not-sure,-but-he-will-have-cargo,-and-it-will-be-about-ten,-he-told,-one-ship."

"What could he have?"

"I-have-no-idea."

"This is interesting."

"I-have-another-issue-to-let-you-know-about.-With-you-in-the-meeting-all-night,-I-could-not-tell-you-earlier."

"What?"

"Her-guards-have-been-setting-explosives."

"Where?"

"Everywhere,-especially-choke-points-and-specific-landing-bays."

"Joxby, send me the information. I will head to my room, Sarge and Tan'cha will join me, and we will discuss this. This place is insane. Every day something."

"Yes,-I-will-send-the-information-on-your-office-monitor."

"Thank you."

Joxby turned to a monitor and started tapping the screen. He sent all the information, surveillance footage from the drones, and the research he had done.

"Tan'cha, we needed to grab Sarge and go over some information from Joxby."

"Sarge."

"Go ahead."

"Meet Tan'cha and me in my quarters; we have some things to go over."

"Finishing rounds and heading your way."

CHAPTER 14

A Warning

The guilds were beginning to arrive. Klavan knew he had the banquet hall ready for all. The landing bays were set, and control had the locations of the guild master's lading bays. The master's new crest was everywhere. The guards had spent a full rotation attaching them everywhere. Each guild master would all see the crest as they exited their ships. Klavan did not understand why She had used Her guards to install the crests and not some of the humanish guards or some of the help. This place just keeps getting stranger and stranger.

Klavan was told by Her he needed to meet and escort every guild master from the time they landed to their quarters. He enjoyed the meeting, etiquette, and protocol of this part of his job the most. The setting up of the banquets, the quarters for the guild masters, etc. The details were the best part. He enjoyed this part of his job. The guard always at his side drove him crazy, but the good always came with some bad.

Control had sent down word that the guild master of the drug cartel and his second in command had just entered orbit. Klavan was headed down to the landing bay assigned to him. The assigning of the landing bays had been tricky as each guild master would demand to be the closest to the main entrance as a sign of influence. Klavan had requested the guild master's personal ship dimensions, and this made things easier as some of the ships were too big to fit close due to landing bay sizes. Klavan had used the main computer to cross-reference the landing bays with ship sizes and had all the guild masters ships set accordingly.

Klavan was glad the first ship was the drug cartel. He knew the master and had known him a long time.

Klavan and his shadow were bound for landing bay one seventeen. This landing bay was the closest large landing bay. The *Vengeful Banshee* was too large to be used as a personal ship, but that was Yegg's style, big and bold. The *Vengeful Banshee* was the largest of any of the guild master's personal ships. Yegg had been the drug cartel's master for dozens of cycles. Klavan had known him before Klavan had become part of the games.

Klavan and the guard arrived at loading dock one seventeen in time to see the *Vengeful Banshee* clear the entry heat ball and begin to cool as she aimed toward the loading bay. It began as a bright spot in the sky and increased in size as it decreased in brightness. It soon became huge, and Klavan began to think it would not fit into the landing bay; he had forgotten just how enormous the ship was. But it hovered over the landing bay for a moment and then dropped slowly into the spot.

The *Vengeful Banshee* was a converted light cruiser left over from one of the many forces involved in the Aashturian Civil War. It was enormous; the fact that it was flat black in color made it extremely intimidating. Light was absorbed by the pure flat black. It would nearly disappear in the void of space. It retained many of the original weapon systems and was the most lethal ship outside of the Assassins' Guild.

Once the ship set down, the landing party exited. The first group in the party were armed guards in full battle gear, armor and weapons, including the much-feared Grazz railguns.

The guards hit the ground and spread out quickly; there were twelve of them; two took station at the bottom of the ramp, four-headed straight to the main entrance of the landing bay, half took up station inside the doorway, and the other two took up station on the outside of the doorway. Four took the ramp up to the rampart surrounding the landing area, and the final two took up station at the back entrance. Ten more guards ran down the ramp in the same armor and holding the same weapons. They reinforced the various positions, another pair of guards at the front, a pair at the rear, and the rest to add to the numbers around the upper rampart.

Then the maintenance team came down the ramp to begin their inspection of the ship and the landing pad. This team had ten members. Four tall figures descended the ramp. They were covered in black from head to foot, the same light-absorbing color of the ship. It was hard to see detail or even figure out which direction they were facing as the figures had no visible form, just an outline of a figure. Two of them walked to the front entrance, and two stood at the bottom of the ramp.

Two more figures in dark green armor, power staffs, and side arms descended the ramp; they were followed by a large group of figures of varying sizes and shapes. These were the guild master and his entourage. The largest was in a dark green vestment identical in hue to the figures with the power staffs. Klavan recognized the figure as Yegg.

"Welcome, Master Yegg," Klavan called out.

Yegg made the bottom of the ramp and looked over to see Klavan; he nodded in Klavan's direction. Then turned and spoke with those others gathered around him.

The entire entourage then walked towards Klavan with the green-clad guards in the lead, followed by Yegg and then the rest of the entourage.

"Klavan, you old Mynog, it has been a while, my friend. How are you?"

"Doing well, Master Yegg," Klavan responded.

"Still the serious protocol. You never change."

"I have your quarters prepared, and as per your usual routine, you are the first guild master to arrive. I have been given word that Hotha, the Hunters' Guild's master, has just entered our system and should be landing shortly."

"Wonderful, you have my quarters set up as I like? Could you arrange a meeting for Hotha and me once he gets settled? I would love to meet him before all the formalities set in. Maybe dinner for us to share?"

"Of course, I could set you up in a private room off the main banquet hall."

"Is this one of Her guards? Did you misbehave?" Yegg said, staring at Klavan's assigned bodyguard.

"Yes, it is one of her guards; Stanton had the brilliant idea of attempting to saddle me with one, which gave Her the idea to assign one of Her personal guards to each of our sides."

Yegg burst out laughing, a boisterous and deep howl.

"Stanton, still a pain in your side. He is such a fool. She must keep him around for entertainment."

"Indeed. This way." Klavan led the party toward their assigned quarters.

This would be Klavans next two rotations, greeting each guild master and their entourages. Showing them their assigned quarters and ensuring they were taken care of properly. Klavan would be ensuring everything would run smoothly until the main event. He loved this. He thought that maybe he could be a peacemaker after all this blew over. Someone everyone trusted to keep the peace and to negotiate for all involved, just as the Game Master was meant to be prior to Her arrival. If Klavan could get the guilds to work together to eliminate Her, he would be the obvious choice to take over. If he could do that, he would gain prestige. He would be as important as he always wanted to be. He could oversee more than just the med lab. He could get rid of Stanton and turn the games once again into a neutral player and negotiator; he may even be able to get the non-aligned cartels and guilds and maybe some of the more legitimate organizations involved. He could become more prestigious and powerful than he had ever imagined, and it would be nearly legal. All he had to do was remove the Master rather than wait for Her to make the move.

---------------- * ----------------

Traxon was pleased with himself; he had found Rags. He was proving to be more resourceful than he had thought he could be. He was now packing the few belongings he had in preparation of leaving this planet. He was raised here in the back-alley ways and the garbage and had never thought he would rise to be the number two of a Dwayan. But just as he had risen, he had seen it all fall apart. If not for Zhuni and his team Traxon would be dead, just like all his friends. But Traxon was innovative and had built himself quite a fortune skimming credit of Stanton. He truly did not know what to do with all those credits but was glad he could do something worthwhile with them. Once he was off this planet with Zhuni, Tan'cha, and Sarge, it would not matter about the credits. Where they were headed, they would not need credits. This made Traxon nervous and excited as he had never been off the planet.

Traxon liked the med lab and the crew here. He could see himself making life with them all. From what Tan'cha said, the planet was gorgeous. Lots of fascinating creatures, delicious foods, crazy climate, and all.

Traxon only had two rotations, and they would be leaving, space travel sounded boring, but it was something new. Traxon had disliked change working for Stanton because it was always dangerous and chaotic, but with this crew, it was safe; everyone helped each other through changes, so traveling through space, going to a new planet, and starting a new life would be better with the support of everyone. Maybe Traxon could learn some new skills during the spaceflight that could help him be more useful to everyone. This is going to be good.

———————— * ————————

"Interesting. It looks like She is targeting the command structure of each guild. Using the crests and once again using that nasty material Boartine. She wants to cause as much shock and damage as possible. There are more than forty of these crests around, one at each landing pad of a guild member or master and at various high-traffic areas. It is like the terror wrought by the collective during the Aashturian Civil War," Sarge informed them.

"It is interesting that She is using Boratine and tactics similar to the collective. It definitely solidifies the fact that She was pictured with Mord. He used these tactics also," Zhuni added.

"Good point; I completely forgot about those pictures," Sarge responded.

"So, what are we going to do?" Tan'cha asked.

"First, we need to figure out how to nullify the explosives. That must be done. They will not affect our plans, but they could kill hundreds. We cannot claim to be doing the right thing saving lives if we do not stop these," Sarge commanded.

"You are correct. How do we do that?" Zhuni asked.

"We need Joxby to figure out the frequency the crests are activated by. The collective sent an activation code to the bombs, and that armed their bombs, then the targets' own communication signal would cause the bomb to explode," Sarge stated.

"Wow, that is fascinating," Tan'cha interjected.

"Yes, it was brilliant; it worked to great effect. They would activate the bomb, and then the equipment used to find the bombs or the teams searching for the bombs would set them off with their own signals," Sarge said.

"How do we eliminate them or neutralize them?" Tan'cha asked.

"During the war, we used signal scramblers that worked most of the time, but occasionally the scrambler would send the correct signal, and the bomb would explode. The best way would be to have the communication signal frequency of each guild and their personal signals. If we put out a scanner, we should be able to figure them out," Sarge stated.

"That will be Joxby once again," Zhuni said.

"He will be able to figure something out, and knowing him, we will get word soon that he has it figured out," Sarge said.

"Should we get the guilds involved?" Zhuni asked.

"I believe that could work to our advantage if only one or two guilds were appreciative of our information that would take pressure off of our travel plans," Sarge implied.

"Good point. Klavan has to personally contact each guild master and other guild representatives as they arrive. He could be a tremendous asset by informing them of the danger. Maybe their own crews could neutralize their bombs," Zhuni affirmed.

"At least they would know we were looking out for their best interests," Sarge stated.

"That could go a long way. It could make our travel plans run smoother," Tan'cha said.

"The only issue would be Klavan getting that information to them with his bodyguard by his side," Zhuni stated.

"Klavan could figure out a way; he is on most of their good sides and has met with most of them several times in the many cycles he has been here," Sarge ensured.

"Then we will have to get word to Klavan," Tan'cha said.

"Now, how is everyone doing preparing for the main event? Joxby said he was contacted by the ship. It is the *Palti*. I do not know much about the different ships, but he seemed excited."

"Excited, Joxby is always excited. But the *Palti* is an amazing ship. She has been both a smugglers' ship and has become prevalent in the Freighters' Guild following her feats during the Aashturian Civil War. She was the first ship to get across Aashturian space. This is the ship that was able to counter Aashturian-mined space before anyone else realized what was happening. She was even brave enough to transmit the information to the smugglers and the freighters before more ships and crews were lost to the mines. Of course, the Assassins' Guild hates the *Palti* because the assassins supported the collective," Sarge educated them.

"That is good to know. So, we have a great ship and crew to get us to Kashtuu, even going through Aashturian space?" Zhuni asked.

"As long as I can see my home world, I don't care what ship we take," Tan'cha blurted out.

"The only crew or ship that could be better getting through Aashturian space would be an Aashturian. And you should care what ship takes you; the wrong ship will kill you before you ever get to your home world," Sarge scolded him.

"Whatever it takes," Tan'cha snapped.

"Traveling through space is a common occurrence, but so are accidents, reentry disasters, space debris damage, etc. It is still dangerous; the correct ship and crew lower your odds of a deadly mistake or accident. We could not be in better hands," Sarge stated.

"So, we will be fine," Tan'cha chuckled.

"Thanks to Rue, he got us this ship. It is amazing how things are coming together for us," Zhuni told them.

"We have some important and talented individuals ensuring our travel plans work out," Sarge revealed.

"With so many working to help us, are we doing our part to ensure we are ready?" Zhuni questioned.

"The tunnel is complete; they have the cliff cavern being opened up a bit to allow a staging area for the passengers. The homing beacon will be set up and activated. We just need them to set down, and we can begin loading," Sarge said.

"The passengers and their families and the supplies are ready. The supplies have been positioned in the tunnel as it has been completed," Tan'cha mentioned.

"Good, the explosives and the transports are ready?" Zhuni asked as he looked at Sarge.

"Yes, Traxon arranged the payments, and he said Stanton would be responsible. At least, that is what I understood from him," Sarge replied.

"Who would have ever thought that Traxon would be the one paying for this excursion?" Tan'cha blurted out.

"Not me, that is for sure," Sarge exclaimed.

"Nor me, but again, it is as if it is our destiny to get to Kashtuu," Zhuni stated.

"It is more than destiny because I do not believe in that stuff. It is divine intervention. No over-explanation. Abijah said the Creator watches over those that follow Him; maybe we are doing the right thing by getting her and her brother home," Sarge disclosed.

"I thought you didn't believe in the Creator Abijah spoke about," Tan'cha said.

"I don't know, but I do know that since working with you guys, I have started seeing things come together in ways I do not understand. I see creatures helping and caring for one another more than I have ever seen in my life. I am convinced that being kind to one another is the reason it is all working out, and I am beginning to believe Abijah is correct with this one God-Creator story," Sarge declared.

"Dagz, I am glad you said that," Tan'cha muttered.

"Why?" Sarge asked.

"Because I am beginning to believe the same thing, and I thought I was going crazy," Tan'cha announced.

"Oh, you are crazy, but you went there a long time ago."

"Shut up," Tan'cha growled.

"Dagz, you two are like two little Mynogs fighting over scraps. Always fussing. Can we get back to our discussion?" Zhuni snarled.

"Yes, sir." Both affirmed.

"Do we have a checklist? Are we missing anything? What concerns do either of you have, Tan'cha, stop pointing at Sarge," Znuhi growled.

---

*

"I can do that; if we can get the guilds on our side, your trip should be uneventful. My only concerns are the Assassins' Guild and the Commerce Guild," Klavan was in his private quarters speaking to Zhuni over the vox.

"If you want the position and you think you can make it a mainstream, not just a black-market program, the Commerce Guild may help that happen," Zhuni informed him.

"That is a good point. I will be meeting with Yegg of the Thieves' Guild and Hotha and Kamon of the Hunters' Guild for dinner. I can inform them. The other guild masters are expected in shortly," Klavan stated.

"Good, then you inform them. Joxby is working on a signal isolator or something like that, he said. It should prevent the activation signal from reaching the crests. This should prevent them from exploding at Her signal," Zhuni announced.

"I will head out to dinner now; I will get the information to them. I believe if we get them to know how dangerous She is, they may stand against Her," Klavan said.

"That is our thinking, plus if you are the one informing them, you will build their trust. Then when you need their support to take over as the new Game Master, you will have them in your corner," Zhuni implied.

"I am off. I will touch base in the early morning," Klavan told Zhuni.

"Good night," Zhuni replied.

Klavan left his quarters to start down the hallway to the banquet hall. He would swing through the kitchen to touch base with Katool, the kitchen manager, and ensure she was ready for the massive banquet coming tomorrow.

Klavan walked into the kitchen to see Dooble cooking a full Banteest,

"Dooble, how are you?"

"Klavan, you are killing us with these banquets," Dooble chuckled.

"The banquets are my favorite part," Klavan shot back.

"I know; I dread the day you become the Game Master; you will close them down and open a restaurant!" Dooble cackled.

"You are hilarious; where is Katool?" Klavan asked.

"She is checking supplies in cold storage; want a platter of Banteest?"

"No, thank you, I am having dinner with those in the side room."

"Yes, always socializing and ensuring everyone and everything is in correct order. One day when you are in charge, things will go perfectly."

"When I am in charge?"

"Yes, we all hope one day you will become the Game Master, and then everything will run smoothly and sincerely. You would have this place running right, and everyone would enjoy being here. We all hope when that day comes that you will release those of us who are slaves just as you did Zhuni."

"Yes, of course. When I become Game Master, I will take care of you all," Klavan chuckled.

"Yes, sir, you get to your meeting, and I will get back to my cooking."

Klavan found Katool just stepping out of cold storage.

"Hello Katool, how is everything going?"

"It is going as well as can be expected. I have so much to take care of; it is crazy. All supplies are on hand; the banquet hall is set up, the staff is ready, and the menu is set. I have not been this stressed in a long time. Too many big wigs wandering around, and the main event isn't even for two more rotations. Now I have a pair of guild masters needing their own dining hall for a special meeting. Not the type."

"That is actually me. I had the dining hall set up. I may be using it several times prior to the main event."

"Wonderful; thank you for the prior notice," Katool grumbled.

"Just keep it set up; I will only need one or two servants to work it. Just clean and reset, bring in drinks and food; there will be no more than five or six in there at a time."

"Well then, since it is for you."

"Thank you. I am heading there now; if there is anything else you need, let me know."

"I will, Klavan, but I think we have everything under control."

"Very well; I will see you soon."

Klavan walked to the side room, paused at the door, and ordered the guard to stand at the exterior entrance to the room to protect him and allow only the servants in or out. Klavan was surprised the guard did as told.

"Good evening," Klavan said, stepping into the side dining hall.

The room was a miniature version of the main banquet hall. The ceilings were tall and highly polished sandstone. The flooring was a different stone of a light brown and orange stone with sparkling specks of gold. There were two large chandeliers of a gold tone to match the flecks in the floor. The large central table was set for six individuals but could hold as many as a dozen. The table was a large oval shape with the ends across the room, offering the side to the main doorway. This setup allowed both guild masters to seat themselves at either end without either having their back to the door. Most guild masters never sat with their backs to doors; in their line of work, it was dangerous not seeing people entering a room.

The food and drinks had been set up along the sides of the room to allow buffet-type eating and allow complete privacy from servants. Each guild master had a few attendants with them who would retrieve their food or drink as needed. Yegg also had two of his personal guard dressed in matching colors, the dark green, which was his personal color. Hotha had two guards of his own. The two sets of guards faced each other across the room.

"Klavan, good to see you again," Yegg greeted, standing and sweeping his arm in a show of welcome. Dressed as before in his dark green robe.

"Yegg, I see you and Hotha are already getting acquainted," Klavan stated, glancing at Hotha.

"Yes, what a wise one he is," Yegg announced.

"Quite also," Klavan stated, smiling and looking at Hotha.

"Yes, it is better to be quiet and allow others to speak," Hotha responded, still sitting but nodding towards Klavan. Hotha was also dressed in his guild master's robe of a royal purple hue.

"That is often the case. I have much to discuss with the two of you. Yegg, I have known you a long time, so you know me fairly well. Hotha, you are a wise leader, I have been told. I need you both to understand the importance of this meeting," Klavan began as he sat down.

"I was wondering why you called us to meet. Yegg and I have little in common other than being guild masters," Hotha stated.

"Yes, there is a reason. The guilds are in danger. The guild masters, in particular. The Game Master is evil and has shown Her desire for control. She killed another master in front of all at the last main event; there is also talk that She killed Droughlok, the Assassins' Guild's Master. She has placed Her crests around the facility, and these crests are bombs. She wants to assassinate all the guild masters and become the all-controlling Master. This will cause instability that could destroy the galaxy as we know it. The last guild war caused the deaths of billions and lasted for hundreds of cycles. The Wreckoning. If She kills the masters, it will be utter chaos."

"We have all been discussing this fact. The guild masters are divided as to how to handle this. Some believe the strong need to survive, and if some guilds die, so be it. Others believe no matter what happens, there will be another war. Some guilds will step in to stand by Her side, and others will attempt to destroy Her. Either way, we do not see a way to prevent a guild war," Yegg explained.

"The guilds cannot stand with Her; She wants full control. A war is coming. We need to destroy Her, and when She is gone, we will turn on each other. Or we can pretend She will allow us to remain in charge as She kills each of us," Hotha explained.

"Yes, Hotha, you are correct. The greatest threat to all of us is She. I see it each rotation. Her thirst for power that I have never seen in another. She will stop at nothing until She has full control," Klavan announced.

"What do you propose?" Hotha asked.

"She has set bombs everywhere; my team is working on neutralizing them. These bombs are the decorative crests we see everywhere. They are made of Boratine. Once that is done, the guild masters will have to stand together to destroy Her. When we remove Her, the guilds will be able to negotiate a settlement. I would assist in brokering that agreement," Klavan informed them.

"So, this is your power play? It is not to protect the guilds?" Yegg asked.

"What? What do you mean, my power play? Yegg, you know me; I do not desire power. I want peace and things to be the old way prior to Her arrival. The Game Master was a neutral party; the games were established to be a neutral meeting ground for all."

"No, power is not your desire; prestige is," Yegg implied.

"Yegg, think about it. Who is more trusted and neutral than Klavan? I have heard of his ability to work with all parties. Imagine him as the Game Master. He would be a fine diplomat. His ability could save the guilds and provide a safe location for disputes. I am sure all the Masters would agree," Hotha declared.

"Yes, Hotha, you are correct. Forgive my assertion, Klavan. I do know you better than that," Yegg apologized.

"Times are stressful for all of us; no offense taken, my friend," Klavan replied.

"We do have the problem of a guild war; the Assassins' Guild wants revenge. They still want to be the guild above all others," Yegg said.

"The Commerce Guild will most likely remain uncommitted. There will be no profit for them joining either side during a war. The Smugglers' Guild may side with the Assassins' as will the drug cartels. We would be able to pull the Miners' Guild to our side once She is removed," Klavan stated.

"Klavan, you have work to do. We will assist with Her removal, but you will need to get the other guilds on board. You are in deep with the Freighters' Guild; they will stand with us?" Yegg questioned.

"I am certain the freighters, the miners, and even the Renegade Guild will join. I must negotiate with the smugglers. I am convinced the Renegade Guild will join anyone opposing the assassins. So that would give us your guilds, the renegades, the freighters, the miners, and possibly the smugglers against the assassins and drug cartels, most likely with the Commerce Guild's backing. We may be able to negotiate an agreement before shooting starts," Klavan said.

"We must protect all of the guild masters, even those who may oppose our actions. Serving and protecting the other masters will go a long way in the negotiations, plus it will leave us with known commodities," Hotha implied.

"Good point. Do we know the Assassins' Guild master?" Klavan asked.

"I have heard it will fall to Droughlok's firstborn," Yegg stated.

"Arioch?" Klavan asked.

"Yes," Yegg bemoaned.

"If that is true, we must be prepared for war. He is an evil and a vile individual who makes Droughlok look sweet. Arioch will think of nothing but hateful revenge. This will be the most vicious Assassins' Guild in history. Imagine Arioch's vengeance. He will turn it on all. He may even be preparing an attack now," Klavan declared.

"Looks like war is coming," Hotha told them.

CHAPTER 15

The Exodus Begins

The *Hatred* was docked on the far side of the loading docks. It would be a quick getaway being so far from the facility, but getting the Starch there would be an issue. Boshduul may need to hire a transport. He may also need to hire a few more guards to unload quickly.

The *Hatred* was a small ship and had a crew of five. Jasp was the flight engineer and copilot. The pilot and ship's captain was a humanish named Birsha. Birsha looked to be mean and controlling; the rest of the crew followed him out of hateful respect. The name of the ship matched his personality. The navigator was a Takchee who went by the name Zimp. Another member of the crew was the loadmaster and gunner, a humanish named Bune. The last crew member is just a laborer. This laborer was a humanish also and named Raca. Overall, it seemed a capable crew but also one that should be easy to dispatch when they were back at Boshduul's homeworld.

The *Hatred* was a small to medium-sized ship shaped like an oval saucer with two tails jutting out at an angle on the rear of the ship. The loading bay opened with a large and wide ramp under and behind the split tail. The cockpit was a hump at the front of the ship. There were blisters all over the ship, which housed everything from communication equipment to weapons systems. The ship was a greyish brown with lighting bolt crossing a hammer painted just below and behind the cockpit. The ship would be perfect. Now to hire a transport.

Boshduul would hire a transport to load the Starch, have the humanish guards load it, drive it to the *Hatred*, and have it enter the *Hatred* with no unloading, no delay. Boshduul may have to get rid of the transport driver, but that would be fine to do once it is loaded; plus, it would influence the humanish guards, and there would be no trouble from them.

Bosduul would have to find the right size transport for this job. A midsize would work. With the transport, he would have less Starch, but the quick getaway would prove more important. The midsize transport would still cover his retirement.

———————— * ————————

Klavan would be entertaining the guild masters until the main event feast. This would give Her plenty of time to put Her plan into motion. She would detonate the explosives immediately after everyone ate. Once the masters' ships were destroyed, there would be no escape. They would either bend to Her will or die. Simple. The guards would then control the guild masters. They and their personal bodyguards would be no match for Her guards, especially when She informed them that the guild masters' guards would not be allowed any weapons other than power staffs, and Her guards would be armed with Blaster rifles; this would put them at a decidedly disadvantaged position. With all the guild masters and their bodyguards and the possibility of a misunderstanding or an argument, She could convince them to limit their weapons.

She would imprison all the seconds, so once the guild masters had been killed or had abdicated, She could use the number twos as Her representative leaders. They would then join Her for the main event; after seeing their masters' bodies, hearing about their ships being destroyed, and seeing Her control two monsters, She would be in total control.

Her guards had been reinforced with more guards, and all had been upgraded. With the upgrades, they would be faster and more accurate with their rifle fire. She had downloaded pictures of the guild masters and their bodyguards; with that information, Her guards would be able to quickly and accurately target the correct victims.

———————— * ————————

The tunnel was complete, the staging area had been increased in size, and it was time to set the homing beacon and have the *Palti* arrive. The foreman had a tanker ready to fill their water tanks and another with the other chemicals they had requested. The foreman was impressed by what Joxby had told him about the engineering done to the *Palti*. They had rigged it to provide multiple atmospheres for their guests. Not many ships used filtered exhaust fumes to discharge vapors to create environments for different creatures. Most ships just expected those who needed a different atmosphere to wear a pressure suit. The *Palti* had built several different environments. Most breathed the oxygen-based air of the planet Agón, but several dozen had to wear pressure suits. They would still need to until they reached their quarters. The more the foreman heard about the *Palti*, the more he wanted to be a part of the crew. Maybe he could work his way in as they made the journey.

The foreman and three workers wired the beacon and started it. They adjusted the transmitter and set it to the coordinates Joxby sent them. The beacon was at the edge of the cavern and mouth of the tunnel. It was barely able to transmit past the mouth of the cavern; Joxby had calculated the spot where it would be unseen and yet provide a clear signal for the *Palti*. The foreman hoped it was correct. Joxby had yet to be wrong. The foreman sent the workers back to the loading dock area to continue the preparations for departure.

The foreman stood by, watching the sky for any sign of the *Palti*. It did not take long to see a bright spot in the sky.

———————— * ————————

"Captain, we have the beacon," the communications officer informed the captain.

"Navigation, calculate our approach. Helm adjust course. All stations prepare for atmospheric entry," the captain ordered.

The main engines rumbled as the ship swung around and adjusted her position. She was now in a nose-down attitude and began her ascent to the planet's surface. Once the ship began to feel the pull of the planet's gravity, the captain ordered main engine shutdown. The ship shook slightly, and then the vector engines started to maintain the proper angle and heading. The heat shields had to be in the correct position to protect the ship as it entered the atmosphere.

The *Palti* was now in Agón's lower atmosphere and was no longer in need of the heat shields' protection. The landing engines were started up, and the ship began the approach to the cavern. The *Palti* dropped low to the water, too low for radar to pick up but high enough to prevent a large plume of water spray. Joxby had calculated their approach, low over the water but far enough off during entry so as to not be visible to the facility nor the spaceports radar.

The *Palti* had to rise up to the cavern.

"To port there, helm. Do you see our landing?"

"Yes, Captain. It is going to be tight."

"Helm, rotate and back her in."

"Yes, Captain."

The *Palti* rotated and smoothly slid backwards into the mouth of the cavern; the landing engines and vector engines began to wind down. She was set down lightly.

The *Palti* was a former battle cruiser that had been heavily modified. The engines and operating systems had remained. Some weapons systems were still intact, as were many defensive measures. The main change had been to the interior of the ship. The armory, the crews' quarters, and the training and gunner solutions centers had all been removed. This left the ship with a massive open interior that could hold more cargo than any other medium freighter, but she had the speed and firepower to take on a ship of the fleet if need be. The *Palti* was a unique ship.

The captain smiled as the *Palti* set down. This was going to be a journey for the record books. The captain knew there was something very different about this run. It was more than having a Drazine; it was as if this ship and this crew had been specifically set up for this exact mission. No other ship in the Freighters' Guild had the capability of this ship. She was originally scheduled to be on the opposite side of the galaxy at this time, but the Aashturians had done something unheard of. They had accepted an updated contract for the client the *Palti* was scheduled to work for. This meant the *Palti* did not have to evacuate the client, so the *Palti* had been sitting dormant, awaiting orders. Strange how everything came together as if by some plan. The *Plati* was idle, had just brought on a science officer who had been explaining how to use the ship waste chemicals and exhaust to create atmosphere for different creatures, how a freighter loaded with exotic foods had blown a main engine and could not make the delivery, but the Commerce Guild had asked the load to be dumped to get the ship repaired. The *Palti* was standing by when the contract was complete and realized the food matched the needs of this journey and just offloaded it all at no cost. The same ship had picked up extra welders for the journey but didn't need them, so the *Palti* took them on to make all the modifications the science officer needed.

Things like this never happened. Was someone somewhere planning all this?

————————— * —————————

"Zhuni,-the-*Palti*-has-landed," Joxby informed them through the vox.

"Great. Let's get the plan started," Zhuni said to Sarge, Tan'cha, and Joxby.

"I will inform the families and the supply loaders. I will get the families staged and the loaders to start loading the staged supplies," Tan'cha said.

"I will get security set up," Sarge said.

"Remember, we need to keep it quiet. We only have this one rotation to get everything loaded and get off this planet.

"We know," Sarge and Tan'cha replied in unison.

"Joxby, have we got our problems figured out?"

"Many-problems-many-fixed."

"First, the bombs," Zhuni continued.

"Yes,-fixed-found-frequencies-I-placed-drones-as-scramblers."

"Did you and Elu figure out the EMPs?" Zhuni questioned.

"Yes,-again,-we-scrambled;-they-change."

"So, we are a go for the main event?"

"Yes,-and-the-run-away-problem-fixed."

"Good."

"Just-need-shooter."

"We will take care of that. Then we just need to load it."

"Yes,-good-luck-with-that."

"Thank you."

—————— * ——————

Zhuni had told Traxon to go to the ship and check in to get his quarters. Traxon had never been on a ship before, and this one was huge. He had seen them at the loading docks, but this was different.

He was not certain if this was a good idea. He knew he had to go with them but was wondering if he could do it without going on the ship. He was scared. He had been scared before, but this was scary because he had no idea what to expect. What if he went and things were the same? He was a little Mynog everyone picked on. He didn't feel that would happen; most who were going had treated him well. It was the complete lack of knowing what was going to happen that scared him.

Traxon walked to the passenger loading ramp.

A tall Krodent was holding a tablet that he checked as everyone came up to him.

"Yes, sir. What is your name?"

"Traxon."

"Traxon, yes, here you are. You will be quartered on the flight deck. That is at the front of the ship. You are in the VIP section. All the important people are there, including our captain's quarters."

"No, I Traxon, not important."

"This is your picture, correct?" the Krodent asked, showing Traxon the ID photo used to identify passengers. It was Traxon.

"Yes, me, not important."

"Well, sir, I do not organize the sleeping arrangements and the quartering; that is someone over my head. I just have you set up to be in the VIP section; someone thinks you are important."

"Me, important?" Traxon asked.

"I would say so. Welcome aboard, sir. Now just follow the virtual bot to your quarters."

A small hologram of a robot appeared in front of Traxon and beckoned him to follow.

"He will lead you to your cabin," the Krodent informed Traxon.

Traxon followed the hologram deep into the ship.

"Next," the Krodent hollered.

They had been up since the last rotation. All were exhausted, but the ship had to be loaded, and the families had to be placed on board. The Game Master would not be looking for family members of staff with everything She had going on. That is why the supplies were loaded first from the pre-staging area in the tunnel, and now the families were being loaded.

Tan'cha had organized everyone well. Joxby had submitted the list of passengers along with photos from their IDs while the *Palti* was in orbit. This allowed the *Palti*'s crew to organize the quarters.

The supplies had been loaded, and now the first of the families were loading. This was going to allow them to be on board and out of harm's way when the trouble started. The fighters would be loaded next as their fights ended. By the time the Drazine were fighting, everyone but Zhuni, Sarge, Tan'cha, and a handful of others would need to get on board the ship.

The first of the fights was starting. The day of the main event had arrived. Tan'cha was by Zhuni's side at the med station just outside of the main arena gate. The first round of fights had gone well, with no major injuries. Zhuni was worried someone would get seriously injured or killed before they left the planet. Those fighters had been sent to join their families on the *Palti*.

The transports were ready, the explosives were set, and the other ships were ready to go. The force generator was set up. The crests She had set were neutralized. The security teams all had the EMPs Joxby and Elu had prepared, and Elu was on the *Palti*, ready to take over for Joxby when the time came. They had planned it all to a tee. Now they just hoped it all went as planned and that Klavan had been able to convince the guilds to remove Her. The guilds would most likely still go to war, but at least the med lab and the Drazines would be gone.

They had lost communication with Klavan. He was unable to speak much as there were ears everywhere, and especially his newly assigned guard, this one, stayed close to Klavan at every moment. Klavan had said all was going as planned on several occasions, which led Zhuni to believe it was Klavan's way of ensuring Zhuni knew to continue.

Klavan had said something earlier in the day while walking the back hallway that the dessert carts would add some excitement. Zhuni did not know what that meant but trusted Klavan to be taking care of his part.

Zhuni heard Abijah speak to him from the holding area she was kept in before the fight. She had made an attempt to speak with her brother, but his mind was too clouded. Abijah felt it was because he had been in stasis for so long, or maybe they had some type of medication to keep him under control. They had planned for his escape also, and Rue was standing by, ready to track the Drazine down once he did escape.

The plan was fairly straightforward but relied on so many moving parts.

"Joxby, are you ready? Your time is coming soon. The fights are beginning to wind down, then they will have the banquet, and then She will release Abijah's brother."

"Yes,-my-team-is-ready;-when-She-sends-the-signal-for-Her-explosives,-I-will-act," Joxby replied.

"Good, be sure to let us know. Sarge, are you good?" Zhuni asked.

"Yes, force generator set, transports awaiting go, tunnel secure. Rue and team in position."

"All right then, it is now or never; begin countdown," Zhuni said.

"Joxby, the *Palti* is ready for departure?"

"Just-spoke-with-the-captain—the-families-are-all-aboard,-and-the-first-group-of-fighters-are-on,-including-the-wounded-you-sent-to-them."

"Here we go."

———— * ————

The warm-up fights ended, and it was time for all to join the feast in the banquet hall. She had been waiting for this moment. Once everyone was in place, She would blow up their ships and march Her guards in, all of them.

The guild masters all took their seats on either side of Her at the head table; Klavan was checking on the final prep details. He would join them in just a moment. She would wait for him to be by Her side before blowing the place up.

"Your Grace, several of the guild masters have asked for you to make a speech to welcome them. I informed them that that was not Your way," Klavan told Her.

To his surprise, She pushed him aside and stood up.

"To the guild masters," She said as She raised a glass.

"Tonight, the guilds change. I have set explosives at each of your ships; I will destroy them as we speak, leaving you no way to leave the planet." With that, She threw the drink across the table, shattering it and sending shards of glass flying everywhere. With the same hand, She reached into Her armor and pulled out a controller; she flipped the safety cover off of it and flicked the switch. She was expecting a roar or the muffled sound of far-off explosions, but there was none.

"We knew of Your plan; we were informed of Your crests and took necessary precautions to disable them. You have now shown

Your true intentions, and the guilds will destroy You," Arioch yelled at Her. The room roared with approval.

The doors flew open as Her guards poured in. The room fell silent for a moment, then all those present dove under their tables or under the side tables to reach their weapons that She had forbidden from being brought into the banquet hall. Klavan had used the dessert carts and other food carts to smuggle the weapons in.

The room lit up and became a cacophony of explosive weapons fire as the guilds fired on Her guards, and the guards returned fire. Guild masters and their entourages battled the guards, guards taking multiple hits but not stopping. They returned the fire to great effect. The guilds' ranks were thinning. They were caught in crossfire and had armor unable to stop the weapons blasts of the guards' guns. The guards' armor was effective against all but the Grazz weapons of the Thieves' Guild. The Thieves' Guild's weapons were taking a terrible toll on the guards. But there were too many guards.

The Game Master looked around the room and realized Her plan had been foiled. It was time for Her to leave. But She had another weapon up Her sleeve. The Drazine would take care of these fools. She looked at Klavan, nodding for him to follow; She left the room with six of Her guards and Klavan following close behind.

Hotha motioned for one of his bodyguards to blast a hole in the wall. The guard did so, then bolted through the hole to secure the other side. Hotha motioned for his other guards to follow the first. They all made the break into the hallway, followed by Hotha.

"Now we must cover the Hunters' Guild master and his team along with the Freighters' Guild and the Renegade Guild. They are our allies." Hotha looked at one guard and commanded him to get back to the ship, have the crew get ready for immediate departure, and send a squad to cover their retreat.

Hotha poked his head back into the room.

He spotted Yegg.

"Yegg, this way, we have an opening!"

Yegg looked up to see Hotha; he turned to command his team to make it to the opening. He led the way. As he ran, he yelled for the other guild masters to follow.

Yegg made it to the gap and out into the hallway.

"Thank you, my friend. That is turning into a slaughter," Yegg stated.

"They will figure our escape out, and your Grazz rifles are the only weapon that is taking these guards down. Get one of your men to the end of the hall to cover our escape," Hotha instructed.

"Go!" Yegg yelled to the first trooper through the gap. He immediately ran down the hall to take a cover position to watch over those in the hallway.

"We have to move, or this hallway will become a killing zone also," Hotha said as he and his team got up and bolted down the hall.

They reached the end of the hall and turned back to see Telore, the second of the Freighters' Guild, coming down the hall, followed by Qua, the Sargent at Arms for the Freighters' Guild.

"It is insane in there; thank you for breaking us out. We need to get to our ships. We should set up a defensive position to cover the others as they retreat."

"Yes, we must," Hotha replied.

"Yegg, get to your ship, but leave your guards to cover the others," Telore hollered.

"I am heading the Banshee; I have another squad on their way," Yegg replied.

A hole was blasted through the wall from within the banquet hall between the hole Hotha had created and the end of the hallway. For a moment, they thought the other guild masters were breaking out. But then, three guards stepped through and started blasting.

Yegg's guard took one guard down with a well-placed shot but was, in turn, killed by the two remaining guards. The guards stood between the guild masters and freedom. The guards raised their weapons...

———————— * ————————

"Zhuni,-She-attempted-the-activation-of-the-crests."

"Now? I thought She was going to do it during the main event. This means we have to move our timetable up to now."

"Problem-in-the-hallway-by-the-banquet-hall;-guild-masters-stuck...-no...-with-no-escape;-we-must-help-them."

"Sarge, hear that? Send a team. We must help them."

"I am on my way with a heavy response team and EMPs," Sarge replied.

"Tan'cha, get the fighters going; they need to get to the *Palti*. There will be no main event. I am going back to the med lab; we need everyone there now," Zhuni stated.

Sarge and his team raced out of the med lab to the loading dock, across the open area, and back into the main loading area. They then grabbed the lift and took it to the banquet hall level. The doors opened to the sound of screams and heavy weapons firing. They dashed out of the lift, down the hall, and past the service area. The sound of fight only got louder. Sarge raised his hand in a fist to stop the team as he glanced around the corner. He saw the backs of two of Her guards and the body of one of Yegg's bodyguards.

"EMPs, two," Sarge yelled. The first team member reached to his waist and grabbed what looked like a small grenade. He handed them to Sarge.

Sarge grabbed both in one hand, used his thumb to depress the arm button, and tossed it towards the guards. It bounced just behind them and rolled to their feet. The device screeched an ear-splitting sound, and the guards dropped to the ground motionless. Sarge rushed over to the first one and reached down, grabbed its head, and wrenched it off. There was no blood nor bones; it was, as they feared, an android. Sarge then pulled his bolter pistol out of the holster, shoved it up under the helmet of the second guard, and pulled the trigger. Bits and pieces of metal and ceramasteel careened across the hallway.

Sarge looked to the other end of the hallway to see several of the guild masters huddled together, surrounded by their bodyguards, some dead and some wounded.

"Grab your wounded and go. My team and I will cover you. Get to your ships and get out of here," Sarge ordered.

The Masters stood up, barked orders to their men, and rushed down the now-open hallway. Their bodyguards followed, carrying the wounded.

"You three, enter the hall through that opening, cover and protect as many as you can. Save some EMPs for our escape. You two with me, we will enter through that opening up there and cover the escape of as many as we can. You three, secure this hall and the lift. Now."

———————— * ————————

The chaos has begun early, Boshduul thought. He had the transport ready, and he was getting the muscle gathered. Might as well start now.

"The music is playing; let's dance," Boshduul announced. He walked out of the loading dock area with the six humanish guards he had hired to load the Starch. They all sprinted towards Stanton's office.

They reached the main doorway to Stanton's office and raised their rifles to blow it open. The doors blasted open, showering debris throughout the office and injuring three of Stanton's attendants. The attendants were struggling to understand what was happening when the humanish guards stormed in and shot them.

"There," Boshduul screamed at the guards, pointing towards the back door where Stanton had told him the Starch was.

The guards blew that door open and rushed in. Just as Boshduul had thought, they all threw their weapons down and started loading their arms with the boxes of Starch. Boshduul had counted on their greed and knew when the transport was loaded and ready, their greed would be their demise.

"Get as much as we can into the transport as quickly as we can. Once it is loaded, that which is left, you all can split as a thank-you bonus," Boshduul teased.

The guards rushed as quickly as they could. The small transport was filling quickly.

"Grab that crate of credits also," Boshduul commanded.

"What about these other crates of credits?" one of the humanish asked.

"I told you, once the transport is loaded, you can split what is left," Boshduul responded.

Bosduul could hear blaster rifles and screaming all around the loading docks. He could also see people scrambling. Time was running out.

"We are fully loaded, drive this to the *Hatred*, and load it onto her. I will be there shortly with the balance of your payment," Boshduul informed the driver.

Boshduul went back to Stanton's office, and just as he had predicted, the humanish were fussing and arguing about what was whose and how much each was going to walk away with.

Sometimes it is too easy, Boshduul thought as he walked into the nearly empty space. He reached into his rags and grabbed a detonator, flipped the switch, and tossed it. He calmly turned and walked back to the loading dock as the detonator exploded.

Boshduul had to navigate the chaos as he made his way to the *Hatred*. There were dozens of guild members running around loading ships, preparing them for lift-off, arming themselves, and taking up defensive positions to guard the ships.

He could see the *Hatred* sitting in her docking bay. The transport must be on board as the loading ramp was closed, and the ship was preparing for departure.

Boshduul saw the passenger gangway was down, and Bune and the transport driver were standing at the bottom.

"Here is your delivery guy. I have to help Raca secure the cargo," Bune said as he started up the gangway.

The driver walked toward Boshduul.

"You owe me the balance of the charges for the delivery, plus I will need extra to cover the transport," the driver screamed.

"Calm yourself, I have your balance right here," Boshduul said, reaching under his rags and flipping out his blade, which he quickly plunged into the driver's throat, twisted the blade, and caught the body as it fell towards the ground. Boshduul lowered him to the ground into a kneeling position. If the crew of the *Hatred* saw the driver, they would think he was looking at something on the ground, so Boshduul threw some credits down and walked up the gangway. He reached the entry, operated the switch that brought the gangway up, and sealed the hatch.

———————— * ————————

She screamed at the handlers to open the gates. They hesitated, which cost them their lives; She cut the three of them down with Her pistol in three shots and one smooth swinging motion.

She commanded Her guards to open the gates and told Klavan to escape the corridor to the left.

They were down on the arena level, and She was having the guards open the back gates to the Drazine's cage.

"Once they are clear, we will release the monster out of the loading dock area to wreak havoc on all those still around. I have programmed several of the facility defense turrets to destroy any ship attempting to take off. We can and will still take control of this situation."

"Your Grace, if we release the monster and it destroys the loading docks, how will we resupply? What good will control be if the area is destroyed?" Klavan asked.

"I thought you were a long-term thinker. When we gain control, it doesn't matter what is left, it matters who is left, and that will be us in control," She corrected him.

"What about the other monster? Is it in the med lab?" Klavan asked.

"One step at a time, my friend. We release this one and then release that one from the opposite side of the facility. That will surely catch all those attempting to stand against us by surprise," She insisted.

Suddenly one of Her guards flew down the corridor as if shot from a cannon and shattered against the far wall.

"Ah, good, it is awake. Now to shut down the force generator," She reached down to Her belt and flipped a switch. There was a noticeable flicker and then a brightening of the corridor lights.

They both leaned against the window overlooking the docks that were in the stairwell. Dozens of creatures fled the loading dock area.

Then the monster appeared. It was a large Drazine, larger than the one in med lab. It was a silver and blue-toned beast. The front claws and feet were enormous, with webbing between claws. The eyes were small, with large brows over them. The beast had a broad flat head with large ears and number of spikes or horns sticking out the top and side of its head. The mouth was turned back in a permanent snarl exposing massive fangs. The creature crawled out of the loading dock (it barely fit) and into the open. It was massive.

"Now we will have some fun," She stated. She reached inside Her armor and removed a remote control, similar to the one She used to control the creature in med lab, She pushed a button on it, and the beast outside became enraged.

The creature's face became distorted, and it began to swing its gigantic tail in a crazy manner, throwing shipping containers and loading equipment aside. The creature bellowed an ear-shattering roar, which could be felt in the chest.

"That is my baby. Go destroy everything," She cackled.

---------------- * ----------------

"Zhuni,-we-have-a-problem," Joxby yelled.

"What now?" Zhuni replied.

"The-monster-is-out," Joxby yelled excitedly.

"Abijah is in the med lab. We are getting ready to load her in the transport, just waiting…" Zhuni was cut off by Joxby.

"Me-to-signal-you-that-Her-guards-are-coming,-I-know,-but-She-has-released-the-other-Drazine-out-the-far-side-of-the-loading-dock," Joxby screamed.

"Dagz! Sarge, did you hear that?" Zhuni shouted.

"Yes, but I am a bit busy attempting to save guild masters, you know." Sarge snapped weapons firing and the sound of combat in the background.

"Well, if we don't get Rue on the new problem, the guild masters may not be able to leave. And they may walk into an angry Drazine, which could be a problem," Zhuni insisted.

"You think? Joxby, what is Rue's location?" Sarge inquired.

"I-do-not-have-his-location;-I-will-contact-Elu," Joxby replied.

"Let me know when you have him," Sarge demanded.

"Will-do," Joxby said.

"I can go; Joxby, get me Rue's location now!" Tan'cha yelled.

"Elu-said-Rue-is-at-the-mouth-of-our-tunnel,-heading-to-landing-bay-mark-ten-forty-five," Joxby blurted out.

"I am going that way, heading from the *Palti*. Can Elu contact him?" Tan'cha asked.

"Elu-has-informed-Rue-of-the-situation," Joxby replied.

"I can see him; he is running out of our loading dock area. I am after him," Tan'cha reported.

"If he is aware of the situation, Tan'cha, I could use a bit of help here in the service hall," Sarge interjected.

"Coming your way," Tan'cha replied.

"Good, we could use the help. Zhuni sent a sled; I have one down. I need to get him to the *Palti*'s med team now. I am not going to lose anyone this close to departure," Sarge ordered.

———————— * ————————

The shooting started, and She left with Klavan. *She did not even look at me*, Stanton thought. Now here he was, hiding under the large dining table, awaiting his death. This was not how things were supposed to go. The guards were going to kill all the guild masters, and She was going to be the ultimate power with Stanton by Her side. But no, that Sarge character and his special boys had to show up and start to drive the Her guards back and save the guild masters.

Sarge and his team had pushed their way into the banquet hall through the holes in the walls and driven the guards back to the main entrance. They had also used detonators of some type to disable more than a dozen of Her guards.

383

Sarge and his team seemed to be out of those devices; they were not using them. The guards were now starting to push back. The Assassins' Guild's new Master Arioch was using a power sword to dismantle the guards himself. Stanton was certain the Game Master would now consider the Assassins' Guild as Her enemy. Of course, Sarge and his boys had ruined everything, showing up just in time to save the worthless guilds, Hotha had gotten out on his own, followed by Yegg, then Telore had escaped. That left the Assassins' Guild, Freighters' Guild second, and the entire leadership of the Renegade Guild trapped along with the Smugglers' Guild and the drug cartels. Sarge had gotten the entire counsel of the Renegade Guild out and now seemed to be pulling back.

Stanton thought if She had left him, and Sarge had left the other guilds, maybe Stanton should make some play to be helpful to these guilds left in here.

Sarge and his team started to slip through the holes in the walls. They were leaving. Interesting, now the Her guards were pulling back. Both forces were now gone.

Stanton raised up over the table to be sure.

Stanton could see that the battle had taken out many attendants and guild assistants but none of the guild masters, it seemed. There were dozens of dead and dying about the room. Stanton was surprised; he thought there would be more dead.

He could see that the Assassins' Guild master, Arioch, was standing tall, barking orders to his men. He wanted a group to follow the guards and keep track of them; the rest of his men were to follow him back to their ship, the *Termination*, and regroup.

Stanton looked across to the far side of the room where he had last seen Thana, the drug cartels master. There was a pile of broken tables, so Stanton got up and walked that way. Behind the pile was Thana. He had taken a blaster rifle shot to the chest; he was gone. Kol, his second, was missing his head. Looking at their position, Stanton realized they had been at the dessert table together when the shooting started and had no cover. When they attempted to create cover, they had set up in a crossfire between Arioch and the Game Masters guards. Arioch and his retinue did not care who was in their line of fire.

Stanton looked at one of the guards that Sarge had killed. Stanton looked closer and realized it was not dead; it was destroyed. It was a machine. Stanton had to leave and get back to the safety of his quarters. This evening was too much; he was useless at this point; he knew he was not a fighter.

Stanton wandered out of the banquet hall and down the service corridor. There were three of Her destroyed guards in the hallway and the body of Yegg's guard. The hallway had fresh blood along with fluid of some type draining from the guards' hulks. Stanton made it to the lift and took it to his personal quarters level.

He exited the lift, turned the corner, and saw the doors had been blown open. He studied the debris and damage as he stumbled down the hall. His legs were weakening as he got closer. He entered the chamber, saw the three bodies of his attendants, and collapsed to the floor when he saw the doors to his Starch and credits storge also blasted open. He turned a pale bluish-grey color.

She had left him to die in the banquet hall; She had taken Klavan with Her. The guilds were fighting Her and each other; he had his Starch and credits taken, and his chambers were ruined. He had no power, no prestige, no credits, nothing. He was ruined. He did not even know what was going on at the moment, was She in control, were the guilds in control, was She still alive? He was ruined. Everything he had worked for was gone. All color drained from him.

*

"Captain, Joxby just contacted us and stated that things have gone sideways," the communications officer of the deck stated.

"What do you mean?" the captain of the *Palti* asked.

"Things have gone wrong in too many ways as of now; Joxby stated that we may have to depart without the entire team."

"Get him, let him know we are standing by, and if we can assist in any way, we will. We will not leave prematurely. We will wait. The plan is good on our end; we have no problems."

"Yes, Captain."

"Flight control, get fighters prepared to launch, security, prepare three reinforced squads for the planet. I want two ready to add their muscle to our client's forces and one to hold the tunnel until all clients arrive. Weapons systems, check and charge. All systems set ship for departure. Plotting, set course to match arrival vectors."

"Yes, Captain," all systems replied in unison.

"Comms, get me Joxby."

"Working."

"Comms, also patch in Lemuel," the captain demanded.

"Comms, aye."

*

"Why noise?" Traxon asked the closest crewmember.

"That is the departure Klaxon. It means to prepare for lift-off," the crewmember informed him.

"Too early, not ready, missing friends."

"You need to let your friends know they need to get here in a hurry."

"I need find," Traxon announced as he hurried down the corridors of the ship back to the passenger ramp.

Traxon did not need the hologram to lead him back. After a lifetime of hiding and living in the shadows and sneaking around, his sense of direction was impeccable. He arrived at the ramp and was attempting to push past the various individuals getting on board.

"Hey, where are you going? If you leave now, you may not get back on; you hear that? That is the departure warning," said the Krodent, who had earlier given Traxon his boarding assistance.

"I find friends, not leave without," Traxon yelled back as he finally got through those getting on board.

"Be quick; good luck," the Krodent yelled.

Traxon ran past the dozens of creatures checking in and boarding. He ran out past the loading crews and equipment, which was placing everyone's personal belongings on the ship. He entered the tunnel and scurried towards the loading dock and med lab.

With everything Zhuni, Sarge, and Tan'cha had done for him, there was no way he was going to leave without them.

He could hear a dreadful noise as he neared the end of the tunnel, there was screaming and sounds of destruction, rifle and pistol fire, explosions, crumbling and crunching, and a strange roar he had never heard and could not identify. He had to get there and help. He was scared but more determined than ever to help.

He ran past the loading dock and was certain he did not want to know what was going on. He just hoped Zhuni was in the med lab or at the arena. If Traxon could find Zhuni, everything would be okay.

CHAPTER 16

Monsters Controlled

Rue could see the monster. It was going to be a harder shot than he had planned. He only had two chances. The creature was smashing everything near it. There was so much debris Rue did not know where to go to get the shot.

The creature was heading towards the landing bays; maybe Rue could get out in front of it. There was an open area just past the facility's security fencing. Rue ran toward the fencing, raised his blaster rifle, and fired at the base of one of the posts. The lower third of the post and a large chunk of the fencing blasted apart. Rue took a second shot and increased the damage. He ran to the hole and stomped on the remaining fence, pushing it to the ground as he stepped across it. He was not in the open area prior to the landing bays. If the monster maintained course, Rue was in a good position.

The humanish guards and the dock workers in the facility were running in every direction. None of them were making any attempt to even slow down the creature, so many cowards. Rue was so glad he had never had to work with them. He would never have had the patience. These creatures disgusted him.

Here it came, just as Rue had hoped. Just a moment, and it would clear the fence line. He should have a good clean shot.

Rue leaped to the top rampart of the first landing bay closest to him. He had lined it up perfectly. The creature was coming directly at him. In fact, Rue realized the beast saw him and was coming after him. Not at all what Rue wanted, but it would allow a clear shot. If he could just figure out what to do after the shot to make certain he would survive, that would be a good thing.

The beast increased its speed and rushed towards Rue. It broke the fence line and still headed directly toward Rue; there was now no question it wanted Rue.

Rue dropped his blaster rifle to his side; it was sling mounted, so it fell to his side but was easily accessible. He quickly drew the other blaster from his back, pulled back the lever, slid the first capsule in, and closed the lever. He raised the rifle and fired. The capsule flew towards the target and found its mark. Rue's shot hit the monster directly between the eyes, exploding in a cloud of mist. Rue was taking no chances and was already closing the lever for the second capsule. In the blink of an eye, the second capsule hit the same spot, exploding in a second misty cloud. Rue took this moment to drop down behind the rampart and bolt to the closest exit. He had the wall between himself and the monster, hopefully giving himself enough cover to make his escape while the monster was attempting to clear its sight.

If Joxby was correct, and the capsule worked as advertised, nanobots would work their way to the probe implanted in the creature's head. These nanobots would destroy the spikes locking them into the beast's brain. Once those were gone, Rue would have to blast the back cover off, and theoretically, the probe would slide out.

Now Rue would have to work his way behind the creature to blast the cover off of its head, releasing the probe the Game Master controlled. It would take a while for the nanobots to do their work. This could be a long afternoon.

"Elu, get ahold of Joxby and let me know how long I have. The capsules have been delivered."

"Yes, sir."

The rampart where Rue had just been exploded. The beast's head followed through the blast. It was attempting to locate Rue. Rue jumped through the exit doorway and cut left towards the creature. This should throw the creature off. Rarely would a predator's prey run towards it. Rue was banking on this strategy.

"Joxby said that Mazalla designed the nanobots. They were entered through the orbital nerves, which lead directly back to the base of the probe. There are marker bots to direct the removal bots. The removal bots are designed to target and destroy the Boratine. They should get to work almost immediately," Elu informed Rue.

"Great, what does all that mean? How much time before I can shoot the cover off?"

"Almost immediately," Elu stated.

"Almost?" Rue rounded the corner to the front of the rampart he had just been on moments ago to see the hind end of the creature begin to enter the landing bay. The tail followed as the creature made its way deeper into the landing bays.

"Yes, you can take the shot anytime," Elu said.

"I am taking the shot as soon as I get it," Rue yelled.

"As soon as you do, get out of there," Elu told him.

"That is my plan," Rue said as he edged around the rubble to track the creature.

———————— * ————————

"Guards, to the med lab," She ordered.

"Your Grace, I do not think there will be much left to control if you release both creatures," Klavan voiced as he attempted to understand how he had gotten into this situation. If he was seen as being with Her after the attempted assassinations, his chance to be the Game Master may evaporate.

"I no longer need this facility. I have used it to my advantage and will destroy whatever I need to," She turned towards Klavan and raised Her blaster pistol.

"Your Grace?" Klavan raised his hand as to block the pistol.

"You have served me well, but it is time to end your service, goodbye," She fired the pistol and sent a blast directly at Klavan's chest. Klavan was blasted across the corridor and slumped against the far wall, motionless.

The Game Master looked at Klavan's lifeless body for a moment, turned with Her guards, and continued down the corridor.

The corridors were oddly empty. There were only a few human-ish guards wandering. She was wondering where everyone was. Had they known She and Her guards were coming?

They reached the med lab's main gate. It was locked. *Where are the fighters who should be here? Why is there no one here?* The fights were still scheduled.

"Blast it," She ordered the guards.

———————— * ————————

"Zhuni," Traxon screeched across the med lab.

"You should be on the *Palti*. What are you doing here?"

"Chaos, dangerous; I come help," Traxon replied.

"Well then, help get the last of the med records there with Mazalla. We need to have the medical records. Thank you. My friend," Zhuni stated.

"Traxon, friend." He smiled.

"Joxby, you need to get out. We are moving. This will be the last run. I have Abijah loading onto the transport. There is just Mazalla, me, Traxon, and the security team here. You need to contact Elu," Zhuni said.

"I-have-transferred-control;-She-coming,-Traxon?" Joxby stated as he shut down the last monitor. He grabbed a remote and slid it into his tool pouch and hopped to the exit of the security center.

"Yes, Traxon left the ship to come help. The security team is ready. I see you are coming down now. Do you have the detonator?" Zhuni inquired.

"Detonator-in-pouch;-lets-go," Joxby said, descending the stairs. He joined Zhuni just as Zhuni started the force generator.

"That should slow Her and the Guards down," Zhuni exclaimed.

"Sarge, Tan'cha, what is your situation?" Zhuni spoke into the vox.

"We have sent the sled to the *Palti*. We are falling back and on our way to the exit," Sarge said.

"Good; everyone is on their way and ready to meet at the rally point," Zhuni informed them.

"Anyone hear from Rue?" Sarge asked with concern.

"Last I saw, he was tracking the Drazine," Tan'cha said.

"Elu-said-Rue-hit-the-target-with-the-capsule-and-was-getting-lined-up-for-last-shot," Joxby said.

"Anyone know his plan for meeting with us?" Sarge asked.

"Elu-said-Rue-would-join-us-later," Joxby blurted out.

"There is no later; we are all leaving now," Sarge added.

"He said he will join us in orbit," Zhuni stated.

"Roger that," Sarge replied.

"How in the Dagz is he going to do that?" Tan'cha asked.

"Who knows, he has a plan or will figure something out," Sarge said.

A massive explosion knocked Zhuni, Joxby, and the security team to their knees. The main gate exploded into the med lab. Debris was scattered across the entire entrance. There stood a dozen of Her guards. She stepped between them and entered the Med-lab.

Zhuni and Joxby helped each other up, and the security team turned to face the threat.

"Her timing is perfect," Zhuni said to Joxby.

"Yes,-very-reliable," Joxby chuckled.

She glanced at them, but Her eyes focused on Abijah, who was being loaded onto a transport.

"What are you doing?" She screamed.

"That would be our cue to leave," Zhuni yelled.

"Yes,-indeed;-She-seems-to-be-upset," Joxby laughed as he leaped to the rear of the med lab making his exit.

"Stop them!" She commanded.

Several of Her guards rushed forward while several others began to fire their blaster rifles. The charging guards hit the force generator and were thrown back into the guards who were shooting. Shots ricocheted all over the med lab.

"Dagz! Shut down power to the med lab! Get outside and cut them off!" She screamed at Her guards.

Several of the guards picked themselves up and rushed out of the main entrance and into the corridors to circle around behind Zhuni and his team.

Zhuni was followed by the security team out to the loading dock; he waved his arms to signal the transport to head out.

"Joxby, now!" Zhuni hollered.

The entire security center at the top of the med lab exploded. Rubble and debris came crashing down; it was immediately followed by the back section of the med lab exploding and collapsing. The Game Master and Her guards had to fall back and dodge the rubble.

"Get that transport!" She screamed.

Zhuni saw Tan'cha, Sarge, and his team at the mouth of the tunnel. He signaled them to get to the *Palti*.

The transport left the loading dock, followed by four more. Zhuni and the security team rushed down the tunnel along with Abijah.

"Final charge," Zhuni yelled.

There was a massive blast that destroyed the loading docks and brought down the first third of the tunnel. Now the tunnel, the loading docks, and the med lab were buried under massive amounts of rock and debris. No one would be getting through there for a long time.

"You have saved so many from their evil servitude. You and your friends have done so much. We have a long way to go, but this is an amazing start," Abijah stated.

"We are working to get you home," Zhuni continued.

"And my brother," Abijah implored.

"Yes, we still have a long way to go. I am not sure when your brother will be joining us. I am not sure how that will work. Will you be able to speak with him?" Zhuni asked.

"I have not been able to communicate with him. But you have been able to. We may need you to speak with him," Abijah stated.

"Me? Why would you think I would speak to him?" Zhuni pondered.

"You are an Ancient; you shared his dreams," Abijah reminded Zhuni.

"What am I going to say?" Zhuni asked.

"If you connect once he is free, you will know."

*

"What do you mean there are several transports? Find the one with my pet!" the Game Master screamed at Her guards.

Several of the humanish guards were also assisting with attempting to find Zhuni and the Drazine.

"Your Majesty, they used five different transports, which all went in different directions; in all the confusion, the explosions, the other monster on the loose, and the guilds leaving, we were unable to tell which transport was the one with the monster," the head humanish guard said.

"Find my pet!" She shrieked.

"Yes, Your Majesty, we are working to do just that. It is going to take time to figure out which transport was which and where they went," he reported.

"They went to a ship; they are attempting to escape with my pet, you insolent Mynog!" She drew her sword and removed his head in one swift, smooth arc. The humanish guards stood still.

"Who is in second?" She wailed.

A battered and worn and enormous humanish stepped up, bowed, and swallowed hard. He looked to have been in every war in history. He was tall; Tan'cha tall and had massively broad shoulders. He wore an olive drab jumpsuit of a flight crew member, which seemed a size or three too small.

"I am the second in command, Your Excellency. I thank you for the opportunity to serve you directly," he slowly rose from his bow.

"What is your name?" She asked.

"Kaloon, at Your service," he responded.

"Kaloon, you are now *my* second. I appreciate your style and your understanding of my position. I will not hold you responsible for your former commander's mistakes, but I will hold you responsible for finding out where my pet is and where Zhuni is."

"Your second, my Grace, I am but a lowly guard; Klavan, I understood, was your second. I could not possibly replace him," Kaloon insisted.

"Klavan is no longer with us, and until I find someone of his caliber, you will do."

"Thank You, Your Excellency; I will find Your pet," Kaloon bowed deeply and turned to those assembled.

"Gentlemen, we must find each transport. We know they all went to the landing bays, so spread out and report in as soon as you find them," Kaloon ordered.

A humanish guard rushed up to Kaloon, and he bent down to listen.

"Your Excellency, I have just been informed a ship that had a transport load on to it in bay one twenty-six was shot down by your automated defense system. They are searching the wreckage now."

"With the guilds cowards escaping or attempting to escape, the system will stay on. We will take down as many of them as we can," She informed them.

"Yes, Your Excellency, my concern is if the system takes down the ship with Your pet or with Zhuni, we may only discover bodies," Kaloon stated.

"So be it!"

A messenger arrived and spoke with Kaloon. Kaloon put his massive right hand to the top of his head and rubbed it as he turned to address Her. He was slightly ashen in color. It did not look like good news.

"They have discovered the skeleton of a massive creature and at least a half dozen humanoid bodies in the wreckage," Kaloon stammered.

"My pet?" She asked.

"I do not know; we are looking into it," Kaloon stated.

"You, take me there," She commanded Kaloon.

"This way, Your Excellency." He stepped to Her side and guided Her out to the destruction of the main loading area.

"Track down Sarge, Tan'cha, and the others. I want them all," She ordered Her guards.

---------------- * ----------------

Rue was now behind the beast, just as he had wanted to be. He lined up the shot. He squeezed the trigger and watched as the beast swung its head, and his shot ricocheted off the back of the beast's skull. It noticed the shot and spun its head around to see what was happening. Rue dropped down behind the rubble, hoping the beast had not seen him.

Rue raised his head slightly and could see the beast looking around over its gargantuan shoulders. It turned back to its original facing and started off on its path of destruction. As it swung, its massive tail swept around and nearly crushed Rue as it removed the rubble pile he was hiding behind.

Rue rolled out of the sweep of the tail and kept his distance, realizing he now had to watch the tail also. As he did so, his earpiece slipped out and hit the ground. He set down and lined up the shot again. This time he would watch the tail. He would also anticipate the beast's head swing. He switched the selector to full auto. This time he would pour the shots on target; he now knew the shots would not harm the beast.

The rifle barked out dozens of shots, all connected with the cover, which was blasted apart. The beast stopped in its tracks. Its shoulders sagged, and the creature slumped forward. The stem slid out the back of its head and dropped to the ground. The beast dropped to the ground. Had he done some harm to the beast? No, the shots just bounced off the beast's head; there was no way his shots had harmed the beast. Rue had accomplished this mission. Now it was time to take care of some personal issues.

Rue turned and stalked his way back towards the loading dock area. He was approaching the fence line when a battery of defense weapons opened fire; Rue spun to see what was incoming when he realized the battery was targeting a ship lifting off. This would be a huge danger for all attempting to leave. Rue now had another mission. To save lives.

"Elu, come in," Rue said.

He realized the earpiece was gone, and he was on his own. This would make the mission a challenge. Rue craved challenges.

———————— * ————————

"Zhuni," Abijah spoke.

"Zhuni," Tan'cha shouted. Tan'cha was already coming back to check on Zhuni when he saw Zhuni collapse.

Tan'cha was at Zhuni's side. He looked up at Abijah; she looked down at him with sad eyes. Tan'cha knew he could not speak to her, but he knew by the look in her eyes there was a problem. Tan'cha picked Zhuni up and looked to Abijah; he nodded for her to follow. They started toward the *Palti*.

The security team and Sarge were waiting for them, as was the *Palti*'s ground team.

"What happened?" Sarge asked.

"I have no idea; I ran back to check on them and saw Zhuni just collapse," Tan'cha reported.

"Was it like in the med lab? Did he grab his head before he dropped?" Sarge asked.

"Yes, exactly," Tan'cha said.

"Rue completed his mission. We have been unable to contact him. He must have run into some issues. Abijah's brother may be attempting to contact Zhuni. We can't leave until they contact each other. Abijah, do you hear your brother?" Sarge asked as he pointed at her and pointed to his ear and then made like a monster, arms swinging around as if he were knocking things about.

Abijah understood and smiled, then shook her head back and forth to say no.

"See, she understands," Sarge said as he pointed to Zhuni and then his ear.

Abijah understood Sarge was asking if she and Zhuni were communicating.

She frowned and shook her head.

Sarge motioned back and forth between himself and Abijah as to say, "Let us know when you do."

Abijah nodded.

"Okay, so she is not communicating with Zhuni, nor is she communicating with her brother, but she will let us know when either happens," Sarge assured them.

"So, what, we just wait?" Tan'cha asked.

"Yes, we told her, and Zhuni promised her we would not leave without her brother. Zhuni has been through this before; we know how tough he is. We will monitor him the best we can. Set up a sled here, and we will wait," Sarge demanded.

"How long?" Tan'cha asked.

"It is still chaos out there; they are most likely still chasing the transports. It will take them a while to figure out the various diversions. We have time. Have we heard from any guilds?" Sarge asked.

"The captain was going to inform us of any contacts," Tan'cha said.

"I will inform the captain of our delay," Sarge stated.

———————— * ————————

"I need you and your guards to assist my guards in finding my pet, Zhuni, and the others while also taking out as many guild members as possible. With the defense system programmed to shoot down all departing ships, there is no escape. I will reward each of your men who bring me the skulls of those they disposed of. I advise your men to encircle the landing bays and dispatch those within one bay at a time," She suggested to Kaloon.

"Wonderful plan, Your Excellency. You heard our Queen; gather skulls," Kaloon ordered.

"Queen, oh, I do like that," She crowed.

The entire entourage continued their march across the loading dockyards and toward the fence line. They were still heading to the wreckage of the first ship, which was shot down. The roar of other defensive batteries firing informed them that there would be more wreckage to investigate. They could see one ship rise up close to them and sweep across the first rampart, drop to nearly ground level, and head toward the marketplace. Batteries turned to attempt to target it but could not bring their guns to bear. The ship was a small blockade runner that disappeared into the alleys of the marketplace.

"Clever, but I do not think it will make it out past the ring defenses," She muttered.

A larger ship attempted the same maneuver, but due to its larger size, it took continuous fire to the upper part of the craft. It took enough damage to start smoking. It hit the ground hard just prior to the marketplace. Its smoking hulk slid a bit and stopped, blocking any smaller ship's ability to use that as an escape route. Several humanish guards could be seen rushing the ship. The defensive turret on the rear of the ship opened fire and tore through the humanish guards. Several others charged the bow of the ship and the sides; these were met with fire from several other turrets on the ship.

"Get several teams loaded into the armored troop trucks and use their weapons to open that ship up!" Kaloon yelled at the closest humanish guards. The guards ran off towards the motor pool.

A moment later, the engines could be heard starting up; then, four armored personnel carriers roared by. The first exploded in a fireball as the rear turret of the downed ship found the target. The second troop carrier careened into the rampart of a landing bay, the third dashed around the burning hulk of the first and rolled just out of the fire arc of the ship's turret. The fourth carrier continued on past until it was taking fire from the side turrets.

The troop carrier at the rear of the ship opened fire with its own turret and destroyed the rear turret of the ship, humanish guards then poured out of the troop carrier, and one ran up just under the ship's now defuncted turret and slapped a breeching charge onto the hull. The guard ran to the side of the ship just as the charge went off. Several humanish guards ran towards the breech in the hull but were cut down before arriving by those within. The guard who had placed the breeching charge now slid along the rear of the ship to the breech and tossed an explosive charge in. This exploded, and humanish guards rushed the hole, making entry.

Guards unloaded from the carrier, which crashed into the rampart, and they added their numbers to the breech.

"Why do I not hear my second pet? It should be out here destroying everything it sees," She asked Katoon.

"I do not understand either, my Queen. But I will find out," Katoon assured Her.

He turned to the guards standing next to him and, pointing at one, told him to run ahead and get up on the highest rampart to see if he could locate the monster.

She could see destruction everywhere. Klavan had been right; there would be little to control once She finished Her rampage. But the guilds would also be without leadership, and She would fill that void. The gaming facility was just a means to an end. She did not care if it was razed to the ground nor if hundreds or thousands were killed, it all led to Her total control of all guilds. She needed to find Her pets, and there would be no stopping Her.

"Katoon, let's not delay further. I am anxious to get to the wreckage," She ordered.

"Yes, my Queen, this way." Katoon motioned Her forward and also motioned to the troop carrier, which had just dispatched the ship's rear turret to drive to them. The troop carrier eased back, turned, and roared its engines as it drove in their direction.

"A Queen should not have to walk such a distance," Katoon implied.

The troop transport drooped its rear ramp allowing Her to step into the carrier along with Her four guards, Katoon, and six of the humanish guards.

She paused for a moment and looked toward the rampart of the first landing pad; Her pet had obviously crashed through that spot on its way. She had a strange feeling someone was watching Her from there, but She could not see them. Strange, who would dare track Her?

"Katoon, send a squad to that rampart and landing bay and have them search it," She ordered. Pointing out the spot.

"Yes, my Queen. What are they looking for?" Katoon asked.

"An assassin, I believe," She said.

------------ * ------------

"How long will it take? We need to leave while the chaos gives us cover," Tan'cha stated.

"I agree, but what can we do? We cannot even get out of the tunnel unless we go to the cliffs; then, we would have to climb them and hike back to the facility. That would take kolts," Sarge said.

"Too bad we can't just take the *Palti*; that would cut our time to nothing," Tan'cha exclaimed.

Abijah sat there watching them banter back and forth. She wished she could understand them.

"Why don't you take them to the facility? You could climb past the *Palti* and fly to the facility." Abijah had a voice she had never heard speaking to her. It had to be an Ancient but who?

"Who are you? Where are you speaking to me from?" Abijah could tell this Ancient had spoken to Drazine before. It was a female Ancient.

"Go, find your brother; defend them as they find their friend. The *Palti* will not leave without you and Zhuni; you are too valuable to the mission. I will contact you when Zhuni awakens. Your brother will most likely let you know, also. Go," the Ancient said.

"I will."

Abijah lowered her head and pushed against Sarge, then Tan'cha.

"What?" Sarge asked.

"What is she doing?" Tan'cha asked, looking at Sarge.

Abijah pushed harder, forcing them toward the *Palti*.

"I think she wants us to board the ship," Tan'cha said.

But when Tan'cha started up the ramp, Abijah knocked him off the ramp and pushed him past the ramp.

"Tan'cha, I think she wants us to go to the end of the tunnel," Sarge said, breaking into a run.

"Okay, let's go," Tan'cha ran with Sarge.

Abijah fell in behind them. They reached the tunnel mouth and were overlooking the sea far below. Abijah stepped to the edge of the cliff and folded her wings and lowered her massive shoulder; looking at Sarge and Tan'cha, she nodded her head as to say get on.

"Come on, she is going to take us to the facility. We can help her find her brother and see if we can find Rue," Sarge said as he stepped up to her back.

"I don't know about this," Tan'cha stammered.

"What do you think she wants us to do other than go with her," Sarge asked.

"Yup, maybe you should go; I am not sure I will be much help," Tan'cha mumbled as he looked over the cliff edge.

"Come on, don't be afraid. You and I can take anything on. Without you, none of us could have gotten this far. We are a team, and I need you," Sarge informed Tan'cha.

"Yea, but…" Tan'cha muttered as he looked over the edge again.

"Imagine the stories you can tell when we get to Kashtuu. Tan'cha, the Drazine rider," Sarge exclaimed.

"I don't know," Tan'cha said timidly, climbing up to grab onto Sarge.

"I will grab her neck; you hold onto me," Sarge said, leaning forward and reaching his arms around Abijah's massive neck. His hands just reached, enabling him to lock fists.

"I don't know about this," Tan'cha reaffirmed his uncertainty.

Abijah crawled closer to the edge until her entire upper body was out over the cliff. She lowered herself and dropped off the cliff spreading her massive wings.

There was a moment of weightlessness as they dropped toward the sea. Then her wings caught the wind as she flapped them inward, and they rocketed skyward.

"Owww," Tan'cha screamed.

They swung out to sea, then turned back to the cliffs and up and over them. They could see smoke rising from several locations, and they could see small blockade runner at ground level heading their way.

"We need to find her brother and see if we can find Rue also. Keep an eye out for both," Sarge yelled.

"Zhuni is becoming restless. Your brother may be awakening," the Ancient's voice came to Abijah.

"We are reaching the edge of the facility. We do not see anything yet," Abijah told the Ancient.

"Remember, to those at the facility, you are a monster. Use that to your advantage; also confuse them by assisting those you can. Between that and the chaos of the battle between Her and the guilds, you should be able to find your brother and get him out safely. Also, look for Rue; he may need help," the Ancient said.

"I will do all I can. We will find them," Abijah said.

———————— * ————————

Rue saw them exiting the facility and dove for cover. She was with a massive humanish, several of Her guards, and a dozen other humanish guards. They were heading this way. Rue would have to set his rifle back to single shot and make it count. He slid behind cover then worked his way back to the top of the rampart. This would be a good spot to take the shot. She should step into the open shortly, and he could take Her out. That would save so many lives.

The entourage was stepping through the fencing and entering the open area.

A small blockade runner zipped over his head, so close he could have touched it. He had to duck so he was not knocked off the rampart. The ship flew down the open area towards the marketplace. It skimmed the ground; that was a tremendous pilot. He was mere feet from alley walls and the ground. He flew just under the arc of the defensive batteries.

The Master was getting closer. Rue wished he had his sniper rifle with him; the shot would have already been made. Now he would have to wait for them to come into range.

A larger ship swooped in low and attempted the same path as the small blockade runner, but it was not successful. It was shot down and caused a melee of activity as the humanish guards attempted to board it. A small battle broke out, and reinforcements arrived from the motor pool. *Great, nearly there, just a bit more, and I can take the shot.*

One of the armored troop carriers arrived at the entourage, and they started to board it. Rue put the sight on Her but could not make the shot; She paused for a moment and looked directly at his position. *Has She seen me?* The armored troop carrier closed the ramp and drove off. He had missed his opportunity, and now there were guards headed his way. They stopped and looked over Rue's position into the sky. Then broke into dead runs as they scattered. Rue turned to see the monster from med lab flying toward him. *Are there people on it?*

———————— * ————————

Zhuni had a massive headache. He was exhausted. He did not know how long he had been out, but he knew the feelings of confusion were not his. He glanced around and realized he had been moved from the tunnel to his quarters. He was hooked up to monitoring equipment. He knew where he was, so the confusion must be Abijah's brother.

Zhuni concentrated to make the connection. It was foggy in his mind's eye. He could see the vague shape of a figure ahead of him. It looked like a massive Drazine. Zhuni headed toward it. He got closer, and it clearly became a Drazine, a massive one, larger than Abijah. Zhuni got so close he could touch it, then it disappeared, and Zhuni realized he was in the mind of the Drazine.

"You sent your dreams to me when you were in stasis. I am Zhuni, an Ancient and a friend. Your sister Abijah sent me," Zhuni thought.

"Yes, I remember connecting with you for a time. What is happening?" the Drazine asked.

"You were grown to be a monster in the arena of combat. We are in the process of escaping and want you to join us. We have freed Abijah of her chains and want to help you," Zhuni informed him.

"How do I join you; I do not know where I am?" the Drazine spoke.

"I will guide you. Follow my voice," Zhun instructed.

"Where is my sister? Is she safe?" the Drazine asked.

"Yes, she is boarding a ship to take all of us back to your homeworld. Reach out to her; you may be able to contact her. She is near," Zhuni said.

"Why can I not speak to her?" the Drazine asked.

"Abijah thinks it will just take some time for you to connect with her. I was the only one you could connect with for a time, so you may have to open your mind to reach her. What is the name you were given?" Zhuni asked.

"I am Aslaug," the Drazine said.

"Well, Aslaug, slow and steady towards the cliffs; they are to your left, swing around and follow my voice," Zhuni insisted.

"I am confused; I am not sure," Aslaug stated.

"I understand. Remember the dreams you had of the experiments and the scientists? Those were real; that is what you have been subject to in the past. That is why we need to get you away from here. This place is not safe for you or your sister. You had a control device installed in the back of your head. A friend removed it," Zhuni explained.

"I saw him. He needs help. Many chasing him. He shot me; why should I help him? He tried to kill me," Aslaug said, getting upset.

"No, he did not attempt to hurt you. You were under the control of the Game Master; we had to remove the device. The only way to do that was to shoot it off. Rue knew you might kill him, but he took that chance to free you," Zhuni told him.

"Why would he risk his life for me?"

"That is what we do; we take care of each other."

"I need to turn around and help him."

"No, we need to get you out of there. He is an expert at getting himself out of bad situations, and he will do it this time. We are counting on it," Zhuni declared.

Aslaug spun around, got a bit dizzy, and stumbled but continued.

"I am going to help him. He is in trouble," Aslaug stated.

Aslaug picked up his pace as he headed back to where he saw the Swaklin known as Rue.

———————— * ————————

Tan'cha tapped Sarge and pointed toward the monstrous beast; it was even larger than Abijah. Abijah saw it at the same time. It was heading back to the facility.

Abijah swooped down to catch its attention, but it seemed confused and did not even look up. Abijah twisted in the direction the beast was headed and spotted a figure dropping down off a rampart. Zhuni had described Rue in their previous conversations, and Abijah was certain this was him. He had several dozen humanish guards bearing down on him. Abijah thought finding her brother again would be easy, but finding that little figure in all this would be difficult. She swung towards him.

"Now, where are we going?" Tan'cha asked.

"Look there." Sarge pointed towards Rue.

"Looks like he is in trouble," Tan'cha said as he saw the guards heading towards Rue's position.

"Not anymore," Sarge said as the guards looked up, saw them, and scattered.

Abijah sat down in the landing bay and dropped Sarge and Tan'cha down off her back. Then lifted off and made her way to Aslaug.

"Nice ride," Rue chuckled.

"We were worried about you," Sarge said.

"I missed her; she got in an armored troop carrier before I could get the shot off. I need to find her," Rue exclaimed.

"Where did it go?" Tan'cha asked.

"It headed into the landing dock area. Toward the marketplace," Rue told them.

"Sarge," Zhuni's voice crackled over the vox.

"We have Rue," Sarge replied.

"Good, I have made contact with Abijah's brother, and I am speaking to both of them now," Zhuni said.

"Great, could you send them this way so we can get back to the *Palti* and get off this planet," Tan'cha chimed in.

"Sending them now," Zhuni answered.

"I need to get her Sarge, and we need to shut down these defense batteries, or no one is going anywhere," Rue stated.

"Zhuni, tell them we need to eliminate the defensive battery controls, or more are going to be shot down," Sarge said.

Abijah swopped down into the landing bay and lowered her shoulder. Sarge climbed on; she immediately flew off.

"I guess that isn't our ride," Rue grumbled.

Aslaug's head appeared over the back side of the landing bay. He lowered it for Rue and Tan'cha to climb on. Once they were on, he turned around and walked in the direction of the cliffs. He leaped and moved quickly. Rue and Tan'cha were having a difficult time staying on.

Sarge pointed toward the control tower so Abijah could destroy it. She took a deep breath and blew a plume of molten fire, which obliterated it. Nothing was left but a smoking pile of melted metal. Sarge could see the closest defense battery drop gun tips down; he could see several at the same angle.

Sarge called Zhuni.

"The tower is down. The defensive batteries are inactive, and it is safe to launch," Sarge told him.

Zhuni must have informed the guilds as dozens of ships started to lift off. The sky filled with ships. Large ships and small ships were all attempting to use the same airspace to leave. Two medium ships slammed into each other, one crashed to the ground at the marketplace, and the other started smoking heavily; it was losing altitude but was aiming for an open area in the marketplace square. It slammed into the ground and, for a moment, looked like it had suffered little damage but then burst into flames and then erupted into a massive fireball.

Now would be the perfect time to escape. Abijah swung back around toward the cliffs. Sarge looked down to see several troop carriers open fire on a couple of ships. He could see that the carriers were scattered around the landing area and began to fire on all ships attempting to leave.

"Zhuni, let her know we have to dispose of these troop carriers. If not, several more ships will not make it out. Plus, one of them contains her," Sarge announced.

"She is going to take them out," Zhuni replied.

Abijah made another sweeping arc back to the battle. It was getting crowded as ships were shooting up from the landing area, and

Abijah nearly took two out as she swung around. One medium transport was caught in the crossfire of three troop carriers and exploded, crashing to the ground and into another transport lifting off. The second transport sputtered as it attempted to get off the ground but slipped into the surrounding rampart, causing further damage.

Abijah targeted the first troop carrier she saw. A stream of liquefied fire drowned the carrier into a puddle of alloy.

She shot a short burst onto the next closest, and it exploded. She continued to target as many as she could. A dozen smoking melted hulks were now where troop carriers once had been.

There were more at the motor pool, so she swooped across the open space and belched more flame upon those carriers stored there. She could see one at the far end of the landing areas but decided it was time to go. She flew out towards the cliffs. Leaving the ships to escape the best they could. They had opened a way for them.

Abijah descended to the cliff entrance and landed in a crouch, allowing Sarge to step off.

Sarge turned to Abijah and proceeded to perform a low bow to say thank you.

Abijah smiled.

They could see Aslaug entering the back of the *Palti*. They both walked back to the *Palti* and entered. The main cargo ramp closed behind them, and the main engines fired up. The *Palti* lifted and slid out of the tunnel, dropped closer to the sea, nosed up, and shot off.

*

She watched as Her pet lay waste to Her defenses. The guilds were leaving, and there was not much She could do to stop them. The ships were leaving in mass; She could only chuckle as some crashed into others.

She had that feeling once again that someone was watching Her. It made Her nervous. She started looking around, but She could not locate where it was coming from.

She looked at the wreckage and could see the enormous skeleton in the debris; She could also see the bodies. Something seemed familiar. She stepped closer and realized the one body was one She saw before. It was one of the contractors that had built the new stations for the guards She had brought in. All of the bodies were the contractors, and upon looking closer, She realized the enormous skeleton was a few Banteests placed together. Someone had gone to a lot of trouble to deceive Her. There was that feeling of being watched again.

The first shot bounced off Her shoulder, nearly taking Her head off. She saw the flash and turned to see another flash. That is all She ever saw again. The shot blew Her head off.

_____ * _____

Rue had leaped off Aslaug when he saw the troop carrier and chased it down. It had stopped to unload the guards, and as he made it to the top of the rampart several landing bays away, he saw Her. He set up with a clean shot overlooking the wreckage.

Rue pulled the trigger just as she turned Her head, so he immediately fired a second round.

He had just pulled off the most important mission of his life. Now he needed to get off the planet. That would be his next mission.

Glossary

Characters

Abijah—the female Drazine known prior to speaking to Zhuni as Brynja Ajal (black or dark death). She is a fire Drazine. Her breath can be an inferno of steel melting flame.

Arioch—the Assassins' Guild's young new master. He gained the position when the Game Master killed his father, the former guild master Doughlok.

Aslaug—the male and younger Drazine from the game facility. Hatched from an egg and operated on to understand Drazine biology. The experiments on him allowed the Game Master to create the control device. He is a plasma Drazine. His breath weapon is plasma, which is devastating to nearly everything: the exact opposite of Abijah, the fire Drazine.

Boshduul—the Gehenna assassin hired by Stanton to assassinate Klavan—is later hired by the Assassins' Guild to dispatch Klavan and Stanton.

Brynja Ajal—the name given to the Drazine; she fights in the arena and is indestructible. Pure evil creature controlled by the Game Master. The term means black or dark death.

Joxby—the Monsee electronic and security expert for med lab. (Introduced on page 63.)

Kaloon—leader of the humanish security forces at the arena, becomes security leader when the guild war begins.

Klavan—the Septorian executive assistant and cultural attaché to several Game Masters and the one who watches over Zhuni in a protective and fatherly manner. The one who developed the idea for the med lab.

411

Kowstee—a small medical attendant to Brynja Ajal and a former fighter pilot during the Aashturian Civil War; he performed the healing procedure on Klavan. (Introduced on page 113.)

Sarge—the former night guard shift leader who is transferred to be in charge of security for the med lab. (Introduced on page 30.)

Slaza—Swaklin second in command to Sarge in med lab security. (Introduced on page 57.)

Tan'cha—gladiator who becomes Zhuni's friend and bodyguard. Tan'cha is from the source planet of Kashtuu. He is a Toochuk; he has blue fur, snow leopard grayish spots, four arms, and stands nearly nine feet tall. (Introduced on page 5.)

Tazlon—assistant medic at the arena who assisted Zhuni when the Pantaas attacked in the corridors. He took over the med lab when Zhuni and the team left.

Traxon—Chrodentian, who was right-hand man to Stanton, and who ran Stanton's henchmen. He was saved by Zhuni during his early development as an arena medic. (Introduced on page 20.)

Zhuni—the young male human that is a medic and is to develop and lead the med lab. He is the only human in the arena, facility, or spaceport. He is gifted in his medical knowledge and quite natural leadership skills; others follow him. He also has an ability to quickly and easily understand and communicate through several languages. (Introduced on page 6.)

Races

Aashturian—a massive creature, twelve to fifteen feet tall, powerful build. Broad shoulders with a large head sunk into the neck and shoulders and long arms that nearly touch the ground as they walk. Grey skin tone. Collectors of all knowledge and destroyers of many cultures and worlds. One of the most technologically advanced races. Profits from their continuous wars.

Ancient—the first race, humans.

Chrodentia—small rat-type creatures. Four feet tall, timid, and frail, but in massive numbers, can be intimidating.

Foehlan—tall, thin, and elegant creatures covered in feathers.

Jursdiak—tall, slender race of humanoids that have instantaneous reflexes, speed, and grace and are covered in a thick grayish-green smooth skin, large black eyes, small slits for mouths, and sharply pointed ears. Due to their tremendous reflexes and speed, they make great assassins.

Kalahar—a humanoid race about the same size as humans. A less developed race who wore clothing of processed animal hide. They were known by their large bluish-black eyes. Two small vertical slits under a small snot in the middle of their face (which is their olfactory) and large round ears. Every generation of Kalahar produced two to three dozen special individuals known as trackers; they had incredible abilities that enabled them to track items and creatures throughout the vastness of space.

Krodent—roughly eight-foot-tall reptilian race of powerful build. Thick-skinned and strong-boned. Colors vary depending upon birthplace. Colors range from blues and greens to reds and oranges; females usually lighter in color and smaller than males.

Lokrogh—small creature (Ohmdod).

Maxta—a peaceful race that is vegetarian. Roughly seven feet tall with four arms. Their face has four eyes, two large eyes at the same place as humans, and two smaller eyes set in their temples. They have large, pointed ears and their mouths are small with small flat teeth.

Monsee—a rarely seen small race. These creatures are adept at electronics and detailed work. Built with strong legs and a powerful tail. Moves about with hops and balances on its large tail. Covered in tiny scales except for its face, throat, chest, and mid-region. Typically, bluish-gray color for males and grayish-green for females.

Ryanlian—a small but strong and quick reptilian race. Used by the cartels and guilds as their goons. Often hyped up on Starch that heightens their war-like behavior and skills.

Salvon—small humanoids (smaller than Chrodentia), broad and strong build, most often engineers or miners due to their natural engineering skills and small size.

Septorian—tall lizard-type race from the planet Septor. They are roughly seven feet tall and armored with thick metallic skin. The males are typically dark teal in color with crème colored chest and throat, while the females are typically an ocean blue tone with slightly yellow chest and throat.

Skrenoch—the Skrenoch were extremely intelligent creatures and were known to study any and everything. Many races went to them to gather knowledge. They were collectors and dealers of knowledge. Physically they are roughly the same size as a human, with smooth greyish-purple furless skin. Dainty in build (the Skrenoch were not strong nor physically menacing) and having much longer arms than humans and hands with only three fingers and a thumb. Their heads are twice the size of a human's and look much too big for their thin necks. They have large black eyes, which blinked sideways, and their eyelids were vertical. Skrenoch move with a slow, graceful purpose.

Swaklin—the Swaklin are large, nearly seven feet tall, with enormous and muscular upper bodies topped by broad heads, which seemed to be extensions of their chest and shoulders. The head seemed to be mostly a mouth with multiple rows of large pointed, triangular, and serrated teeth. Their eyes are widely spaced and a bit large for their heads. They are able to see extremely well in the dark as they have a dark red protective eye cover that they can use when needed. Fearless warriors often used in security or mercenary positions around the known galaxy.

Takchee—a creature who was about eight feet tall. They have a green-brown exoskeleton. They walk on its back four legs. Their upper body has two appendages, like arms, one with small hands, which had two fingers and a small thumb, and the other pair with claws. They speak in a series of hisses and whistles.

Toztat—a stocky built humanoid about five feet tall on average with stocky powerful build, making them great workers in the mines throughout the galaxy. Most members of the Mining Guild were Toztat. Toztat start life with rich brown skin color, which fades to nearly white as they age. They have flat squarish heads on short wide necks. Their ears are small and low on the sides of their heads, their eyes are widely spaced and small, and they have two vertical slits just above their small-lipped mouths, which serve as their nostrils. They often have short fur covering their head and down to their lower back.

Toochuk—aliens from the world of Kashtuu. Males have blue to teal-colored short fur covering them and stand roughly nine feet tall; females tend to have orange to red short fur and are shorter at roughly seven to eight feet tall. Both sexes have four arms and are extremely strong. Both sexes have horns wrapping around the front of their heads from the back and have large disks on the side of their heads that are their extremely sensitive ears. The horns assist in directing sound vibrations to the base of their ears.

Terms

Actas—a measure of time; seconds.

Ceramasteel—a compound that is a ceramic with the tensile strength of steel, often used as armor or used in place of steel in high-temperature environments, such as heat shields for reentry or in engine exhausts.

Cycle—a solar year, the time it takes for the planet to make a full rotation around its sun.

EMP—electromagnetic pulse. Used to disrupt and, if strong enough, destroy electronics. Joxby created several small handheld devices (grenades) to take out the android guards.

Kolts—measure of time; hours.

Partions—measure of time; minutes.

Rattons—measure of time; weeks.

Rotation—measure of time; one day, a full planetary rotation.

Slansteel—a lightweight and extremely flexible metal. Mainly used in construction for cargo netting, safety straps, and barriers. Used wherever extreme strength, flexibility, and lightweight are needed.

Starch—a tuber grown on Kashtuu. For the native creatures, it has a highly concentrated nutritional value that stores well and survives the extreme conditions of their planet. For non-native species, it has numerous effects. Some are performance enhancing, such as highly increasing reflexes, tremendous strength, and/or heightened senses. For others, it is an instantly addictive hallucinogenic. For other species, it has no effect at all. Peddled by the drug cartels as it is so addictive and can become life-sustaining to those addicted.

CPSIA information can be obtained
at www.ICGtesting.com
Printed in the USA
BVHW071915130223
658422BV00012B/123